RAVE REVIEWS FOR RICHARD LAYMON!

"I've always been a Laymon fan. He manages to raise serious gooseflesh."
—Bentley Little

"Laymon is incapable of writing a disappointing book."
—*New York Review of Science Fiction*

"Laymon always takes it to the max. No one writes like him and you're going to have a good time with anything he writes."
—Dean Koontz

"If you've missed Laymon, you've missed a treat."
—Stephen King

"A brilliant writer."
—*Sunday Express*

"I've read every book of Laymon's I could get my hands on. I'm absolutely a longtime fan."
—Jack Ketchum, author of *The Girl Next Door*

Other *Leisure* books by Richard Laymon:

INTO THE FIRE
COME OUT TONIGHT
RESURRECTION DREAMS
ENDLESS NIGHT
BODY RIDES
BLOOD GAMES
TO WAKE THE DEAD
NO SANCTUARY
DARKNESS, TELL US
NIGHT IN THE LONESOME OCTOBER
ISLAND
THE MUSEUM OF HORRORS (anthology)
IN THE DARK
THE TRAVELING VAMPIRE SHOW
AMONG THE MISSING
ONE RAINY NIGHT
BITE

RICHARD LAYMON

THE LAKE

LEISURE BOOKS   **L**   NEW YORK CITY

A LEISURE BOOK®

November 2005

Published by

Dorchester Publishing Co., Inc.
200 Madison Avenue
New York, NY 10016

ISBN 0-8439-5620-8

Printed in the United States of America.

Visit us on the web at www.dorchesterpub.com.

THE LAKE

ONE

Tuesday, April 27

Verna Lavette clapped her hands.

"My *favorites!*" she squealed.

Almond marzipan, walnut whirls, and those *scrummy* caramel creams . . .

"Oh, *thank* you, she said, her chubby face wreathed in smiles.

"No problem, sugar," the man said. "My pleasure—as always."

Verna looked sheepish. "Can I have one, now? Before . . ."

"Sure. Have one, two, or three. Makes no difference, but . . ." He glanced at his wristwatch. "Best make it snappy. No time to lose."

Sucking on a caramel cream, Verna looked at her benefactor. Well, she pondered, he ain't *really* my benefactor. *I* give *him* plenty, in return for his dough—ooh, yes, and the candy. Don't forget the candy.

She made a face.

Sure, she did her bit.

Got the scars to prove it, too.

Yessir. All things considered, the Candyman got pretty much what he wanted.

He must like what I do—and how I do it, she told herself. Keeps a-comin' back for more.

Like now.

The room was dark except for the anglepoise spotlight by her bed. He was telling her to take off her slip, all slow and sexy, like Marilyn Monroe.

It always began like this.

Then the action moved on to . . . other things. . . .

Some guys have weird ideas, and her Mr. Candyman was no exception. At times she wondered if it was worth her while. The things he made her do, an' all.

She sighed. In *her* job, never mind the way she *looked* these days, she needed every goddamn cent she got— while she could still get it.

And, no question, the Candyman paid her good.

She watched him adjust the spotlight so it lit up her left side. Feeling around in his holdall, he brought out a Polaroid camera.

He put it to his eye, squinted into the lens, and ran off a couple of shots. Testing for light conditions. Verna knew the score inside out.

He waited a moment. The mechanism whirred and spewed out the Polaroids.

He peeled off a picture and watched it color up.

Frowned, muttered "Shit!" and tossed it on the bed.

The result was not to his liking.

The second one turned out okay.

Mr. Candyman grinned approval. His teeth gleamed briefly in the lamplight.

That's my baby.

Now. Down to business.

Sweat broke out. Speckling his upper lip.

Placing the Polaroid camera on Verna's nightstand, he brought up a small silver one from out of his holdall.

Verna smiled. *One a' them classy Japanese jobs—nothin' cheap about this guy.*

Dollar signs danced before her eyes.

The Candyman was naked.

Verna stared at his erection. Tilting slightly, stiff and strong, poking out from all that dark curly hair.

I wish, she thought, hungrily, the familiar tingly rush teasing her center like crazy.

Do things right the first time—and maybe, just *maybe,* Verna gets to taste some a' that.

She sighed. The Candyman wasn't into sex; he was interested only in his goddamn pictures. God knows she'd *tried* to play it for sex, but he just got angry. He'd slugged her in the kisser a coupla times.

If he weren't so good-lookin', he'd be just your average creep, she decided. But a mighty good-lookin' creep, I'll say that for him. The quiet type, too; don't say much.

Bastard sure knows what he's doin' with a camera, though.

Verna shivered. A gal could go off the boil, time it takes . . . She studied the Candyman's face. It was set. Engrossed. Maybe he's one a' them porno guys, she thought, making heaps a' dough selling dirty pictures. She'd done a few porno flicks in her time, so she knew the score. Hell, there were plenty of big bucks in that game.

On the other hand, maybe the shit jacks off on 'em, all on his lonesome in a dark little room someplace. . . .

Who cares? I do the job 'n' I gets my fee . . .

Tossing back her blond hair, Verna swung into action.

Ready for my close-up now, Mr. DeMille.

She posed. Bunched up her lips. Lifted her shoulder, looked at the camera, and smiled coyly. She crossed an arm over her breasts and slipped off a shoulder strap.

Candyman focused the lens.

"Let it fall, slowly. Hold your breasts, sugar. Play around

with them . . . like you're making sweet love to yourself. . . . That's it. Now, for the next shot . . ."

Verna had done it all before. Many times. She'd lie on the bed, spread out, like one a' them sacrificial virgins you read about in history books.

Oh, yeah?

She almost laughed out loud.

One thing's for sure. Verna ain't no fuckin' virgin!

Candyman took a few shots. Then he straightened up and replaced his camera on the nightstand. He opened up his holdall. Put the Polaroid job inside it. His pants and T-shirt were already in there.

Neatly folded.

Out of the way.

He came up with a knife.

Verna shuddered. One false move with that baby, an' I can kiss my candy good-bye.

He leaned over the bed, blocking the light from the lamp.

Her heart beat faster.

She looked at the blade. Felt a sharp, stinging thrill between her legs. Got her juices going, all right, but it sure was scary.

Too goddamn scary. Not really knowing what the fuck he was gonna do next . . .

With a forefinger, he traced a line from her throat right down to her pubic bone. For a big man he had a soft touch. Light as a feather.

She wriggled, and shivered.

"Ooh, that tickles . . ."

"Ssshhh. Not a sound, sugar. Mr. Candyman's about to create a masterpiece here."

Verna closed her eyes.

Let him have his kicks.

Any which way he wanted. After all, he was the guy with the dough. . . .

"Heyyyyyyy whadyal . . . ? AAaahhhggg . . ."

Blood sprayed the Candyman's face.

He grunted, opened his mouth, and licked his lips.

The knife slicked down Verna's torso, jerking a little going past her breastbone. The Candyman slowed down, then dug in deep, opening her guts like she was a sheep in a slaughterhouse.

Verna's red mouth sagged a little in surprise.

Her baby blues snapped wide, then quickly glazed over.

Fascinated, the Candyman stared into them. He liked the way Verna fixed her eyes. All that black eyeliner. And those long black lashes. Way back, she told him she'd been a singer at some club in downtown Frisco. Yeah, it figured. Gals in Verna's line a' business knew all about makeup.

He stood back, tilting his head.

An artist surveying his masterpiece.

He liked what he saw. Verna was a work of art.

Picasso's "red period."

He stared at his creation.

Opening her up made her breasts flop over, each pointing outward, either side of the bloody ravine down her middle. Her breasts were big and white and splashed with red.

How 'bout that?

Candyman's "red period."

His lips curved in a tight smile.

All that blood . . .

He dug the way it flowered beneath her, like some exotic jungle orchid.

A strand of black hair peeked out from beneath the blond wig. He removed the wig, watching the way her head wagged, all loose like a rag doll. Her lids drooped. She coulda still been alive. Asleep.

He tossed the wig to the floor.

Carefully, he stroked her long black hair, smoothing it into place over her shoulders.

He rearranged her arms so they stretched out from her body. Engrossed in his work, his mouth opened slightly.

Verna's legs gaped apart; blood oozed from her orifice.

It was still pumping from her belly.

Should be slowing down about now . . .

Mmmm. She looked like a five-pointed star.

Interesting.

"Doing the bitch a favor," he murmured, "rearranging her like this. Only way *she'll* ever get t'be a 'star'!"

Neat, huh?

Grinning, he stabbed the knife deep into Verna's middle. Her body shook; her breasts wobbled precariously. Spats of blood sprayed up from her guts. Landed on his belly.

Glistening gobs of it clung to his pubic hair.

His head buzzed inside. Like it was full of swarming bees.

He got angry. Couldn't stop stabbing . . .

"You fuckin' bastard, evil bitch!

"Rot in HELL! You hear me?"

Sweat beaded his brow, droplets stung his eyes. His breath came out in harsh, wheezy grunts.

Seconds later, he'd calmed down.

Wiping his hands on Verna's bedsheet, he picked up his camera and clicked away.

TWO

Wednesday, June 30

The footsteps got closer.

He, *it*, was almost *on* her now.

Her legs pumped hard. Her lungs gagged for air.

The thing followed with superhuman speed.

Christ. I can't go fast enough—or far enough!

Heaving, panting, she drew to a halt. . . .

A bony hand clawed her shoulder.

Hooked her throat.

NO. My God. NO . . . PLEASE!!!

* * *

Deana jerked awake, heart pounding, nightgown twisted up above her waist, clinging like a live thing to her sweat-soaked skin.

Her breathing evened out a little.

Puffing out a gusty sigh, she relaxed.

It was only a dream.

Dream?

Try a fucking *nightmare!*

She sighed again—in relief this time. Turning her head on the sodden pillow, she saw familiar shapes in the weird half-light. She relaxed some more.

Then . . .

What was that?

Her heart began racing again.

She could hear *something.*

Footfalls.

Soft, scrunching sounds on the gravel outside.

Her eyes darted to the window. The filmy curtains stirred in the breeze. . . . Moonlight filtered pale gray beams across her bed.

She scanned the window. Saw a tall, hunched shape move across it. Shaggy hair sticking out from beneath a long floppy hat.

This is for real.

I'm not dreaming now.

The shadow paused, stiffened, and turned, looking over its shoulder like it was scared of being followed.

Then the big hook nose pointed forward again.

Like a giant bird of prey . . .

It carried a hatchet on its shoulder.

Oh my God!

Can this *really* be happening?

It's my nightmare come true!

Deana clamped a hand over her mouth, stifling the scream rising in her throat. Her breath huffed out in ragged, hurting gasps.

"Ah'm a-comin' to getcha, baby . . ."

A harsh, breathy voice. She couldn't believe it!

If this really IS a nightmare, I gotta wake up fast.

Sliding a hand under the bedsheet, she found her thigh. She pinched it, hard.

Ouch! *Shit!* Okay, so I'm not dreaming. I'm awake.

Jesus. If I *am* awake . . . who is *that* outside my window?

A burglar?

Carrying a hatchet?

Killers carry hatchets . . .

Mad ax murderers!

But why pick on me?

Who'd want to kill *me?*

Nobody I can think of would want me dead.

Except maybe that bitch Nancy Guildenschwarz—she *hates* me like hell after Allan ditched her and dated me instead. . . . Even so, Deana reminded herself, Nancy's short, plumpish—*and* she's a girl.

Not a tall, thin *man.*

Unless Nancy's people put out a contract on me.

There's a thought.

Wouldn't put anything past that bitch. Always boasting her dad had connections . . .

Name like Guildenschwarz, he sure *needed* connections.

Like a mouse in a maze, Deana's mind scurried through her past, searching for a tall scarecrow man who hated her enough to sneak around her house in the dead of night.

With a hatchet for company . . .

Nah. Nobody hates me *that* much. Do they?

Jeez, I hope not.

If she yelled for Mom, he might smash through the window and hack her to death before Mom could get to her.

Best stay quiet, she thought. Pretend I'm not here.

Deana shut her eyes tight, held her breath, slid down under the bedsheet, pulled it over her head, and lay there, heart racing, till she almost suffocated.

Then, peeking from under the bedsheet, she scanned the window again.

Nobody there. Only the moon, casting ghostly rays onto her bed.

Perhaps the thing with the hatchet never happened?

Oh yeah?

Deana wiped her face with a corner of the sheet.

It was awfully hot.

Hot, shitty, oppressive, and muggy.

Another summer night in Marin County.

'Cept it wasn't just "another summer night."

A mad axman's out there, sneaking past my window.

Stalking me.

Looking for me. Wanting to hack me to death.

Deana listened, willing her heart to slow down.

A warm mistral rose up from nowhere, whispering into the night, tossing the leaves of the citrus outside her window. The rustling sounds should have been familiar and friendly.

Tonight, they didn't seem that way.

In the past, she'd loved that big old tree.

At age ten, when she and Mom first came to live in this house, she'd imagined small furry creatures hiding away up there; birds, nesting in its branches. Mornings, she'd lie in bed watching it. At night, she went to sleep listening to its quiet, scurrying sounds.

Now it shivered and rustled like something in a horror movie.

It was so scary.

Her gaze switched to where she'd last seen the intruder.

Hoping she wouldn't see him again.

Trying to convince herself the shadowy shape didn't exist. Hadn't really happened at all.

She waited . . .

But there was no Mr. Hatchet Man. Just her tree. Its leaves stirring softly in the night breeze . . .

Making long black shadows on her ceiling.

Raising her head off the pillow, she squinted at the clock on the nightstand.

12:10.

Past midnight.

A good time for nightmares.

And weird dreams.

She stretched, letting her tense, coiled-up limbs ease out, running her tongue over bone-dry lips.

Her eyes darted nervously to the window.

Just checking.

Fearful the same spooky sequence would start over again.

Wide-eyed, waiting, she counted to thirty . . . forty . . . fifty . . . sixty.

No sign of the Hatchet Man.

Swinging out of bed, she peeled off her nightgown. It was soaked with sweat. She spread it over the bedrail, grabbed her robe, and shrugged into it.

It felt soft and comforting to her damp, chilled skin.

She tied the sash tight.

Wouldn't do for Mr. Hatchet Man to catch her naked.

Mr. *who?*

That was a nightmare, dummy, and don't you forget it.

Still her breath came hard and fast.

Calm down, she told herself.

You're safe.

The doors are locked.

Mom's in the next room . . .

Everything's okay. Honest.

In the busy flickering shadows, familiar things greeted her like old friends.

She made for the kitchen.

Opening the fridge door, she reached inside and took out a jug of lemonade.

It felt good and cold.

Mom made it only yesterday. From fresh lemons. It was her own special brew, and Deana knew it'd taste bitter-sweet, tart, with just a dash of honey.

The way I like it.

The glass jug clouded up. It felt deliciously cold in her hands. Licking her lips, she watched the pale liquid swish around inside it—almost *tasting* that first almighty swig as it hit her throat.

First, she set the jug on the table and went over to the sink. Turning on the cold faucet, she cupped her hands and splashed water over her face.

Then she grabbed a hand towel, patted herself dry.

Feeling better, safer, all the time.

It was only a nightmare, she told herself again.

Deana downed two glassfuls of juice, knowing she'd probably spend the remainder of the night in the bathroom.

Who cares? I'm awake, I'm alive, and I'm all in one piece!

Back in her bedroom, she caught that same weird figure slink past the window.

Again?

NO!

Frowning, she stared hard. But saw nothing.

Just the curtain, stirring softly.

And her tree, murmuring in the breeze.

Wonderful. I'm going crazy. My mind's playing tricks . . .

She set her refilled glass on the nightstand, took off her robe, and climbed into bed.

She yawned, glad the nightmare was over.

She felt safe again.

And sleepy.

Her lips curved in a smile.

As her lids closed, she thought about the party tomorrow night. . . .

Tomorrow night?

Tonight, she reminded herself.

Deana yawned again, going through the scenario of telling Mom how she and Allan would be going to the movies after dinner. Mom'd be furious, but she'd soon simmer down. Hey. She knew how it was; she'd been there herself, hadn't she?

Once upon a time.

So she keeps reminding me.

Deana smiled sleepily. It felt good, touching her naked body beneath the sheet, the soft breeze wafting through the window.

Thinking about the dinner party—and afterward, when she and Allan would bunk off together.

"Mmm . . . ," she whispered. "Tonight, we're gonna have the time of our lives!"

THREE

"If I were the suspicious type," Deana said, "I might think that car is following us."

"But you're not," Allan said.

"A little bit, maybe." She looked over her shoulder. The other car was still beyond the last curve, its beams dim and barely visible through the narrow rear window of Allan's Mustang. Seconds later, the headlights appeared. One was out of alignment, throwing its beam crooked and high. Deana didn't like the cross-eyed look. It made the car seem a bit demented.

"How about turning around," Allan suggested. "You're making me nervous."

"It's making me nervous."

"Probably just some guy on his way to Stinson Beach. Once you're on this road, you're on it for keeps."

Deana faced the front. Her hands were sweaty. She wiped them on her kilt. "Maybe you should slow down and let him pass."

"You've seen too many *Friday the 13th* movies."

"*You* dragged me to some of them."

"I love the way you squeal and cover your eyes . . . and peek through your fingers."

"Maybe we should have gone to a movie," Deana said.

"Losing your nerve?"

"It's awfully dark out here."

"It's supposed to be."

"How soon's the turnoff?" Deana asked.

"It's coming up."

"Well, if he makes the turn, too, I say we forget it."

Allan turned his head toward her. She couldn't see his expression in the darkness, but he obviously wasn't thrilled by the idea of forgetting it. She couldn't blame him. He had suffered through the dinner with Deana's mother and grandparents, which must've been quite a drag for him, probably able to keep his spirits up only by reminding himself of what was planned for afterward.

"One more thing," she had told him on the telephone before the party.

He had responded with an "Uh-oh."

"This isn't an 'uh-oh,' pal, this is an 'ah-ha.' Once dinner's over, you and I will be free to amscray. I was thinking of somewhere very dark and very secluded, perhaps in the vicinity of Mount Tamalpias. You might want to bring a blanket."

Maybe dinner hadn't been such a drag for him, after all, Deana thought. If the nervous, excited looks he gave her were any indication, he was too busy imagining sex in the woods to be bored with the family gathering. She'd had a difficult time, herself, keeping her mind on the festivities. By the time they were clearing off the dishes, she was such a wreck that Mom asked whether she was upset about something.

Well, see, Mom, it's like this. Allan and I aren't actually going to a double feature. We thought we'd find a place over by Mt. Tam where we'll have a little privacy; we've only done this kind of thing once before, and we were both a little loaded then, so this will almost be like the first time, and I'm a little tense.

Just a little tense, that's all.

The clicking sound of Allan's turn signal brought her back to the present. She realized she was gripping her thighs and trembling. Calm down, she told herself. This is nothing to be scared about.

"It went right on by," Allan said after making the turn. For a moment, Deana didn't know what he was talking about. Then she remembered—the car that had been behind them.

"Well," she said in a shaky voice, "I guess we're in luck."

Allan downshifted, the car growling like a determined animal as it started to climb the steep road, headbeams pushing into the darkness. Deana felt herself sink deeper into the bucket seat.

"Wouldn't a breakdown be fun about now?" Allan asked.

"A laugh riot."

Maybe this area is a little too secluded, she thought. And too dark—and scary. She found herself thinking about last night. *Nightmare on Del Mar,* starring, tadah . . . Mr. Hatchet Man. Uhhh . . .

She turned her eyes to the safe, familiar green glow of the dashboard instruments.

"We should've gone to a Holiday Inn," she muttered.

"I thought you were against motels."

"Yeah, well, I might be changing my mind."

"Man, I wish you'd changed your mind half an hour ago. Want me to turn around?"

"No, that's okay. We're already here."

"I don't mind. A bed. A shower. Heyyy."

"Maybe some other time."

"Is that a promise?"

"It's a thought. We'll think about it, okay? It still seems kind of . . . I don't know . . . tawdry."

"Tawdry?"

"Look it up."

"You're definitely weird, you know that? It's all right to fool around in a car or in the woods someplace, but you do the same thing in a motel room and it's tawdry. Does that make sense?"

"It must," Deana said, "or why would I feel that way?"

"Because you're nuts?" Allan suggested.

At the top of a rise, the road leveled out. Ahead was a wide, moonlit clearing—the parking area for the outdoor theater. When they'd been here last month for a production of *Othello,* the lot had been packed with cars.

Now it was deserted.

"Looks like we've got the place to ourselves," Allan said.

"I figured we might."

Allan drove to the far end of the lot. He stopped at its edge near the start of the footpath leading through the trees to the theater. He turned off the engine. "Well, here we are," he said, sounding a little nervous himself. He killed the headlights. Darkness closed over the car. He took the key from the ignition, pushed the key case into a front pocket of his corduroy pants, and rubbed his hands on his legs. Twisting around, he reached between the seat backs and brought the blanket through the gap.

Outside, the night breeze chilled Deana's legs and seeped like cool water through her sweater. Shivering, she gritted her teeth. She wrapped her arms across her chest. Allan joined her in front of the car. "Cold?" he asked.

"A little."

He fluttered open the blanket and draped it over her shoulders like a cape.

"There's room for two," she said, holding out one side.

He huddled in close against her, drawing the blanket across his back and slipping an arm around her. They walked slowly toward the path. The blanket felt warm and good. So did his hand stroking her side. They were just a few steps along the path before his hand found its way beneath her sweater. She moaned as it moved over her bare skin. It roamed higher.

"Hmmm?" A surprised, questioning sound.

"Fooled you," she said.

"You were wearing one at dinner."

"My last stop in the john before we left. It went in the hamper."

With a sigh, he reached and caressed her breast.

"God," he whispered. He drew her around to face him. She lost her end of the blanket, but let it fall as Allan hugged her tightly, both hands now under her sweater and rubbing her back, his mouth open and urgent against hers. Breathless, Deana tugged out his shirttails. She sucked his tongue. She stroked his bare back. His hardness was a stiff bulge against her belly, the feel of it stirring a warm, moist tremor deep inside her.

He eased Deana away and lifted her sweater. Her skin, bare to the night breeze, crawled with goose bumps. Her nipples, already erect, grew so hard they ached, and then his hands were on them. Warm. Enclosing her breasts. Squeezing. The heat in her breasts was almost like pain, and she threw back her head, squirming.

His hands loosened as if he feared he might be hurting her.

"Toss anything else in the hamper?" he asked in a husky voice.

"Could be."

He reached for Deana's hips, but she danced backward, out of range. She pulled her sweater down. "Not here," she said.

"Where?"

She shrugged. "We're too close to the parking lot." She waved a hand in that direction. She could see moonlight on the windshield of Allan's Mustang. "Let's go in farther."

"Over by the theater?"

"Yeah."

"How about on the stage?"

She flung out her arms. "All the world's a stage, and all the men and women merely—"

"Props," Allan put in.

"The bard you're not."

"Can you see it? There we are, right in the middle of the theater, surrounded on every side . . ."

"You're being redundant."

"Surrounded by all those high rows of seats, empty seats, while we . . ."

"Make the beast with two backs."

"Screw our heads off," he said, curling a hand over the back of Deana's neck.

"Yeah," she sighed.

"And as we lie there," he whispered, "our naked bodies sweaty and tangled . . ."

"Gleaming in the moonlight . . ."

". . . from off in the distance, high up in the seats, comes . . ." He took his hand off Deana's neck and slowly clapped.

She stared through the darkness at him. He kept on clapping. "Christ," she muttered.

He clapped again and again.

"Cut it out, you're scaring me."

He stopped. He laughed softly.

"Let's go back to the car," Deana said.

"You're kidding."

"No I'm not."

"Deana, it was a joke."

She turned away. He caught her from behind and wrapped his arms around her belly. She settled back against his warmth.

"I want to get out of here, Allan. It was a rotten idea in the first place."

"Man, that's the last time I'll tell *you* a story."

"Yeah, well, somebody *could* be around here. How do we know?"

"We don't." His hands moved up to her breasts.

She stroked the backs of his hands as they caressed her through the sweater. "We'll go someplace else, okay?"

"Like where?"

"Someplace that isn't . . ." Allan gently pinched her nipple, and she caught a ragged breath. ". . . isn't so dark," she said in a shaky voice. "A street near home."

"In the backseat?" She nodded.

"Wouldn't it be better . . ." His voice stopped. His fingers spread out, hands still holding her breasts but motionless.

"Allan?"

"Shhh."

"What?"

Then Deana heard it, too. "It's just the wind," she whispered.

"It's a car."

Deana's insides went soft and loose. She tightened herself.

If it was a car, where were its headlights? Allan took a hand off her breast. The warmth went away. He pointed. At first, Deana saw only strips of moonlit parking lot in the spaces between the trees. Then a dark shape crossed one of the strips. More like a chunk of shadow than a car.

"It's probably someone like us," Allan whispered.

"What do you mean?"

"A couple. You know. Looking for a good place to mess around."

"God, I hope so."

"Let's get back to the car." He picked up the blanket. Deana stayed close to his side as he walked along the path. She still heard the car, but she couldn't see it. Just before the end of the path, Allan crossed to a tree. She followed. Ducking behind its trunk, they looked out at the parking area.

The Mustang was only a few yards away. The other car

was directly behind it, motionless near the middle of the lot. Its headlights were off. Its engine idled. The glare of the moonlight on the windshield prevented Deana from seeing inside.

"What do you think?" she whispered.

"I don't like the way it's just sitting here."

"Do you think he can see us?"

"I doubt it."

For a while, they watched the car in silence.

"This is crazy," Deana finally said. "Why doesn't he go away?"

"Maybe it *is* somebody making out."

"With the engine going?"

"It's like he's waiting," Allan said.

"Yeah. For us."

"Don't worry. Nothing can happen as long as he stays in the car and we stay here."

"What if he gets out?"

"Comes looking for us?"

"Yeah."

"It'd be easy to hide from him. He wouldn't know where to start looking. Maybe we could even double back to my car."

"Maybe we should just go to your car. Right now."

"You think so?" Allan asked.

Her heart pounded so hard, it made her chest ache.

"At least we'd get it over with. We can't wait around all night. And we don't really know what he's doing in there."

"Maybe just enjoying the scenery," Allan suggested in a nervous whisper. "You want to give it a try?"

"I don't know."

"It was your idea."

"Yeah, well, I'm not so sure about it."

"It's either that or we try to wait him out." Allan looked over his shoulder at Deana. "Maybe we should go ahead with our original plan."

"I'm glad you haven't lost your sense of humor."

"He might be gone by the time we get back."

"And if he isn't and he nails us," Deana said, "at least we'll have shared a few moments of bliss."

"Bliss?"

"Shit," she muttered.

"Ditto."

"We're going to feel like a couple of prize idiots after we stroll out to the car and drive off and he's still sitting there."

"Does that mean you want to do it?" Allan asked.

"No, I don't want to do it, goddamn it, I'm scared shit-less, but what sort of choice do we have?"

"We'd only be out in the open for a few seconds."

"Yeah. What's he going to do, spray us with lead?"

Allan pushed himself away from the tree trunk and stood up straight. He took a deep, loud breath and blew it out. He had the wadded blanket under his left arm. He dug his right hand into the pocket of his cords, took out his keys, and picked through them until he found the car key.

"Did you lock your side?" he whispered.

"Yeah. I always do."

"Okay, you take the keys. Once you're in, reach across and unlock my door."

"Don't give me this 'ladies first' stuff. You're quicker than me."

"Deana." He sounded ready to argue, but paused. He was silent for a few seconds. "I know what we'll do," he said. "You wait here. I'll go out to the car and bring it right up to here. Sideways, so it'll shield you. Then you just jump in, and off we go."

"Don't be a . . ." She shook her head. That's right, she thought, snap at him for offering to take all the risk. Leaning closer, she kissed him softly on the mouth. "You're all right," she whispered.

"You too."

She stroked his cheek. She almost said that she loved him, but decided it would sound too sappy and melodramatic. This is it. End of the road. I love you. Violins. Hand in hand, the lovers stride toward their rendezvous with death.

An hour from now, we'll be laughing about this.

Sure. Maybe in a week.

"We go out together," she said.

"I really think . . ."

"You and me, pardner. Butch and Sundance."

"Please. *Not* Butch and Sundance."

"Let's get it over with." She took the blanket from him. He didn't put up a fuss, apparently realizing that they would have to rely on his quickness if something went wrong. She held his hand. It felt wet and cold.

They stepped out from behind the tree and walked through the high grass, straight toward the front of his Mustang.

The headlights of the other car came on. Deana's stomach gave a cold lurch. One of the beams was high. It crossed the other. She moaned.

"Just act normal," Allan said.

A foot in front of the bumper, they parted hands and split up, Deana walking to the passenger door while Allan stepped to the driver's door. She gripped the handle, thumb on the latch button, ready. Forcing her eyes away from the other car, she looked across the Mustang's low roof and watched Allan bend over. She heard the rasp of his key entering the lock, the quiet thump of the button popping up. Allan swung his door open.

The other car sprang forward, roaring. Allan's head snapped toward it. He was bright in the glare of its headlights, hunched over, mouth wide.

"Get in!" Deana yelled. Dropping the blanket, she ducked and peered through the door window. The ceiling light was on. Allan dived at the driver's seat. The car got his legs, yanked him out. Deana lurched back, numb, as the speeding car ripped off the driver's door.

It was slow motion.

It was impossible.

It was the door flipping upward, twisting, skidding across the hood of the Mustang with a trail of sparks and the car rushing past with Allan in front, hooked over the bumper, out of sight from his waist down, the rest of him draped across the side of the car, arms flapping loosely overhead.

Brakes screaming, the car had too much speed to stop before the edge of the lot. It bumped over the grass and smashed into a tree. The tree caught Allan in the rump. He was thrown backward from the waist, hair flying, arms flinging out.

The backup lights came on. The car shot backward. Allan rolled loose, hung in the air for a moment in front of the one working headlight, then dropped and tumbled.

Deana was numb, frozen. But there was a lucid corner of her mind that somehow took control. She peered through the window of the passenger door as the other car shot backward. Allan's keys lay on the seat where they must have fallen when he was hit. Though she knew her door was locked, she thumbed the latch button anyway and jerked. The door stayed shut. The other car had stopped slightly ahead of the Mustang. Its door opened.

Deana ran.

She ran for the woods, not looking back.

FOUR

Dad sat at the kitchen table, drinking coffee and puffing on a cigar, while Mom helped Leigh with the dinner dishes. Most of the dishes, after being rinsed, went into the dishwasher. The crystal glasses, however, Leigh didn't trust to the machine. Those were done by hand, Mom washing them while Leigh dried.

It didn't take long, because there were no cooking utensils to contend with. The food had been prepared by the chef at the Bayside, delivered and served by two of Leigh's best waiters, who had since returned to the restaurant.

When the last crystal wine goblet was dry, Leigh suggested after-dinner drinks. Dad, stubbing out his cigar, asked for Scotch and water. Mom wanted Bailey's. Leigh stayed in the kitchen to prepare the drinks while her parents headed for the living room.

The evening had gone quite well, she thought. Dad and Mom both seemed to be in excellent spirits, as if oblivious to the rather scary fact that Dad was now only a year short of sixty.

Hell, they're young. Damn young to have a thirty-seven-year-old daughter and a granddaughter who will be starting college in the fall. They're both in good health. They've got plenty to be happy about.

Me, too.

She took her time pouring the drinks.

I've got two great parents, a beautiful, intelligent daughter, a thriving restaurant considered the finest place to dine in Tiburon. Not to mention the house. Fabulous house.

So what's this jittery feeling in my stomach like something's wrong? Nothing is wrong. Probably just that Deana's out. It's impossible to relax completely when she's gone at night. So much could happen. A breakdown . . .

Allan seems reliable, though. He'll take care of her.

That amused Leigh.

Other way around: Deana would be the one to take charge if a problem came up. Nothing *will* come up. She'll waltz through the door around one o'clock—after the movies are over.

If they went to the movies at all.

Leigh set the glasses on a silver serving tray. She knew she was a bit tipsy, so she concentrated on holding the tray steady as she carried it past the dining area and down the single step to the living room. Mom was in the stuffed chair, Dad standing by the glass wall staring out at the view. He turned around as Leigh set the tray on a low table in front of the sofa.

"I can't get over your view," he said.

"Me, either." Leigh had lived in this house for eight years and still found herself staring out at it daily.

"That was a lovely dinner," Mom said.

Leigh handed her a snifter of Irish cream. "Beef Willington is Nelson's specialty."

"It's such a shame that Deana had to leave early."

Leigh smiled and fought an urge to roll her eyes upward. Mom had to start on that. Well, she could be counted upon to start on something, especially after a few drinks. "Mom, she and Allan canceled a dinner reservation so she could be here."

"Why would she have a dinner reservation for *tonight?* Didn't you tell her . . . ?"

"We originally asked you over for last night, remember? But you and Dad had the club banquet."

"It still wouldn't have killed her to stay."

"She has a life of her own," Dad said. He took his Scotch and water from the tray and sat on the sofa. Leigh lifted her glass of Chablis off the tray. Holding it carefully, she lowered herself onto the sofa beside Dad. "I'm sure she has better things to do," he continued, "than spend Friday night with a bunch of old fogeys."

"We're hardly old fogeys," Mom pointed out. "It wouldn't have killed her to spend one evening with her family."

"She sees you all the time," Leigh said. "It's not as if you live in Timbuktu."

"Wherever the hell *that* is," Dad said. Smiling, he took a drink.

"What do you know about this Allan?" Mom asked.

"She's been going with him for a couple of months. She met him in drama class."

"He's an *actor?*"

"I think he intends to be an attorney."

"Great," Dad said. "We could use a lawyer in the family. You know what they say—every family needs a lawyer, a doctor, and a plumber." He grinned. "And a restaurateur, of course."

"He's hardly part of the family."

"I don't know, Helen, they looked pretty serious to me."

"Don't be silly."

"And it is probably no coincidence," he added, "that they both plan to attend Berkeley in the fall."

"Berkeley," Mom muttered. She rolled her eyes upward. "Don't talk to me about Berkeley."

"I don't think it's the same as when I was there," Leigh told her.

"Well, thank God for that."

Dad settled back against the cushion and crossed his legs. He looked at Leigh. "You turned out pretty well for a radical hippie chick."

"Let's drop *this* subject," Mom said. "Uhhh. The absolute *hell* you put us through. Do you have any idea of the *hell* you put us through?"

Leigh sighed. She didn't need this. "It was a long time ago," she said.

"Your senior year in high school. That's when it all started. You were just Deana's age. She's such a fine young lady. You don't know how lucky you are."

"We're all pretty lucky," Dad said. He patted Leigh's knee and gave her one of those looks that said, *Sorry about this. You know how Mom gets.*

"How do you think you'd feel if Deana came home one fine day, dressed up like one of those 'punks' you see on the street corners in the city? How would that make you feel if her lovely hair was all chopped off and spiky like a bed of nails, and *green?* Or orange! Or maybe she comes home with a Mohawk, looking like Mr. T!"

Leigh couldn't hold back her smile.

"You'd be smiling out of the other side of your face, young lady. Suppose she had a safety pin in her cheek?"

"I never did any of that," Leigh told her.

"Only because it didn't happen to be 'in' at the time."

"What movies did they go to?" Dad asked.

"I'm not sure. A double feature in San Anselmo, I think."

"We went to see—"

"You should've seen yourself," Mom interrupted. "You looked like one of those Manson girls."

"Mom."

"Helen."

"God only knows what might've become of you if we hadn't shipped you off to Uncle Mike's." A pause. "And then look what happened."

Leigh felt as if an icicle had been thrust into her belly.

"Damn it, Helen!" Dad snapped.

"Well, it's the truth. You *know* it's the truth." Her eyes watered up. Her lower lip began to tremble. "Don't raise your voice at me," she said with a tremor.

"You push it and push it. We're supposed to be here for a good time. The *last* thing Leigh needs is to have that summer thrown into her face."

Mom took a drink of Bailey's. She stared into the snifter, weeping quietly. "I was . . . just trying to make a point."

Leigh got up from the sofa. Crouching next to her mother, she said, "Hey, it's all right." She had a lump in her throat, tears in her own eyes. She stroked her mother's hair. "That was so long ago. Everything's fine now, isn't it?"

"You put us through such hell."

"I was pretty much of a creep there for a while. But now is what counts. The present. I'm not so bad now, am I?"

"Oh, honey," she said, sobbing. "I love you." She pulled Leigh's head down and kissed her. Leigh stayed at her side while she took out Kleenex and wiped her eyes and nose.

Her mascara was smeared, making her look a little weird, somehow reminding Leigh of Bette Davis in *Hush...Hush, Sweet Charlotte,* though Mom didn't look nearly as old or weird as Charlotte. "The beef Willington was absolutely delicious," she finally said, signaling her recovery.

"It's Nelson's specialty," Leigh said. Hadn't they been through this before? She didn't mind. "You two really should come to the Bayview more often," she said, returning to the sofa and picking up her wine.

"We don't like to take advantage," Dad said, looking vastly relieved. His eyes were red. He, too, must have been weeping.

"You're not taking enough advantage," Leigh told him.

"You'd see us there more often if you'd let us pay for our meals occasionally."

"If that's what it takes," she said.

Some of the tension remained, and they soon got up to leave.

"I wish we could stick around till Deana gets back," Dad said, "but that might be a while, and I've got eighteen holes waiting for me in the morning."

They walked toward the door.

"Why don't you and Deana come over next week," Mom suggested. "We'll barbecue, and the pool's nice and warm with all this hot weather we've been having."

"That sounds nice."

"And tell Deana to bring her friend."

"All right."

"We really didn't get much of a chance to visit with her tonight."

"I know. I'm sorry about that."

"You should bring a friend too."

Let's not start on that, Leigh thought. The one touchy subject that had fortunately been avoided until now.

"Really, darling, you're thirty-seven and—"

"We'd better be on our way," Dad interrupted. He

hugged Leigh and kissed her cheek. "I had a wonderful time, sweety. Thanks so much for the dinner and presents. And give our love to Deana."

"I will. Happy birthday, Dad." He patted her rump and turned away to open the door.

"Next Saturday, all right?" Mom asked.

"You're on."

They hugged and kissed.

Leigh followed them out to the driveway, waited there while they climbed into their Mercedes, and waved as Dad backed the car up the steep driveway.

Inside, she shut the door, leaned back against it, and sighed.

Over.

At least Deana hadn't been around to witness Mom's tantrum.

She gathered up the glasses, took them into the kitchen, and rinsed out the milky residue of Mom's Irish cream. She would wash them in the morning.

She had the house to herself. It felt good. If only she could get rid of that nervous feeling about Deana. From several years of experience, however, she knew that wouldn't go away until Deana returned.

She looked at the clock. Not even ten-thirty. The first movie was probably just ending. Deana probably wouldn't be home till one. A long wait.

So make the most of it.

Out on the deck, shivering as the breeze found its way through her gown, Leigh twisted a knob to heat the water in her redwood hot tub. She hurried back inside and walked down the long hallway to her bedroom at the far end of the house. There, she slipped out of her clothes and put on a soft, bulky bathrobe.

There was a greasy stain on the breast of her gown from a glob of Hollandaise that had dripped off an asparagus spear. She took the gown into the bathroom and scrubbed at the spot with hot water. She threw it over a bedroom chair. It would have to go to the cleaners. She tossed her undergarments into the hamper. She lined up her shoes on the closet floor. No hurry. She wanted the water in the redwood tub to be good and hot before she ventured out again.

Dropping onto her bed, she checked *TV Guide*. One of the local channels would be showing a repeat of an old *Saturday Night Live* show at 11:00. She remembered watching one of the current *SNL*s with Deana a couple of weeks ago. Deana had found humor in strange places.

Generation gap.

She thought about her mother.

Mom's right. I'm damn lucky Deana hasn't gone freaky, the way I went when I was her age.

Pretty harmless stuff, though.

Except for that sit-in. That's what got to them, the idea that their wonderful daughter almost got herself thrown in the slammer. That's what did it. That's why they sent you to Uncle Mike's. . . .

Her stomach knotted cold.

Quickly, she rolled off the bed and took a towel from the closet. She hurried down the hall.

Don't think about it.

Do not.

I'll watch the TV when I come in. A toss-up between a *Cagney & Lacey* rerun. Or *Titanic*. Again. Or . . . anything that takes my mind off what Deana is up to right now.

Leigh left the foyer light on, then made a circuit of the kitchen, dining area, and living room, turning off all the lights. Stepping outside, she slid the glass door shut behind her. She flicked a switch to start the bubbles, climbed the three stairs beside her tub, and dropped her towel onto the platform. She took off her robe. Gritted her teeth at the feel of the breeze.

Quickly, she stepped over the side of the tub. The warm water wrapped her leg to the knee. Not bad, but it would get better as the heat increased. She lifted her other foot over the edge, stood on the submerged seat, then stepped off and crouched, covering herself to the shoulders, sighing with relief as the water eased her chill. For a while, she didn't move. The water swirled, its warm currents caressing her like gentle, exploring hands.

Then she glided forward, stretching over the front rim and peering over the top, higher than the deck railing, so she had an unobstructed view.

Below, most of the houses at the foot of the hill were lighted. A lone car circled the cul-de-sac and pulled into the Stevensons' driveway. Off to the left, a car crept up Avenida Mira Flores, turned toward her, and dipped down the slope. Much too early to be Allan's car. Over the tops of the hills, she could see a piece of Belvedere Island rising out of the bay, dark except for a few specks of light from streetlamps, house windows, and cars.

Beyond Belvedere, far off in the distance, the northern end of the Golden Gate was visible—red lights on top of its tower, cables sloping down. The bridge was often shrouded in fog, but not tonight. Nor was there fog sneaking over the tops of the hills beyond Sausalito. Too bad. The fog was always so lovely in the moonlight, glowing like a thick mat of snow and always moving, always changing. She watched the headlights of cars on Waldo Grade, then lowered her eyes to the lights of Sausalito.

Leigh rarely went to Sausalito anymore. It was no longer a town, it was a traffic jam. She shook her head, remembering how she used to love that place. Back in her high school days. A century ago. God, the hours she used to spend there, wandering around. It had street people then, not just tourists. It had the Charles Van Damm: The ancient, beached stern-wheeler was a coffeehouse in those days, and she used to sit in the smoky darkness far into the night, listening to the singers. The guy with the twelve-string who did "The Wheel of Necessity." Leigh sighed. She hadn't heard that song in about twenty years.

Staring out at the swath of Sausalito lights, she could

hear it in her head—the pounding thrum of guitar chords, the raspy, plaintive voice of the singer. What had become of him? What was his name—Ron? He was the best. "The Wheel of Necessity." She'd forgotten all about that song. It must have been Mom's talk about the early days that helped stir her memory.

Ah, the water felt good. Releasing the tub's edge, she eased backward to the far side. The bench rubbed her rump. She sat low, stretched out her legs, and let the roiling water lift them. She held on to the edge of the seat to keep herself from drifting up. The water was very hot now, wisps of steam rising off its surface.

She closed her eyes.

"The House of the Rising Sun"—that was another one the guy used to sing. Sometimes, she hadn't been able to force herself to leave. On a couple of occasions, she didn't get home until almost two o'clock. No wonder she drove her parents crazy. If Deana ever stayed out that late . . .

She wondered what Deana and Allan were up to. If they really stayed for both shows, they would have to drive straight back here to arrive by one o'clock. Deana had said she would be back by one, and she was reliable that way.

What they probably did, they split before the second feature so they'd have some time to make out. Deana was usually straight with Leigh; on matters like this, however, she might bend the truth a bit. Only natural, Leigh thought. The girl wouldn't want to announce she was fooling around.

Just be careful, honey.

Yeah, like I was.

Pregnant at eighteen. Not exactly a picnic. It worked out, though. It worked out fine.

Charlie.

No.

Her eyes sprang open. Her heart raced. She took deep breaths.

No. That's one little trip down memory lane you don't want to take.

32

You filthy whore! shrieked in her face.

Leigh groaned. She stood up fast.

I'm not going to remember, she told herself.

Her warm wet skin, hit by the breeze, turned achingly cold from shoulders to waist. She started to shake. Gritted her teeth. Crossed her arms over her breasts. Drops of water rolled down her back and sides.

The shock treatment did its trick, forcing her mind into the present.

The memories of that time didn't come often, but when they did they could tear her apart if she let them. Fortunately, there were the tricks. She had taught herself plenty of ways to stop the assault before it went too far. This was a new one, and hurt less than punching the nearest wall or digging fingernails into her leg.

If she relaxed into the warmth, however, the memories would start again. Once that terrible door in her mind was open, it stayed that way for a while. The thoughts had to keep busy with other matters.

She started to sing "Waltzing Matilda." She sang it quietly in a shaky voice as she climbed from the tub, toweled herself dry, and put on her robe. She kept on singing it while she turned off the bubbles and heater.

In the kitchen, she looked at the clock.

Eleven-fifteen.

She wished Deana were here.

Probably parked somewhere—maybe nearby. If they left the movies early, though, they'd be careful not to return too early and blow their cover.

Leigh smiled.

The kid was no dummy.

Hope she's smart enough to use something. If she had taken care of that little matter, she had kept it to herself.

Don't depend on the guy, for godsake.

Maybe I should have another talk with her.

Hell, if she hasn't gotten the message by now, it's probably too late.

In her bedroom, Leigh took off her robe. She put on a light, silken nightgown.

From the way Deana and Allan acted around each other, Leigh was pretty sure they had already made love. The idea of that, shocking at first, no longer bothered her. Hell, the girl was eighteen. What kind of girl *hasn't* done it by eighteen? And Allan seemed like a good kid.

Just don't knock her up, that's all I ask.

Save the bambinos for after college.

In the den, she inserted a tape of *The Way We Were* into her VCR. Before turning it on, she got herself a glass of wine from the kitchen. Then she started the television and sat on the sofa.

When her glass was empty, she stretched out. A pillow propping up her head, she watched the movie. She had seen it many times. The hot tub, followed by the wine, had left her feeling languorous. After a while, she let her eyes drift shut.

The jangle of the telephone startled her awake. Thrusting herself up, she grabbed the phone off the lamp table. "Hello?"

Deana.

It wasn't Deana.

"Leigh. It's Dad. 'Fraid we'll have to call off that date next Saturday, hon. Had a message to say your aunt Abby had a heart attack. She's in intensive care. So Mom and I are catching a flight to Boulder just as soon as we can."

"Oh, Dad . . ."

"It's okay, Leigh. Don't you worry none about your aunt Abby. She's in safe hands, and we'll be looking after her when she comes out of the hospital. Sorry to spring this on you, honey—after such a wonderful evening an' all. We both enjoyed it so much. Now this. Matter of fact, your Mom's packing as we speak, so . . ."

"Sure, Dad. Have a safe flight. And tell Aunt Abby she has our love."

"Speaking of which . . . Young Deana, has she—"

"Deana's okay, Dad. Tucked up in bed right now . . ."

A white lie; reasonable at a time like this. Can't have Mom and Dad worried about Deana. 'Sides, she's gonna show up any minute now. . . .

"She shouldn't worry you like this, Leigh. Get to grips with the situation before. . . ."

"Before she ends up like I did at her age?"

"You know what I mean, young lady. Now, sounds like my presence is required elsewhere. . . ."

"Okay, Dad. Safe journey. Love to Mom."

"Sure. Catch up with you later, honey."

Leigh's stomach began to churn. Something was not quite *right* about tonight; she was sure of it. And it wasn't only the news about Aunt Abby, either. Put it down to Deana, she told herself.

For godsake, Deana. *Where are you?*

The phone jangled again. Leigh caught a ragged breath.

Deana. Something's wrong . . .

She snatched up the phone again.

A man's voice said, "I'd like to speak to Leigh West."

"This is Leigh West." Her heart pumped hard. She felt dizzy.

"This is Detective Harrison of the Mill Valley Police Department. I'm calling about your daughter. . . ."

FIVE

Glancing over her shoulder as she made her break for the woods, Deana saw him leap from the car. He was tall and cadaverous, with strangely long arms. He loped after her, waving a meat cleaver overhead. He was dressed all in white. He wore a chef's cap that wobbled and flopped as he ran.

Whirling away from him, Deana dashed onto the path. She had a good head start. She was in good shape from running every day before school. If he wasn't fast enough to overtake her quickly, she might get away.

I *will* get away, she thought. I have to.

If he catches up, he'll kill me.

She couldn't hear him. He must be far behind, but she didn't dare slow down.

She pumped her arms, threw her legs out quick and far, felt the breeze in her face.

I'm really moving. He'll never get me.

She looked back.

He was three strides behind her, a white silent phantom grinning in the moonlight.

No!

Deana lunged to the right, leaving the path, her only hope to lose him in the trees. The underbrush tried to snare her feet. But it'll slow him down, too, she told herself. She jumped over a dead branch, hurled herself through a narrow gap between two trunks, made a quick turn, and scurried up a slope. Near the top, the slope became very steep. She clawed at weeds for handholds. Her feet slipped on the dewy ground.

A quick tug at her waist. Clutching the weeds, she twisted her head around. He was beneath her, a hand clenched on the hem of her skirt.

"Ho ho ho," he said, and yanked.

Deana clung to the weeds. With a raspy tearing sound, the skirt released her. It whipped down her legs, jerked her toes from the ground. The man cried out. Skirt in his hand like a dark banner, he flew backward and tumbled to the bottom of the slope.

Deana scampered to the top. Panting for air, she leaned over the edge and saw him start to climb again. She stepped back. The forest floor was dappled with moonlight. She found a fallen limb and picked it up. Raising it over her shoulder, she crouched near the edge.

Seconds passed. She listened to the rustling sounds of his climbing. Then his head appeared. He had lost his chef's cap in the fall.

He had the cleaver clamped in his teeth.

Deana brought the limb down with all her strength. It cracked against the top of his head. Losing his hold on the weeds, he dropped backward. His arms waved. His back hit the slope and his legs kicked up at the darkness.

He somersaulted down the slope.

He was still falling when Deana threw aside her limb and rushed away. As she ran, she wondered if she should have followed him to the bottom and hit him until he couldn't get up again—until he was dead. Too late for that. But maybe the single blow had been enough.

She couldn't count on that.

At least she had given herself some time. If she could just find a hiding place . . .

Climb a tree, she thought.

Slowing down, she glanced at the nearby trees. One had a fork in the trunk that looked low enough to reach. She rushed over to it. Leaping, she grabbed the thick branch and pulled herself up. She wrapped the trunk with her bare legs. Writhing, she hugged the branch. She twisted, kicked, hooked a foot over the crotch of the trunk, and finally managed to squirm onto the branch. Straddling it, she let her legs hang down while she scanned the woods.

Her pursuer was nowhere in sight. Maybe he still lay at the bottom of the hill, unconscious or dead. If the blow with the stick hadn't done it, maybe he broke his neck in the fall or struck his head on a rock.

Tipping back her head, Deana looked at the branches above her. If she got high enough, she would be safe. He would never be able to spot . . .

Cold fingers wrapped her ankles.

Her breath burst out.

He was beneath her, grinning up.

"Now I gotcha," he said in a low voice.

Impossible! Where had he come from?

"No! Please!" she gasped.

He pulled, forcing her down hard against the branch between her legs. Deana shoved at the branch with both hands, trying to ease the hurt.

He swung by her ankles, his weight a torture, his momentum scraping her on the bark. Blood spilled from her, splattering his face. Gazing down, she saw a split crawl out of her pubic hair, widening as it climbed to her navel. Her sweater was gone. She was naked, and the fissure was moving toward her chest. She felt the thickness of the branch tearing her insides, driving into her like a wedge. Her rib cage broke open. And still he swung beneath her. . . .

In horror, she saw her breasts on each side of the branch. *When it reaches my neck, my head will pop off.* "Please stop!" she shrieked, and woke up gasping.

Deana was in bed, in her own room. Wiping sweat from her eyes, she looked at the alarm clock. Almost three o'clock in the morning. She was tangled in sweaty sheets.

She unwrapped herself and sat up. Her sodden nightgown clung to her body. She peeled it off and tossed it to the floor. The air felt good on her hot skin.

Crossing her legs, she held on to her knees and took deep breaths. Her heart began to slow down. She remembered the nightmare vividly. A strange nightmare—such a horrible, distorted version of what happened that night.

If only the reality, too, had turned out to be a nightmare.

Allan.

In her mind, she saw the car carrying him through the night, smashing him against the tree. She shivered at the memory and wrapped her arms across her chest.

According to the police, Allan had died almost immediately from the massive injuries. But Deana hadn't known that until later, while she was waiting in the police station.

Fleeing through the woods, she had ached to return to

him, get him into the car and rush him to a hospital. But the other was back there, pursuing her. So she raced on, then hid for a long time high in a tree, and later made her way down to a road where a teenaged couple on their way back from Stinson Beach gave her a lift to Mill Valley. She didn't even ask them to take her back to the theater parking area.

For all she knew, then, Allan might still be alive. But the man might be there, waiting, and Deana couldn't ask these strangers to risk their lives. She was afraid for herself, too. She had escaped, and the thought of returning filled her with terror.

It wouldn't have done any good, going back. She knew that now, but the guilt remained and would probably be with her for a long time. The fear, too.

Sleep had been a refuge. She'd slept through most of the day after getting home, and gone to bed early last night. She wished she could go back to sleep now, but she felt wide awake and she was afraid of the dream. What if it came back?

What if it returned every night?

And maybe that *other* nightmare she'd had, had been a portent of things to come. It was too spooky to think about.

Swinging her legs off the bed, she reached up and turned on a lamp. She crossed her room to the dresser, took out a jersey nightgown, and put it on. The clinging fabric felt good against her chilled skin. She left her room and made her way down the dark hallway to the bathroom. After using the toilet, she returned.

With pillows behind her back, she sat in bed and opened a book. As she started to read, a quiet sound from the hallway made her stiffen. She darted her eyes to the door. A moment later, her mother appeared.

"How are you doing?" Mom asked.

She shrugged.

"Want to talk?"

"Sure."

Mom sat near the end of the bed, turning sideways to face Deana, a leg drawn up beneath her nightgown. "Trouble sleeping?" she asked.

"I had this lousy rotten nightmare."

"Rough, huh?"

"It wasn't fun. He caught me. Split me right up the middle." Trying to smile, she drew a finger up the front of her nightshirt. "The mind plays funny tricks."

"Hilarious tricks," Mom said.

"Does it get any better?"

Mom shrugged.

"How did you . . . cope with it when my father was killed?"

"I guess you helped pull me out of it. When I found out I was pregnant, it gave me something new to worry about, so I stopped dwelling on the past."

"Maybe I should run out and get pregnant."

"I don't recommend it." Lowering her eyes, Mom frowned. "There was something else, too. Your father . . . It's hard to think of him as your father. . . . The young man who got me pregnant . . ."

"Charlie Payne," Deana said.

"I didn't know him very well. I didn't actually love him. That must've made a difference. I took Charlie's death pretty hard. I mean, I was there and it was partly my fault, so I had plenty of guilt to deal with, but I know it would've been a lot worse if I'd actually loved him."

"What is there, a family curse or something? Look at us. Both of us lost boyfriends—lovers. You were eighteen, I'm eighteen. It's kind of weird, don't you think?"

"There isn't any curse." Something about the tone of Mom's voice made Deana wonder.

"Just bad luck?"

"We were both taking chances, honey. Going where

maybe we shouldn't have been. It doesn't take a curse." Mom patted Deana's leg through the blankets and stood up. "The important thing is not to blame yourself for what happened."

"Not so easy."

"I know. Don't I know." Bending over, she kissed Deana. "See you in the morning, honey."

As she headed for the door, Deana said, "You'll come with me to the funeral, won't you?"

"Of course. We'll go out tomorrow and buy you something appropriate."

SIX

The mother's face was hidden behind a black veil, but she felt the eyes on her, watching her, hating her. The preacher, standing beside the grave, spoke calmly of the sure and certain hope of resurrection. The mother, voiceless, damned her.

It's not my fault. *Please.*

"And so," the preacher said, "as the coffin sinks slowly into the ground, we bid a fond farewell . . ."

The mother started to move. She walked around the end of the grave, slowly.

Stay back.

No, don't point at me. Oh, my God!

She took a step backward as the mother approached, but bumped into someone behind her.

"You! You did this to him. You filthy whore!" The pointing hand opened and darted, smacking her face. "You murdered him with your lust, you whore! Monster!" To the others, she shouted, "Look at her! Look at the monster! This is what murdered my boy!" The hands clawed at her, ripped her blouse open, tore it from her shoulders, grabbed her naked breasts.

Crying out in agony, she squirmed and tried to pry the fingers loose.

"*You* should be dead, not him! Not my boy!"

"No! Let go!"

"You killed him, whore!"

She was dragged forward by her breasts, whimpering. Then the mother twisted and flung her. She hit the edge of the grave with her knees. Wildly flailing her arms, she caught her balance. But a shove from behind sent her down.

"*That's* where you belong!"

She fell and fell.

She wanted to scream out her terror, but she couldn't get a breath.

Why is it so deep?

It always is.

She'd been here before. She realized that now. Familiar territory, this bottomless grave.

Only, it's not bottomless.

She knew that. And she remembered what was below. Choking out a whimper, she flapped her arms and kicked, desperate to stop, to take flight, to get the hell out of here.

Pitch dark. Grave dark.

But she could see in the dark.

The coffin didn't have a lid. There had been a lid when it was lowered, but not anymore. He wore a necktie and brown suit. His feet were bare. His face, as pale as chalk, glowed beneath her.

Okay now, don't, she thought as she fell closer. Please don't.

Oh, but he will.

Oh shit he will he always does but they were dreams before and this is real and he's really dead so he won't open his eyes this time, not this time, or reach up like a goddamn zombie to grab me, not this time.

The holes where his eyes had been opened wide.

He reached up.

"NO!"

Leigh heard her voice and opened her eyes as she thrust herself away from him. Below was her powder-blue pillow. She was on her hands and knees, gasping.

It *was* a dream. Of course.

Thank God.

And thank God morning was here.

Still braced on stiff arms, Leigh lowered her head.

Scratch one nightgown, she thought.

It used to happen a lot. But the last time, Deana was about four.

Talk about Allan's funeral, that's what did it. The last thing before sleep.

Leigh rolled off the bed. When she stood, the nightgown slipped the rest of the way down. She stepped out of it, picked it up, and inspected the damage. The gauzy fabric was split down the middle, breast to belly, and one of the straps had been wrenched from its seam. One for the rag bag.

No, better get rid of it. You don't want Deana seeing it. Deana didn't know about the dreams. Or about the funeral of Charlie Payne. And finding out wouldn't do her any good.

Leigh looked down at herself.

She groaned.

Edith Payne didn't grab her for real in nightmare-land and do this. Leigh had done it to herself.

But this was a new twist.

Not even in the old days when the dream came regularly did she ever wake up to find fingernail marks on her breasts.

Tiny little crescent moons.

They looked a lot like the ones Edith Payne gave her the day of the funeral.

SEVEN

When Deana woke up, she heard bathwater running. It was unusual for Mom to take a bath first thing in the morning.

She remembered the shopping trip. To buy a black dress. For tomorrow's funeral.

Her fresh, morning eagerness collapsed. Her stomach went jittery and she knew she had to get up fast or she would lie here immobilized, sinking.

She swung her legs down, sat on the edge of the bed, and wondered if she could force herself to go running. She always went running as soon as she got up. She loved it—the peacefulness of the quiet streets, the smell and feel of the morning air, the way it felt when she was pushing to make it up a slope, and especially when she reached the top and there was level road ahead and she would really go all out.

Night. The woods.

Deana went numb.

She saw herself racing through the darkness, dodging trees. She felt the terror.

You weren't going to think about that.

It was the running that saved me.

She rubbed her thighs, trying to make the goose bumps go down. As she rubbed, she stayed away from the bruises and scrapes she got shinnying up the tree.

I *will* go running, she decided. She had to do something, and maybe it would wipe her mind clean, at least for a while.

Pulling the nightshirt over her head, she stepped to the dresser. She put the nightshirt away and opened the drawer where she kept her running clothes. The faded red shorts, neatly folded on top, were Allan's. His gym shorts from Redwood High. Deana lifted them from the drawer and held them up by the waistband.

He wore them that day on the Dipsey Trail. They were too small for him, and the seat ripped when he squatted to catch his breath. It happened at the top of those endless stairs. They weren't even out of Mill Valley by then, and still had miles to go before reaching Stinson Beach—including a stretch through Muir Woods that was certain to be crowded with tourists. When the ripping sound came, he reached back and felt around. "Uh-oh," he said. "We'd better go back."

"We can't." She reminded him that Sally and Murray would be waiting at the beach that afternoon, to give them a lift back to Tiburon.

"We can *drive* over and meet them."

"Oh, come on. We can't let a little rip stop us."

"It's not so little."

"Let me see."

"Are you kidding?"

"It can't be that bad."

"I haven't got any . . . uh . . . just a supporter."

"How tacky."

"Ha ha ha."

"Take off your shirt. You can tuck it in back there—eclipse the moon, so to speak."

"I've got very fair skin," he said. "I'd sunburn. How about if I use your shirt instead?"

"Normally, I'd be glad to give you the shirt off my back." Mimicking him, she added, "I haven't got any . . . uh . . ."

"I know, I know."

Allan finally took off his T-shirt and wore it like a tail the rest of the day. Later, he gave the shorts to Deana, gift-wrapped but still torn, as a memento of the journey.

Elbows on the dresser top, the shorts pressed to her

face, Deana tried to stop the crying that had begun when she started to remember. She wiped her eyes dry, but they filled again.

The seam in the rear looked almost as good as new where she had stitched it with the sewing machine.

Maybe best, she thought, to put the shorts away. Hide them in the bottom of a drawer or something, so they wouldn't be around to remind her of Allan.

Hell, I don't want to forget him. If the memories hurt, it's only because they're *good* memories. I'll wear these shorts till they fall apart, and then I'll still keep them.

Sniffing, Deana stepped into the shorts and pulled them up. The wet seat clung to her skin.

She put on a bra. God knows, *that* hadn't come from Allan. It was an elastic harness made for running—the female equivalent of a jockstrap. He liked the flimsy, transparent kind that unhooked in front. Or none at all. The look on his face that first time she didn't have one on and he didn't know it until he reached under her sweatshirt and touched her breast instead of fabric.

In the mirror, she saw herself smile. Just a bit. She looked like hell with her eyes all red and puffy.

Allan hadn't said anything. He'd moaned.

Deana pulled a T-shirt over her head, took socks from the drawer, and sat on the edge of her bed to put them on.

After that night, she'd started making a game of it. Sometimes she wore a bra, sometimes she didn't. It drove Allan nuts each time they were together, until he found out one way or another. He never came right out and asked. He observed. He pulled little maneuvers such as running his hand down her back. If he determined that she was wearing a bra, he relaxed. If she wasn't, he spent the rest of the evening watching her chest at every opportunity—apparently eager to catch a jiggle of breast or evidence of nipples pushing against her clothes. If she wore a loose top, he kept trying for glimpses down the front. And Deana would help him by bending over a lot. Obsessed, that's what he was.

Was.

Oh shit oh shit.

Deana sprang from her bed. It's okay to think about him, she told herself. Just not all the time.

She took her shoes from the closet. She put them on quickly, grabbed the front-door key off her dresser, and hurried down the hall, slipping the long key chain over her head. She dropped the key down the front of her shirt. It felt cold for a second against her skin.

"Back in a while," she called out through the silence.

"Hey!" came her mother's voice. "I want to talk to you."

"Mom."

"Come here."

Deana backtracked to the master bedroom. She crossed to the bathroom door. It was open a crack. "Yes?"

"You're not going out to run, are you?"

"That was the plan."

"I wish you wouldn't."

Keep it light. "Gotta stay fit, Ma."

"Not today, all right?"

"Why not?" She knew why not.

"Because."

"Mom."

"I just don't think it's a good idea."

"You want to turn me into a hermit?"

"You know what Mace said."

"Mace? You mean Detective Harrison?"

"Yes, Detective Harrison."

"I know what he said. He said to be careful. I'll be careful."

"I don't want you going out alone. Not for a few days, anyway."

"I *need* to run, Mom."

She heard some quiet splashing sounds from behind the door. Then Mom said, "Okay, but I'll go with you."

Deana didn't want to wait. She didn't want company. It

wouldn't be the same. "You'd never be able to keep up with me."

"You're talking about the gal who wipes you off the tennis courts."

"You don't want to get sweaty after your bath."

"I'm not kidding about this. I don't want you going out alone. I mean it."

Deana sighed. "Is it all right if I wait for you out front?"

"Where out front?"

"On the driveway. I'll just warm up while I wait."

"Where on the driveway?"

"At the bottom."

"All right. But keep your eyes open."

"Yes, ma'am."

"I'll be right out."

Deana started away. Christ, Mom thinks the guy's out there. Ready to pounce on me. Or run me down.

What if she's right?

That is just what I need on top of everything, a good case of paranoia.

"I don't want to frighten you," Harrison had said. *Mace.* "You and the Powers boy might very well have been random victims. On the other hand, it's possible that the assailant knew precisely who he was after. If he was after *you*, Deana, then he might make another attempt. You and your mother need to face that possibility and take precautions. Do you understand?"

"He wasn't after me. I mean, it had to be random like you said."

"Not necessarily."

"I already told you, I haven't dumped any boyfriends, I don't have any enemies, I—"

"This could be a guy who spotted you at the supermarket and followed you home. It could be a guy who stopped beside you at a traffic light, or sat behind you one night at the movies. And seeing you triggered something. Maybe you wear your hair the same way as a girlfriend who jilted him. Maybe you've got his mother's blue eyes, and she used to abuse him. It could be a hundred things. Do you understand? There's a good chance it *was* random, but you have to act as if you were the intended target. At least until we nail this guy. I don't want you to end up . . . hurt."

He had sounded as if he really meant it, as if he cared. And somehow as if his lecture, though addressed to Deana, was actually spoken for Mom's benefit. Something going on there. A subtle undercurrent.

It must have made an impression on Mom. Calling him Mace.

Deana opened the front door, pulled it shut behind her, and stepped over the *San Francisco Sunday Examiner and Chronicle*. She looked back at the paper. Part of her routine was to bring it down from the top of the driveway each morning when she finished her run. She always found it near the top of the driveway—sometimes hidden in the geraniums. This was strange. No matter how good his arm, the paper man couldn't possibly have winged the *Chronicle* all the way to the front stoop. You can't even *see* the stoop from the road. He had either driven or walked down the steep driveway to get it here. Really going for brownie points. Christmas is six months away. Maybe it's somebody new.

Maybe *he* did it.

Deana felt a chill crawl up the back of her neck.

Paranoia must be contagious. Like the flu.

She scanned the ice-plant-covered slope across the yard, the hedge at the top, and the weed-choked stretch of hillside behind the Matson house. It all looked normal. The hedge up there was a bit too skimpy to conceal anyone.

At least this is taking your mind off Allan.

She walked past the kitchen windows and stopped on the broad, concrete apron in front of the garage.

The paper man got ambitious, that's all.

One steep mother of a driveway. Narrow, too.

She shook her head.

The geraniums along the sides of the driveway were not skimpy.

Get off it.

Deana stepped closer to the garage. Facing the driveway, she took a deep breath. The morning air smelled sweet and clean. She did a few jumping jacks. When she started the toe-touching exercises, her rump brushed the garage door.

Thataway, back to the wall. Nobody's gonna sneak up on *you*. No-sirree.

Chicken shit.

She took five steps forward—count 'em, five.

That's better.

That wasn't better. She felt exposed.

What's keeping Mom?

You wanted to go running alone, remember?

She sat down. The concrete, still in shadow, was cold through her shorts and worse against the backs of her legs. She leaned forward, stretching, grabbing her shoes.

I would have been just fine except for Mom's little talk. And she had to remind me of what Harrison said.

The way you wear your hair.

Bull.

She touched her forehead between her knees.

Saw a madman in a chef's cap bounding down the driveway waving a meat cleaver, and looked up fast and saw no one.

Where'd you get this chef's cap nonsense?

Oh yeah, the dream.

Lovely little dream—and all that weird shit the night before.

Legs spread wide, she leaned forward, touched her right hand to her left toe, left hand to right toe. The stretching muscles felt good.

She flinched at a sudden bumping sound, then realized

it was only the front door shutting. Mom. That was pretty quick, actually. She got to her feet and hitched up the shorts that had been inching down her rump during the exercises.

"What took you so long?" Deana asked.

"Are you kidding? I'm still wet."

Deana stared. Mom looked so normal. So *good*. As if this were just any other fabulous Marin County morning. Except for the blue ballcap covering her pinned-up hair, she was dressed in white—knit shirt, shorts, socks and shoes, all white. Which made her fair skin look almost bronze.

Deana had rarely seen her with her hair up.

"My gosh, Mom, you've got ears."

"Anything wrong with them?"

"They're rather large, is all."

Mom grinned. "Have you looked in a mirror lately?"

Deana's own smile slipped.

Sure have, Mom.

She remembered it well. A red-eyed girl clutching gym shorts.

"Not to change the subject or anything, I thought you promised to stay down here."

"I did."

Mom raised an eyebrow. Then she swept down from the waist, touched her toes, and made a quick catch as her ballcap dropped.

"Oh, you mean the newspaper."

"That's right, Watson. Here, hold this."

Deana took the hat.

Mom resumed touching her toes. She had a few drops of water on the backs of her legs. No cellulite. She *was* in terrific shape. Always had been. Maybe that was one reason why Deana started running last year. She'd been getting a bit pudgy, and it was damned embarrassing to have a mother who looked better than you in a bikini. Some of her boyfriends—take Herb Klein, for instance—spent more time ogling Mom than . . .

"At least you didn't *leave* without me," Mom said.

"I didn't bring down the newspaper. I didn't touch it."

"How did it get there?"

"I suppose the delivery guy was feeling energetic."

"Geez," Mom said, "and Christmas isn't for six months."

"Maybe he's angling for a Fourth of July tip."

"Weird." Mom swung her arms around, then took the hat from Deana and flopped it onto her head with the bill high. She squinted up the driveway. Looked at Deana. Raised one side of her upper lip to show her distaste for the chore ahead. "Well, I'm ready when you are."

"I'll take it easy on you."

"Oh, thanks. You're so thoughtful."

Deana started up the driveway, leaning into its slope, not pushing. Mom stayed at her side.

It was like climbing a stairway. Taking the stairs two at a time.

She thought of the stairs at the start of the Dipsey Trail. They sure nailed Allan. Let's try not to think about Allan for a while. Let's just think about running, the good feel of working muscles. And getting closer to the top.

Halfway there.

Three quarters. No sweat. She glanced at Mom. Mom smiled.

The mailbox at the top came into view.

Then the car.

Mom said, "That's a great place . . . to leave a car."

It didn't block the driveway. It was parked on the other side of the street. But nobody ever parked there because of the blind curves.

Deana didn't see anyone inside.

She stopped at the edge of the street.

"What's the matter? Pooped?"

"Mom."

The tone of Deana's voice turned her mother's face strange.

Deana's gaze swept the street and hillside as she walked on numb legs toward the old, red Pontiac Firebird. She stepped in front of it. The grille and headlight on its right side were smashed in. "My God," she muttered.

Mom grabbed her arm, pulled her. "Quick. Back to the house."

They ran.

EIGHT

"It needs something."

"*You* need something," she said. "A frontal lobotomy."

"That's no way to talk to the man who's going to immortalize you."

"My foot," she said.

"Precisely."

"You'd better hurry. If I fall in, I'll tear your face off."

"Behave." Still squatting on the bank of the stream, he raised the Nikon to his eye and studied the situation again. "Nah, no good."

"Kee-rist."

He stood up. "I've got it. Come on back."

Mattie reached out her hand. He grabbed it and pulled as she leaped across the running water. Her bare feet landed on twigs, and she winced.

"Right back."

"Where are you going?" she asked.

"My first-aid kit's in the car."

"Good idea, Charlie. You may need it."

"Buck up. We'll be done shortly."

Mattie rolled her eyes upward and planted her fists on

her hips. "You know," she called at his back, "real models get big beans for this kind of shitski."

"Don't think I'm unappreciative."

"No, not you."

He made the top of the wooded embankment, jogged past a deserted picnic table to the parking area, and opened the trunk of his Trans Am. He glanced around to be sure nobody was nearby, then lifted his .12-gauge Ithica shotgun, raised a corner of the blanket on which it had been resting, and took out his first-aid kit.

He hurried back to Mattie.

"What's the big plan?" she asked.

"A Band-Aid on your toe."

"You jest."

"Not me. Mark my words, it's just the touch that's needed. An air of vulnerability to an otherwise perfect foot." He opened the plastic case, took out a bandage, and offered it to her.

"You'd better apply it. You're the *artiste* around here."

"Fine. Sit."

"Where?"

"On the ground."

"It's *wet*." She wrinkled her nose. Then, with a heavy sigh, she sat. "You owe me for this, Charlie."

"You'll sing a different tune when your foot's hanging in the De Young." Tearing off the wrapper, he crouched at Mattie's feet and picked the paper away from the adhesive strip.

"Why can't you be normal and shoot nudes?" she asked.

"Leaves nothing to the imagination, my dear."

She wiggled her toes. "That turn you on?"

He nodded. The bandage on the big toe might be a little too obvious. The third toe seemed best, though the Band-Aid was really too large for it.

Mattie leaned back, bracing herself up on stiff arms.

Yes, the third toe. He reached for it.

Mattie raised the knee of her other leg and swung it far to the side. "Does *this* turn you on?"

He looked. The cutoff jeans were very cut off—no more than a frayed seam remained between the legs. "How inelegant," he said.

Mattie chuckled. She kept her left foot fairly steady while the bandage was being applied, but waved her bent right leg from side to side, whispering, "Now you see it, now you don't. . . . *Now* you see it, now you don't."

"All set." He patted the bottom of her foot. "Assume the position."

"Bet you can't stand up straight."

"Matter of fact, I already am."

He pulled her hand, and they both stood up. Mattie bent over to check him out. "Well, shitski, hon, you could knock me over with a feather. Want me to take care of that for you?" She didn't wait for an answer. "I know, I know." Turning away, she stretched out her leg until her foot found one of the small, flattopped rocks a yard from the bank. Arms out for balance, she pushed away from shore with her other foot. Once she was perched on the rock, she carefully pivoted until she was facing him. Then she swept out her right foot, planted it on a nearby rock, and took a deep breath. "Fire away."

Crouching, he framed the foot, the water shimmering around the rock. "Beautiful," he muttered. He snapped the shot. The camera's automatic advance buzzed. He clicked, straightened up a bit for a new angle, took another shot, sidestepped to the left and took more, stood up straight, took more, then waded out with the cool water filling his sneakers, bent down, and snapped a few extreme close-ups.

"What dedication," Mattie said.

He waded ashore, changed the lens setting for six feet, picked up a stone, and tossed it underhand at Mattie's midsection.

"Hey!" she yelped.

She caught the stone. But her quick movement was enough to upset her precarious balance. She flapped her arms as she fell backward.

He got it all on film—Mattie's stunned expression as she snatched the stone, her flapping arms, her splash when she hit the stream back-first, feet flying into the air. Then her furious drenched face as she sat there scowling at him. He kept clicking away as she staggered to her feet and waded toward him. "I suppose you think you're cute."

He lowered the camera so it hung by the strap, and protected it between his arm and side. "Don't do anything foolish," he warned as she approached. Mattie had a brown belt in judo. She could throw him ass over head into the stream, and he had no defense short of decking her with a punch. He wouldn't do that.

He didn't like the way she was grinning. "Mattie, my camera."

"Pity."

"My beeper."

"Oh, your precious beeper."

"My revolver."

"A little water won't hurt that."

"It'll *ruin* my holster."

"Not to mention your ego, big man." She grabbed the front of his shirt. Instead of dropping backward, planting a foot in his gut and sending him on a trip, Mattie pulled him against her and kissed him. He put his arms around her. The wetness soaked through his shirt.

"I'm going to wait," she murmured against his mouth. "When you least expect it, *wham*."

"Fair enough."

"Now, how about tooling me over to my place so I can get out of these duds?"

"You may feel free to get out of them at my place."

"*Haw*."

"We'll give them a spin in the dryer, they'll be good as new. Which isn't saying much."

She swatted his rump. "Let's move it, then, Charlie." She stepped into her sandals.

They climbed the slope. They were nearly to the top when his beeper sounded.

"I don't believe it," Mattie muttered. "There goes our Sunday."

When they reached the car, he opened the trunk and pulled the blanket out from under the shotgun. Mattie wrapped the blanket around herself, then sat in the passenger seat. "Maybe it's a wrong number."

"Most likely." He called headquarters on his cellular phone. "Harrison," he said.

"Mace, you just got a call from a Leigh West. She said it regarded the Powers case."

Mace took the number, broke the connection with headquarters, and put the call through.

"Hello?" The woman's voice sounded taut.

"Miss West, this is Mace Harrison."

"I'm sorry to bother you, but you said we should call if anything suspicious happened, and the car's out on the street right in front of our house."

He didn't need to ask what car. "Any sign of the driver?"

"We didn't see anyone."

"Is your house locked up?"

"Yes."

"You're in Del Mar on Mark Terrace, right?"

"That's right." She gave him the address.

"I'll be there in ten minutes."

"We're not absolutely sure it's the same car, but . . ."

"I'll be right over." He put down the phone. "The Powers case," he told Mattie as he swung his Trans Am around. "That was the mother of the girl. There's a car in front of her house. She thinks it's the one that ran down the boy. Want to come?"

"Like this?" She plucked the wet shirt away from her breasts.

"I can drop you off."

"Hell, I don't want to miss anything."

"Didn't think so."

She bent over, lifted the hanging blanket, and brought her shoulder bag up from beneath her seat. She took out a comb and brush. Then she twisted the rearview mirror in her direction. Mace's rear visibility was gone, but he didn't protest.

"Guess I shouldn't have stoned you," he said.

"Those photos better just not show up at roll call."

"On my honor." He accelerated to make it through an amber light on Throckmorton. There wasn't much traffic in downtown Mill Valley. He knew he would make good time.

"Should we notify Tiburon PD?" Mattie asked.

"We'll check it out first."

"You think *he's* up there?"

"If he is, he hasn't made his move yet. They're secure in the house."

"Unless he's inside with them."

It was a disturbing possibility, one that Mace had already considered.

Leigh hung up the phone and turned around in time to see Deana slide a butcher knife out of its walnut holder. "What're you—"

The girl pressed a finger to her lips. She walked quietly across the kitchen to where Leigh was standing. "Follow me," she whispered.

"What is it?"

"Shh. Come on."

Confused and growing alarmed, Leigh followed her past the dining area. What was happening? Had Deana seen something, heard a noise? My God, does she think the killer's in the house? He couldn't be. The doors . . .

Don't kid yourself, anybody who wanted to get in . . . maybe the guest-room windows.

She scanned the living room. Deana was several strides ahead of her, shoes squeaking on the foyer tile. Leigh rushed to catch up. Beyond the girl's shoulder, she saw the narrow, shadowed hallway stretching ahead of them.

Deana *wasn't* planning to search the place?

Leigh almost reached out to grab her, but Deana made a quick lunge into the bathroom, caught Leigh by the hand, and yanked her through the doorway. She swung the door shut, locked it, then hurried to the tub and checked behind its frosted-glass shower panels. Turning to Leigh, she let out a loud breath. "Just being careful."

"Do you think he's in the *house*?"

"He might be. I mean, I don't really think so, but who's to say he isn't? I just think this'd be a good place to wait until your policeman gets here."

"He's not *my* policeman."

"Then how come you called him instead of the Tiburon police?"

"Because this is his case. He knows what's going on."

"Uh-huh."

Leigh shook her head. Deana boosted herself up and sat on the counter beside the sink. "You know what some people have," the girl said, "is a safe room. Some actress has one. Victoria Principal? It's the bathroom. You have a reinforced metal door put in, with special locks. You have a telephone put in. That way, you've got someplace to go if there's trouble. You can call the cops, and nobody can get to you. The lock on *this* door wouldn't keep out a four-year-old."

"I wouldn't want to live like that," Leigh said.

"You don't have to *live* in the john. It's just so you have a place to go. . . ."

"No pun intended?"

Deana grinned. Lowering her head, she scraped the knife over her thigh. "This thing isn't very sharp."

"It isn't supposed to be a razor."

She lifted the knife away and ran her hand up from her knee to her shorts. "I'm gonna start looking like a werewolf. You're lucky you're a blonde."

"You've got lovely hair," Leigh said, stepping past her.

"Yeah, everywhere. What did my father look like, King Kong or something?"

Leigh felt a cold ripple in her stomach. She took off her ballcap and started to unpin her hair.

"You don't talk about him much," Deana said after a while.

"There's not much to say." Crouching, she took Deana's blow dryer from the cabinet under the sink. "Mind if I use this?"

"Help yourself." Deana reached down beside her knee, slid open a drawer, and took out her hairbrush. "Here."

"Thanks."

"Gotta fix yourself up for your policeman."

Leigh plugged in the dryer, turned it on, and started to brush her hair as the hot air blew against it.

"You never told me how he died," Deana said in a loud voice.

"Yes I did."

"I mean, not *how* it happened."

"It's a long story."

"Okay, so?"

"Mace'll be here in a minute."

"Well, that's . . ." She stopped. Frowning, she leaned forward and peered at the bathroom door. "Turn it off, Mom."

Leigh silenced the dryer. "Did you hear something?" she whispered.

"I don't know. That thing's so loud."

Leigh stood motionless, holding her breath. She flinched at the sudden sound of a thud.

A car door shutting.

"It's probably Mace," she said.

Deana hopped to the floor, cranked open the bathroom

window, and looked out. Leigh gave her hair a few final strokes with the brush. She heard footsteps on the walkway leading to the stoop.

"It's him," Deana said. "He's got a gal with him." She stepped away from the window. "You think it's his wife?"

"I wouldn't know."

"Don't worry about your hair. Hers is wetter than yours."

The doorbell rang.

"Just a second," Deana called out. She picked up the knife.

"Why don't you leave that here?"

Deana raised an eyebrow, kept the knife, and held it at her side, blade forward, as she stepped to the bathroom door. She turned the knob slowly, keeping the lock button depressed so it wouldn't ping out. She jerked the door open fast. Nobody there. Leaning out, she looked both ways. "The coast is clear," she said.

The *ghost* is clear, Leigh thought, following her out. That's what Deana used to say when she was about four and didn't know any better. It didn't seem like very long ago. Now she's eighteen, and looking after *me*.

Deana led the way to the front door and opened it.

"Come in," she said, lowering the knife.

Mace stepped in, followed by the woman. The woman's short brown hair was slicked down. Her blouse and cutoff jeans looked wet. "Any trouble?" Mace asked.

"We haven't seen anyone," Leigh said. "We were worried he might've gotten into the house, though, so we waited in the bathroom."

"It's about the only door with a lock," Deana added.

"Good place to wait," Mace said. "Ladies, this is Sergeant Blaylock. Sergeant, Leigh and Deana West."

They nodded greetings.

"I'll take a look around," he said. He turned away. As he walked up the hallway, he lifted his shirttail and pulled a small revolver from a holster at the back of his belt.

Sergeant Blaylock stayed.

"You got one, too?" Deana asked.

She patted her shoulder bag. Her head moved slightly as she scanned the living room. "I heard you own the Bayview," she said, glancing at Leigh before returning her gaze to the room beyond. "That's a fabulous place."

"Thank you."

"Anytime some guy wants to impress me, that's where he takes me. Works, too. Maybe I could hit you up for the veal scaloppine recipe. Or is that classified information?"

"I'll get it for you," Leigh assured her. The recipe *was* to be kept secret, but she liked Sergeant Blaylock. She felt a bond with this slim, attractive woman who looked as if she'd just lost a sorority tug-of-war. She didn't know why she felt this bond. Maybe it had to do with the sergeant coming to her home on a Sunday morning, ready to put it on the line for her. "For your eyes only," she added.

"Fair enough."

"Are you Harrison's partner?" Deana asked.

"Used to be. When we were in radio cars." She frowned toward the corridor. "Mace!" she yelled.

"Yo!" he called back.

"He might take all morning," she said, "but when he's done you can bet your petuties you won't have anyone creeping out at you."

"Are you two on duty?" Deana asked.

Leigh wished she would quit.

"We are now," the sergeant said.

"How come you're all wet?"

"Sorry about that." She looked down, apparently to see whether she was dripping. "You know the Old Mill Stream in Mill Valley?" She fluttered the front of her blouse. "This is it, Charlie."

Charlie.

What *is* this, Leigh wondered, a conspiracy to keep dredging up Charlie Payne?

"We came right over, so I didn't have time to change."

"If you'd be more comfortable in dry clothes," Leigh said, "you're welcome to something of mine."

"No. Thanks anyway, Ms. West."

"Leigh."

"Leigh it is. I'm Mattie."

"I'm Deana."

"I caught that."

"You called me Charlie."

"Yeah, I do that."

"My father's name was Charlie."

Here we go again, Leigh thought.

But it didn't go any further, because Mace came striding down the corridor. He held his short-barreled revolver close to his shoulder, pointed at the ceiling. "It's all right back there," he said. Before reaching them, he stepped down into the den and disappeared behind the fireplace area that separated the den from the living room.

A little while later, he walked past the rear of the fireplace and made a circuit of the living room, checking the sliding glass doors and looking behind furniture. At the far side of the living room, he unlocked the door, ran it open, and stepped outside. He vanished, then reappeared, walking the deck that stretched along the entire rear of the house.

When he came back, he headed for the kitchen. Leigh heard his footsteps on the floor, then the squeak of the door opening into the garage.

Finally, he returned. "The place is secure," he said, and put his revolver away. "That's to say, nobody's here but us. There's no indication of forced entry. You've got drop pins on your sliding doors, which is good. You should do something about the windows, though. Pick up some quarter-inch dowel rods to drop in the runners, that's the easiest way. Cut them off in lengths that'll let you open the windows a few inches for fresh air, but no farther."

"We'll have to take care of that," Leigh said.

"You might want to invest in an alarm system that'll tie in to a private security patrol. Oh, and the gravel strip under the windows is a good idea. Announces the presence of intruders in that area. If and when, of course."

Leigh nodded.

"Let's take a look at the car." He opened the front door. "Do you have your keys?" he asked.

"I do," Deana said, pulling a chain out of her T-shirt. A house key dangled at its end.

They stepped outside. Mattie shut the door.

"That's another thing," Deana said, pointing at the newspaper on the stoop. "It's always up at the top of the driveway. When I came out this morning, it was right here."

"Okay. We may want to have the lab check it." They crossed to the driveway. A shiny, black Trans Am was parked in front of the garage. "What time did you first notice the car?" Mace asked as they started up the sloping pavement.

"Around eight-thirty," Leigh said. "Just before we phoned."

"We were to go running," Deana added.

"What did you do when you saw it?"

"Hauled ass back to the house."

"Deana."

"Sorry."

"Did you hear any unusual sounds? Last night or this morning?"

"No."

"Nothing."

Just before they reached the top of the driveway, Leigh saw the old red Pontiac. Even in the bright sunlight, it looked ominous. It reminded her of that movie *Christine*. The car in that movie was red, too, but not a Pontiac. It had a life of its own, and she imagined this one starting up with no one inside. It won't, she told herself. It damn well *better* not.

They crossed the road. Squatting, Mace touched the exhaust pipe. Then he peered through the open driver's window. Mattie, beside him, looked into the backseat. She opened her shoulder bag and followed Mace to the front, where he bent down and inspected the smashed-in areas.

Mattie took out a notepad. She started writing.

"The damage appears consistent with the facts of the hit," he said. He dug a pocketknife out of his pocket, pried out a blade, and scraped at the bent metal grille. His knife point came away with a tiny pile of powder that looked like rust. He fingered it off, rubbed the dust with his thumb, sniffed and tasted it.

Deana looked at Leigh and wrinkled her nose.

"We'd better have a crime-scene unit come out," he said.

"Then this *is* the one?" Leigh asked.

"I can't say for sure. It's a strong possibility, though." He looked over his shoulder at Mattie. "We'll notify the Tiburon PD. They'll need to be in on this, but they'll probably be agreeable to letting our people handle the detail work."

"Save a lot of back-and-forth," she agreed. She hurried across the road and started down the driveway.

"Doesn't she need my key?" Deana asked.

"She can call from the car." Mace put away his knife. Getting down on his hands and knees, he lowered his head almost to the pavement and looked under the car. Then he stood up. He brushed gravel off his palms.

"What now?" Leigh asked.

"We wait for the lab people to do their work. It won't take long to find out whether the blood down here matches up with the Powers boy."

"Shouldn't somebody search Del Mar?" Leigh asked.

"This car has been here for hours. He's long gone. But he left the car behind, and that was a big mistake. It'll help us nail him."

"It's probably stolen," Deana said.

"Undoubtedly. But we'll get some physical evidence from it. Maybe fingerprints, maybe hair samples, maybe fabric particles. When we run down the car owner, we might find out if he witnessed the theft—if that's what it was. All this will take time, though. I don't want you two staying in the house."

Leigh felt her stomach flip as if the street had suddenly dropped from under her feet.

Mace looked from Leigh to Deana. His gaze settled on Leigh's eyes. "I don't want to alarm you, but . . ."

"You're going to do it anyway."

He smiled a bit. "Afraid so. You know what it means, of course, the car being here."

"Exactly what *does* it mean?" Leigh heard a tremor in her voice.

"It means, A, the killer knows where Deana lives, and B, he paid her a visit."

"Why?"

"Unfinished business."

"Jesus," Deana muttered.

"He was here," Leigh said, "so why didn't he *do* something?"

"We don't know what he did or didn't do."

"I can think of a couple of things he *didn't* do," Deana said, and tried for a smile. The corner of her mouth trembled for an instant. She licked her lips, wiped them with the back of her hand.

"He might have left the car here as a message," Mace suggested. "A warning that he can get to you if he wants. Or maybe he's toying with you."

"Toying?"

"This guy is not a normal person. He's probably totally different from anyone in your experience."

"You mean like a psycho?" Deana asked.

"That's what I mean."

"Move over, Norman Bates."

"So there's no telling what he might do."

"You think he left it here just to scare us?" Leigh asked.

"Anything's possible. But . . ."

"They're on the way," Mattie said, striding across the street.

"What were you about to say?" Leigh asked Mace.

"I think you should check into a motel, unless you have friends or relatives who wouldn't mind putting you up for a while."

"That isn't what you were going to say," Leigh challenged him. "It was something about the car and why it's here. To scare us or *what*?"

"It would just be a guess."

"I want to hear it."

"All right." He looked uncomfortable. He lowered his eyes for a moment, then met Leigh's gaze. "That unfinished business I mentioned earlier? I think he came here intending to finish it. Last night. But something went wrong. The car's still here. I suspect the reason it's here is because it quit on him. He realized he couldn't count on it for his getaway. That's why he didn't go through with his plan."

NINE

"Do you have a plastic bag large enough for this?" Mace asked, looking down at the thick edition of the Sunday newspaper that lay flat on the stoop, tied with string.

"A wastebasket liner?" Leigh asked.

"That'd be perfect."

"You want to get one for us?" she asked her daughter. The girl went to the door.

"Why do you need the paper?" Leigh asked.

"There's a good chance your visitor put it here." He stepped onto the grass, and Leigh followed him along the front of the house. "Maybe he was good enough to leave us some prints."

"Can you get fingerprints off newspapers?"

"These days, you can get them off almost anything. Our lab people have chemicals that interact with the body oils left by . . . Look here." Stopping, he pointed down at the flower bed. The soft soil had been mashed down by shoes.

A glance at Leigh's feet convinced him that she hadn't made these impressions. Her feet were too small. And the daughter, who was only a bit taller than Leigh, probably didn't have feet this large, either.

The footprints led through the flower bed to the guest-room window.

Mace looked at Leigh. She was standing rigid, gazing at the ground, the fingertips of one hand stroking her lower lip.

He felt sorry for her. He could imagine what she must be feeling—scared and vulnerable. The bastard had actually crept right up to her house last night while she and her daughter were inside, maybe fast asleep. Maybe he'd even seen them.

From where Mace stood, he couldn't spot any damage to the window or frame. "It doesn't look as if he tried to break in."

"But he could've," Leigh said, "couldn't he?"

"It wouldn't have been too difficult."

Leigh shook her head slowly. "It's just getting worse. What do you . . . Do you think he wants to kill her?"

"Either that or take her. I think I mentioned Friday night that he might have some kind of obsession. Maybe he wants her."

"God," Leigh muttered.

"Don't worry. We'll see that he doesn't get another chance."

They both turned toward Deana as the girl approached with a white plastic bag. "What's up?" she asked. "Did you find something?"

"He was here," Leigh said. She pointed to the ground.

Deana looked at the footprints. "Oh, wonderful," she muttered.

"We should be able to get a good estimate of his height and weight from these," Mace said.

"Not to mention his shoe size," Deana added in a quiet voice. She didn't like the way things were turning out.

Mace led the way to the stoop. Taking the bag from Deana, he crouched over the newspaper and carefully slipped his fingers under one of its strings without touching the "Blondie" comic strip beneath. When he raised it, the paper tilted.

Out of its folds slipped a small, white knob, maybe a bone or a polished rock. It hung at the edge of the newspaper, held in place by a rawhide strip that ran through its center and stayed trapped inside the paper.

With a ballpoint from his shirt pocket, Mace hooked the rawhide and eased it out.

The thong was knotted at its ends. It swung from the tip of his pen like a strange, primitive necklace.

"Mom!"

Mace looked, saw Leigh with her eyes rolled upward, her knees folding. He sprang at her, thrust his hands under her armpits, and slowed her fall as she sank to the stoop, unconscious.

TEN

When she got home late that afternoon, she had a story ready: A purse snatcher had grabbed her shoulder bag when she came out of the movie theater on Market Street, she had fought him off, and that's how the sleeve of her granny dress got torn.

One look at her parents and Leigh knew that the story

wouldn't wash. They were standing in the living room like a couple of mannequins left behind in a hurry—Dad sideways near the window, head down and turned her way, one hand on the back of his neck, Mom in front of the fireplace, facing her, the fingers of both hands mashing her lower face. Mom's eyes were red, accusing. Dad's eyes were haggard, blank.

Obviously, they both knew.

Leigh forced a smile. It felt crooked. "I guess I'm in for it now," she said.

Dad's eyes stopped looking blank. "If you see an amusing side to this situation," he said in an icy voice, "I would appreciate your filling us in. We fail to see the humor."

"Do you have any idea what you've put us through?" Mom asked, lowering her hands and clutching them in front of her waist.

"I'm sorry," she mumbled.

"You're sorry," Dad said. "Well, so are we."

"How . . . how did you find out?"

"They interrupted the Giants game," Dad said.

"My God, how could you do such a thing?" Mom blurted.

"And there you were."

"It made your father physically ill."

"I'm sorry I lied. But you wouldn't have let me go if I'd told you about the demonstration."

"You're goddamn right about that."

Leigh cringed. She'd rarely heard her father use profanity.

"Kids are over there dying, for godsake, and here you are in a getup like some kind of hippie freak, holding hands with a bunch of long-haired creeps who want nothing better than to destroy a way of life—"

"Nobody wants to destroy anything."

"Bull*shit!*"

"We just want the war to stop."

"I'm not going to debate the war with you. That isn't the issue."

"It is, too."

"How do you think Colonel Randolph would feel," Mom asked, "if he saw how you—"

"He'd still *have* his son," Leigh snapped, "if it weren't for that murdering bastard in the White House."

Dad turned white. He crossed the floor so fast Leigh didn't have time to move, and slapped her hard across the face.

She was stunned. Dad had never slapped her before.

Whirling around, she ran to her room, slammed the door, and threw herself down on her bed.

She had stopped crying by the time Dad came in. He sat on the edge of the bed. He had been crying, too. He stroked Leigh's forehead, lightly brushing the hair aside. "I'm sorry," he said.

"I know. Me, too."

"Your mother and I . . . we try to understand. If we didn't love you so much, do you think we'd care one way or the other if you were out there? . . . You could've been hurt. . . ."

"Maybe I was. Did you ask?"

"No. *Were* you hurt?"

She shook her head.

"Well, that's lucky. How did your dress get torn?"

"One of the . . ." She almost said "pigs," but she didn't want to start him up again. "A cop grabbed me. But I got away from him. Then I took off. I was supposed to *let* them bust me, that was the idea, but I figured you and Mom would really hit the ceiling if you had to come and bail me out."

"You're right."

"I guess you hit the ceiling anyway."

"I spent four years of my life fighting for this country, honey. I can't help it, but my blood just starts to boil when I see a bunch of pampered kids who never worked a day in their lives spitting on everything that—"

"Don't get started, okay?"

"Burning the American flag."

"Dad."

"Mouthing off about 'the establishment.' My God, it's the dreaded 'establishment' that puts the food in the bellies of these people. . . . *I'm* the establishment. Me and all the other people who worked our butts off so that our kids could maybe have it a little better than we did. And *we're* the enemy? Am I a warmonger? Is Colonel Randolph? Do you think he *likes* this war? My God, the man's been devastated by it."

"Then he should be out there marching against it."

Dad shook his head, sighed. "I would never wish anything bad on you, honey. I certainly hope you don't have to learn this the hard way. You're all idealistic right now, and you're sure that peace and love will rule the world if you just march around and sing a few songs about it. But I'm afraid you're in for a rude awakening. There are bad people in this world."

"Tell me about it," she muttered.

"I intend to, whether you like it or not. There are people out there—and governments—that would be more than happy to wipe out you and me and your mother, our country if they're given half a chance. Guys like your pals Castro and Ho Chi Minh."

"They aren't my pals. Neither is LBJ."

He ignored that and went on. "Guys like Charles Starkweather and Richard Speck."

She'd heard of Speck but didn't know who Charles Starkweather was.

"Do you think your pacifism would work on them? Turn the other cheek on them, and they'll cut it off for you."

"I get the message."

"Do you? I doubt it. I think your mind's been so twisted around by all your long-haired friends that you don't know which end is up anymore. We've been pretty lenient with your weird outfits and anti-everything buttons and staying out till all hours at that place in Sausalito. But we trusted you to have more sense than to get involved in something like this today. We brought you up to know better."

"You brought me up to do what I think is right," Leigh said. "And I think it's right to protest the war."

"Well, you're mistaken. And it's high time for a crackdown."

"Let me guess. I'm grounded."

"At the very least, young lady."

"Whatever happened to freedom of speech?"

"You can feel free to *speak* whatever you like, but I will not allow you to march with the Great Unwashed and get yourself thrown in jail."

"I didn't get thrown in jail."

"Not this time. And believe you me, you won't get another chance at it. Not while you're living under this roof."

Leigh pulled the pillow down over her face. "Are you done?"

"We just want what's best for you, honey."

"Yeah, sure.".

"You'll understand someday when you have kids of your own. Now why don't you get cleaned up for supper. We'll try to start out on a new foot, okay?"

"All right," she muttered.

When he was gone, she took her robe into the bathroom. She pulled her dress over her head, turned it around, and looked at the buttons pinned to the front. A peace button. One with Uncle Sam pointing, not his finger but a revolver. One read, "Make Luv Not War." Another, "The Great Society: Bombs, Bullets, Bullshit." Another, "War is Unhealthy for Children and Other Living Things." Dad had called them "anti-everything buttons." He was so blind. Couldn't he see that they were pro-peace and -love?

Leigh let the dress fall to the floor. She moaned from her aches as she bent down and untied the leather thong around her left ankle. The bell strung through it jingled softly. She set it on the counter.

Reaching behind her neck, she untied the other thong. She held it up and stared at the dangling ornament. She had found the thing in the sand near Point Reyes Station a few months ago. She didn't know what it was. Maybe that was why she had kept it. The small, rounded thing with one side curled inward seemed too light to be a stone. It looked and felt like ivory. She suspected it might be some kind of shell or fish bone, though its shape was so peculiar that she couldn't imagine what kind of creature it might have once belonged to.

It came with a hole through the middle, so she had strung it on a rawhide lace from one of her old hiking boots and made herself a necklace.

She thought of it as her "sea-thing" necklace. Sometimes as her lucky necklace.

It hadn't brought her much luck today.

She set it down carefully beside the ankle bell and looked down at herself. Pressing in on her left breast, she flattened it enough to let her see the reddish-blue mark across the ribs just beneath it. A police nightstick had done that. The same nightstick, wielded by the same pig, had left a bruise the size of quarter on the jut of her hipbone.

That fucking Gestapo pig.

Leigh had seen lust in his eyes when he went at her, ramming low with the end of his stick. He was aiming between her legs. But she moved fast enough so it pounded her hip instead.

Leigh turned around. She looked over her shoulder at the mirror and saw three strips of bruises across her back. The seat of her panties was shredded and speckled with blood from when they had dragged her by the feet. She pulled the panties down and wrinkled her nose at the sight of her scraped buttocks.

Yeah, Dad, she thought, tell me about the bad guys.

* * *

Three days later, Leigh was on a TWA flight to Milwaukee.

From her parents' point of view, the Bay Area was a hotbed of radicalism. A month with her uncle Mike and aunt Jenny, two thousand miles away from it all, would keep her safe from such influences and give her a chance to learn how people look at things in the solid, down-to-earth Middle America.

She didn't *have* to go, of course. They wouldn't force her. If she refused, however, she would be restricted to the house for the entire summer.

Leigh decided to take her chances with the boondocks.

Once she agreed to go, Mom and Dad changed. They seemed a little giddy. The Prodigal Daughter had returned. Instead of slaying the fatted calf, they took her out to dinner at the White Whale on Ghirardelli Square. Leigh let herself slide back, at least for the time being, into the role of the well-bred daughter. She didn't want to spoil their mood. Besides, acting rebellious would have been difficult; she enjoyed fine restaurants too much. The dim lights, the quiet sounds of people dining, the pleasant aromas and delicious food. She could never walk into one without starting, right away, to feel good.

Her parents seemed to forget that the trip to Wisconsin was a ploy to remove Leigh from harmful influences. It was a special vacation for her. She would love it—the woods and lake, the swimming and boating and fishing. They wished they could go with her, but of course Dad's job made that impossible. On second thought, maybe they could arrange to come up for a week later on. It would be terrific.

Mom took Leigh shopping the next day. At Macy's on Union Square, they bought a conservative dress and shoes for the flight, two sundresses, an orange blouse, white shorts, a modest one-piece bathing suit, and an assortment of undergarments. Leigh went along with her mother's suggestions, though she fully intended to spend most of her time in T-shirts and cutoffs.

At Dunhill's, they bought a soft leather tobacco pouch and a tin of Royal Yachtsman tobacco for Uncle Mike, a pipe smoker. At Blum's, they bought a box of candy for Aunt Jenny. They ate lunch there and finished with a dessert of Blum's fabulous lemon crunch cake.

Leigh expected to be taken home when they returned to the car after lunch. Instead, Mom drove her to North Beach. "You'll need some reading material, I think." They went to the City Lights, then to a secondhand bookstore across the alley. Mom waited while Leigh loaded up with paperback editions of *Franny and Zooey, Soldier in the Rain, Boys and Girls Together, The Ginger Man, In Cold Blood, Love Poems of Kenneth Patchen, Just You and Me,* and *The Strange Case of Charles Dexter Ward.* Mom raised an eyebrow at the selection but kept her opinions to herself and paid for all the books.

Leigh woke up on Tuesday morning feeling excited. The trip, to be sure, was a form of banishment. But she found herself looking forward to it anyway. The trip would be an adventure. She'd be on her own during the flight and, if her aunt and uncle would stay out of her hair enough during the visit, she might even be able to enjoy herself. At least they weren't her parents—maybe they wouldn't try to control her life while she was there.

At the boarding gate, Mom wept. Dad gave her a fierce hug.

"Be on your best behavior," Mom said.

"Save some fish for us, honey," Dad told her.

"You're definitely coming out, then?"

"We wouldn't miss it."

Leaving them, she hurried along the boarding ramp with light, quick steps. She almost started skipping. She felt free and wonderful.

When she reached her seat, she opened her purse and

took out her peace button. She pinned it to the top of her crisp, proper, Macy's dress. Then she tied the rawhide behind her neck, opened her top button, and slipped the seathing in. It was smooth and cool on the skin between her breasts.

The pin and necklace let Leigh feel more like herself.

They can change where I go and who I see, she thought, but they can't change who I am.

ELEVEN

Leigh hadn't seen her aunt and uncle since their trip to California when she was twelve, but she recognized them immediately when she stepped through the gate.

Uncle Mike looked a lot like Dad, especially his eyes. He was bigger, though—built like a football player. And, unlike Dad, he sported sideburns and a bushy mustache. His hair was considerably longer, too. Dad wouldn't have approved of his brother's appearance. Leigh felt relieved. She gave him a hug. His corduroy jacket smelled of pipe smoke.

She kissed Aunt Jenny on the cheek. The woman was surprisingly short. She used to be the same height as Leigh. Now the top of her head came only to Leigh's chin. She was still as slim, however, and she still had a humongous bosom. She no longer wore the weird, harlequin glasses she'd had six years ago. Now she wore round lenses with wire rims. Granny glasses. A very good sign.

"You sure have sprouted up," Aunt Jenny told her. "I considered it, myself, but chose not to. I enjoy conversing with belly buttons."

Uncle Mike reached for Leigh's carry-on. "Let me take

that for you." They started walking. "So how was your flight?"

"Just fine."

"They feed you?" Jenny asked. "We've got a pretty long haul ahead of us."

"We've got snacks. Or we can stop along the way." Mike smiled around at Leigh. "Are you still crazy about McDonald's?"

"Not quite like I used to be."

"God, I remembered you hogged my fries."

This might not be so bad, Leigh thought as she walked with them toward the baggage-claim area. Then she thought, Don't kid yourself. Maybe they're not as uptight as Mom and Dad, but they're the same generation. They'll have a lot of the same hang-ups, even if they do seem pretty cool for people their age. So you'd better watch out.

Their car was an old, battered station wagon. Mike loaded Leigh's luggage into the rear, tossed in his corduroy jacket, which must have been smothering him in this hot, muggy weather, and came around to the passenger side. "Don't see why we can't all pile into the front," he said.

Leigh sat between them.

"So," Mike said as he started to drive, "we hear you've been dabbling in hippiedom."

Here we go. "A bit," she admitted.

"I don't see that the movement's produced any worthwhile literature."

"I wouldn't say that," Jenny told him. "Hey, hey, LBJ, how many kids did you kill today?"

"Ah, but where are the Ginsbergs, the Ferlinghettis, the Kerouacs, the Gary Sniders?"

"Mike misses the Beatniks," Jenny explained.

"I was in Ferlinghetti's bookstore just yesterday," Leigh said.

"The City Lights? No kidding. We stopped in there

when we were out visiting you folks. We sandwiched it in between the McDonald's, so to speak. Do you remember that?"

"I don't think so."

"It was the high point of the trip for Mike," Jenny said.

"Who've the hippies got? Kesey? He's all right. *Cuckoo's Nest* is all right. But who else?"

"Ginsberg's still writing," Leigh said. "Yeah, but he's not a true hippie. He's an over-the-hill Beatnik. There's a difference."

"Not a whole lot," Jenny said. "Do hippies wear berets? Do hippies play bongos? Do hippies recite poetry in coffeehouses?"

"Mike's a closet Beatnik."

He started to declaim "Howl" in a deep, thundering voice.

"Oh, geez, spare us."

Leigh started to laugh.

After a few stanzas, Mike quit his recitation. He and Jenny started asking the questions Leigh expected from relatives she hadn't seen in years. How were her parents? How was school? Did she have a boyfriend? What did she like to do in her spare time? What did she plan to major in at the university? Did she have a career in mind?

They talked about themselves: the high school where Mike taught English and Jenny taught music; their cabin on Lake Wahconda; the new Cris Craft they'd bought two weeks ago; a drowning the previous summer when a fisherman's boat capsized in a sudden storm; a legendary muskie named Old Duke that was said to inhabit the lake.

By the time they'd been on the road for an hour, Leigh felt completely at ease. Her aunt and uncle seemed easygoing and good-humored. They didn't talk down to her. They treated her like an adult, a friend.

"Are you getting hungry?" Mike asked.

"I'm okay," Leigh said.

"Thought I heard your stomach growl."

"Not mine."

"Well, I'm pretty sure there's a McDonald's around the next bend."

Leigh doubted it. They were traveling along a two-lane road deep in the woods. The Big Bass Bait & Tackle Shop was the last business establishment Leigh had seen. That was ten minutes ago.

Mike steered around the bend. "Guess I was wrong. I remember I was wrong once before."

"You can remember that far back?" Jenny asked. "Admirable."

"You'd better break out the provisions, Tink."

Jenny turned around. Kneeling, she reached down behind the seat. She handed back three cold bottles of Hamms to Leigh.

Mike started to sing the Hamms beer commercial about lakes and sunset breezes. Leigh pictured a cartoon bear playing a log like a tom-tom.

"We thought you might appreciate an authentic native snack," Jenny said, twisting around and sitting down again. She had a box of Ritz crackers in one hand, a pottery crock in the other.

The crock contained smoked cheddar, which she spread on crackers while Leigh broke open the beers with a can opener from the glove compartment.

"Now, we know we're corrupting you here," Mike said, "but we rely on your good judgment to keep your folks ignorant about this."

"Mum's the word," Leigh promised.

"Don't tell your mum, either," Jenny warned.

The beer was cold and good. Maybe it was her hunger, but Leigh thought she had never eaten cheese and crackers half as delicious as these. She drank, ate crackers, passed some from Jenny to Mike, and later took over the cheese-spreading chores when Jenny knelt on the seat again to get three more bottles of beer.

She already felt light-headed, a little numb behind her

cheekbones. So she watched herself, being careful to hold her giddiness in check and pronounce her words correctly when she talked. It wouldn't do at all for them to think that the beer was getting to her. During the second beer, the numbness spread to her cheeks. The cheese and crackers tasted better all the time.

"I've about had it," Jenny finally said.

"More for the rest of us," said Mike, clamping his beer between his legs and taking another cheese-mounded cracker from Leigh.

Soon, the knife was coming out of the pottery crock with no more than a thread of cheese along its edge.

"Better swoop up the rest of it with your finger," Mike advised.

"That would be gross," Leigh said.

"You're among friends."

So she cleaned out the remaining cheese, licking it off her finger.

When her beer was finished, she folded her hands on her lap, sighed, and settled down in the seat. "That really hit the spot," she mumbled. Soon, her eyes drifted shut.

When she woke up, the car was passing a lake. A boy standing in a motorboat was handing a tackle box to a man reaching down from the dock.

"We're not there yet," Mike said.

"A couple more hours," Jenny told her.

"You guys must really live far out."

"Far from the madding crowd," Mike said.

Later, they stopped for gas at a place called Jody's with two pumps in front and neon beer signs in the windows. A thin, red-haired man in bib overalls stared down at them from a rocker on the porch. "Mary Jo," he called in a flat voice.

The door swung open. A girl wandered out and squinted toward the car as if she couldn't quite puzzle out where it might have come from. "Don't just stand there collecting dust."

With a shrug, she trotted down the porch steps. She didn't look older than twelve. Leigh took an immediate dislike for the man—sitting on his butt and ordering the kid to do the work.

"Help you?" she asked at Mike's window.

"Fill her up with ethyl."

The girl went around to the rear. "I don't know about you guys," Mike said, "but I'm going to make a pit stop while I've got the chance."

The man watched them in silence as they left the car and climbed the porch stairs. Leigh was glad to get inside, away from him.

"A real charmer," Jenny whispered.

"His kid's no prize, either," Mike said.

They walked past a deserted lunch counter. At the far end were two doors, one marked "Pointers," the other "Setters."

"Well, I'll be doggone," Mike said. He smirked and opened the Pointers door.

Jenny motioned for Leigh to go first. Inside the rest room, Leigh bolted the door. The window was open. She looked through the screen to make sure the man wasn't skulking around. Behind the building was a jumble of weeds, then the forest.

The toilet seat looked clean, but she didn't sit on it. She braced herself above it until she was done. After washing her hands, she held on to a paper towel as she unbolted and opened the door. She didn't want to touch anything in this place.

Jenny entered. Mike was already at the other end of the lunch counter, wandering among shelves at the other side. Leigh went to join him. This part of the room had groceries, souvenirs, and sporting goods. "Something for everyone," Mike said.

The man came through the door and stared at them. Leigh stepped closer to Mike.

"Help you?"

"Just looking around, thanks."

"Gas comes to eight-fifty," he said, and stepped behind the small counter next to the door.

Leigh went to a wire book rack as Mike headed over to pay him. The paperbacks were mostly Westerns and mysteries. Some had bent covers and white lines down the spines as if they'd already been read.

"Where you folks headed?" she heard the man ask.

"Up to Lake Wahconda."

Leigh wished Mike hadn't told him. Then she felt foolish. What was she afraid of? Did she think the creep would pay them a visit?

After paying the man, Mike wandered over to a wall map near the door.

What was taking Jenny so long?

Leigh returned her gaze to the book carousel. The man stayed behind the counter. He seemed to be watching her, but she forced herself not to look at him. She would not look. Her eyes slipped sideways. He was staring at her, all right. Not at her eyes, though.

At the peace button?

She wished she had left it in her purse.

Hearing quiet footsteps, she turned her head. Jenny was striding between the lunch counter and tables. "All set?"

With a nod, Mike opened the door.

"Don't be strangers," the man said, a smile on his flushed face.

Leigh hurried to catch up. With Jenny on the porch and Mike outside holding the door, Leigh was alone as she passed the man.

" 'Bye, now," he said.

She looked at him as he stepped back from the counter. She tried to smile, and thought for an instant that he was missing an arm. Why hadn't she noticed that before? She started to feel sorry for him. Then she realized that he wasn't an amputee at all. His right arm, from the elbow down, was inside his bib overalls. The bulge of faded denim made by his arm angled down to his crotch. There, the jutting fabric stirred with the motions of his hand.

Leigh rushed outside and dodged just in time to avoid a collision with Mary Jo. "Sorry," she muttered.

The girl narrowed her eyes, stepped past her, and went through the doorway.

"Are you all right?" Mike asked.

"Yeah, fine."

"You look a little shaky."

She shrugged.

Before climbing into the car, she glanced over her shoulder. No one came out of Jody's. She didn't look again. Safe between her aunt and uncle, she gazed at the dashboard. The car bumped over ruts, then moved along the smooth pavement of the road and soon rounded a bend.

She felt frightened, violated.

When Mike turned his head slightly to check the rearview mirror, Leigh twisted around and looked back. A pickup truck was close behind them. Reflections on its windshield prevented her from seeing inside. The pickup swung into the other lane, gaining speed. Her stomach tightened. As the truck pulled alongside their car, a young woman nodded a greeting through the passenger window. Leigh glimpsed the driver, a heavyset man in sunglasses, wearing a ballcap with its bill tipped up. She settled back into her seat as the pickup sped by. A safe distance ahead, it eased back into the northbound lane.

"Something wrong?" Jenny asked.

"Just that guy back where we got the gas. He gave me the creeps."

"You and me both," Jenny said. "Not that he did anything in particular to deserve it."

Oh no? Leigh thought.

"Too much isolation," Mike explained. "It has a way of warping the mind."

"He was warped, all right," Leigh muttered.

"I feel sorry for his daughter," Jenny said.

"Who?" Mike asked. "Mary Jo? What makes you think she's his daughter? She and her folks stopped by for gas last summer. Ol' Jody bashed their heads and planted 'em out by the woodpile, kept the girl."

"That's not very funny, Mike."

"I guess not. You've got to admit, though, some pretty weird goings-on go on around this neck of the woods." He glanced at Leigh. "There was a fellow a few years ago, Ed Gein—"

"Don't get into that," Jenny warned.

"Well, I don't want to frighten you, Leigh."

"Then don't," Jenny told him.

"But I want you to keep your eyes open while you're staying with us. Just because you're not in the big city, don't let your guard down. We've got our share of weirdos."

Mike was Dad's brother, all right. This lecture had a very familiar ring to it.

"Mike is right about that," Jenny said. "We've never run into any problems, ourselves, but . . ."

"I wouldn't exactly say that."

"Nothing serious. But you do want to be careful, especially if you go around anywhere by yourself."

"I will be," Leigh assured them.

As she gazed at the tree-shadowed road ahead, her mind traveled back to Jody's. The guy there had wanted her to see what he was doing. That's why he spoke to her as she was leaving, so she would look at him, see his overalls sticking out like a tepee. His hand in there. Moving around. Rubbing himself. While he stared at her.

Mike's story took hold. She finished in the bathroom and opened the door, and stumbled over Mike's body. Jenny was sprawled atop the lunch counter, screaming as the man plunged a hunting knife into her belly again and again. He stopped. He turned to Leigh. His face was splattered and dripping blood.

"Now you're all mine, sweet thing."

Licking blood off his lips, he stepped toward her. The knife in his left hand carved slow circles in the air. His right hand tugged his zipper down, reached inside, and freed his huge, engorged penis. He slid his hand up and down, slicking his shaft with blood.

I'd bite it off for him, Leigh thought.

No, I'd make a break for it.

She pictured herself whirling around and locking herself inside the bathroom. He kicked at the door. Her only escape was through the window. A tight squeeze, but maybe . . . She boosted herself up. Started squirming out. And saw the girl, Mary Jo, standing in the weeds below with an ax in her hands. "Oh no you don't," the girl said, and grinned. "We got her cornered, Pa!" she yelled.

Leigh's heart was thudding. Her mouth was dry. How in hell would she get out of *this?*

Don't worry, she told herself. It didn't happen, and it won't. He's a goddamn pervert, but we're out of there. We're all in one piece.

If he had tried something, Mike would have fixed him.

Unless he took Mike by surprise.

Don't get started again.

Why did Mike have to tell him where we're going?

He *isn't* going to come.

He could leave Mary Jo behind to pump gas, run the grill, and look after the shop. Take a gun and knife out to his pickup truck.

"You goin' after that gal?" Mary Jo asked.

"Prime stuff, weren't she?"

"Well, bring some back for me, Pa. You know how I like gizzards."

Good Christ, Leigh thought. I must be going nuts, thinking up this kind of garbage. "Hey," she said, "maybe we ought to sing something."

"Great idea," Jenny said.

"Do you know 'Waltzing Matilda'?" Mike asked.

"Just the refrain."

"Well, you're with a couple of teachers."

"Yep," Jenny said. "We'll teach you the words."

"Singing's dry business," Mike told her. "Better break out some brews."

TWELVE

Her experience at Jody's stayed in Leigh's mind like a spider huddled in a ceiling corner—a black speck, always there and vaguely disturbing, but not much of a threat. So long as it didn't start to travel.

During the first few days at Lake Wahconda, Leigh watched for the man. She went nowhere by herself. She knew he would not show up. But he might.

Even if he didn't, Leigh had no guarantee that someone with a similar warp might not be lurking in the woods.

The western side of Lake Wahconda was fairly well populated: a vacation camp with a lodge and a dozen small cabins near the south shore, and a chain of eight or ten cabins and A-frames, with a good deal of woods between them, extending up to the north shore. The nearest island had a large stone house on it. The rest of the islands were uninhabited.

It was as if civilization had captured the western shore and the single island, then ventured no farther. Except by boat. Out fishing with Mike and Jenny, Leigh sometimes saw rickety docks, ancient rowboats, cabins and shacks hidden among the trees. She occasionally heard wood being chopped, a distant crack of gunfire. People lived along these shores. A few, anyway. But Leigh didn't spot any of them; she didn't want to.

As the specter of the man from Jody's diminished, Leigh began to take the canoe out by herself. She enjoyed the peaceful solitude, the feel of her working muscles, the challenge of making the canoe glide over the water. But there was something more—a sense of anticipation. Alone on the lake, paddling the length of its western shore, she felt as if something mysterious and wonderful might happen at any moment.

The feeling was vague and without definition at first. On the fifth day of her visit, however, that changed.

They had gone out fishing in the Cris Craft early that morning until almost noon, so Leigh missed her morning canoe trip. After lunch, Jenny had driven into town for supplies. Mike stayed at the cabin to watch a baseball doubleheader on television. Leigh, invited to go into town with Jenny, had declined. She felt restless and eager. She wanted to be on the lake.

"I think I'll take the canoe out for a while," she told Mike.

"Fine," he said, looking up from the television. "Have fun."

Outside, she made her way quickly down the path to the shore. The outboard was tied at the dock, the canoe beached where she had left it yesterday. She tossed her rolled towel into the canoe, then lifted the bow and pushed. The aluminum hull scraped over the sand, then slipped easily onto the calm surface of the lake. Leigh hopped in. She scurried in a crouch to the stern. There, she knelt on a flotation cushion, picked up the paddle, and swept the canoe past the dock. Her sense of impending adventure was stronger than ever. It gave her flutters in the stomach.

Fifty yards out, she turned the canoe southward. The sun blazed down on her.

Soon, her blouse was clinging to her back and she felt sweat trickling down her sides.

On her morning trips, she was always perfectly comfortable in her blouse and cutoff jeans. But she had anticipated the afternoon heat, so she was prepared for it.

Resting the paddle across the gunnels, she looked over the glinting water at the shore. She was across from Carson's Camp. She saw people on the diving raft, a few swimming, others sunning themselves on the pier. The sounds of laughing, yelling kids and a distant, scolding mother came over the water to her. All the kids she had seen there during the past few days were young. Too young. The oldest boy she'd spotted seemed no older than twelve or thirteen.

Which did not necessarily mean that a guy closer to Leigh's age wasn't among them.

And maybe watching.

Her fingers trembled as she opened the buttons of her blouse. She pulled the damp blouse off, dropped it across her knees, and struggled out of her cutoff jeans.

She was wearing her white bikini, not the one-piece suit that Mom had bought her at Macy's. The sun felt hot on her bare skin, but there was a mild breeze that felt very good.

She took a deep, shaky breath, bent forward, and slipped a squeeze bottle of suntan oil out of her rolled towel. She forced herself not to look toward shore as she spread the oil over her shoulders and arms, over her chest and the exposed tops of her breasts.

She felt her nipples harden, a low tremor, and moving, liquid heat.

Suddenly, she understood.

Those restless feelings. That sense of expectation.

What she was expecting was to meet a *guy* while she was out here alone in the canoe.

A guy on vacation, most likely staying at Carson's Camp. Someone lean and tanned and handsome to spend her time with. Someone who would fall for her. The lake and woods were so romantic, especially at night. She needed a boyfriend, a lover, to make it all perfect.

So where *are* you? she wondered, looking toward shore.

How come you're not swimming out to meet me?

Here I performed this nifty striptease for your benefit.

You've got to be there. Right? So where are you?

She saw only kids, a few older guys who no doubt had

wives and kids in tow. She didn't want an older guy. That would be scary. And wrong. She wanted someone her own age, or close to it.

Leigh picked up the paddle, dipped its blade into the water, and sent the canoe sliding forward.

Maybe *he* was watching her right now, wondering about her, wanting to meet her.

She couldn't expect a total stranger to come swimming out like Tarzan or something. Though that, she supposed, was exactly the type of adventure she'd been anticipating all along, even if she hadn't realized it until now.

More likely, he would arrange an "accidental" meeting. Position himself out here in a boat, tomorrow, pretending to fish while he waited for her to come along.

Dream on, she thought. This is Boondocks U.S.A., and the chances of running into Frankie Avalon out here are about zip.

Frankie Avalon isn't such a . . . Troy Donohue, *he'd* be more like it. Since you're dreaming, dream big.

She smiled and shook her head at the irony of it. Hey Mom, hey Dad, get a load of your reactionary kid paddling around a lake with visions of Troy Donohue dancing in her head.

Nearing the southern shore, she turned the canoe around and started back. How come I've suddenly got boys on the brain? she wondered. It wasn't that way at all, back in Marin. She hadn't gone regularly with a guy since Steve when she was a sophomore, and that hadn't been any great romance.

She would still be a virgin if it weren't for that time she got high with Larry Bills last November. They shared a joint in his station wagon after leaving the Charles Van Damm. She hardly even liked Larry Bills. But that night, she was feeling lonely and horny, and the grass made her *very* horny, and it just happened. It wasn't too bad, either. But she'd made up her mind, after that, not to get it on with anyone unless she really liked him. A lot. She found plenty of guys she liked, and scads of them who obviously wanted to make it with her, some calling her uptight when she refused, but she'd found no one special enough. Which had suited her fine. The need just wasn't there.

So why is it *here?* she wondered. How come I'm suddenly hot and bothered, and scouting the shores for a handsome prince?

The fresh air. The heat. The woods. The lake. The balmy nights. The moonlight on the water. It's this *place.* Must be.

I'd better get myself under control, is what I'd better do.

Blinking sweat out of her eyes, she stopped paddling. As the canoe glided along, turning slowly with the current, she scooped up water with her hands and splashed her face. It felt icy on her heated skin. She flung water onto her shoulders, squirming as it streamed down her back and chest.

She was across from Carson's Camp. Of course.

Anybody watching?

Where are you, pal?

She arched her back, stretched her tightening muscles, then lifted the paddle and continued along her way.

She didn't turn in at Mike and Jenny's place. Instead, she continued northward past the neighboring homes. A woman in a red halter waved at her from a pier. She waved back. A motorboat with a couple of middle-aged fishermen crossed her path. She waved at them, too, and wished she had her blouse on. Her canoe bobbed as the wake washed beneath it.

After passing the boathouse that marked the end of the populated western shore, she did put on her blouse. With a feeling of disappointment, she headed home.

That evening, after supper, she took a walk along the dirt road behind the cabin. It led through the woods along the rear of Carson's Camp. A family with three small kids was having a barbecue beside one of the cabins. The smoke and grilling hamburgers smelled wonderful. Leigh walked by, smiling at the wife, who looked up from setting a picnic table.

She felt good, but a little jittery. She had bathed and shampooed her hair before supper. She wore the orange blouse from Macy's and her legs looked sleek and tawny between the white of her new shorts and the white of her socks. Her skin glowed with the heat of a mild sunburn.

She had considered using makeup, but her reflection in the bathroom mirror had convinced her to leave it alone. A couple of dabs of cologne, and she'd been ready.

Ready for her big night out.

Ready to venture to the source.

If this fails, she thought as she strolled past another cabin, I'm out of luck. Well, maybe not. Most people probably only spent a week or two at Carson's Camp before heading home. Then new vacationers would arrive. She could take some consolation in the steady turnover.

Leaving the dirt road, she took a footpath toward the lodge. The trees opened up. She gazed out at the lake. Though she was in shadow, the early-evening sun still fell on the water, and trees on the nearest island looked dusted with gold. A few boats were out, people fishing in the calm. The peaceful beauty of it all made Leigh stop. She stood there, saddened, wanting somehow to be part of it, not just a spectator.

Well, she thought, go for it.

She turned away, walked the final distance to the lodge, and opened one of its heavy doors. The lobby was deserted except for a lone boy in a wicker chair. He glanced at Leigh, then returned his gaze to the television. She followed the sounds of conversation and clinking silverware to the dining-room entryway.

Only about half the tables were occupied, mostly those near the windows, the ones with the best view of the lake. Her eyes wandered from group to group, starting with the closest table and moving down the room until she had seen everyone.

Maybe she'd missed him.

She had missed no one.

So damn much for summer romance.

Lower lip clamped between her teeth, she turned away and hurried outside.

It was too much to hope for. She was being silly.

But it hurt.

Hell, who wants to get involved anyway? If you did meet a guy, it'd all be over in about three weeks and you'd probably never see him again. Who needs that?

The next day, she met Charlie.

THIRTEEN

Quiet knocking aroused Leigh from her sleep. She raised her head as Jenny called through the door. "Time to rise and shine, if you want to go after the big ones."

"I don't know," Leigh told her. "I didn't sleep very well."

"That's fine if you'd rather catch some extra z's. If you change your mind, though, we won't be leaving for fifteen or twenty minutes. Either way's fine."

"Thanks," she said, and lowered her face into the pillow.

She felt bad about lying to Jenny. She had slept well. She just didn't want to go out with them. Not this morning. She didn't want to do anything.

I should go along, she thought. What's wrong with me? It'll be great out on the boat. I don't really want to stay behind. Once they've gone, I'll probably wish I was with them.

You'd better get a move on, then.

What for? I'm not going.

She rolled onto her back. The window was open, the gauzy curtains billowing inward and flapping. The breeze brought a mild scent that reminded her of Christmas trees. From the feel of it, she guessed the sun hadn't been out for long. Drawing the sheet aside, she felt it stir over her nightgown and bare skin.

She heard quiet voices beyond her door. Through the open window came birdsongs, the soft sounds of leaves rustling in the breeze, the sputtery hum of a motorboat like a power lawn mower far away. After a while, she heard the screen door of the porch slap shut. Climbing from the bed, she stepped to the window. Mike and Jenny, loaded with fishing gear, were heading down the wooded slope. She watched them walk onto the pier. Mike stepped into the Cris Craft and set down his gear. Jenny handed her rod and tackle box to him, then untied the mooring lines while Mike started the twin engines. She hopped aboard. Mike, standing in the cockpit, backed the boat around the arm of the L-shaped pier. The pitch of the engines rose. The bow tipped upward and the boat headed out, churning a frothy wake.

Leigh stood at the window long after the boat was out of sight. She wasn't sure what to do with herself. She should have gone with them.

Her eyes lingered on the lounge chairs and table at the end of the pier. A couple of evenings, she had sat out there with Mike and Jenny after supper. It was pleasant then. It would be nice now, while the sun was still low.

At the bureau, she took off her nightgown and opened the drawer where she kept her white bikini. In a corner of the drawer was her necklace, the leather thong with its sea-thing ornament. Her good-luck necklace.

Leigh could use some good luck.

She knotted the rawhide behind her neck. The bonelike ornament felt smooth and cool between her breasts. She hadn't worn it since the day of her arrival.

The man at Jody's.

So what makes you think it's a good-luck charm?

The jet didn't crash, did it?

The guy didn't grab me.

Don't start thinking about him.

His overalls sticking out, his hand inside.

Mary Jo. Maybe he closed up as soon as we left, and . . . No. She's only a kid, probably his daughter. In spite of what Mike said.

Stop this.

She put on her bikini.

The girl had walked right in. She must have seen what that guy was doing.

Leigh's stomach hurt. "There is a house—in New Orleans," she started to sing. She picked up her sunglasses and a paperback and left the room, still singing to block out the thoughts.

She smelled coffee. She spent a few minutes in the bathroom. With her hair in a ponytail, she pulled her beach towel down from its rod, rolled her suntan oil inside, and went into the kitchen. She poured herself a mug of coffee.

Then she walked down the slope to the pier.

The boat was out of sight, either hidden from view by an island or in one of the many coves around the borders of the lake. The painted slats of the pier felt cool under her bare feet. They creaked as she walked out. The warm breeze felt wonderful on her skin. She set her coffee mug, book, and suntan oil on the wicker table, then spread her towel over one of the lounge chairs.

Turning, she scanned the shore. To the right, three piers up, someone was swimming with slow, balletlike strokes. It had to be a woman. Far beyond the swimmer, a motorboat was chugging out, trailed by wisps of bluish smoke. She guessed that the two men were the same who had passed her yesterday afternoon. To the left, a kid was sitting at the end of the nearest pier, fishing with a cane pole. Beyond him, at Carson's Camp, a family was loading one of the dozen motorboats available to the guests.

At the pier's end, a boy and girl, side by side, dove at the same instant. Leigh heard their splashes. They raced out to the diving raft that floated on metal drums about thirty yards beyond the pier. Leigh waited to see who won. The girl did. "That-a-way," she whispered.

Then she straddled the lounge chair, sat down, and leaned back. Drinking coffee in this position, she realized, would be a neat trick. So she sat up straight and folded her legs. She picked up the mug. Steam still drifted off the coffee. The breeze caught it and twisted it away. She took a sip. The coffee tasted rich and good.

The swimming woman was far out and turning back toward shore. The motorboat with the two fishermen was moving past the point of the nearest island. Far off, near the northern shore, was a rowboat—someone getting his or her morning exercise. Leigh couldn't tell, at this distance, whether the rower was male or female.

Nearby, a motor sputtered to life. She didn't bother turning to look. It had to be from the boat of the family at Carson's Camp.

She took another drink, set the mug on the table, and reached for the plastic bottle of suntan oil. Before touching it, however, she stopped. The stuff was messy. It would cling to her hands no matter how hard she might try rubbing it off, and end up on the pages of her book. So she left the oil alone and picked up the paperback.

It was *Boys and Girls Together,* a book she'd bought at the City Lights. William Goldman was the author. She'd bought two books by him that day, because she remembered how she'd loved his first one, *The Temple of Gold.*

Boys and girls together.

Don't you wish.

At least you'll be able to read about it.

A fly settled on her leg. She waved it away, and noticed some hair curling out from the edge of her bikini shorts. Real cute, she thought. She fingered it out of sight, and decided she had better give herself a trim the next time she was in the bathroom. Or shave it off entirely.

What if you have to go in for a physical before it grows back?

You already had your annual checkup.

What if you got in an accident?

Just explain you didn't want it sticking out when . . .

Explain? What's the doctor going to do, tell on you?

She took another drink of coffee.

The rowboat was closer now. The person at the oars didn't seem to be wearing a shirt. Probably a guy, she thought.

Finishing the coffee, Leigh set the mug aside. She uncrossed her legs, stretched them out, and leaned back. Through her sunglasses, the cloudless sky was a deep blue-green. A mallard flapped by. She opened her book, raised it high enough to block out the sun, and began to read.

Soon, she was caught up in the story. She was *in* the story, living it with the characters, though part of her mind was aware of herself enjoying the book, aware of how good she felt with the soft cushion beneath her and the sun hot on her skin, the mild breeze roaming her body. She turned the pages. Her arms, muscles still aching from all the canoeing over the past few days, grew heavy from holding the book high enough to shade her eyes.

Maybe go back up to the cabin and get a hat. Get a refill of coffee while you're at it.

Wait till the end of the chapter.

She kept on reading.

"Baskets!"

The voice made her heart lurch. She lowered the book.

The rowboat was straight ahead, no more than sixty feet off the pier. It was loaded with baskets, some the size of clothes hampers, others that looked like picnic baskets, fishing creels, bread baskets. The young man in the center seat held the boat broadside, barely moving its oars.

"Selling them?" Leigh asked.

"Sure am."

He wore a black hat with a high, rounded crown, a wide brim, and a red feather on each side of its headband. The feathers stuck up like horns.

"Handmade," he said. "Can't buy no better."

Leigh sat up straight and took off her sunglasses to see him better. His face, shaded by the hat brim, was lean and handsome. He had a slight cleft on his chin. His bare torso was slim and muscled, his sleek skin glossy with sweat. He wore jeans so old and faded they were almost white. Their knees were in shreds.

"I can show 'em to you," he said.

Leigh nodded. "Yeah, okay."

"I'll beach her."

She watched him turn the bow. He leaned far forward to start rowing. His back muscles rippled, gleaming. His jeans were low. She glanced at the shadowy crevice between his buttocks and wondered if he wore underpants.

Come off it, she warned herself.

Her heart continued to pound fast as she watched him bring the boat closer. Her mouth was parched. Standing up, she put her book and sunglasses on the table. She plucked the sweaty seat of her bikini away from her skin. Looked down at herself. Fine. Nothing showing that shouldn't be.

With glances over his shoulder, the young man guided the boat around the end of the pier. He headed for the beach area where Leigh kept the canoe.

She forced her eyes away from him as she walked down the pier. She didn't hurry. She strolled along, head up, back arched, keeping her belly muscles tight though she knew she was too slim to bother with that.

For godsake, she thought, calm down.

He's gorgeous.

He's a local.

So what?

So plenty. Maybe.

Stepping from the pier onto the sand, she watched him ship the oars. As the boat glided silently toward the beach, he hopped out. He grabbed a gunnel and waded, towing the boat beside him. He dragged it onto the sand. Let go. Straightened up. Turned to face Leigh.

She tried not to let it show. Her shock.

He had three nipples.

She looked quickly to his face and walked closer. "Let's see what you've got," she said. Her voice trembled a bit.

"Got real fine baskets," he told her. "All shapes and sizes. Homemade." Turning away, he lifted out one of the large ones. He set it down in front of her. It held several smaller baskets. Reaching inside, he took out two of them.

It wasn't a nipple. Thank God. It was a red, heart-shaped tattoo above and slightly to the right of his left nipple. Scrawled inside the heart design, in small, flowing red letters, was the word *Mom*.

Leigh took a deep breath. "Did you make these baskets yourself?" she asked, feeling her shock subside.

"I just sell 'em," he said. "Mom makes 'em."

"They look very nice."

He handed her one. "Can't get something this fine in no store. My family's been making 'em going back a hundred years. Maybe longer."

The basket in her hands was long and narrow, just the right size for a loaf of sourdough. It was woven of reedlike wooden strips, a deep brown instead of the straw color she was used to seeing. The top edge was neatly rimmed with heavier strips fastened into place by tiny nails. She didn't know much about baskets, but this one did look a lot nicer than the ones her parents had at home. It would make a nice gift for Mom. "What does something like this cost?"

"Twelve dollars."

Not exactly cheap.

She had to buy a basket from him, though. At least one.

"Look at the others before you make up your mind. The smaller ones, they don't cost as much." Bending over the boat, he lifted out one with a hooped handle. It looked like an Easter basket. "Something like this, it's good for candy or nuts." He nodded toward a picnic basket near the stern. It had double handles and the kind of lid that flaps up from hinges in the center. "That's the most popular, that picnic basket there. It goes for twenty-five."

It was identical to one owned by Mike and Jenny.

"Have you sold baskets to these people here?" she asked, nodding toward the cabin.

"Sure, I sold 'em some. There's not much of anybody on the lake I haven't sold some to."

He looked into Leigh's eyes.

She felt a low, pleasant tremor.

"You a relation?" he asked.

"I'm their niece. My name's Leigh."

"You were water-skiing Monday."

She nodded.

"I saw you."

A blush warmed her face. "I hope you didn't see me fall down."

"You had on a white swimming suit." He looked at what she was wearing. "Not this one, but it was white like this one. There was more to it."

"Oh."

"This one here's better."

"Thanks." She swallowed hard. "About these baskets. I'd like to buy this one."

"I'm Charlie. Charlie Payne. That's P-a-y-n-e, not like a hurt."

"Nice to meet you, Charlie."

"You said your name was Leigh. What's your last name?"

"West. Like the direction."

He nodded. He smiled. He had extremely white teeth.

"My money's up in the cabin. Why don't you come along and get out of the sun?"

He nodded.

Leigh turned away and started walking. She glanced back. He was following, but staying a distance behind her as if wary of getting too close. "Do you live on the lake?" she asked.

"Over at the other side."

The eastern shore, where the only homes were those creepy-looking shacks.

And not many of them. Leigh had suspected that he came from there. Still, having it confirmed made him seem even more alien. He was from a different world, a place that seemed both mysterious and somewhat sinister.

She didn't feel threatened, though. Nervous, excited, but not threatened.

She climbed the shaded path, the breeze cool on her damp skin. Though she didn't look back again, she was certain that Charlie must be studying her. The feel of the fabric taut across her moving buttocks kept her aware that she was nearly naked.

Maybe he was getting turned on.

Or maybe his people didn't dress this way and he found it offensive.

No, he'd said that he liked the bikini.

At the top of the slope, she followed an offshoot of the path to the cabin. Charlie's footfalls stayed behind her. She climbed the wooden stairs, opened the screen door of the porch, and held it wide.

Charlie stopped.

"You coming?"

"I better wait here."

She thought of her parents' strict rule about not having boys in the house while they weren't home. Well, this isn't their house. Mike and Jenny had imposed no such restriction.

"It's okay," she said. "Nobody's home."

"Mom, she don't want me going in folks' places."

"What she doesn't know won't hurt her."

His eyes narrowed.

He doesn't trust me, Leigh thought, annoyed. "Suit yourself." She turned away.

"Guess I can wait on the porch," Charlie said.

She held the door open for him and watched him approach. He had brown, curly hair starting at his navel and spreading downward like a triangle to the waistband of his low jeans. Leigh stayed in the doorway while he climbed the stairs. He turned sideways to avoid touching her as he stepped by.

He looked around the porch.

Leigh gestured toward the swing suspended by chains from the ceiling. Obediently, he went over to it and sat down. The chains groaned and creaked quietly.

"Back in a second."

Leigh carried the basket into her bedroom and tossed it onto the bed. With trembling fingers, she opened her shoulder bag and found her billfold. She took out a ten and two ones. Then she hurried into the kitchen. The lower shelves of the refrigerator were loaded with cans of soda and beer. She hesitated, then folded the bills, tucked them under the elastic at her hip, and took out two cans of beer.

She had swung the refrigerator door shut and started out of the kitchen before she changed her mind. Mike and Jenny might not approve of her serving beer to Charlie. On top of that, she didn't want Charlie getting the wrong idea. So she put the beer away and took out cans of black cherry soda instead.

She opened them and carried them out to the porch. Charlie's hat was on his lap. His brown hair was plastered to the top of his head and stuck out, unkempt and shaggy, around the ears.

"Would you like a cold drink before you go?" she asked.

"Don't want to put you out none."

"You'd better take one," she said. "They're already open, and I can't drink them both." She handed one of the cans to him.

"Thank you."

He was sitting near the middle of the swing, an arm draped over its back. Leigh considered asking him to move over, but that seemed a bit too pushy. Besides, if she joined him on the swing, it would make looking at him awkward. So she stepped away and leaned sideways, shoulder against the door frame.

"Your mother makes the baskets, and you sell them to people around the lake?"

He took a drink and nodded.

"Are there enough people around to make it worth-while?"

"Don't need much." His gaze flicked downward, then back up to Leigh's face. "There's four lakes. Did you know there's four of 'em?"

"No."

"Wahconda, Circle, Goon, and Willow. There's channels. You can get from one to the other. I sell on all of 'em. There's places like Carson's where you've got folks coming and going all summer. That's where I sell the most.

"New folks all the time, and they like Mom's baskets. They got money, too, a lot of 'em. Made sixty-five dollars off just one lady a couple weeks back."

While he talked, his eyes kept straying down Leigh's body. Then he would look elsewhere fast as if he feared being caught.

"It sounds lucrative," she said.

He lowered his gaze to the top of his soda can. "That lady didn't want just baskets."

"What else did she want?"

"Well, she liquored me up."

Leigh was suddenly very glad she'd decided against the beers.

"Then she went grabbing at me, but I made her quit. Mom, she give me a good switching."

"How did your mother find out?"

He shrugged. "Smelled the liquor on me. I told her I made the lady quit, but she hided me anyhow. It didn't count I sold five baskets. See, I went in her place and got a snoutful and put myself in the path of temptation." He didn't sound resentful against his mother, more as if he had strayed and deserved the punishment. "She'd likely switch me," he added, "if she found out I was here."

"Well, I hope you're not planning to tell her."

"I don't guess I will," he said, and looked up at Leigh with wary eyes.

"Don't worry, I won't liquor you up and grab you."

The red of a blush showed through his tan.

"Your mother sounds pretty strict." Sounds like a regular bitch, Leigh thought.

"She just don't want me doing wrong."

"Does she let you date?"

Charlie looked confused.

"You know, go around with girls."

He shook his head, looked back down at his can of soda, and took a drink.

"You mean you never had a girlfriend?"

"Just never mind," he muttered.

"Okay. Sorry." She sipped her black cherry soda. As she tilted the can down, a cold drop fell to her breast. It trickled down. She saw Charlie look up in time to watch her brush it away. "What about your father?" she asked.

"He run off with a tramp. I was just a kid. I don't remember him at all."

"That's rough," Leigh said.

"He was no good."

"Maybe your mother's afraid *you'll* run off with a tramp."

"Not me."

"That would explain why she doesn't like you seeing girls."

"You shouldn't talk that way about her."

"I'm sure she's a fine person."

"That's right."

"I just think maybe you're missing out on a lot, that's all. Most guys your age— What are you, nineteen or twenty?"

"Eighteen," he said.

"Okay, eighteen. Guys your age, that's about *all* they

ever think about, is girls. Don't you feel like you might be missing out on something?"

"I know what you're up to."

"I'm not up to anything," she protested.

"Oh no? How come you keep talking about me and girls?"

"I'm just curious, that's all."

"You want me to do things to you." There was a challenge in his eyes. Leigh felt caught. She wanted to snap out a denial. But Charlie wouldn't believe her anyway. He knew what he knew. "It's crossed my mind," she admitted. "Don't get any ideas, though. I'm not about to let you try anything with me. It's not that I don't like you. I'm glad we met, and I think you and I could be friends if we got to know each other better. The thing is, I've already got a boyfriend. He's back in California, but I'm not the kind of person to fool around behind his back. So we could be friends, you and I, but it would have to be strictly hands off."

"Well, how come you brought me up here, then?"

"I came up to get the money, remember?" She pressed on, confident now that he seemed to be buying her story. "Just because you had one bad experience, Charlie, you shouldn't jump to conclusions. Everyone isn't like that woman who tried to grab you. And you shouldn't go putting all the blame on her, either. If you were looking at her the same way you've been looking at me, it's no wonder she got ideas."

Charlie's eyes widened. His mouth fell open.

"She probably thought you were asking for it."

"I didn't look at her that way."

"Well, you've sure been looking at *me* that way."

"She weren't near as . . ." He stopped himself and scowled down at his soda can.

"Near as what, Charlie?" Leigh asked in a soft voice.

"You know."

"Mean and ugly?"

He shook his head.

"Fat and stinky?"

He smiled, fought it away, and raised his eyes to her.

"She weren't near as pretty," he said.

"Probably not near as naked, either."

The smile broke out again. This time, it stayed. His eyes still had a nervous look. "Not to start out with, anyhow."

"Oh?"

"But what she had weren't something I much wanted to see. It put me off my feed for a week."

Leigh laughed.

Charlie laughed a little, himself, shaking his head. "I seen better-looking tits on a road apple. And she had a hind end . . ." He stopped. His face was suddenly solemn. "I beg your pardon," he said.

"You don't have to beg *my* pardon."

"I gotta go now." He gulped down the rest of his soda, put on his strange hat, and stood up. "Thank you for the drink."

Leigh nudged herself away from the door frame and stood up straight as he came toward her. "I'm glad you came up here, Charlie. It's been nice talking with you." He gave the empty can to her, pulling his hand away quickly as if afraid of being touched. Leigh set both cans on a wicker table. She caught the screen door as it swung shut. "Hold up, okay? I'm going back down."

He waited for Leigh to join him.

"So you'll be selling baskets the rest of the day?" she asked as they stared down the slope.

"Yeah. I'll make a stop at Carson's and then head on away."

"Do you go to all the lakes in one day?"

"I guess I'll just get over to Circle today. It's a full day trip, making Goon and Willow."

"So they're on tomorrow's agenda? How would you like a helper?"

He shook his head.

"I've never been to those other lakes."

"You can't come."

They reached the sand, and Charlie took long, quick strides as if wanting to leave her behind. Leigh quickened her pace. "What are you scared of?"

"I ain't scared."

"You just don't want me with you. That's real nice. It really makes me feel good."

At the boat, he faced her. "It's nothing against you."

"Oh, sure."

"It just wouldn't be right."

"What would be wrong with it? Oh." Nodding, she pointed at the heart tattoo on his chest. "Your mother wouldn't approve," she said softly. Her fingertip touched the tattoo. Charlie flinched but didn't move away. "I wouldn't want to get you in trouble with your mother."

She put her open hand on his chest, feeling his smooth skin, his quick heartbeat. Sliding it down over the firm slab of his pectoral, she felt his nipple stiff under her palm. "Maybe you'll come around again sometime," she said, and took her hand away. She was trembling. "Maybe I'll buy another basket."

"I gotta get going."

Leigh stood on the warm sand until Charlie had pushed off his boat. Then she walked onto the pier and watched him row past.

She raised a hand in farewell.

Charlie looked at her as he worked the oars, but he said nothing.

FOURTEEN

His boat was beached at Carson's Camp. Leigh had watched him unload baskets and carry them up the slope.

She could go over there.

But she didn't want to spook him.

God knows, she had already pushed matters as far as she dared. She'd probably scared him away for good.

Looking back on it, she was shocked by the way she had acted, the way she had felt. What was wrong with her? Never in her life had she come so close to throwing herself at a man.

It might be best, she told herself, if I *don't* ever see him again.

Forget about him.

She turned her lounge chair to face Carson's Camp. Lying back, she rubbed herself with suntan oil, but it was Charlie's hands spreading the slick fluid over her skin.

After a while, Charlie returned to the boat. He loaded some baskets inside, took out two of the picnic baskets, and hurried back up the slope. Later, he returned empty-handed.

Leigh was glad he'd made sales.

He pushed off his boat.

She thought of the canoe.

Follow him.

No.

Just leave him alone. Forget about him.

All day, she thought about him. That night, in bed, she stared at the ceiling and wondered about tomorrow. She knew where he would be: at Goon and Willow. She had found out from Mike where the channel was. She could intercept Charlie, if she dared. She trembled, thinking about it.

I won't go over there, she told herself.

You want to bet?

She pictured him gleaming in the sunlight, strong and sleek, the jeans low on his hips.

Fancy meeting you here, Charlie.

He would know, of course, that it was not an accident.

Get out of here and leave me alone.

No, he wouldn't say that. He would sneak glances at her body. He wanted her, but he was scared.

Stop this, Leigh thought.

Restless, she threw her sheet aside. The breeze from the window cooled her damp nightgown. It smelled wonderful. It felt wonderful. Sitting up, she looked toward the moonlit window. She heard birds and crickets chirping in the night.

Why not go outside and enjoy it, she thought. You're not going to fall asleep anyway.

She stood up slowly, listening to the quiet squeak of the bedsprings, and crept to her door. Her heart thudded wildly as she eased the door open.

What are you jumpy for? You don't have to *sneak* out. Mike and Jenny wouldn't care.

It's not them, she realized. It's this. It's going out alone, at this hour, in your nightgown.

She wasn't afraid, she was excited.

It's no big deal.

Then how come you're shaking like a leaf?

Except for creamy moonlight from the windows, the cabin was dark. She rubbed the goose bumps on her arms, then walked silently to the front door. She inched it open and squeezed through the gap, her breath snagging as the edge of the door rubbed her stiff right nipple. Trembling, she pulled the door shut.

The porch floor was cool and smooth under her bare feet. The screen door groaned, but the noise didn't worry her. She stepped down the wooden stairs.

You're out. You made it.

When her feet touched the ground, she stopped. She took a deep breath. A lightning bug drifted by, glowing and fading. Closing her eyes, she let herself feel the breeze. It stirred her hair, blew softly against her face, stroked her arms and legs, moved the nightgown against her skin. Its touch was subtle and erotic.

Her legs felt weak as she walked down the steep path to the lake. At the pier, she looked both ways. She saw no one along the shore. Water lapped and sloshed quietly around the pilings. To the right, the moon made a silver path over the lake.

She walked to the end of the pier. The breeze was stronger here. It fluttered her nightgown and slipped beneath it—lover's hands, gentle, exploring with tentative, intimate caresses.

Leigh wanted to take the nightgown off, to stand naked in the moonlight and feel the breeze all over her.

Not here, at the end of the pier. Someone might be watching.

From over the water came a quiet groan.

It didn't sound human.

Metallic, almost like an oarlock.

The sound startled Leigh out of her dreamy languor. She stiffened. Her eyes searched the darkness.

The boat was a vague blur on the lake's black surface. In the center sat an upright shape. She couldn't believe that she hadn't noticed it at once; the boat was directly ahead, no more than fifty feet beyond the end of the pier.

It went nowhere.

Charlie?

She almost spoke his name, but stopped herself. What if it's not Charlie?

It might be anyone.

The man from Jody's.

She felt her skin prickle.

Don't be silly.

It might be someone night-fishing.

She couldn't see a pole.

It is Charlie. It has to be.

This is too weird, she thought. Spooky weird.

What's he doing here?

"Charlie?" she asked. She didn't raise her voice. In the silence, it wasn't necessary. She knew the name would carry out to him.

The oarlocks groaned, more loudly this time. She heard the soft swoosh of the blades rising out of the water. The dim silhouette leaned forward and back, beginning to row. The boat turned.

He's coming for me.

Oh dear God.

Leigh's heart felt as if it might smash through her rib cage.

This isn't happening. It's a dream. A very weird dream. You're going to wake up any second.

She knew she was not dreaming.

She locked her knees to keep herself upright.

Calm down, she thought. You wanted something like this. Well, it's happening.

She was a little frightened, but excited. She couldn't stop trembling.

Then she realized that the boat wasn't moving closer. It was heading away.

Charlie had lost his nerve.

He'd been drawn here, late at night when she would be sleeping, only to stare at the cabin, to . . . what, fantasize?

Calling out to him would do no good.

Leigh dove, leaping from the edge of the pier and stretching out, hitting the water and slicing down beneath its surface. The first shock of cold made her flinch. Then the rush of water felt good. She arched upward and broke the surface. Taking a breath, she blinked her eyes clear and spotted the distant shape of the boat. She swam for it.

She knew Charlie must have seen her dive. Rowing away, he would be facing her. He had to see. But would he stop, or row all the harder hoping to get away?

Leigh was a strong, swift swimmer. In a canoe, Charlie would be able to leave her behind, but rowboats were heavy and ungainly. She was sure she could catch up to him, no matter how hard he might row.

She kicked steadily, darting out one arm then the other with smooth, easy strokes, turning her head for a breath on every sixth stroke.

He probably thinks I'm crazy, she thought.

I *must* be crazy.

I could've taken the canoe.

This is better.

A corner of Leigh's mind, which seemed to be observing her from a distance, was admiring her nerve. And was a little amused. You've really gone and done it.

She raised her head.

The boat was broadside to her, not far ahead. So Charlie was no longer trying to get away.

Good for him.

He wasn't wearing his odd, feathered hat.

She lowered her face into the water and kept on swimming.

What if it's *not* Charlie?

She considered taking another look. That wouldn't solve anything, though. Too dark.

It better be him.

What if it's not?

She went tight and cold inside.

She told herself not to worry. It had to be Charlie.

But she was very close to the boat, getting closer with every stroke. She saw herself grab the gunnel and pull herself up. A face above her. A stranger's face. A woman's. Charlie's mother. Her hand clutched Leigh's wrist. *Now I gotcha!*

It was a crazy thought, but she couldn't get rid of it. She stopped. Treading water, she wiped her eyes.

The boat was two yards away.

The man in its center had Charlie's shape, but the face, a dim blur, could have belonged to anyone.

"Charlie?" she asked.

"Might as well grab an oar," he said. The hushed voice was Charlie's. He didn't sound overjoyed.

Leigh kicked closer, caught hold of the slippery oar blade, and pulled herself along its shaft. Then she clutched the gunnel with both hands. "Thanks for stopping."

"What am I gonna do, let you drown?"

"I wouldn't have drowned."

"Well, you gonna climb in, or what?"

"I haven't decided." She thought about her nightgown. Wet, it would be transparent. "What were you doing out here, Charlie?"

"Nothing."

The boat was empty except for an anchor on the deck near the bow. "Not selling baskets, I see."

"I just come out for some fresh air. Too hot in the cabin."

"You rowed all the way over here for some fresh air?"

"Think I come by to spy on you?"

"Something like that."

"Well, you're full of it."

"It's all right, Charlie. I don't mind. I was thinking about you, too. That's why I couldn't sleep and came down to the lake. I missed you. I was afraid we wouldn't see each other again."

"How come you were thinking about me, and not that boyfriend of yours?"

"There isn't any boyfriend. I just made him up. Comin' aboard," she said.

Charlie scooted away to balance the boat, and Leigh thrust herself up. Bracing herself on stiff arms, she waited for the boat to stop its wild rocking. Then she swung a leg over the side and tumbled in. She landed on her back, grunting with the impact. Her knees were in the air, parted, so she quickly rolled to her side.

"Hurt yourself?" Charlie asked.

"I'll live." She ran a hand down her rump and leg. The clinging fabric didn't end until just above her knee. She sat up, then scuttled backward to the edge of the stern seat. She boosted herself onto it. "Graceful entrance, huh?"

Charlie moved to the center of his seat and caught the handle of the oar he'd left dangling. He lowered both handles to his thighs. The oars jutted out like strange, uptilted wings.

Shivering with cold and excitement, Leigh looked down

at herself. As she'd expected, the nightgown was glued to her skin and she could see right through it. She folded her arms tightly across her breasts. She hunched over. "You wouldn't have a towel?"

"You can have my shirt," he said.

"Thanks."

He shipped the oars, swinging them toward Leigh and inward, resting their paddles on the sides of her seat. Then he took off his shirt and tossed it to her.

Leigh draped his shirt across the seat beside her. "Shut your eyes," she said.

"What for?"

"Because I'd like you to."

"Okay."

"They shut?"

He nodded.

Leigh couldn't see whether they were shut. Half expecting him to peek, half wanting him to, she raised herself off the seat and peeled the nightgown over her head.

She wadded it into a tight club and wrung it out into the lake. She set it aside and lowered her gaze. Her skin looked dusky where she was tanned. Her breasts were pale, her jutting nipples almost black in the darkness. Taking a deep, tremulous breath, she picked up Charlie's shirt and put it on. It clung to her damp skin but took away the cold. She fastened the two lower buttons and arranged the hanging front to cover her lap.

Even with the shirt on, she felt naked. It was the painted plank seat, wet and slick against her buttocks.

"Okay," she said. "You can open your eyes." Charlie nodded.

"You didn't peek, did you?"

"No." He fidgeted a bit. "You asked me not to."

"Well, good. Thanks for the shirt. It feels good. I was freezing. Are you cold without it?"

"No. I'm not wet."

"How long have you been out here?"

He shrugged a bare shoulder. "Not real long."

"Does your mother know?"

"She was sleeping."

"What if she wakes up and finds you gone?"

"Well, I guess she'll whale on me pretty good when I get back."

"But you came anyway."

"I didn't . . . I just got in the boat and ended up here. I didn't mean to. It just sort of happened."

"I'm glad."

"You weren't supposed to know."

"Take me someplace, Charlie."

He rubbed his mouth with the back of his hand. "I oughta take you back to your pier."

"You won't, will you?"

Shaking his head, he raised the oars over the sides and lowered them into the water. He held one oar motionless under the surface and stroked with the other until the bow swung around to the opposite direction, then rowed northward. The boat swept along, oarlocks squawking, blades making quiet slurps as they came out. They left straight trails of droplets on the surface until they dipped in again. They stroked back smoothly, silently.

Leigh watched Charlie. He sat with his back arched, legs stretched out, his bare heels planted against the ribs along the inside of the hull. Leaning forward with his arms stiff, he slipped the paddles in. Then he eased back, drawing them through the water, coming forward again as they broke the surface, letting the boat glide as he brought the oar handles toward his belly in a graceful circular motion before extending his arms again and bending far forward to start over.

"You're very good at this," Leigh said.

"Thank you."

She stretched out her legs until her feet met Charlie's. He kept rowing. He didn't try to move his feet away.

"It's beautiful out here at night," she said. "So peaceful. Have you always lived here?"

"Yeah."

"It must be nice."

"Sure. It's okay."

"Do you have any brothers or sisters?"

"No."

"Neither do I."

"I had a twin, but it was born dead."

"I'm sorry."

"Well, it don't bother me. I never knew it, so it weren't like a loved one going toes up on you." He rowed a few strokes in silence. "Would've been queer, having a brother around that looked the same as me."

"I know some twins. They pretend to be each other. They've put over some good ones."

"It's in the lake."

"What?" Leigh asked, uncertain what Charlie meant.

"My old man, he took it out on the lake and tossed it in with an anchor. Guess it's still down there."

Leigh frowned, trying to make sense of what Charlie had said. Suddenly, she realized that "it" was his stillborn twin. Charlie's father had weighted the body with an anchor and left it in the lake.

She'd been *swimming* in the lake. . . .

There wouldn't be much of it left by now, she told herself. That was what, eighteen years ago?

A dead baby down there.

Its bones, anyway.

The lake's dark water with its silver-moon trail didn't look quite as tranquil and beautiful as it had a few minutes ago.

"Funny to think about it down there," Charlie said.

Hilarious.

"You know how sometimes a fish'll jump and you look real quick but you don't see it? There's just the ripples moving around? Well, when I was a kid and that used to happen, I'd think it was 'it' coming up."

"Jesus," Leigh muttered.

"Didn't scare me. I just kept looking quick, hoping I'd get a peek at it. I was mostly curious, is all. One time, I jumped in." He shook his head. Leigh saw the white of his teeth. Was he smiling? "Had it in mind I might dive down and grab the body, get a good look at it."

Leigh didn't want to hear any more. "How far's the high school?" she asked.

"Oh, twenty miles."

"How do you get there? Do they have a bus?"

"I never gone."

"You never went to school?" She wasn't very surprised.

"What do I need school for? Mom teaches me all I need to know."

"Your mom's a teacher?

"She was, a long time ago."

"Well, you'd meet people."

"Don't have much use for 'em."

"You'd meet girls."

"You gonna start on me about girls again?"

"Not if you don't want me to."

"Well, I don't see no point. You're a girl. You're here. What's the point talking about girls I don't even know?"

"None, I guess."

"I never seen one, anyhow, as pretty as you."

"Oh, I bet you have."

"Nope. And I see plenty of 'em, too, going around the lakes hawking the baskets. None of 'em are as nice, either. Mostly, they act funny like they're scared of me."

"Why would they be scared?"

For a few moments, he didn't answer. He drew back, the oars and leaned forward again. " 'Cause I'm not the same as them, I guess. Is that why? You're scared of me, too, so I guess you must know how come."

"I am not."

"Sure. Only difference is, you don't let it stop you."

"If I were afraid of you, I wouldn't be out here in your boat in the middle of the night."

"That so?"

"Yes, that's so. I'm no idiot."

"You're scared, but you're not scared off. Maybe you got a streak of daredevil in you."

"I've sure got a streak of *some*thing, Charlie. And you're the one who gave it to me." She drew in her feet. "Move over," she said. Staying low, she made her way to the center seat, raised the oar handle out of her way, and sat down beside him. "Let's make this baby fly," she said, and started to row.

Leigh matched his movements, leaning forward as he did, dipping in her paddle and drawing it back, feeling her body against his—his arm and hip and leg.

He sped up, and so did she.

The boat skimmed along, faster and faster toward its destination known only to Charlie.

FIFTEEN

With a shush of hull against sand, the boat skidded to a stop. Leigh and Charlie swung their oars in, resting them on the stern seat.

"Well," Charlie said, "here we are."

Leigh nodded, a little breathless from the rowing.

"You like it?"

"Just fine," she said. Except for its opening not much wider than their boat, the inlet was surrounded by high trees. It looked totally isolated. It was a far better place than Leigh had hoped for. She smiled at Charlie. "In fact, it's terrific." Peering over her shoulder, she saw that they had landed on a dim stretch of sand. "It's even got a beach," she whispered.

"That's 'cause it used to have a house. Still does, only no one lives there." He got up from his seat and stepped to the bow. There, he lifted the anchor and flung it. The concrete block hit the sand with a quiet thud.

"I'll be right with you," Leigh said, still in a whisper. This place *made* her whisper. She went to the stern. Bending over, she felt the shirttail slide up, felt the soft breeze on her buttocks, wondered if Charlie was watching.

Her nightgown was a damp wad. She shook it open and spread it on the seat to help it dry, then walked the length of the boat and hopped down. The sand felt soft and warm under her bare feet. She moved closer to Charlie. She was breathing hard now, but not so much from the rowing.

Just beyond the small patch of beach, the trees began. She saw a few lightning bugs drifting among them. Her gaze wandered up the wooded slope. The dwelling was barely visible among the trees: squared-off corners of darkness, a cabin or shack.

"You sure nobody lives there?"

"Want to go up and find out?"

"Not especially."

She stared at Charlie. She wished there were more light so she could see his face. His deep-set eyes were lost in shadow, his lips a blur. For a terrible instant, he was a stranger. Then she touched his face, and he was Charlie again. Her trembling fingers wandered down his cheeks, his jaw. As they settled on his shoulders, Leigh stepped against him, drew him closer, and kissed his mouth.

His lips felt rigid. She slid her tongue along them, and they parted slightly. The tip of his tongue met hers. She flicked at it, then sucked it into her mouth. Moaning, Charlie put his arms around her. He squeezed her tightly and opened his mouth wide, lips pressing, tongue filling her mouth.

Leigh squirmed, caressing his smooth back from shoulder to waist, then clutching him closer. He was tight against her, chest hard against her breasts, flat belly pushing hers as they breathed, the button of his jeans digging into her skin.

Charlie's hands felt enormous on her back. But they didn't move. They stayed up, just below her shoulder blades. Leigh wanted them moving, exploring. She wanted them under the shirt, on her skin.

It's all right, she told herself. He's new at this. He's never been with a girl before, doesn't know what to do, or knows but is frightened.

She slid a hand down Charlie's back and pushed her fingers under the waistband of his jeans. He didn't have underwear on. His buttocks were smooth, firm mounds.

"How about if we . . . take a swim?" he asked.

"Great." Leigh pulled her hand out. "I didn't bring my swimming suit. Neither did you."

"That's okay," Charlie said.

"What will I wear?"

"You can wear my shirt if you want."

"I don't want to get it wet for you."

"I don't mind," he said. He let go of Leigh. She eased away from him. She put her hands on his sides. "Do you want to help me with the buttons?"

He unfastened the two buttons, spread the shirt open, and stared at her. Leigh closed her eyes. She felt the shirt slip off her shoulders, its sleeves glide down her arms. She stood before Charlie, naked, trembling, waiting for his touch.

"I sure wish it was light out," he said in a husky voice, "so I could see you better."

"There's always Braille," Leigh whispered. Charlie just stood there. Opening her eyes, she reached for the button of his jeans.

He pushed her hands away. "Go on and get in the lake," he told her. He didn't sound annoyed, just nervous.

"You don't have to be shy," Leigh said.

"I'll be right in."

"Okay." Turning away, Leigh walked down the sand. The water washed over her feet. She remembered its chill when she dove from the pier. It didn't seem that way now. It felt as warm as the night air.

"Now, don't look," Charlie said.

"Okay, bashful." The water rose around Leigh with mild caresses. She caught her breath when it lapped the joining of her legs. Then she leaned in, left her feet, and glided forward. When she sought the bottom again, the water was neck high. She let her arms drift to the surface. She stared out at the line of trees ahead, the narrow moonlit mouth of the inlet.

Soft splashing sounds came from behind. She waited for Charlie's arms to encircle her, his hands to find her breasts. She waited for the feel of his body against her back.

He swam past her, only his head above the surface, then turned to face her six feet away. "This sure feels good," he said. "Nothing like a night swim."

"Come here, Charlie Payne."

He laughed softly. "Betcha can't catch me."

Leigh didn't feel like playing games. "What are you scared of?"

"Not it! You're it!" His head turned away and he started to swim.

"Damn it, Charlie."

"You ca-an't catch me," he chanted over his shoulder.

"Don't think so, huh?" Muttering, "Shit," she lunged forward, dropped beneath the surface, and swam underwater. She passed through a chilly current. She went deeper. Her lungs hurt, but she kept going.

She pictured Charlie treading water. His long legs. His penis.

She should almost be to him.

The water stirred against her. She heard the muffled sounds of splashes. He was making a getaway.

Seems like he's *always* trying to get away.

Leigh surfaced, gasping, her face splashed by Charlie's kicks. She darted out a hand. Grabbed one of his ankles, pulled. "Gotcha!" Tugging the ankle, she reached higher and clutched his leg. She expected to find skin. Instead, there was denim. "Hey!" She hooked fingers into a rear pocket and yanked. Charlie slipped backward. He twisted around, freeing himself. "What's the big idea?" Leigh demanded.

"Huh?"

"You've got your jeans on."

"So?"

"Well . . . for one thing . . . what makes you think they'll be dry by morning?"

"Guess they won't be."

"You gonna tell your mother . . . how they got wet?"

Charlie didn't answer. Obviously, he hadn't thought about that. Leigh eased herself backward until her feet found the rocky bottom. Charlie moved closer. He stood, the water just lower than his shoulders. "It takes a long time for jeans to dry," she said. "If you give them to me right now, I'll wring them out for you and hang them up. Maybe the breeze . . ."

"I wouldn't have nothing on."

"That'd make two of us."

"You think they'll dry out in time if they're hung out?"

"Maybe."

"All right, but . . ." He didn't finish. His shoulders moved slightly, then he ducked beneath the surface. His movements under the water sent currents brushing against Leigh. He was below for a long time. His head finally popped up with a burst of water. He thrust the jeans toward Leigh.

"Don't go away," she said, taking them and wading for shore.

That little ploy sure did the trick, she thought. She still felt a little annoyed that he'd kept his jeans on in the first place. It was cheating. It was also pretty damned peculiar. How many guys, in his place, would've stayed in their pants with a naked girl waiting in the water? Zip, that's how many.

So what's new? He's been peculiar from the start.

Never been with a girl.

His mother's got him so screwed up . . . Well, this time it backfired on her. If Charlie wasn't so frightened that the wet pants would give him away, he might've never taken them off.

Leigh waded out and stood on the beach, her back to the inlet. The breeze made her shiver. She gritted her teeth at the feel of cold droplets trickling down her skin. As quickly as possible, she twisted each leg of the jeans. She wrung the jeans with all her strength. When she shook them open, the fabric was still wet but no longer dripping.

To reach the nearest trees, she had to leave the beach. Twigs hurt her feet. Undergrowth snagged her ankles. She looked up at the dark shape of the cabin, wondering if it really was deserted.

What if somebody . . . ?

Don't start.

He might be hiding among the trees, watching. A hand inside his overalls . . .

Don't worry, Charlie's here.

Here? Out in the water.

Would he come and help if someone rushed out?

A quiet, crackling sound came from the slope. Leigh stopped. A tree was only a few steps ahead. Her eyes studied the dark woods, but nothing seemed to move. She wanted to glance back and see how far away Charlie was, but she didn't dare. If she looked away, even for a moment . . .

What the hell am I doing here?

You're trying to hang up Charlie's jeans.

What am I doing *here?* My God. I swam out to this guy's boat in the middle of the night and now I'm standing here bare-ass like some kind of maniac. I must be crazy. I should be back at the cabin asleep. I should be home in Marin, asleep. Jesus H. Christ on a rubber crutch, what am I *doing* here?

Trying to get laid by Charlie, that's what.

Which he's afraid to do because his mother wouldn't like it.

And even if he was eager, you're nuts to be going for it this way. You don't even know him. He's definitely a little weird.

Forgetting about the threat from the woods that had so unnerved her a few moments ago, Leigh stepped close to the tree. She reached up and draped Charlie's jeans over its lowest branch.

She turned away and started back. Charlie was still in the lake. He looked as if he'd been cut off at the neck.

Leigh's nightgown was a pale shape spread over the stern seat of the rowboat. She walked toward it.

She pictured herself putting it on.

Game's over, Charlie, take me home.

He wouldn't come out of the water without his jeans.

You could go back for them.

You could leave him here and walk back to the cabin. Just follow the shoreline, then make your way up to the dirt road.

Standing by the boat, she stared down at her nightgown.

Do it, she thought.

She bent over and picked up her nightgown. The breeze caught it, lifting and rippling its weightless fabric.

"What are you doing?" Charlie asked.

I don't know, Leigh thought. God, I haven't the slightest.

She pressed the nightgown to her front and held it there, covering herself.

You're really going to call it quits?

It never should have gone this far. I was out of my mind.

She heard quiet sloshing sounds. "Leigh?" Charlie was wading closer, the black of the water dropping.

"What're you doing?" he asked again.

"I think I'm ready to leave," she said.

You *think?*

"What for? Don't you like it here?"

"It's awfully late," she said.

Late. How lame.

Charlie stopped. He was bare to the waist. Just another step or two, Charlie. "What's wrong?" he asked.

"Nothing."

"You mad at me?"

"No. It isn't you."

"You're mad at me 'cause I left my pants on."

"No, I'm not."

"Well, they're off now."

"It doesn't matter," Leigh said.

She stared at the dark surface in front of him. Of course it doesn't matter, she told herself. Oh sure.

"I should've took 'em off," he said. "I knew I was s'posed to. I was just too yellow, that's all. I'm awfully sorry. I wanted to, that's for sure."

"Charlie, we shouldn't be like this."

"I guess not. But I don't want us to leave, though." He waded out. He walked up the beach, hands crossed to cover his groin. "Cold," he whispered.

Leigh draped her nightgown over the boat seat and went to him.

You were going to leave, she reminded herself. What are you doing?

Her heart thudded. Her mouth was dry. She met Charlie and put her arms around him. His wet skin felt cold. His arms went around her back. His open mouth found hers, and his tongue pushed in. She squirmed against him, moaning with the feel of his penis pressing thick and hard against her belly.

Where their bodies met, the chill went away. The skin of his back was still wet and cold. Her hands moved down to his buttocks. Charlie, following her lead, moved his hands down to her rump. They felt big and warm.

Soon, Leigh took her mouth away. Kissing the side of his neck, she reached behind and took his wrists. She eased away from him. She lifted his hands to her breasts, and trembled at their touch. His hands were calloused but gentle. Leigh closed her eyes. She clung to his hips as he caressed her. The hands glided over her breasts, enclosed them, held them tenderly, tightened and squeezed, roamed them, exploring, then squeezed again.

"Kiss," Leigh muttered.

He crouched. She held his shoulders, and he kissed her left nipple. His tongue thrust. Leigh moaned as he sucked the nipple into his mouth, tongue swirling and probing.

Fingers in his wet hair, she urged his head closer. Her breast felt engulfed.

He rubbed her thighs. His mouth went to her other breast, and his hands moved higher as he licked the nipple. Higher until his thumbs stroked the creases of her groin.

Leigh's grip tightened on his hair. Charlie made sucking noises tugging at her nipple. His hands swept over her hips, around her buttocks, the backs of her legs, then up again, curling in and pressing. With a gasp, Leigh locked her knees to keep her legs from buckling. Her breast was drawn deep into his mouth. One of his hands went away and came to the front. Its edge pressed her vagina. She shuddered as it sawed back and forth, rubbing, opening her, sliding between her folds, slick and hot. His thumb rose into her.

"Charlie," she gasped.

His mouth pulled away from her breast, leaving it wet and tingling. "Does it hurt?"

"Hurt? No. Dear God." She hugged his head between her breasts. His thumb pushed and circled. His hand pressed hard, part of it rubbing her clitoris. She squirmed on it.

Then she released his head and squatted. Charlie sank to his knees, his thumb still inside her. He curled his other hand behind her neck to hold her steady. She reached between his legs. His penis felt huge. Her fingers enclosed it, slid down its length. She gently squeezed his scrotum, glided her palm up the underside of his shaft, then let herself fall backward onto the sand.

Charlie loomed over her, kneeling between her bent legs, holding himself up with stiff arms. Leigh stroked his sides. "In me," she whispered. "I want you in me."

"You sure?"

"My God."

"I mean . . . you won't get a baby?"

"It's okay." Probably, she thought. She had already counted. Her period was due in four days.

Charlie pressed down, his hips forcing her thighs even farther apart. She dug her heels into the sand, lifting herself to meet him.

His penis rubbed her. It moved slowly, spreading her, barely inside, sliding along her slit. Then it began to ease in. Leigh thrust up. The penis filled her.

Charlie's tongue pushed into her mouth. She sucked it. His tongue was in her, his penis was in her. She possessed both, and they possessed her. She writhed. His tongue thrust and retreated, matching the strokes of his penis. She gasped through her nose. She heard wet sounds and Charlie moaning. She dug her heels into his buttocks. He rammed deeper, and suddenly went rigid. Leigh sucked his tongue hard. Her insides quaked with the feel of him all the way in, jerking and throbbing and pumping a flood.

She cried out into his mouth.

Sixteen

A gentle rapping woke Leigh up. She raised her head off the pillow and groaned.

"We're going out for the big ones," Jenny called through the door. "Want to come along?"

"Okay," Leigh said. "Time for me to shower first?"

"No problem."

Fishing was about the last thing she wanted to do, but she had made up her mind, in the early-morning hours, to go with them today. If she missed two days in a row, they might suspect something was amiss.

Something was amiss, all right. Every muscle in her body ached when she pushed herself up. Her insides felt battered.

Moaning, Leigh limped to the chair by the window. Her nightgown was draped over it. She lifted the gown and inspected it. It was dry, but dirty. She wadded it up and made her way to the dresser. She hid it at the bottom of a drawer. She could do her own laundry, later, and take care of it. Nobody would be the wiser.

In the mirror, her hair was a straggly mess. She combed out the worst of the snags and brushed it. Sand sprinkled her shoulders.

Back at the bed, she brushed sand and bits of leaves and other debris off the pillow and bottom sheet. She found a small, stiff place on the sheet. She guessed it was dried semen. Checking herself, she found some flaked in her pubic hair, and a patch of it on her inner thigh that felt tight and looked like skin peeling from a sunburn. She left it there and made the bed.

She took her robe from the closet, put it on, and went to the door.

Mike, in the kitchen, was pouring coffee into a thermos. "And how are you this fine morning?" he asked.

"Great," Leigh said. "A little stiff from canoeing yesterday." She tried her best not to limp on her way to the bathroom.

Inside, she hung her robe on the doorknob. She looked at herself in the full-length mirror. Her breasts were a little red. Otherwise, none of the damage showed. Turning around, she looked over her shoulders. Her back was all right except for a few faint red marks on her buttocks where she had lost the scabs from her scrapes at the demonstration.

The cop dragging her.

That seemed like years ago.

It seemed like it had happened to someone else.

She made the water as hot as she could stand and stepped under the shower. The spray beat down on her. It felt wonderful. Sighing, she stretched her sore muscles. Then she slicked herself with soap. She scrubbed between her legs to make sure she got all the semen off.

Probably more inside, she thought.

There must've been a gallon last night.

Four times.

Three, not counting the mouth.

No wonder I ache.

Even her cheeks felt sore.

What a night.

The memories of it rushed through her mind, triggering fresh desire.

She couldn't wait to see him again.

She began to shampoo her hair.

Before parting, they had agreed to meet at three o'clock where the channel from Wahconda entered Goon Lake. He said he knew of a secret place to take her, a place where no one could see them even in daylight. It sounded terrific. She hoped she wasn't too sore to enjoy it.

Her mind was full of Charlie as she finished her

shower, dried, and returned to her room. She wondered what time he would be leaving in his boat to take the baskets over to Goon and Willow. Maybe she would see him. The possibility made her heart race. She parted her hair in the middle, brushed bangs down over her forehead, and gave herself a ponytail. She wanted to wear her good white shorts, but decided to save them for the rendezvous. She put on her cutoffs instead, and a faded blue T-shirt.

Heading down to the pier with Mike and Jenny, she thought she had never felt quite so fine. In spite of her aches. The morning air was sweet with pine. The breeze caressed her. The calm blue lake shimmered with sunlight.

"You're looking pretty chipper this morning," Jenny said.

It showed? "Guess it's the fresh air," she said, and stepped down into the boat.

When the gear was aboard, Mike steered the boat out around the pier. Then he asked if Leigh would like to take the controls. "Sure," she told him, and stepped to the helm. "Where to?"

"Anywhere you want."

Opening the throttle, she swung the boat northward. She watched the shore. Soon, she saw the opening of the inlet where Charlie had taken her. When the boat was directly across from it, she glimpsed the beach.

She felt the sand against her back, Charlie pounding into her.

A few more hours . . .

In the sunlight, they would be able to see each other.

Near the north shore, she turned the boat to the east. The foreboding she used to feel along this side of the lake was gone. Approaching an old dock with broken planks dangling toward the water, she searched the woods until she spotted a shack hidden among the trees. Was this Charlie's place? Probably not. She suspected that he lived farther down, maybe even along the eastern shore.

"Where we going?" Mike asked, appearing at her side.

"How about between those two islands?" she suggested, pointing at the patches of woods far ahead.

"Looks good to me," Mike told her.

Yesterday morning, Charlie had said that he'd seen her water-skiing. Well, she'd been skiing over much of the lake, but the nearest she got to the eastern shore was when she circled those two islands. Maybe that's when Charlie spotted her.

Let's not be too obvious about this, she thought as she neared the islands. You don't want to wind up on his doorstep.

The islands were about a hundred yards apart. As the boat entered the area between them, Leigh cut the engines. "If I were a fish," she told Mike and Jenny, "this is just the place I'd hang out."

Mike dropped anchor.

Jenny opened the picnic basket—one of Charlie's baskets. She poured coffee into mugs, then handed out egg salad sandwiches wrapped in cellophane. It was their custom to eat before baiting the hooks.

Leigh's cheek muscles ached as she chewed, reminding her again of last night—her lips tight around Charlie, her mouth full, the slick smooth hardness of him, her sucking. She'd been on top, Charlie's head between her legs, his tongue . . . Her mouth was too dry for the sandwich. She struggled to swallow, and washed the food down with coffee.

Stop the daydreaming, she warned herself. Save it for later when you're not with Mike and Jenny.

She joined in the conversation. Soon, she was calm enough to finish her sandwich.

They baited their hooks.

The current had swept the boat sideways. Leigh dropped her line over the port side so she could face east while she fished. The wooded islands acted as blinders, blocking much of the lake's shoreline. She could see no pier or dwelling along the visible stretch of shore. Just thick forest, curtains of green drooping toward the water, roots here and there reaching down from the banks. She wondered if Charlie's place was nearby, maybe on the other side of one of the islands.

If so, there was a chance she might see him when he rowed out with his baskets.

The white top of her bobber rode the small waves, rising and falling. She watched it. She watched the lake.

Her thoughts returned to last night. She let the images play through her mind, the feelings come back. It was almost like being with him again.

She *would* be with him again, this afternoon. They would go to his secret place.

I'll take along the suntan oil, she thought.

Charlie would spread it over her naked body, then she would rub it on him. She pictured their skin gleaming with oil. She felt them squirming together, all slippery.

In just a few more hours.

She watched her bobber. She watched the lake.

There was no sign of Charlie.

Maybe he'd started early and was already on one of the other lakes. Of course. He would have wanted to finish his selling rounds as fast as possible so he could be ready to meet her.

At three o'clock.

She wondered if she could stand to wait that long.

At two-thirty, Leigh left the cabin after telling Mike and Jenny she planned to "go exploring" in the canoe.

They said to have fun.

Her heart thudded hard as she made her way down to the shore. She felt tight and trembly inside. She wore her fresh shorts, just as she had planned, and a red sleeveless blouse. She carried a towel. Rolled inside the towel was the plastic bottle of suntan oil.

She pushed the canoe into the water, wading out for a few steps before climbing aboard. She took out the suntan oil, then knelt on the towel and paddled away.

Though Leigh wanted bright sunlight for the rendezvous, there were high clouds shadowing the lake.

If the sun's not out, she thought, we won't glisten.

There wasn't even a cool breeze to compensate for the sun's loss. The air was still and muggy.

Leigh's blouse clung to her back. It was tucked into her shorts, and it pulled at her shoulders each time she leaned forward.

After passing Carson's Camp, she swung the bow eastward. She blinked sweat out of her eyes.

Awfully muggy.

Resting the paddle across the gunnels, she looked around. The nearest other boat was so far off that the people aboard were vague and without features. She tugged her blouse out of her shorts and lifted the front to wipe her face. She wished she could take it off, but she wore nothing beneath it.

Guys are so lucky, she thought. They can take off their shirt in weather like this.

She unbuttoned her blouse, lifted it around her lower ribs, and tied the front.

A lot better.

She picked up the paddle and dug it into the water. The canoe started forward again. Soon, it was shooting over the calm surface.

She kept a close watch on the southern shore. At last, she spotted a field of lily pads with a narrow path of open water down the middle. This had to be the channel to Goon Lake. She swung the prow toward it.

The canoe glided in, a bit to the left of the open water. The lily pads rustled like paper against the hull. Setting down the paddle, she let the canoe drift. She was out of breath, drenched with sweat. She pulled the towel out from under her knees and wiped her face with it. She wiped the back of her neck, and was glad she wore the ponytail; it kept the hair off her neck. Still gasping for breath, she plucked open the knot to let her blouse fall open. She rubbed her dripping sides and belly and chest.

As soon as the towel was gone, her skin felt damp again.

It was the heavy, hot, humid, suffocating air.

Air that smelled faintly of rain.

She wished it *would* rain.

Fat chance.

Leigh paddled farther into the channel. Ahead, there was no sign of Goon Lake. She looked behind her. Wahconda was out of sight.

Dragonflies hovered over the carpet of pads. She saw a green frog hop and splash. The motionless air seemed silent, but she realized it was noisy with buzzes, chitters, water plops, bird squawks, and chirrups. No human sounds; that's what made it seem like silence.

Leigh took her blouse off. She leaned over the side with it, the canoe tipping slightly, the aluminum gunnel pushing hot against her breast, then she plunged her blouse into the water. She lifted it out. It dripped on her thighs. She sighed deeply as she pressed the wet, cool fabric to her face. She dunked it again, shook it open, and swept it against her torso. It plastered her from shoulder to waist.

She peeled it down, soaked it one more time, then struggled into it and tied the front again.

It had felt good while it lasted.

It hadn't lasted long.

She needed to be *in* the water. Swimming. With Charlie. Soon now.

Slowly, she paddled forward.

The channel curved one way, then the other. From the air, it must look like stacked *S*'s. Or a snake, she thought. This is probably a good place for water snakes, though she hadn't noticed any so far.

She kept dipping the paddle in, drawing it back slowly,

trying not to exert herself as she guided it along the twisting channel.

Finally, she came out at the other end. She laid the paddle across the gunnels. As she folded the towel and sat on it, her eyes swept Goon Lake. It was much smaller than Wahconda, maybe half the size. Like Wahconda, most of the piers and dwellings were along the western shore. She saw a skier being towed behind a motorboat, and three other boats off in the distance with people fishing. She didn't see Charlie.

Maybe he hit a delay.

Maybe he was doing a brisk business in baskets and didn't want to cut it short.

There were several small islands. One of them could be blocking Charlie from her view.

She waited.

He was nowhere in sight. Maybe he was still over on Willow Lake.

Leigh considered heading over to Willow, but she had no idea where the channel might be. She supposed she could find it. If she tried, however, there was some chance she might miss Charlie. He could end up waiting here while she was busy searching for him.

This is where we planned to meet, she told herself. I'd better stay put.

The canoe kept drifting back into the lily pads. After paddling it free a few times, she decided to simplify matters by landing. She headed to the right and brought the canoe up against the trunk of a fallen tree. Clamping her towel under one arm, she scurried in a crouch to the bow and picked up the mooring rope. She tied its end to one of the dead, leafless branches. Then she climbed onto the trunk, made her way carefully back toward its cluster of roots, and hopped to the ground.

At a shaded place close to shore, she toweled away her sweat once again, then spread the towel on the ground and sat on it.

From here, she had a full view of the lake.

She still did not see Charlie.

What could be keeping him?

He'll be along. He's only a little bit late.

Probably half an hour late already, and no sign of him in the distance.

Does he have a watch? Leigh had never seen him with one.

I should have brought a book.

She was sitting cross-legged. The ground felt very hard. After a while, her rump and legs began to go numb and tingly. She leaned back, bracing herself on her elbows and stretching out her legs. She kept her head up to watch the lake. That felt a lot better, at first. But soon the strain of her already stiff neck and shoulder muscles became painful. She wanted to lie down.

If you do that, you'll fall asleep.

She had napped for a couple of hours after lunch, but that hadn't been enough to make up for last night.

If she fell asleep now, she might miss Charlie. He could show up, not see her or the canoe, and figure she had either stayed away or given up on waiting.

Moaning with aches and weariness, Leigh got to her feet. She climbed onto the tree, walked along its wide trunk past the place where the canoe was tied, and sat down. The water felt smooth and cool around her feet.

The skier was gone. One of the boats was moving slowly near an island, its motor a faint humm. She spotted a rowboat!

Her heart quickened.

It's about time, she thought.

She gazed at the rowboat. It drew slowly closer, then turned as if heading for one of the piers. A cloud moved briefly out of the sun's way. The rowboat caught sunlight and glinted.

It was aluminum.

Charlie's boat was wood, painted green.

It's not him.

Leigh's disappointment came out in a long sigh.

"Where the hell is he?" she muttered.

He'll be here, she told herself.

Maybe he chickened out.

Or he had to change plans. Maybe his mother wanted him to postpone today's trip for some reason.

Am *I* in the right place? How do I know for sure this is Goon Lake? Maybe this is Circle, where Charlie went yesterday, and he's waiting for me at the channel into Goon and wondering where *I* am.

Mike told me yesterday where to find the channel to Goon.

Maybe Mike was wrong.

Something went wrong, that's for sure.

Trickles slid down her cheeks. She felt like crying, but these weren't tears. She rubbed her face with the backs of her hands. The backs of her hands were wet, too, and only smeared the sweat on her face.

Couldn't there at least be a breeze?

Where is Charlie?

I'm not giving up. I'll wait here till Hell freezes over.

Fat chance of *anything* freezing over.

A tickling drop of sweat slid down her neck and between her breasts. She wiped it away.

And remembered her sea-thing necklace.

She didn't have it on.

Maybe that's the problem, she thought. Should've worn my good-luck charm.

I didn't wear it last night, though, and had plenty of luck without it.

The necklace has nothing to do with luck.

Still, she wished she were wearing it.

Even if you're not superstitious, always a good idea to keep the bases covered.

From now on, I'll wear it.

She kicked her feet, making the cool water splash her legs.

The hell with the necklace, I should've worn my bikini.

She'd thought she wouldn't need it. She'd planned on skinny-dipping at Charlie's secret place, expecting it to be an inlet similar to the one last night, or maybe a stream or pond.

Here, nobody was nearby. But there was no real privacy. She couldn't go in naked.

With a shrug, she pushed herself off the trunk. She dropped into the waist-deep water with barely a splash, took a few steps along the slippery rock bottom until she was clear of the trees, then left her feet. The cool engulfed her. It felt wonderful. She glided beneath the surface until she needed air, then came up. She rolled onto her back. Floating, she closed her blouse over her breasts. Then she shut her eyes.

Buoyed up, it felt like she was lying spread-eagled on a cool, liquid mattress. She had to hold her back arched to keep from sinking, but otherwise no effort was needed. The water turned her slowly, toyed with her limp arms and legs.

I should've done this a long time ago, she thought.

She felt fine and relaxed and drowsy.

Like this, I could wait all afternoon for Charlie.

He'll be along . . .

. . . pretty soon.

A nose full of water startled Leigh awake. Spluttering, she slapped the surface and kicked. A few quick strokes took her close enough to shore so she could stand. She coughed and blew her nose. Then she was all right except for a burning sensation behind her eyes.

Wonderful, she thought. Drown, why don't you.

Wiping her eyes, she turned around and scanned the lake. No Charlie.

It must be four o'clock by now.

He's not coming.

Goddamn it.
She waded ashore and flopped facedown on her towel.
Come on, Charlie.
Where are you, Charlie?
Goddamn it to hell anyway.
Shit!
Leigh began to sob.

SEVENTEEN

Leigh rolled over, sat up, and knuckled the tears from her eyes. Like a kid at school. Despite her frustration at Charlie's absence, the idea struck her as a little amusing. Tears welled up again, but she thought better of it. Wouldn't do for Charlie to catch her like this, eyes all red and puffy from crying.

If Charlie deigned to put in an appearance this side of tomorrow.

Fine. Put it down to experience, Leigh. World's *full* of gals who've been let down—*are* being let down at this very moment, she told herself. But she could *swear* Charlie had been serious last night. Serious enough to come out to look for her, anyhow.

Not today, though.

Must have had second thoughts.

Maybe his mom beat him when she saw his wet pants and he's stayed home.

Who gives a shit, anyway. . . .

She wasn't a gal to hang around after some guy who couldn't stand up to his own mother.

She must be a tough old bitch.

Not like *her* mom.

Leigh imagined her own mom and dad—if they could see her now. Waiting around for this guy who sells *baskets* for a living, how would *they* react? "Don't tell me," she muttered. "They'd be all self-righteousness and pursed lips. Accusing eyes. Mom's would be red with weeping."

"Pull yourself together, young lady," Dad would say, with a pleading glance at Mom, like "We got ourselves a situation here, Helen. She's *your* daughter, too, y'know. Tell me, what *are* we going to do with her?" Mom would just shake her head, wring her hands, stem back more despairing tears.

"What are Mike and Jenny *doing?*" she'd blurt. "Allowing her out on her lonesome like this? Leigh's so vulnerable just now. What with that showdown with the police and everything. Your brother should have had more sense than to encourage her to meet up with this . . . this *basketseller!*"

"*My* brother. That's rich! My brother indeed! I don't recall *you* putting forward any of *your* family to help out with your errant daughter. . . ."

"You mean *our* errant daughter!"

God, what a mess!

For the millionth time (it seemed like the millionth), Leigh lifted her head and scanned the lake. She was weary with waiting. Charlie had either forgotten, or was being held captive by that witch bitch mother of his.

"That's it," she muttered. "Mom found out, locked her precious boy in the closet, and swallowed the key. Jeez. What kind of fool *am* I? Driven to the point of suicide by some kid who can't even stand up to his own *mother?*"

Some kid who's gagging for sex but doesn't even know it yet. Wouldn't know a pussy if it jumped up and bit him. "No," she told herself. "That's not true." She remembered Charlie last night, the state he was in (the state they were *both* in), and knew that no way was that true.

Time to haul ass and head for home, honey. Quit being a prize idiot and just get gone.

She looked at her wristwatch. 5:57. Mike and Jenny

would be getting worried. More than that. They'd most likely be hairless by now. Wondering if they should call Mom and Dad.

Or the cops . . .

No, they wouldn't do that. Not Mike and Jenny. They were okay guys. Sensible. Levelheaded. Teachers, for godsake. Through her tears, Leigh was sorry for what they must be feeling right now. They'd be thinking they had let her parents down.

Let *her* down.

Jesus.

At least she owed them the courtesy of an appearance before they called the police department.

She climbed to her feet. Her back and legs were wrecked; she felt like she'd done a fifty-mile route march.

Aaaghh . . .

She limped over to the canoe. Clambered into it. Sat down and eased the paddle off the gunnel. It was *so* muggy and hot. She unbuttoned her blouse. Her *almost* new blouse, the one she'd worn only twice before. She liked it, too, knew the color red looked good against her fair hair and sun-bronzed skin.

But it wasn't looking so new, or so good, now.

Hanging off her shoulders like a limp rag.

She dragged it together, tied the ends in a knot. Under the thin fabric, she felt the weight of her breasts as she leaned forward, skimming the paddle through the water. She scanned the dark pines and the shining lake spread out before her . . . and saw Charlie up ahead, powering his rowboat toward the shore with strong, well-muscled arms, his back against the sun, his front in shadow.

Like last night, he wasn't wearing his hat.

She could see his gleaming white teeth.

Because he was *smiling,* for chrissake.

The smile did it for her.

Goddamn you, Charlie. I don't *believe* this. All bright-eyed and bushy-tailed, and I've just spent an entire *afternoon* waiting for you. Shit, Charlie. How *could* you?

He steered the boat around, easing its hull onto the sand. All so laid-back . . . and, goddamn it, he looked so . . . unconcerned. He lifted the anchor and let it drop into the water.

Then, effortlessly, like an athlete, he leapt from the rowboat and came toward her. Gleaming muscles, slender hips—and jeans bulging in all the right places. He sure looks mighty pleased with himself, she thought angrily.

"Charlie, you useless piece a' shit. Where *have* you been?"

"Mom told me to take more baskets out on Willow. There's a whole new buncha vacationers over at Carson's Camp, and . . ." He stopped, saw her angry face, and dropped his eyes.

He looked caught, uncomfortable.

"Charlie," she persisted. "You *knew* we arranged to meet today. At three o'clock, we both agreed. It's now turned six. What *is* the matter—can't you tell the time?"

His face reddened, his mouth trembling slightly.

Alarmed, she thought he was going to burst into tears. *Oh my God.*

Don't *do* this to me, Charlie.

I want a goddamn lover, not a crybaby.

Take me in your arms. Sweep me off my feet.

Do *something*. But don't just *stand* there like an idiot.

He looked confused—innocent, like a child; melting her anger like a snowball in the sun. More than anything else in the whole world, she wanted to hold him close. Gather him to her breast; caress him with gentle hands.

And for him to *ram* himself inside her.

Now.

He could have committed murder for all she cared.

Maybe had.

Maybe his mom lay bleeding to death right now, a stained hunting knife tossed to one side. The lifeblood pumping out of her.

All because she wouldn't let him go to the evil bitch who lusted for her precious Charlie's sex.

Give it to me, Charlie. Here. Now. In front of anybody who cares to watch. Just *give* it to me.

Leigh opened her blouse, letting it fall from her shoulders as she moved toward him.

His eyes widened. Then he smiled, shyly, fixing his gaze on her naked breasts. They were heavy and swinging as she walked toward him.

He held out his arms, and with a moan she pulled him to her. Wrapped an arm around his neck and pressed her open mouth onto his. Their tongues met. Her free hand struggled to undo the top button of his jeans.

They're so *tight*.

It's a wonder he isn't raped every time he goes out, she marveled, peeling down the zipper. Easing her fingers in between his legs, she found the hot, pulsating bulge lying there. Waiting for her. With both hands, she reached in farther, cupped his scrotum and penis, and drew them out. He moaned, squirming in her grasp.

"*In* me, Charlie," she breathed.

"The house. Come into the house," he whispered hoarsely.

"Why not here? Anyway, *what* house?"

"My secret place. It's private. Come with me."

She pouted. Annoyed at the interruption, her rim aching with need. If he's gonna play games again, it's finito. I'm outa here.

Still pouting, she followed him up the limb-strewn beach to a house set back in the pines. Watching out for him across the lake, she hadn't noticed it before. He led her across the rickety porch, to the stoop and through the half-open door.

"You been here before?" she asked warily.

"Yeah. Lotsa times," he told her. "Not with nobody else, though. I come here alone. So's I can think."

"Whose place is it?"

"B'longed to some rich New Yorker guy back in the thirties, Mom said. Shot his wife, buried her out back in the woods. Guy hanged himself from that there balcony, y'see up there?"

"How did they know he'd shot and buried his wife?"

"Left a note on the kitchen table confessin' all. Said he'd caught his wife in bed with Jed Johnson, local ranger hereabouts. Nobody'd live in the place after that. It was left to go to rack 'n' ruin. Y'can still see bloodstains on the kitchen floor," he explained with enthusiasm, as if proud to impart this piece of local lore.

The house was dark inside; it smelled earthy and damp. Leigh wrinkled her nose as she caught the moldy odor of decaying wood—*or was it dried blood?*

Shivering, she wished she'd picked up her blouse from off the beach.

It had been wet, anyhow.

Might have dried off by now, though.

A sharp shiver brought goose bumps to her naked flesh. Hunching her shoulders up to her ears, she wrapped her arms around her breasts.

Charlie led the way up the stairs.

"Mind that one—and the next. These old stairs are real unsafe. Don't want you breaking a leg, now."

"God, Charlie. Do we *have* to do this? I mean, this place could put a person off it, y'know. . . ."

She flung out an arm to balance herself, clutching at the balustrade. It was tacky with damp and mold. She dragged back her hand, checking her fingers.

"Yuck. This is *gross*. Charlie, you're doing this on purpose. Tell me you don't want to make love to me, and I'll go. Just fade out of your life forever . . . I don't *need* all this."

Tears of disappointment welled in her eyes.

Disappointment? Try *terminal frustration!* He's playing games with me—just like last night. Who the hell does he think he is . . .

"Charlie?"

They reached the landing, a mezzanine arrangement with several doors branching off into various rooms on the right. Must have been quite a house once upon a time, she thought miserably.

"Charlie . . . !"

He turned, sweeping her into his arms easily, as if she were a child, and carried her into one of the rooms. By its size it had probably been the master bedroom. A tick mattress lay in the center of the floor.

Jagged, broken windows overlooked the pine-fringed lake. It was a mighty fine view, she had to admit.

Any other time . . .

Empty beer cans, food wrappers, and other junk was piled in the corners of the room. Squatters, campers . . .

Even murderers . . . She pictured the New Yorker guy, rope in hand, taking one last look at the lake below. . . .

Charlie put her down, then went over to an old-fashioned dresser. He opened a drawer, took out a folded sheet and an Indian blanket.

Leigh perked up.

Looks like this could be a regular routine.

She felt let down. Cheap, tawdry. She'd *hoped* she'd been his first. Looked like he'd been lying through his teeth when he told her he'd never had a girlfriend.

Guys. What is it with them?

Wondering what he'd come up with next, she watched, hands on hips, eyebrows raised.

"Uh-huh," she murmured, eyeing the bedcovers and wondering who'd used them before she came along.

"Very handy."

"I snuck these in last night, after you'd gone." He looked as if he expected her to pat him on the head and say, "Gee, thanks, Charlie."

She didn't.

He spread out the sheet on the mattress. Then he put the blanket on top.

At least they're clean.

If they'd been dirty, I'd've been out of here, she told herself. Then, immediately, she felt guilty. Charlie had done all of this for *her*. She was sure of it.

He was smiling eagerly. Folding down the bedcovers, he motioned for her to get in.

Still, she was cynical.

"The romance is killing me, buster. . . . Can't wait for dessert."

Cocking his head to one side, he tried to understand her words. Her mood. He hadn't seen her like this before. His eyes shifted to his feet.

"I . . . I thought you'd like my secret place . . . ," he said quietly, disappointed she seemed displeased.

Leigh let out a small "aahh" of guilt. She couldn't *bear* to see him hurt. Innocently, his eyes questioned hers. Like a small boy who'd brought his mom a special gift, only to be told she didn't want it.

She relented, couldn't take his discomfort any longer.

"Okay, Charlie. I give in. This sure is some place you got here."

Moving over to the makeshift bed, she clambered in, hugged her knees, and smiled up at him.

Charlie looked happier already. It dawned on her that in his own special way maybe Charlie was in love with her.

She opened her arms, and he came to her.

They lay there for a while, he stroking her breasts, her belly, her thighs and legs. Doing it carefully, like she was a piece of precious china.

Lying by her side, propped up on an elbow, head in his hand, he looked at her. She smiled deep into his eyes.

His arm dropped down.

They lay together, their bodies touching. The pain, the

hard ache between her legs, began again. He caressed her back, gently. Kissed her lips, her eyelids, her cheeks.

Then tenderly, and with infinite feeling, her lips again.

She sensed the *different* kind of passion.

Not the wham-bam, thank-ya-ma'am stuff that had happened yesterday.

This was a wonderful, titillating foreplay to the main event.

Leigh responded, gently at first, then with impatience and a growing need. She came on top, straddling him, her mouth opening on his, finding his tongue, sucking, sucking, and pulling it into hers. Drawing it into her throat.

Wishing it were *him* she had in her mouth.

Like last night.

She left his mouth. Sliding down, she trailed her tongue over his slick, muscular chest.

His body tasted good; it was hairy and salty with sweat.

She licked harder now, her breath coming in short, hard gasps. Her tongue traveled past his navel and through the dark curly hairs spreading across his hard belly.

Down to his huge erection.

She grasped it and took it in her mouth until he came, writhing, moaning, spurting into her. Sobbing and gagging, she swallowed his come.

Gasping, tears running down her face, she lay with her head between his legs, panting, breathless. Pulling her up against his chest, he massaged the backs of her thighs with firm, smooth strokes.

His mouth found hers again; he took her tongue and sucked at it, hard. As he shifted slightly, his pubic hairs rubbed against her belly. Then, with a strength she wasn't expecting, he shoved a hand inside her.

Aaaaghhh . . .

She cried out. In shock. In pain.

With a catlike movement Charlie was on top, thrusting himself deep into her center. Pounding into her, gouging, shaking her body to the core. She rose to meet him, raw, hurting, pressing herself against him, raking herself up and down his shaft till she could take no more.

He came into her again. And again. Still gasping, crying a little, she lay back on the tousled, sweat-soaked sheet. Charlie lay on his side, looking down at her, hungrily.

Panting. Wanting more.

Playing with her dark, softening nipples.

She felt the hard ache rise again. . . .

"Charlie," she breathed, closing her eyes, lifting her arms to hold him.

But Charlie leapt up, grabbed his shirt, and thrust his arms into it. Fumbling with the buttons, he gave up trying and dragged on his jeans.

Hopping from one leg to the other, he looked almost comical.

Except it wasn't funny.

Leigh was in shock.

Crying out in disbelief: "Charlie?"

Astounded.

Bereft.

"Where are you *going?* You can't leave me now . . . not like this . . ."

"I gotta I gotta . . . ," he stammered desperately. "I promised Mom I'd be home for supper. She thinks I'm out collecting wood for tomorrow. . . . I gotta go . . . I just gotta . . ."

He looked around wildly.

Torn. Willing himself to be somewhere else.

Night shadows had gathered. She couldn't make out his features.

Couldn't see if he was disappointed.

What had gone wrong?

Had she been too forward?

Whatever. Looks like she'd frightened him off. . . .

And now he was leaving her.

But he *couldn't.*

Not when we've had it so good together.

Nothing, *no one,* is gonna keep us apart!

She sprang up and grabbed him; he wrenched away from her urgent, shaking hands grasping his shirt, holding on to him.

"Mom'll be looking for me. She's expecting me. . . ."

They fell to the floor, struggling, fighting. He rolled away from her.

Pushed himself up.

Unable to believe what was happening, she reached out to hold him.

He fell back, away from her, shoving an elbow hard on the floorboards. With a rending, splitting sound the rotten floor gave under his weight.

He plummeted to the ground below.

She stared at the black space where the floor, *where Charlie,* had been.

Hearing his low, hurt grunt as he hit rock bottom.

The dull crack that was a *thud* and a *splish!* all at the same time.

Like a ripe melon bursting open.

Terrified, Leigh scrambled to her feet.

"Charlie oh my God Charlie Charlie! Wait, I'm coming I'm coming."

Naked, she bounded across the landing and took the stairs, two, three at a time.

Ouch.

Shit!

She caught her toe in a broken stair and stumbled.

Flinging out her arms, she clawed at the balustrade, almost falling headlong.

No need to search for Charlie.

His legs sprawled at weird angles in the room facing her.

"Charlie. I'm here. Don't move. . . ."

Then her heart stood still.

She was terribly afraid.

More afraid than she'd ever been in all of her eighteen years.

Her stomach turned to ice.

But she went forward, through the doorway.

To get to Charlie.

Lying there.

So still.

She was in an old-fashioned kitchen. Dark with shadows. Shuttered windows. Narrow rays of the setting sun carving through dust motes rising from where he'd fallen, in an awkward nest of wood and flaking bits of plaster.

She stared at Charlie.

"Oh, God. NO! NO NO NO-OOO!!!"

Forced herself to look at what had been his head.

Clumps of brown hair clinging to slivers of scalp, scattered in a mess of brain and shattered skull.

Slimed with matter, the base of the stove poked through the red mush of Charlie's face. An eye, a bloodshot globe attached to bloody strings, escaped from its socket.

Leigh stared. The eye slipped a little.

Showing the brown iris.

It knows I'm watching it. It's smiling Charlie's smile at me. . . .

Leigh heaved, swayed, doubled over, and slid to her knees on the dusty clay floor.

Breath burst from her lungs in great, ragged gasps.

Hot, chunky vomit rose in her throat.

This, this . . . wasn't . . . *couldn't be* Charlie.

Charlie's beautiful, strong—and he loves me. I know that. *He loves me. . . .*

Taking one last look at Charlie, flaked with dust and plaster like a discarded tailor's dummy, she fled down the passageway, out onto the stoop, and stumbled down the steps.

Whimpering.

Fighting back vomit.

Sobbing, muttering, as she ran.

Straight into the small, rigid figure of a woman.

Charlie's mother.

Thin, birdlike.

Openmouthed.

Shocked. Staring at Leigh's naked body with horrified, accusing eyes, bright as polished stones in the fading light.

The woman skimmed past her. Into the house. Leigh hurried on, toward the canoe, her feet cut and bleeding as she fled over stones and fallen branches.

The scream coming from the house pierced the evening quiet, renting the air like a knife through silk.

Pure. Vibrant. Agonized.

An animal caught in a trap. Then . . .

"Whore; Lilith; poisonous bitch; filthy murderess!"

Under glowering skies, Leigh pushed her canoe into the lake and climbed in. Grasping the paddle, she worked it hard, bending forward and back; dipping, skimming through the dark water. As she traveled, crisp, white wavelets lifted around the bow, telling her the wind had changed direction.

She shivered, feeling its chill on her tear-streaked face, on her cold, trembling body.

Paddling hard, her uneven breaths coming in raw, hurting gasps, she left Goon Lake behind.

The screams of Edith Payne followed her like arrows from hell.

EIGHTEEN

"Hey. Earthling. Anybody home?"

Jenny eyed Leigh over the breakfast table. She didn't like what she saw. Yesterday Leigh had been bright and breezy. Today, it looked like her personal piece of sky had just caved in.

"Sorry, Jenny. I . . . I didn't sleep too well last night."

"Didn't hear you come in." A pause. "We waited to eat

supper, just in case. Then, when you didn't show, we ate your share and decided to turn in." She paused, not wanting to appear heavy—after all, Leigh *was* on vacation. She decided on the concerned-aunt routine, hoping it wouldn't come over too strong.

"Didn't you know that Mike and I would worry if you stayed out late? 'Specially nights . . . What happened, Leigh—or is it a state secret?" Beneath her determined smile, Jenny was worried.

If this is what life with a teen is all about, Mike and I sure missed out on all the excitement.

They'd regretted not having kids, and visiting Jack and Helen on the West Coast once in a while made up for it to some degree. That, and teaching kids at high school, helped them both understand what went on in those young minds.

Leigh hung her head. Put her fork down and pushed away her untouched eggs. Her lip trembled. She scraped back her chair and rushed from the table.

Jenny followed her to the guest bedroom. She spotted Mike coming out of the bathroom and put a discreet finger to her lips. With raised brows, he carried on rubbing his damp hair and went on his way.

Kids, eh?

Jenny sat on the bed and drew the sobbing girl to her. "Come on, now, tell Aunt Jenny," she said gently, cradling Leigh's head against her shoulder.

Leigh let everything go, crying as if her heart would break. Eventually, the great, gulping sobs trailed off and she recovered sufficiently to wonder where to begin her story and what, if necessary, should be left out. The plain, unadulterated truth was just too *awful* to say out loud.

"It's bad, Jenny. It's real bad. . . ." Leigh broke down again, heaving and sobbing into her aunt's soft, accommodating bosom. A cold shiver touched Jenny's spine. This *was* bad. She knew she wasn't going to like what Leigh was about to tell her.

Had the girl been raped? Oh my God! What do we tell Jack and Helen?

"Take your time and tell me all about it, baby," she said in a soothing voice. "Tell your auntie Jenny."

Leigh's parents listened in horror to Mike's story over the phone. "Not that we wouldn't like her to stay with us a while longer," he'd explained in a calm but concerned voice. "It's just that I—we think Leigh needs her parents at a time like this. . . . And, of course, there is the matter of her being questioned. . . ."

Mike met Jack and Helen at General Mitchell International. They'd brought a change of clothes in their carry-ons, expecting only to stay overnight before taking Leigh home.

The journey to Wahconda was not a good one. Along the way, there was a wearing mix of tearful accusations from Helen, interposed by irate remonstrations from Jack—punctuated by Mike's patient explanations. Fielding their rhetoric wasn't easy, and Mike wished like hell Jenny had come along as referee.

He sighed. He'd expected the drive to be a nightmare. It was—and more besides.

They arrived at Wahconda in the early hours, fatigued and more than ready for the fragrant coffee, but, for the aggrieved parents, not the cheese sandwiches and apple pie Jenny put before them. Preparing the snack beforehand, she hadn't reckoned on them doing much eating.

She was right.

Jack and Helen demanded to see their daughter, who'd taken sedatives prescribed by Doc Barton and was lying, pale and barely breathing, when her parents arrived.

"Not a good time to wake her, Helen. The poor dear has been through a lot these last twenty-four hours. Best let her rest while she can." Jenny looked anxiously at her sister-in-law. The last thing they all needed was one of Helen's tantrums.

"You're right, of course," Jack said, placing an arm around Helen and steering her into the hallway. "Come along, dear. Let's get us some rest. Plenty to discuss tomorrow."

"You're not kidding," retorted Helen, glaring at him through red-rimmed eyes. "Leigh had better have a real good reason for going off on her lonesome like that." She darted an accusing glance at Jenny. Clearly, right now, she was blaming her in-laws for the mess they were in.

Daylight found them drinking coffee around the kitchen table again. Still tired, but determined to see this thing through like sensible people.

"At least," Dad said, "Leigh's alive. That's a blessing in itself."

Leigh, pale and dazed from her drugged sleep, joined them in the kitchen. Smiling wanly at Mom and Dad, she avoided their questioning looks and gratefully hugged the mug of steaming coffee Jenny placed before her.

"Good morning, young lady," Dad began.

Leigh groaned inwardly.

This I can do without.

After . . . Charlie . . .

Tears welled and fell down her face. Mom rose and took her daughter in her arms. They both had a darn good cry. Then Mom told her: "We love you so much, sweetie. How could this *awful* thing be happening to us . . . ?"

"Now, Helen," Dad put in. "All we can do is get our little girl through this unfortunate incident. We have to be strong, for her sake."

"Agreed," Mike murmured. "At this stage, recriminations are redundant. Leigh needs all the help we can give her." Jenny nodded, smiling bravely. "That's right," she said. "We must pull together, whatever happens."

"Now, perhaps you'll be kind enough to tell us in your own words what happened back there, day before yesterday." Dad caught Mike's raised brows, realizing that maybe a confrontational attitude wasn't going to work with his little girl. Not this time.

"It's okay, Dad. I'll tell you as best I can. . . . I appreciate you need to know the facts before the cops get here."

Mom and Dad exchanged glances. This was their errant offspring. Chastened and acting grown up for a change.

They listened in stunned silence to Leigh's halting account of her brief affair with Charlie. Afterward, Mom stifled back tears, her cheeks getting redder all the time. She fiddled nervously with the gold cross hanging on a chain around her neck. Dad looked shocked and embarrassed by turns. For the first time in living memory, he had nothing to say to his daughter.

Leigh sank into a bewildered daze, reliving the nightmare of Charlie's death—the way he'd looked—over and over again. It was the most horrendous thing she'd ever experienced; something she'd never, ever, forget even if she lived to be a hundred years old. Tears streamed down her face, and she just couldn't face her parents' wounded expressions.

Just as if it had happened to *them*.

But they had every right to be horrified.

And so, she told herself, had Charlie's mom—*she* had more right to hate her than anyone.

Losing her son that way.

Mom got upset and Mike called the doc, who said it was okay if Mom used a couple of Leigh's sedatives. No problem. They were just your average sleeping pill, he told them. Nothing too strong. But take them only till the intial shock passes over, you understand.

Dad was grimly stoical. Patient. At least there were no more black looks. Leigh couldn't bear it when he looked at her as if she were some kind of stranger and called her "young lady" instead of Leigh. Meanwhile, he spoke urgently with Mike in low tones, while Jenny went around making more coffee, filling in the awkward gaps, and trying to keep tension at bay.

By the time Officers Fallon and Henty dropped by to get the story, Leigh had taken to her bed again.

Apologizing for the trouble, they waited for Leigh to emerge. Meanwhile, Fallon confided that Edith Payne had made wild accusations against the young lady who was, ahem . . . with . . . her son at the time of his death.

"Not that we're paying any attention to all that." He didn't think now was a good time to quote the words Charlie's mom had *really* screamed at them. Like: "Find the whore who murdered my son. Or I will."

No-sirree. Instead, he gave Mom a reassuring smile, telling her that he himself had an eighteen-year-old daughter and so was no stranger to the workings of a young girl's mind—

Mom stopped him short with a sour look.

The officers questioned Leigh for half an hour or so and, at the end of it all, went so far as to say that what they had here was a case of Accidental Death. Not, in their opinion, Murder One.

Relieved that this part was over, Leigh returned to her room.

"Thank ya kindly, ma'am," Henty said, and smiled, nodding briefly at Jenny as she came around with yet more coffee. Fallon turned to Mom and Dad. "We've known for some time that old house out on Goon was a death trap," he admitted. "But," he went on, "the place is in probate and we can't do a dern thing about it. However, in the light of . . . er . . . recent events, we'll try for a court order to take the place down. Demolish it. Clear the site. Leave things as they are," he added, "more kids could get hurt."

"She's asking about the funeral," Mom said flatly.

"Funeral?" Glancing at his partner, Henty decided to lay it on the line.

He did. Confiding that this particular funeral wouldn't

be such a good thing for a young girl to experience.

"Not as if it'll be your regular funeral," he said, sending Dad a level look in a man-to-man sort of way. "We're talking personal tragedy here. Big time. Lotta raw feelings on the loose, that kinda thing. Old Ma Payne's a weird piece a' work. No telling what might happen, under the circumstances.

"Yessir. Best take the young lady on home. . . ."

"And so," the preacher said, "as the coffin sinks slowly into the ground, we bid a fond farewell . . ."

Leigh's heart lurched.

Coming here is not the smartest thing I've ever done, she told herself with a shudder.

Charlie's mother approached. She walked around the end of the grave, slowly. Standing apart from the small group of mourners, Leigh held her breath, watching the small, upright figure dressed in black.

She'd known where to come.

She'd heard Mike tell Dad that Charlie's funeral would be at the Seventh-Day Adventist Church.

Here, on Wahconda.

It services the lake people hereabouts, he'd said.

Keeping her eye on the mother, Leigh shivered some more. No sun reached this desolate plot hidden in the pines just north of Carson's Camp, and she wished she'd worn something warmer.

I shouldn't be here at all, she chastised herself. But God knows, I had to come. *Needed* to be at Charlie's funeral. I owe him that much. If I hadn't gone with him to the old house, everything would've been okay. . . . Charlie's death was all my fault.

Stay back.

No, don't point at me. Oh, my God!

Her heart raced. She took a step backward as the mother approached. . . .

* * *

The following day, Leigh and her parents said their good-byes to Mike and Jenny and flew back to the West Coast. In the days that followed, Leigh waited anxiously for her period.

It didn't happen that month.

Nor the next.

Tests showed she was pregnant.

NINETEEN

"Mom."

"Uh-huh?"

"Johnny Depp just called to ask me for a date. That okay with you?"

"Er . . . what was that?"

"Mom. You haven't been listening to a *word* I'm saying. I could sprout wings and fly away, and you wouldn't even notice. What's up? Your man Mace playin' on your mind?"

"Sorry, hon. Sure, I got things on my mind. What with this guy and his 'unfinished business,' and everything . . ."

"Okay. So this guy and his unfinished business. We keep on our guard 'n' call Macie baby if we get spooked—what else can we do? Detective Harrison seems like a pretty smart cookie to me. He'll catch that weirdo before we even know it."

Deana put her arm around Leigh's waist. Feels like I'm a regular grown-up, she thought. What goes around comes around, I guess. I'm glad Mom was there for me over what happened to Allan—now it's *me* comforting *Mom*.

She liked the warm feeling this gave her. How it should be. Anyway, Mom knows what I'm going through. She's been there. History repeating itself.

Except, *I'm* not pregnant.

I don't think.

Nah.

Didn't get the chance back there in the woods.

Thanks to that madman.

She caught Leigh's sigh and frowned a little. "C'mon, Mom. Tell Deana. What gives?"

"What gives? Isn't all this enough, young lady? Madman on the loose. Nelson sounding off back at the restaurant. Mace playing this whole thing down—but heaven knows, I can tell he's worried. God, Deana. How can you be so *blasé* about it all?"

"Sorry, Mom. I really am. If Allan and I had gone to the movies like we said, all of this wouldn't be happening." Deana's eyes filled, and Leigh softened.

"Baby, don't you worry. We'll get through all this. I promise. . . ." She stroked Deana's cheek and forced a bright smile. "Everything's gonna be okay. Promise."

"Sorry to be such a kid about everything." Deana was apologetic. God knows Mom didn't need all this. "I'm just a bit keyed up, is all. . . .

"Anyway, you should be back at the restaurant. I'll be okay here. Honest. I'm not likely to go wandering off anywhere. Not until everything's cleared up.

"What's Nelson griping about, anyway?" As far as she could gather, Mom left Nelson to do what he did best: create memorable meals.

Hmmm . . . Pretty cool name for a restaurant.

Memorable Meals.

"Nelson? Oh, the usual. Having one of his sulks again. Wants to come from behind the scenes occasionally. Be somebody. Meet the clientele. But, frankly, I'm afraid his appearance might put them off."

"Yeah. With his eye patch and big, hook nose, he ain't no Paul Newman, and that's for sure!"

"Hey. There's the door. Probably Mace with some good news . . ."

"I bet," Deana agreed.

We should be so lucky.

Leigh made for the front door. Deana followed. Saw Mom peek through the small round spy-glass—and drop the door chain. It chittered and clattered swinging to and fro.

Then:

Mom was opening the door.

Reeling back, gasping oh my God . . .

Tripping over the doormat.

My nightmare—all over again.

Nelson.

In his chef's hat, clutching a meat cleaver.

Holding it high.

He's gonna hack Mom.

Then me.

In broad daylight.

And there's no one around to help—to call the cops.

The hedges between the houses were high. Bad news for nosy neighbors; terrific for intruders. "Keeps us nice and private, honey," Leigh told her when they bought the place. "We've cameras and gravel all around to deter intruders. Anyway—one phone call, and the cops'd be here in no time at all."

Yeah. Neat plan. But somehow Deana didn't think it was gonna work today. . . .

Nelson changed his mind.

He dropped the cleaver. It crashed to the floor, the clatter echoing through the hallway.

His arm shot out. He grabbed Mom by the throat . . .

Squeeeezed it tight.

Mom spluttered; a strangled half-scream burst from her lips. It died. Next came this awful gurgling sound.

Deana gasped, her heart pounding. This *can't* be for real. It can't . . .

It can. It is. It's my nightmare come true. . . .

You better believe it.

He'll kill Mom.

Then he'll kill me. . . .

Nelson with a cleaver. Outside my window. Threatening me. Mace was right. It's me he wants. Oh my God, this isn't a dream.

"*I'm coming to getcha. . . .*"

"STAY AWAY FROM HER!" Deana yelled.

Nelson lost it.

Drawing back a bony fist, he slugged Deana on the chin. Hard.

She heard the crack.

Felt the *blinding* pain.

Saw shooting stars.

And slipped into deep black space. . . .

Before she went down, she saw Nelson's black patch and one fierce, protruding blue eye, gleaming hatred, straining from his thin, hollow face.

His mouth was a black gaping hole. Spittle swung from his grizzled chin, trailing and dripping down his chef's tunic.

Paul Newman, he ain't.

Dazed, Deana clamped a hand to her jaw, wincing with pain. She watched Mom wrench away from him, get to her feet, turn and make for the phone.

Nelson's big hand reached out, clawed at Mom's shoulder.

Sending her down again.

Leigh crumpled to her knees, hitting the tile floor with a sickening thud. She rolled away from him, then leaned up on an elbow, shaking her head. Moving in slow motion.

Still stunned and not quite with it.

"Mom!" Deana screamed. "Get up, he's gonna kill youuuu!"

Grunting like an enraged pig, Nelson snatched up the cleaver. Raised it above his head.

Deana screamed: "NO-OOOO!"

Leigh stared. Like a rabbit caught in the thrall of a snake. Watching Nelson's arms slice down . . .

"FREEZE!"

Mace.

And Mattie.

In the doorway.

Behind Nelson.

Guns pressed into his back.

Nelson's hand opened, letting the cleaver drop again. It clattered and clunked on the foyer tiles.

He sprang forward, leaping over Leigh and knocking Deana to one side, lurching down the hallway, toward the back of the house, panting, pushing, shoving furniture behind him as he went.

Mattie raced after him, head down, dodging the flying ammunition.

Shit!

The kitchen door slammed in her face. She felt her nose crack.

Shit shit *SHIT!*

She kicked open the door, cursing as the outer door swung to and fro.

Nelson was gone.

"You *bastard*," she spat. "So you got away. *This* time!"

Mace dropped down on one knee. "Leigh. Leigh. You okay?"

"Uh-uh. Thank God you came—just in time. Guess you saved our lives. You okay, Deana?

"Deana!"

Leigh crawled over to Deana, stretched out on the floor, an ugly red bruise already staining her lower jaw.

Breathlessly, Mattie returned to the others, stabbing out the connection code on her cell phone, cursing to herself as she did it. "Fuckin' bastard got away. How the *hell* he did it, beats me. He just disappeared. Obviously knows the territory."

At the other end, Mill Valley PD picked up, getting an earful of Mattie's dialogue.

"Yeah." She was terse. "You heard me right. Man with a cleaver, attacked woman and daughter. 104 Del Mar, on Mark Terrace. Lost the suspect, but we have the weapon. Try putting out an all points—he's on foot. Maybe. Could be the killer of the Powers boy in the Mount Tam vicinity last night. Yeah. We have two injured people here. Call an ambulance."

Deana groaned. Mace guided Leigh to the living room and settled her on the sofa. Mattie was already busy in the kitchen, wringing out a cold compress to put on Deana's jaw.

Mace strode back to the hallway. Nudging the cleaver with the toe of his shoe, he called out: "Know who this guy is, Ms. West?"

"Do I. His name is Nelson Willington and he's head chef at the Bayview."

Mace and Mattie, both in the living room now, exchanged glances.

"What did ya do, Leigh?" Mattie asked. "Cut his pay in half?"

"You could say that. I fired him a coupla days ago."

Nursing her jaw, Deana perked up. So that was why Mom was so . . . so preoccupied with Nelson.

"You *fired* him?"

Mace, too, was all ears. "How come?"

"He wanted a piece of the action. A partnership in the business. Said if it weren't for his cuisine, I wouldn't be where I am today. One of the best restaurants in Tiburon et cetera, et cetera."

"*The* best restaurant in Tiburon," Mattie put in.

"Thanks." Leigh gave her a wry smile.

* * *

Mattie brought out a plastic sack from her shoulder bag. Shook it open. Put on protective gloves, went to the hallway, and picked up the meat cleaver.

It looked like a nasty piece of work. Honed to a fine sharpness, she guessed it would slice through bone just as easily as it would through butter.

Gingerly, she put a forefinger to the blade.

"Ouch," she murmured, slipping it into the sack.

"Careful, Mattie. Don't want you losing any fingers out there," Mace said lightly.

"Butt out, Charlie. Do either of you ladies recognize this thing?" Mattie carried the cleaver into the living room. It had an intricate dragon design on the handle, winding its way up to the blade.

Before Leigh could answer, Deana said, "Yes. There are two in the kitchen at the Bayview."

"Sure are," Leigh agreed. "Nelson uses them for cutting up sides of beef."

Sirens began to wail. Lights flashed in the driveway. Mattie went to the front door.

"Over here, guys," she called out.

"Maybe I don't need hospital treatment," Leigh said. "I'm okay. But how about you, Deana? You look as if you might have a fractured jaw—best we have it checked out."

"You *both* need checking out, Leigh," Mace put in. "Mattie, go along with the ladies. I'll hang around here a while longer."

Deana pouted. The hospital didn't seem like a smart move right now. Especially as the action seemed to be heating up a little. She flinched as a stab of pain shot through her skull.

"Okay. Okay," she muttered. "I'm going. Macie baby's right. As usual."

"Deana."

"Sorry, Mom," she said thickly. Her jaw throbbed. It felt

like she was talking through cotton wool lips. "We'll miss all the fun, though."

"What fun, Deana? You want that creep to sneak back in, wait till you're in bed, then zap?" Mace slapped the palms of his hands together with a loud crack.

Deana winced. Leigh shot him a cool glance.

"Right, folks. We're ready to roll!" Mattie called out. Sensing the tension, she looked at Mace sharply. "You okay alone here?" she asked.

"Sure. Stopped worrying about boogeymen twenty years back."

"Yeah. I bet." Mattie tossed him a tight smile over her shoulder. She followed the two women to the ambulance. The tip of her nose, where it had collided with the kitchen door, hurt like hell.

"Don't worry your heads none about Mace," she told Leigh and Deana. "Our mad axman catches up with Mace, he'll wish he'd never bothered."

Picturing Mace's well-built, muscular five eleven against Nelson's thin, gangling frame, Leigh almost felt sorry for the chef.

At the hospital, Leigh and Deana were treated for shock. Leigh had bruising to the neck and shoulder, contusions to her elbows, but not much else. Deana had severe bruising to her lower jaw. Thankfully, no fractures. They were issued painkillers and allowed to go home.

Mattie came around early next day.

"Hi, guys. How ya doin'?" She followed Leigh into the living room, waving away the offer of a seat. She got straight to the point.

"As you know, we have the meat cleaver from the scene. Now I'd like you to show me where Nelson keeps his. The ones you say he uses." She shrugged. "Could be there are two, three, or even more in circulation. We need to narrow the field as much as possible."

Deana asked, "Thought you weren't officially on this case. As in, no longer working with Mace?"

"Right," Mattie replied. "I'm here by special request."

"Special request?"

"Uh-huh. Mace put in a request for me to work on this case with him, so I could look after you lucky ladies. And, well, here I am, folks. Personal bodyguard at your service."

Deana looked at Mattie.

"That was good of Mace, being so concerned about us."

"Yeah. Seems like he has a special interest in the Powers case."

Leigh appeared nonchalant, but her heart skipped a beat. It *was* good of Mace to go to all this trouble.

Appointing Mattie as their bodyguard—no prizes for guessing who'd come out on top if she and Nelson happened to meet up.

Mattie drove them to the Bayview. She was an expert driver, Deana noticed. Comes with playing cops and robbers for a living, she guessed as they slid to a halt in the Bayview's private parking lot.

Leigh's pride and joy was a smartly painted, double-fronted restaurant on Main Street, looking out onto the harbor. Brass-framed menus in the doorway offered a wide choice of ethnic and traditional dishes.

Bay-caught fish were a house specialty.

Leigh led the way through the dark interior, then on through to the kitchen. The aroma of fresh bread hung on the air—Leigh prided herself on her bread rolls, ciabattas, and French sticks, freshly baked on the premises.

She shivered.

The place felt oddly strange without Nelson.

No lanky figure leaping about, mixing, mincing, creating his famous dishes, his one good eye rolling round in its socket like a billiard ball.

Instead, Nelson was on the run. With his cleaver.

They looked around the kitchen. Leigh went to the

metal stand where Nelson hung his array of choppers, knives, and other kitchen implements.

Both cleavers were missing. Looked like Mattie had Exhibit A, the one Nelson dropped when he fled; then he'd sneaked back into the restaurant to pick up Exhibit B. So now Nelson, plus cleaver number two, were out there seeking vengeance.

The women exchanged glances.

"We need to nail Nelson, pronto," Mattie said briefly.

Leigh met Deana's eyes. "I'd say that was the understatement of the year, Mattie."

TWENTY

Brrring . . . Brrring . . .

Leigh's fingers felt around the nightstand, then stretched out to reach the telephone. Her grazed elbow twinged. She made a face, squinting at the red numbers on the clock.

11:22.

Christ. Who *is* this?

At this hour?

She fumbled around some more and clicked on the bedside lamp.

Something's happened, she thought. *They caught Nelson. They've . . .*

"Yes?"

"Hi, Leigh. Mace here. Called to see if you're okay."

"Uhh . . . I was asleep, if that's what you mean."

"Sorry. Just thought you looked a little wrecked earlier."

"Well, thanks a lot, Mace. You woke me up to tell me *that?*"

"No, Leigh. It's just that I don't want you worrying yourself over that maniac. Is all."

"Cheers for that, Mace. But I'm—we're—okay. Truly.

Right now, I need some rest. Took one of those bazookas an hour ago and I'm sleepy as a kittycat."

"Yeah. Sure. Sorry for the intrusion. You phone me if you have any problems. Or need to talk. Y'hear me, now?"

"Sure, Mace. Sure. G'night."

Smiling, she put the phone down.

What a jerk! But quite a *nice* jerk . . .

She smiled, snapped off the light, turned over, and closed her eyes.

And opened them again.

God, much as I like the guy, I wish he hadn't called.

'Cause now I'm *really* awake.

She sighed.

Take another sleeper.

No, don't.

Doc said only three a day. I've taken three already.

She twisted up on an elbow and gasped a little.

Ouch! That hurts.

Making a face, she punched and plumped up her pillow. Then sank back into it.

Mmmm . . . That's better.

Gradually, her lids drooped and her breathing evened out.

Brrinng . . . Brrinng . . .

GOD! MACE! What *now?* I'll swing for that guy. Doesn't he *ever* give up?

"Mace?" she yelled into the phone.

"Ms. West."

Her heart leapt into her mouth. Pounding, hard.

Racing like a traction engine.

"Nelson." A breathless pause. "What d'you want?"

"You shouldn't have done it, y'know."

Mustn't let him think I'm scared.

"Done what? Whatever did I do to you that wasn't completely justified? Tell me that!"

She was sitting up now. Shaking. Rocking with terror,

her free arm hugging her knees. Almost screaming into the phone.

Deana burst through the door.

"Mom!"

Leigh shook her head.

Put a finger to her lips.

Shush, Deana. Quiet!

She pointed to the extension phone in her hand, then stabbed a forefinger at the open door.

Deana frowned.

Leigh rolled up her eyes.

She mouthed, *"Deana. Pick up the other phone!"*

Deana raced out of the room.

"I was the best thing you had, lady," Nelson whimpered. He seemed lost, uncertain, and Leigh relaxed a little. She could handle a pathetic Nelson. "An' you didn't know it," he went on. "You didn't *'preciate* me. Called me an oddball and then *FIRED* me." His pace spiced up a little. "ME! The finest chef in the whole of the Bay. I coulda cooked at 'Frisco's finest, and you know it!"

Let him talk. I can deal with that okay.

Maybe.

"Nelson, calm down."

Leigh heard a faint click as Deana lifted the phone in the hallway.

"Whass that?" Nelson was suspicious. Twitchy. His tone upped a couple of octaves.

"Just the line, Nelson. I should get it fixed. Been playing up on me for a week or so now."

"Sure. You do that. Where's that kid a' yours?"

"Deana? Oh, she's spending the night with a friend—"

"You lie!" he shrieked. "The light was on in her room a half hour ago. Don't you lie to me, Leigh West. Or you'll *both* regret it."

His voice dropped. He spoke slowly, spelling it out: "You'll *both* wish you hadn't. Geddit?"

"Nelson, *please*. Why would I lie to you?" Leigh knew she was pleading and hated herself for it.

But she'd best play it his way.

Plead. Beg, if she had to. She smiled grimly.

He'd like that.

Christ. He'd been creeping around the house only a half hour ago?

Where the hell was Mace?

On the phone. Asking me if I was okay. Jesus, Mace. You shoulda been out there protecting us!

No. That's not fair. Mace has to go off duty some time. Not his fault.

"You still there, Leigh?" The voice was low. Derisive. Mocking. Like he knew he had her in the palm of his hand. Running scared.

Her heart started to pound again.

She was panicking; couldn't control the way her breath came out, all huffy and shallow.

She turned away from the phone, hoping he couldn't hear her quick, uneven breathing.

Please God. Don't let him hear me.

For a split second, she paused, steadying herself.

"Yeah. Sure. I'm still here, Nelson."

"Y'know, you said some pretty hurtful things back there, Leigh. An' all I ever wanted was *recognition* for my work. I deserved better. I know I'm not much to look at, but I'm an *artiste* in my own right. My creations *made* the Bayview the place it is. . . . And my beef Willington's a masterpiece." He choked out a sob. "Everybody says so. . . ."

Leigh calmed down a little. Nelson wasn't angry, spiteful, or threatening anymore. Just downright pitiful.

"You *knew* my worth," he went on. "You knew how *good* I was."

Leigh listened to his pathetic whining. Not quite sure how to handle it now. Thinking that this entire conversation could go horribly wrong; change into something bad. . . .

Mustn't offend him, she thought.

Play him like a fish.

Placate him.

Let him spit it out. Whatever it was he had to say.

"All I wanted was to hit back at you." His voice wavered. Leigh was finding it difficult to hear him now.

". . . An' make you worry like crazy. So the way I figured, I should follow your girl and scare the *shit* outa her. . . ."

His sobs were noisy, heaving gulps, vibrating over the line.

She moved the phone away from her ear. When she listened from that distance, Nelson's voice made thin, tinny sounds; ineffectual squawks coming from a long way off.

He was crying, too.

"Nelson. Don't go on so."

She heard Deana's gasp of horror.

Jesus. Quiet, hon. There's my girl . . .

"I didn't mean that boyfriend of hers should get killed. I didn't want for that terrible accident to happen. I was so riled up, I couldn't help myself. I'm sorry. . . ."

Listening to him groveling, Leigh grew more sure of herself. "Nelson," she said. "What you did was really bad. You killed that young man. You deprived him of a fine future. But if you're as sorry as you say you are, all you have to do is give yourself up. You'll have a fair trial, Nelson. Believe me."

Sure. All things considered.

A fair trial.

The guy's a maniac. Not a pervert.

Not an obssessive killer at all.

What he needs is a straitjacket. Not the chair.

Her thoughts flew back to Deana.

Hope she has the sense to call Mace on my cell phone. . . .

"Nelson, where are you? I mean, are you close by?"

Hope to God he's not outside the house.

Could be.

She heard a wet, gasping sob.

"Christ, Nelson. Where are you?"

Deana, use my phone, for godsake.

Call Mace.

"Just wanted to get it off my chest . . . how all of this happened. So you know it was *your* fault. You coulda told me you didn't want me for a partner. Not just *fired* me . . ." The whining tapered off. Then:

"Coulda lived with *not* bein' a partner."

A long pause.

"I been feelin' real tuckered out lately. I worry about my work an' all . . ." Nelson sounded beat now. "Anyways. I won't be botherin' you no more, Ms. West. You'll be fuckin' rid of me for good! But I hope you'll remember, as long as you've breath left in your body, that *you* brought it on your own fuckin' self—"

"NELSON! What d'you mean? I'll be rid of you. . . ."

Silence. Then:

"Ah'm goin' away, Ms. West. Forever. You'll not hear from me again."

"Nelson."

Say something. Anything. Just keep him talking.

"Was it you who returned my necklace? You took it, didn't you? From the restaurant?"

Nelson wasn't listening.

The phone fell from his grasp. It dangled, swinging to and fro on its connection cord. Fascinated by the pendulum-like movements, he watched it for a moment, his toothless mouth making a small black O.

Somewhere deep inside his mashed-up brain, a smile began. A grimace of triumph that tried but didn't quite make it to his tear-streaked face.

He'd told her, all right.

He'd told that high-handed bitch what for.

Spittle swung from Nelson's chin. Snot dribbled into his mouth. His tongue came up and licked it away. The stuff tasted good and sweet.

Lurching away from the pay phone, he crossed the sidewalk and teetered along the edge, his arms outstretched for balance.

Cars came at him from nowhere.

Like bats out of hell.

As he squinted in the glaring headlights, his face lifted to meet the cool night breeze.

It felt all right.

Clean.

He was a boy again. Out on one of them lakes beyond Point Reyes Station. Fishing with his pa. Taking in great gulps of fresh, clean air. Hearing the squawk of Pa's oars in the oarlocks, the slap of wood on water, making ripples and waves dance around their smart new rowboat.

And the fish he brought home.

Yes-siree Bob! Ma sure knew how to cook her boy's fish. Tender as a baby's smile, they fell to pieces soon as look at 'em.

Fog shrouded the far end of the Golden Gate Bridge.

Nelson grinned and walked toward it.

TWENTY-ONE

"He's gone, baby." Leigh shrugged into her toweling robe. She drew the belt tight around her, giving a long sigh of relief, grateful the ordeal with Nelson was over.

He'd sounded weak. Beaten.

Not a threat anymore.

Please God.

She looked up as Deana appeared in the doorway, wrapped in her robe, hugging it around herself. "Wow," she breathed. "That was something else. Nelson sure flipped this time."

Hope to Christ he's gone for good.

She gave a small yelp and clamped a hand to her jaw. "Ouch. This really hurts, Mom."

"I know, honey. Just take it easy, now."

Leigh knew it had been a shock for Deana to hear her shouting into the phone like that.

Poor kid. She doesn't need it. Not after Allan . . .

All because of my upset with Nelson.

Guilt merged with a growing sense of urgency.

"We gotta call Mace. Tell him Nelson—"

"Been there. Done that."

"You have?" Leigh felt relieved. And proud. Of *course* Deana would call Mace. She was a smart kid, her daughter.

Leigh relaxed—then jumped as the doorbell rang.

It sounded extra loud.

And strident.

This time of night.

"That's Mace now."

"You sure about this, Mom? Could be Nelson coming back to finish what he left off. . . . Remember last time you answered the door?"

Leigh hurried into the hallway. "Mace?" she called through the door.

"Leigh. It's me. Mace. Open up."

Leigh almost fell into his arms as he stepped into the foyer.

Deana made a face.

Mom, she cringed, d'you *have* to do that? Get all swoony like some dopey kid in high school?

"It was Nelson . . . ," Leigh said.

"Gathered that from Deana's call. Smart move there, kiddo."

Deana glared grumpily at Mace. She was in no mood to be patronized. Digging her hands into her robe pockets, she snatched another look at him. He wore a white T-shirt, tight black jeans, and a black leather biker jacket.

Apart from his weapon bulging out of his hip holster, he wasn't looking much like a policeman tonight. She stared a while longer.

Mmmm . . . Sexy, or what?

Oh yeah?

That'd be wonderful. Making a fool of myself with Mom's boyfriend. Pardon me, Mom's not-quite but soon-to-be boyfriend.

How can I be such a *shit,* anyway? Allan's only just . . . Her eyes watered up.

But Mace sure looked attractive. Tanned complexion, sun-streaked hair. A regular California surfer look.

The Beach Boys.

Yuck.

Nowhere near as *ancient* as the Beach Boys.

Mace's maybe thirty-six—going on thirty-eight?

Same age as Mom?

He *is* sexy, though . . . in a tough, die-hard kinda way. A body like that, he must work out pretty much every day.

Mace's eyes held hers briefly.

A tight smile flicked across his face before he returned his attention to Leigh.

"Could be we're getting closer," he said. "Not often perps get to call their victims and apologize for their misdeeds."

"No, I guess not," Leigh said. "Coffee?"

"Thought you'd never ask." Mace grinned.

"Sugar?" Leigh asked as the coffee started to perk.

"No," Mace said. "Gotta keep in shape, y'know."

"Mmm, some shape," Deana murmured.

So soon after Allan . . . What kind of schmuck am I? Forgive me, Allan. Please.

Leigh sent her a warning look.

Deana threw a quick glance in Mace's direction. Had he heard her last remark? Watching him settle back into the sofa, she decided there was no way of telling if he had.

She *hoped* he hadn't heard.

If he had, it would be too embarrassing for words.

Anyway, where's Mattie tonight?

Or is this a *personal* visit?

Mace accepted his coffee from Leigh. No cream. No sugar. Deana pictured his abs. Taut. Toned. A regular Rocky. A regular *blond* Rocky.

Suddenly, Mace was all cop. "Now, ladies," he said. "Tell me again what happened when Nelson called."

There's your answer, Deana. He's here on business. . . .

Deana and Leigh pieced together the conversation as best they could. Finally, Leigh said, "And I just *know* he took my lucky necklace. Must have been a coupla weeks ago. I was real upset about it at first—thought I'd lost it for good. Then I remembered I'd left it at the restaurant. Nelson didn't admit it, but I somehow *know* he'd taken it, just to spook me."

"And now he's disappeared." Mace's tone was brisk. He was more interested in Nelson's future plans than in Leigh's shell necklace.

"Yeah. He *did* sound pretty downbeat." Leigh hesitated as another possibility struck her. "D'you think he's going to *kill* himself?"

"Maybe. Sounds like he confessed—or apologized, whichever way you look at it. Had a fit of the guilts and aimed to pull the plug. You said he maybe left the phone hanging. Didn't terminate the call?"

"No 'maybe' about it," Leigh told him. "Nelson said he'd seen the light in Deana's bedroom half an hour before his call. My guess is, he was lying; that he hadn't been here at all." She shook her head.

"He just wouldn't have had the time. To be outside our house and then make the phone call from the Golden Gate Bridge at the time he did."

"The Golden Gate?"

"Yes. I held on to the phone for a while and heard traffic zooming by. Nonstop and a lot of it, I'd say.

"And I could swear there was a foghorn in the distance."

TWENTY-TWO

"Mace is quite a guy, don't you think?"

"Deana!"

"No worries, Mom. *I* don't want him. Believe me, after . . . you know . . . I need some space for a while. 'Sides, he's too old for me!"

"Just remember, my darling daughter, that Mace is here to do a job of work. As in nailing Allan's killer."

Leigh had had a special meal brought in from the restaurant. We both deserve a break, she'd decided. These last few days have been a nightmare.

Beef Willington may have been off the menu, but Carl, her new, hastily appointed chef at the Bayview, had produced a wonderful dinner of marinated swordfish topped with spicy mango and tomato salsa.

Squishy chocolate dessert followed.

Deana's favorite.

"Here's to us! One door closes, another opens," Leigh proclaimed with a wry smile. She took a sip of cool sparkling Californian wine. "Mmmm. This is good. And Carl's doing great, too."

"Yeah. Good riddance to you-know-who."

"Well, not exactly, honey. Nelson *did* have his moments. And he'd made a name for himself. In Tiburon, at least. Apparently, his previous experience came from working with some fancy Italian supremo at a top joint in New York. So he told me."

"Pity he hadn't stayed there."

"Mmmm . . ." Leigh was more relaxed than she'd felt since Mom and Dad departed after the family get-together.

Only it hadn't turned out to be a *proper* family get-together.

All that awkward stuff with Mom . . . And Deana and Allan leaving so soon after dinner . . .

Thank *God*, Mom and Dad had gone off to Boulder to be with Aunt Abby. Before everything happened.

Leigh glanced fondly at Deana. So young to have gone through such an awful experience. But, apart from her bruised jaw and a faraway look in her eyes now and then, Deana seemed to be holding up.

As funerals went, Allan's had been pretty tense and grim. Understandably, she reckoned. Mary Powers, a single mother, so it turned out, was pale, tearful, and near to collapse. Luckily, there'd been a sister, Allan's aunt Beth, to support her and help her through the ceremony.

Both had been distant with Leigh and Deana, darting just brief looks of recognition at the outset.

Nothing more.

Unlike Leigh's own nightmares over Charlie's funeral . . . *Charlie.*

After eighteen years, memories of his death still lingered. *Maybe there is a curse on us, after all. . . .*

Leigh dismissed her gloomy thoughts and looked over at Deana. She gave a contented sigh. It was good, sitting here in the candlelight, chatting, eating nice food.

Despite the cloud of Allan's death still hanging over us . . .

Not wanting to spoil tonight for either of them, she made a determined effort to lighten up, recalling another event.

One that had happened only that day.

A vivid reminder of the past.

Cherry.

"Cherry. Cherry Dornay!"

The red-haired girl looked up.

"Leigh West. As I live and breathe."

"How're things, Cherry? And," Leigh paused, "how's Ben?"

"Oh, Ben's okay. Never married, of course."

There was an awkward silence. The red-haired girl moved on, hastily. "And you? I recall you were set on owning your own restaurant all those years ago."

"Yeah. I was. And I did."

"Huh? You mean . . . all *this* is *yours?*"

Leigh gave a pleased smile, and Cherry said, "Wow!"

They chatted.

About this and that.

The old days.

How things had changed. Cherry taught art now, and was living in the San Fernando Valley. Ben was in IT—and still in San Diego.

They laughed a lot, reminiscing together. Yet Leigh still felt an awkwardness, a barrier that time had placed between them. She smiled at Cherry, remembering the seventies. San Diego. Lazy days on Mission Beach; meeting up with the crowd at Pepe's Place on J Street. That trip to Tijuana when Ben had lost his precious guitar . . .

So *much* had gone on since then.

A lot of water had gone under quite a few bridges.

She thought of Ben. Strong, gentle; fair curly hair, worn shoulder length, hippie style. And the beard. Don't forget the beard!

Yeah. Ben had been quite a guy.

Leigh and Cherry exchanged telephone numbers.

Promising to keep in touch.

Maybe.

"Mom. The door. I'll get it."

Deana left the table and went into the hallway.

"Wait, honey. Don't open up yet."

Deana looked through the spyhole.

Mace.

Does the guy never give up?

"Well?" Leigh asked.

"It's Mace." Deana pouted. Ordinarily, she would have

been a little excited. Tonight she was disappointed. She'd had Leigh all to herself—and they'd been sharing some rare intimate moments.

Precious mom-and-daughter time.

Till around thirty seconds ago.

Screw Mace.

Was he redundant, or what?

Leigh opened the door.

"Why, Mace!" Her head lifted. She laughed, raking a hand through her hair. "This *is* a surprise."

"Yeah," Deana muttered. "Fancy seeing you here."

Stepping inside, Mace threw her a beamer, not missing a beat.

He fished around in his pocket and came up with a palmful of sunflower seeds. He tossed them into his mouth, watching her all the time. His jaws worked around the seeds.

Deana frowned back.

Who does he think he is, Fox fuckin' Mulder?

Still grinning, his lips peeled back, showing her his rows of straight white teeth.

But his eyes stayed cool. Alert.

He turned to Leigh.

"Dropped by to say we backed your hunch that Nelson maybe *was* in the Golden Gate vicinity last night. We have a coupla police launches patroling the area—in the unlikely event they find his body."

Mace and Leigh sauntered off into the living room.

Deana followed, suddenly feeling left out.

Looked like Mom and Mace were already an item.

Christ!

Okay. Maybe Mom *does* need a boyfriend.

But *Mace?*

She pictured Mom and Mace making mad, passionate love. His mouth on hers. Running his hands over her naked body . . . Mom panting a little, pushing him into her . . .

Deana squirmed at the thought.

"Oh. I'm sorry," Mace said, eyeing the table. "Were you two having dinner? I'll be on my way. Have to catch up with Mattie, anyhow. This time of night and she's *still* at the depot. Spends more time on her computer these days than she ever did when we were out on the streets."

"Thought you and she were history. Like, you're no longer partners?"

"Right. Mattie got a little bored in the car all day. Cramped her style, she said. Got herself an office job instead." Mace huffed out a harsh little laugh.

Looking at him, Deana got the feeling there was probably more to Mace and Mattie than met the eye.

Maybe they *had* been an item, both on and off duty.

"Deana," Leigh put in. "How about some coffee?"

Trying to get rid of me, Mom? Okay, but please don't make a fool of yourself. I'm not jealous. Just don't want you getting hurt. . . .

"This is my first day back at the restaurant," Leigh was telling Mace.

"That so? Sure you're up to it?"

"Yeah. Got to make a start sometime. Besides, what else can I do to solve the mystery of Nelson's disappearance? It's up to you guys now."

She changed the subject.

"Seems like the new chef is shaping up real good. Thank heavens." Leigh gestured toward the remains of their meal—and the wine.

"Oh, I'm sorry, Mace. Would you have preferred a glass of wine rather than coffee? I do apologize. But, naturally, I thought you were still on duty. . . ."

"I'm not, as it happens. But coffee's fine. Just mighty pleased to see you and Deana are coping so well. Under the circumstances."

"Well, we've felt better, I can assure you. But we're getting there. We'll be okay when you find Nelson. He seemed like a man at his wits' end—so maybe he won't be much of a threat to us anymore."

"Can't be too sure about that, Leigh." Mace met her eyes candidly. For a moment, her heart warmed. He was being very thoughtful. And she was grateful for that.

Briefly, she considered the yawning gap in her life. The space that one day, she hoped, a partner would fill.

Admit it, Leigh, she told herself. A man in your life could be a lotta fun.

Yeah. In my dreams!

There *had* been guys.

After Charlie.

A handful. Maybe even more. But her life had always been too busy for a full-on relationship.

Because there'd been Deana. Not counting the restaurant. Plus the hard work that went with all of that.

The late nights. Early mornings.

There'd been no time, no place for a permanent man in her life.

Looking back, there'd only been one who'd even remotely fitted the bill. He'd have married her like a shot if she hadn't been so goddamned intent on her career.

Ben.

What a fool I've been.

He'd have made the perfect partner.

Meeting Cherry today brought all those memories flooding back. . . .

"Something on your mind?" Mace placed a warm hand over her cool one.

She started. "Sorry. I . . . met someone today. Someone from the old days. Triggered off a few memories, I guess. A blast from the past, you might say."

She smiled into his eyes. They were dark; she hadn't noticed *how* dark before. Looking into them now, she saw warmth and concern—and behind that, a raunchy twinkle.

He likes me, Leigh told herself.

Mace likes me.

A squirm of excitement stirred between her thighs. It had been far too long. . . .

"Come and get it!" Deana bustled in with the coffeepot, cream, and sugar on a serving tray. She paused, sensing the atmosphere.

Seems like I'm interrupting a special moment here.
Good.

"Uh-huh." Clearing a space on the table in front of them, she plonked the tray on it.

"I feel a date with my TV coming on. According to TVS, *Sleepy Hollow*'s showing after the news. So it's coffee for two, I'm afraid, folks."

"Oh, *that's* a shame." Mace almost sounded sorry. "Well, don't wait up. I'll stay and chat with Mom a while longer."

Deana threw Leigh a questioning glance.

Is this *really* what you want?

Leigh's face stayed bland.

"Okay, honey. Try to get some rest, now. I won't be long." With a thoughtful face, Leigh watched Deana go.

"Hey. The kid'll get over it. Kids do. It's been a real bad experience for her—for you both—but she's a survivor. She'll be okay."

"Think so, Mace?" Leigh seemed unsure. She concentrated on pouring the coffee. Black for Mace; white, no sugar for herself.

"Right on. Few weeks from now and it never happened."

She still wore a worried frown, and he took her hand in his.

"Nice place you got here, Leigh. Great view of the Bay. I'd sure like to take some shots. All that perspective, sweeping down to the Gate. Wonderful vantage point—best I've seen."

"Shots?"

He laughed. "Not *those* kinda shots. Shots as in photographs."

"Oh, you take pictures. Professionally?"

"Nah. Just a hobby. But I like to think, once in a while, they'll be good enough for exhibition. Had one or two in an L.A. gallery last year. Got some okay reviews."

"Nice going, Mace. And sure. Feel free. You're welcome to take shots from my window anytime!"

They exchanged glances and smiled.

Sharing the joke.

They lapsed into silence. It was one of those rare, comfortable moments when Leigh felt at peace with the world.

It was a good feeling.

"Mace?"

"Uh-huh?"

"This is great. Y'know that?"

"Mmmm . . . Yeah. Suits me, too."

"Do you . . . have anyone? I mean, anyone special?"

"Me? Nope. Girl I met at college was the last *special* one that I recall. Wanda Baker, her name was. Yeah. She *was* something special. Till she got herself carved up, that is."

"Mace! What*ever* happened?" She glanced at his face. It looked dark. Closed. She shivered a little, then said, "There's no need to tell me if you don't want to."

"That's okay. I don't have a problem with that. Not anymore."

He leaned forward, studying his Nike sneakers, arms resting on his knees, hands hanging slack between his thighs.

"She was the prettiest little thing," he said. "Blond. Five two and a bit, and neat with it. Y'know? Her dad died when she was a year old. Her mom committed suicide, so she was brought up by an old aunt.

"Wanda was an old-fashioned kinda girl. Quiet. Kept to herself." He eased back into the sofa, staring through the glass wall into the night.

"Oh, Mace. What a terrible story. And for her to get murdered . . ."

"You move on, Leigh. Have to. Otherwise you break. Anyway," he said, looking deep into her eyes, "you said you met someone from *your* past. Tell me about it."

"How about a Courvoisier?" Leigh asked him.

"Long story, huh?"

"No. That time of night, is all."

"Sure. I'm not on duty. A drink'd be fine."

Leigh stepped over to the bar and decanted cognac into two balloon glasses. She handed one to Mace, took the other, and sat sideways on the sofa, facing him.

"It was eighteen years ago. I was pregnant with Deana. Mom and Dad sent me to an aunt in San Diego. . . ." She caught the question in his eyes. "I was eighteen and single," she explained. "I needed somewhere to have my baby."

Mace frowned.

"I had my baby. Made a life for myself. Oh, I was capable, all right. Knew it all. Rebellious. Anti-everything, so Dad said. Practically a member of the Great Unwashed . . ." She grimaced at the thought. "I went on marches, though. Did demos."

Mace grinned. "You were a hippie?"

"Looking back, I suppose you could say that. But it wasn't all flowers in the hair, peace, man, and all that jazz. Sure, I did demos. Got involved with the cops.

"Anyway, that was here in Tiburon. Before I got myself pregnant. After that . . ." She paused. "When I went to San Diego, I met a young art student, Cherry Dornay. She was a great kid. Free as the wind, happy, and a real pleasure to be around, I guess.

"She had a brother, Ben. Now, *he* was a real hippie. Long hair, beard, wild shirts, Jesus boots. Into the Beatles. The works."

She broke off, embarrassed. She felt awkward. Guilty, divulging this piece of her personal past to a comparative stranger. She hadn't even told *Deana* about her friendship with Cherry and Ben.

Mace was smiling at her. She relaxed again. The mood was just right: warm, friendly, with more than a hint of sexual awareness, which she knew they both were feeling. Her heartbeat quickened, bringing a flush to her cheeks.

"Sounds like you really enjoyed life back there," he said.

"Yeah, I guess I did."

"And you met this girl again, today?"

"Right. It was a . . . wonderful surprise. We had a lot of catching up to do."

"You never kept in touch?"

"No," Leigh gave a wistful smile. "I guess I was too busy. Too busy making plans. Set my heart on having my own restaurant. Not easy, with a baby. But I managed; Mom and Dad helped me financially. Kept us both clothed and fed . . ."

"You didn't go back there. Home, I mean?"

"Not straightaway. I was proud. Wanted to prove myself. Wanted to *redeem* myself, I guess. Show Mom and Dad I could be a success. Show them I'd grown up and could look after my daughter okay."

"You've sure done all of that, Leigh. You've got a great kid who's going to college in the fall, and a successful restaurant. Your folks must be real proud of you."

Leigh saw a shadow cross his face.

Maybe not. Trick of the light, she guessed.

Sighing, she glanced at her wristwatch.

Almost midnight. Deana's probably asleep by now.

"I can take a hint. Time I was somewhere else, Leigh. Thanks for the drink. And your company," he whispered. "My treat next time. You choose the place—and we'll make a date."

"I'd like that, Mace."

"You would?" He smiled eagerly.

"Yes, I would. Very much."

He bent his head and kissed her lightly on the cheek.

" 'Night, Leigh. Take care, now."

Her heart raced again.

She saw him to the door, then watched the taillights of his black Trans Am snake away into the night.

TWENTY-THREE

Deana lay in bed.

Listening to Mace go.

She heard Mom's voice. Light. Laughing a little. Then Mace's, low and intimate.

Looks like he got Mom on the hop.

Bastard!

It was one of those nights again, hot and muggy.

I sure could use a shower.

She shoved the sheet down with her feet and lay still.

Feeling the sweat go cold on her body.

She lifted her nightgown away from her breasts and blew down inside the bodice. It made her feel hotter.

"Phewww!"

A night like this when I had my dream . . .

That was no *dream*. It was the real thing.

Nelson and his hatchet.

Sorry. Meat cleaver.

What's the difference?

Either way, you end up the same—a chopped-up body.

Could've been *my* chopped up body.

Oh God. Let them find him soon.

Mom thinks he threw himself off the bridge.

Hope so.

Then we'd all be safe.

But he *was* out of his tree.

Anyone could see that.

Those wild eyes. Mistake. *That* wild eye. Slobbering mouth.

Uhhh. Yuck!

She swung her legs out of bed and stood up.

The breeze whispering through the open window felt good. Lifting her nightgown over her head, she let it drop to the floor—changed her mind, picked it up, wadded it, and tossed it in the hamper.

She looked down at her body, pale and slick with sweat. Her full, firm breasts, flat belly, and long, muscular legs.

Gleaming in the darkness.

No full moon tonight.

Not like the night Nelson paid me a visit.

Nelson. Fucking maniac.

If it weren't for him, Allan'd still be here. . . .

She opened the nightstand drawer, pulled out Allan's gym shorts, and buried her nose in them.

She took a deep, deep sniff.

And couldn't believe it.

Allan's smell was gone.

So soon.

How could a person's *smell* disappear like that? It was like it had died with him.

Bit by bit, piece by piece, Allan was going away.

Leaving her behind.

This is how it's gonna be. I'll forget what he looks like next. Except I have that photograph of him I took at Stinson Beach a couple of weeks back.

The one where he looked like a young Robert Redford. Tousled blond hair, broad smile, gorgeous teeth, eyes crinkled up against the sun.

He was wearing those tight, shiny swim trunks. . . .

Oh God, Allan. I'll never forget you. Never. I promise!

Knowing that Allan was gone forever hit her hard.

Again.

Tears stood in her eyes, then coursed down her cheeks. She wiped them away with the shorts.

She sighed, fighting back a sob. Gently, she folded the shorts and replaced them in the nightstand drawer.

Allan's smell may have disappeared, but she would always have his shorts to remind her of the good times they'd had.

Could *still* be having—if it weren't for that sick fuck Nelson.

Loud, hurting sobs broke through, bursting from her throat.

She threw herself on the bed and lay weeping into her pillow, drawing up her knees till they touched her chin. She rocked and sobbed, her tears drenching the pillow, hopelessness sweeping over her like a tidal wave.

Allan was gone.

Forever.

I'll never forget you, darling. . . .

The tears gradually subsided. She felt calmer now and turned over on her back.

Staring at the ceiling.

Watching the shadows from her tree spread across it like giant fingers.

If I could find Nelson, I'd kill him. That's what I'd do. If I saw him tonight and killed him, nobody would know.

I could slit his goddamn throat. Stab him to death. Then hide the body.

Roll it away into someone's garden.

Or into the stand of redwoods, back of the house.

Nobody'd ever think of looking there.

She leaned over Nelson's body, blood streaming from the wound in his gut, pouring from his mouth. Sobbing and choking at the same time, he pleaded with her to stop, get help.

He hadn't meant to do it.

Oh no?

He was *sorry*—he hadn't wanted to *kill* anyone. . . .

She laughed at him scornfully, kicked the knife into the bushes, and strolled back into the house.

She sat back on the bed, planning her next move.

Knife. That's what I need, a knife.

Her mind flew to the kitchen.

Mom's vegetable knife.

It was lethal. Short, strong, with a pointed blade. You could lose a finger and not even notice.

I could handle it, though.

Deana pictured Mom holding the knife.

Chopping carrots.

Quickly, expertly, like a machine, the root falling away from the knife like small orange counters.

Yes, Mom's vegetable knife could kill Nelson okay.

No problem.

Deana swung herself off the bed, shivering with excitement. The idea of killing Nelson was scary, but it was turning her on.

It would be *so* easy.

And she'd get away with it.

Nobody'd suspect her.

If they did, well, she was a girl, wasn't she—still distraught at the death of her lover.

They'd say she didn't know what she was doing.

Maybe they'd think a young girl like her wouldn't have the courage, the strength to kill a grown man. . . .

Nelson won't be hanging around, though, waiting to be killed.

Not if he has any sense.

Or would he?

Maybe he *has* got this fatal attraction for Mom and me.

Maybe he won't be able to stay away.

She crept to the door.

Listening out for Mom.

Seems like she's already in bed. Having cleared away the supper things, got into her nightgown, cleaned her teeth. . . .

Probably went to sleep thinking of Mace.

Yuck.

The silence was everywhere, except for the rustling tree outside her window.

Reminding her of Nelson, the way he'd scared the daylights out of her. . . .

I'll scare the butt-ugly bastard shitless. If and when I find him.

She dressed quickly, her resolve to find Nelson growing by the second. She pulled on a black, long-sleeved sweatshirt and matching tights.

Bundled her thick hair into a knot.

Dragged a black knit cap over her head, safely anchoring the hair in place.

No black sneakers, though.

Damn! Then:

"Yes!"

Brilliant!

A brain wave . . .

She picked out black knee-length wool socks from her drawer and pulled them over her white Nike running shoes.

I look like a cat burglar!

Cary Grant in *To Catch a Thief.*

Slipping quietly into the kitchen for the knife, she *felt* like Cary Grant in *To Catch a Thief.*

Holding her breath, she stood still, listening.

No sign of Mom stirring.

Tiptoeing over to the cutlery drawer, she pulled it out carefully.

It rattled slightly. Drawing in a quick breath, she held still for a moment. Then she took out the vegetable knife and ran her fingers lightly over the steel blade.

Wow!

It was *really* sharp.

She closed the drawer, freezing as it rattled, louder this time, on its way back into the cabinet.

A gurgling sound belched behind her. She caught her breath again—and let it out with a gasp.

Phew . . .

Water in the pipes.

I think.

I hope . . .

Through her soft sweatshirt, she fingered the door key on its chain, lying in the deep cleft between her breasts.

Might need this in a hurry if things go wrong.

Like I'm standing over Nelson's bleeding body . . . and someone sees me holding the knife dripping with blood . . . and I have to run like crazy to make it home before they call the cops.

Must be an idiot to think that Nelson'd be hanging around.

Waiting to get stabbed to death.

But you never know.

I got this feeling I could be in luck tonight.

One way or another.

Anyway. I'm out there for a run, aren't I?

Not aiming to kill anybody.

I'm taking the knife along in case Nelson happens by.

Then I promise you, Allan, I'll kill the bastard.

She slipped out the front door, holding the knife blade outward. She ran lightly down the driveway.

The knife felt awkward at first. Then she got used to it, pumping in and out in her hand as she ran.

The socks were great. Like this, she could run on in silence. No one would hear her muffled steps.

Blending in with the shadows, she felt like one of them herself. Part of the scenery.

Black clothes make perfect night camouflage, she told herself.

Wearing black made her feel a lot safer.

But it was still spooky out here.

Scary.

And it was hot. Her head was sweating already.

I'll take off my cap in a minute. . . .

She paused to work out her strategy.

She'd reached the end of the drive. Now, which way, up or down?

If Nelson's around, which way is *he* likely to go?

Might be coming up to the house.

Got himself another car maybe? The cops have his old one.

Something rustled in the juniper bushes to her left.

She stiffened, not daring to breathe, flattening herself against the shrubs by the gatepost.

Yeoowwww . . .

A cat streaked out in front of her. She gasped; then, feeling relieved, she laughed a little. Fuckin' cat!

Okay.

Start running.

Downbank?

Best go upbank; it'd make for an easier journey on the way home.

After I've annihilated Nelson.

She turned and jogged upbank, gently.

Looking around her.

Is someone watching?

Wondering what the hell that girl is doing out at one a.m.?

Asking for trouble . . .

A thrill buzzed in the pit of her stomach.

It *was* spooky.

But it was exciting, too.

She could meet *anybody.*

Or *anything.*

Dressed in black, the odds were that no one could see her anyway.

On the other hand, there could be some guy out there, thinking about what he'd do to her if he caught her. . . .

She hastened her step.

Maybe she should turn around?

Go back home . . .

Not yet.

I'm not *that* scared.

Keep on truckin', Deana. . . .

And eyes front, all the way.

It'd be a dumb move to look around, enjoy the scenery as she ran along.

Yeah.

Asking for trouble that way.

Mostly, it'd make her feel scared, worrying about *who* or *what* could be out there.

I should worry. I have a knife.

Mom's vegetable knife.

Don't make me laugh.

Some karate kid comes along and kicks the knife outta my hand.

Then what?

Then you get jumped, raped—or worse, you dope.

Murdered.

Raped *and* murdered.

You're an idiot, Deana West. What *are* you doing out here, anyway?

Mom'd have a fit.

If she knew.

She'll never know.

I'll be home in ten minutes. Fifteen and I'm tucked up in bed. No one any the wiser.

"Hey."

A shout.

Ringing out in the night. Echoing loudly.

Deana gasped, melting into the shadows of a redwood spreading out from a driveway.

Her grip tightened on the knife.

She stood poised, ready for action.

"Hey. You want to look where you're going?"

A German shepherd dog sprang up out of nowhere.

Knocking her to the ground.

Pounding the breath, the *life*, out of her.

Curling into a tight ball, Deana shielded her face with her arms feeling the dog's weight as its heavy front paws pinned her down.

She kept still.

Do that, and the dog won't eat me.

At least I *hope* it won't.

You never can tell with dogs. . . .

She moved position and the knife skittered away, its spinning blade glinting in the darkness.

Mom's vegetable knife.

How quaint.

"Here boy. Sabre. Heel!"

Deana peeked though her hands. The voice didn't *sound* like it belonged to a rapist.

Or a murderer.

It sounded strong. Ordinary. Youngish.

The dog backed off, its long tongue lolling over some seriously pointed teeth. The dog fixed its gaze on its master, like it was waiting for the next command.

Deana blushed in the darkness.

It's only a *dog*, for chrissake! Just a big stupid mutt.

The mutt turned its attention to her curled-up legs. Snuffling around some, giving her a steam clean with its big slobbery nose.

Yuck. The *beast!*

Deana scrambled to her knees. Stood up, then bent down quickly to pick up the knife.

In the shadowy darkness, the blade flashed embarrassingly bright.

"What's this?" The guy grabbed her hand, twisting it backward. Her grip loosened and the knife clattered to the sidewalk.

He yanked her wrist again, making her yelp with pain.

"What d'you think you're doing?" he demanded.

She regained her balance, drew back a leg, and aimed a kick at his crotch.

He danced back. Just in time.

Then, holding up both hands in mock surrender, he laughed.

"Hey. You're looking at a friend here. Not foe!"

"What the hell you doing with that dog? It could kill a person, jumping out at them like that!"

She scowled at the dog. It was hauled in on a short lead now, sitting quietly by his master's feet, tongue lolling out of mean-looking jaws. . . . Hot breath clouding the night air.

"Sorry. I'm Warren Hastings. This is Sabre, my trusty sidekick." Warren held out a hand. "You must have been really scared."

Deana ignored the hand.

"You aren't kidding. That's a *monster* you've got there." She was still fighting back tears of relief.

"That's no monster. That's my mutt. Let me tell you, there's a kittycat lurking beneath that rugged exterior. Right, boy?"

"Some kittycat. He scared me half to death, I'll have you know."

Warren smiled.

"You dropped your knife. Make a habit of carrying a knife? Make a habit of midnight runs, come to that?"

"A girl's gotta stay safe. Never know who she might meet up with. And yes. I like to run at night. Got a problem with that?"

"Nope. But why not run during daylight hours? Safer that way, so they tell me."

"What's it to you? What were *you* doing out here, anyway?"

He laughed, a warm, infectious sound. "Why don't I offer you a mug of cocoa. To make up for my marauding mutt?"

"Thanks, but no thanks."

"I make a mean mug of cocoa when I've a mind."

Warren tilted his head to one side. His smile was infectious, too. Deana found herself relenting and grinned back at him.

Steady on. Mustn't let him think I'm easy meat.

"How do I know . . ."

"That I'm not a rapist? Or a serial killer? That the problem?"

"About the size of it."

"Look. That's my house, there. The one with two redwoods in front. Moved in just a coupla days ago.

"Here's the deal. I make us some cocoa and you fill me in on the neighborhood. Might even run to a cookie or two . . . ?" He smiled, showing nice white teeth.

"*Your* house? You live there alone?"

"Not alone. There's my sister, too. She's called Sheena. You'd like her."

"I really oughta go. Mom'll be worried. . . ."

"Does Mom know you're out?"

Nice one, Warren. You sure know how to press the right buttons. "Sure she does. She doesn't mind me running at night."

"With a knife?"

"Just let me pass. I gotta get on home."

"As you wish. Take a rain check on the cocoa, though. Finest on the West Coast. Got Best Frothy Choccy Drink Award last year . . ."

"Good night, Warren."

"Let me walk you home. Sabre'll defend us from would-be rapists."

Don't keep using that word. Makes me scared.

"No, thanks. Only a block to go and I'm there."

"Suit yourself."

"Yeah. Good night."

"Good night, O nameless lady in black. We shall meet again, maybe."

Deana turned and ran swiftly downhill, her sock-covered

feet beating a muffled rhythm on the sidewalk. By the time she got to her driveway, she was breathing hard.

Running lightly down the slope, she reached the stoop, steadied herself against the doorpost, and felt for the key. It nestled hard and warm between her breasts.

She hauled it up, lifted the chain over her head, and felt hair.

Shit. I left my cap on the sidewalk!

After the trusty Sabre jumped me.

Carefully, she slid the key into the lock.

She cringed slightly. Sometimes the lock made a loud, metallic scraping noise.

But not tonight.

Thank God.

Wouldn't do to meet up with Mom.

Deana snuck into her bedroom.

She closed the door and leaned back on it, breathing a deep sigh of relief.

Her legs were shaking. Her heart still pounded.

Must be the excitement of her nocturnal adventure, she guessed. Not the exercise; she'd had too much practice for that to be a problem.

Warren.

She gave a wry smile.

Looks like I made a new friend.

Allan's image flashed before her.

I went out there to kill Nelson, Allan. To kill your murderer. I got waylaid, though. But we'll get him, soon.

She flooded her mind with thoughts of Allan till, suddenly, he was there.

She tilted her head and sniffed, catching a whiff of his scent. It eddied all around her.

Then it was filling the room.

Allan's here!

His hands cupped her breasts; his upturned thumbs stroked her nipples.

Shuddering with ecstasy, she remembered how he liked doing that. How he loved the feel of her skin. Warm, silky, so *ultra-sexy,* he'd told her.

For a long time Deana stared at the window, at the soft billowing drapes and the flickering shadow of the tree. . . . Thinking about Allan.

Slowly, she undressed, piling her sweats back into the drawer.

Throwing herself onto the bed, she stared at the ceiling for a long, long time, feeling hot salt tears stream down her cheeks.

Allan would always be special to her.

She'd never forget him.

How could she?

"Even when I'm old," she whispered. "I'll *always* remember you, Allan . . . and cherish the memories of the good times we've shared."

Yeah. The good times.

Before the horror of *that* night took them all away.

Before Nelson . . .

No. She'd never, ever, forget Allan.

Some adventure she'd had tonight, though.

Warren was quite a guy.

Bet he *did* make a mean cocoa.

She smiled . . .

He had a nice voice. Warm and friendly.

Good teeth, too.

Hadn't seen much more in the dark.

Maybe, soon . . .

The mutt would have to go, though.

Deana sighed.

Didn't get to kill Nelson.

Fuck Nelson. I'll hack him to death some other time.

With Mom's vegetable knife . . .

Oh no!

It was on the sidewalk. With her cap.

TWENTY-FOUR

"Oh God. This gets worse. I've gotta go out there and get the knife. Can't go back now, though. Warren'll be asleep. And his dog. Fat chance I have of sneaking into his house to see if Mom's vegetable knife's in there, with Sabre around.

"Maybe it's on the sidewalk. Maybe someone kicked it into the bushes."

No way. An urgent little voice told her the knife was now in Warren's house. She stared at the curtains, billowing inward. Felt the soft breeze. Sniffed at the air, thinking she'd caught a whiff of Allan's scent again.

Stop it.

Now!

She let her eyelids droop. Wriggled her shoulders. Relaxed her body right down to her toes. Breathed deep. In, out, in, out . . .

But her special relaxation technique wasn't working tonight. She couldn't get the knife out of her mind.

Mom's gonna miss her knife. She uses it almost every day.

She's gonna think that someone stole it.

No way would she think she'd *lost* it. . . .

She always puts it back in the drawer.

Hope Warren did find it.

Probably took it indoors, intending to return it later.

The knife *and* my cap.

Doesn't really matter about the cap.

Idiot. Warren doesn't know where I live.

Didn't give him the chance to *ask* where I lived.

Didn't want to tell him, either. He could've been a rapist.

Nah.

Not with a dog that size. Rapists creep about on their lonesome.

Preying on girls.

Dog like that, a would-be rapist wouldn't have a victim to rape. They'd be dead with fright, or halfway down the street.

Only one thing for it. Wait till Mom goes to bed tonight, then sneak out.

Again.

If I'm lucky, I'll catch Warren walking his dog.

Then I'll ask him if he saw the knife, and did he happen to pick it up. And if so, please can I have it back?

Make it easy on yourself, Deana. Buy a new one.

Can't do that.

Mom'd notice the difference.

She'd wonder why she's suddenly got a new knife in place of the old one.

Phweww . . .

What a tangled web . . .

Only one thing for it.

Gotta go out there and find Warren.

Sample his cocoa.

Maybe. Whatever. Just get the knife back.

TWENTY-FIVE

Nelson shivered.

It was dark and getting colder all the time.

Blinded by the glare of headbeams, he couldn't make out where he was walking.

His pirate patch was long gone; his sewed-up eye looked like it had been sucked back into his skull. Hot tears welled up in his good one.

He was exhausted; his head throbbed with a muzzy ache. The tears made everything blurred and hazy. He lifted a hand to dash them away.

Christ, this is one mean mother of a headache. . . .

He'd lost his floppy chef cap, and his tunic was all dirty from when he'd last fallen.

Clutching the hatchet, he held it, blade up, like a rifle on his shoulder. Just *having* it there gave him a warm, safe feeling.

"Anybody messes with me 'n' I'll use it," he muttered to himself. "Bank on it, you fuck pigs out there; I'll hack ya t' pieces, jes' like a cut a' meat."

Nelson stumbled off the sidewalk. Into the path of an old Ford truck. Brakes slammed home. The truck screeched to a halt. Then, with a crashing of gears, it swerved around him, almost knocking him off his feet.

Through a hazy blur, he caught the driver's face, bloated, maniacal, mouthing profanities. The near-side window dropped down. The man shook a meaty fist at Nelson.

"What *are* you, punk—a fuckin' loony, or WHAT? You wanna die? Do us all a favor, lemme help ya do it!"

The driver's big face shoved itself through the window. A wad of phlegm shot out like a bullet, hooking itself on Nelson's tunic.

Noisy blasts and honks peppered the air.

Sobbing, Nelson hurled himself back onto the sidewalk. The hatchet escaped his grasp and clattered to the ground. He scrabbled around on his knees, his hands circling the gritty path. Then, with a cry of relief, he caught the blade, fingered it carefully, and felt his way down till he found the heft.

Cradling it lovingly to his chest, he rocked back and forth, his face turned skyward.

"Thank you, Lord," he said, sobbing huskily. "I found my cleaver. The only thing left . . . from Nelson's *magnificent,* goddamn career . . . His dear old cleaver . . ."

* * *

He rocked a while longer, crying like a baby, then wiped his eye on the sleeve of his tunic.

That's better.

His good eye was clear now.

"Thank you, thank you . . ." He wagged his head up and down. The Lord was on his side, he knew it.

Raising his arms in triumph, he hoisted the cleaver high, its blade shining in the glare of the streetlamps.

A siren wailed behind him.

He jerked around.

Cops!

Pressing into the shadows, he became one of them.

Bastard cops!

After him.

The shadows suddenly gave way to an embankment. He scrambled upright and tentatively put one foot over the edge. Then the other . . .

Soon he was slipping and sliding down over rough grass. Clutching at weeds, stretching out his arms, hanging on to the cleaver; trying not to tumble headlong into the awful darkness below.

Crying out, his feet caught at tangled roots and bushes. He lurched forward, slipped again, lost his footing, and landed smack on his butt. He slipped down some more and panicked. No way could he stop.

He plummeted down.

Still clutching the cleaver.

"Yo . . . What have we here?"

Grabbing at the weeds with his free hand, Nelson shoved his heels into the turf. He shuddered to a halt and went quiet. His heart lurched. He gripped the hatchet tighter.

Whoever's out there, he thought, will think maybe I'm a drunk. Or a dopehead . . . If I'm lucky, they'll leave me be. If'n I'm not lucky . . .

A throaty chuckle rumbled in the darkness.

A hand grabbed his ankle. Yanked him farther, *much* farther down the slope.

Into a deeper, darker place.

The smell was awful. Rank. Like bad meat.

He scrabbled and clawed at weeds and tufts of grass frantically trying to halt his progress. . . .

The hand pulled harder.

Someone sniggered.

"S'matter, boy? Don't ya want to join us down here? My, aren't *you* the party pooper? *We* want ya to join us." The voice rose a notch. "Don't we, guys? Always a hearty welcome for new blood around here . . ."

Nelson sobbed. His heart lurched again; this time it bounced around his chest like a big chunk of rock.

"Please . . . let . . . me . . . GO!"

Another yank and he was on the move again.

Undergrowth tore at his face, burning the flesh in raw, hurting patches.

He struggled like a mad thing, rolling from side to side, wrestling to free himself from the viselike grip.

The hand held firm.

It dragged him across more rough ground. Garbage—jagged cans, glass, sharp objects—scraped and cut into him as he bumped and jolted along.

Still gripping his hatchet.

Can't let it go. . . . Gotta use it to hack my way outta here. . . .

Suddenly, the hand let go. Nelson broke free rolling over and over . . . and over. Into a stinking ditch; into water that was thick, cold, and slimy.

Acrid odors hit his nostrils.

Oil and . . .

Sump oil, seemed like . . . but what else?

He scrambled out of the ditch, his shoes filled with slime, the bottom half of his pants clinging to his legs.

He heard uneven, panting breaths coming from behind;

feet chugging steadily through the undergrowth; sounds of kicking, cans and other stuff being scattered out of the way.

More gasps and pants . . . They, whoever they were, were catching up. Hands clawed at his tunic. Sour breath warmed his neck.

"Fuck! Gerroff me, ya fuckin' bastard, he's mine—arrghhh . . ."

The whiny voice cut off short; growls of *others* joined in, arguing like a pack of starving hounds.

Christ Jesus! How many of 'em are there?

The trolls came to a ragged halt. Whispering, sniggering.

Listening out for me, most likely.

"C'mere!"

The voice came up close. Right behind him.

Terrified, Nelson held his breath, hugging the cleaver tight to his chest.

Then:

Can't breathe—dear God . . . I can't—breathe. . . .

His heart rocked, lurched, fluttering around like a big wounded bird.

A goddamn angina attack!

Cold beads of sweat broke out on his forehead.

Rolled down. Dripped through his brows.

Itching, irritating. Falling into his good eye.

Stinging like salt.

Then:

"Hey. Quit that, you *filthy* fuckin' pervert, you."

A woman's voice. Sharp. Imperative.

Sounding scared. Very scared.

A male voice now.

Gruff, threatening.

"You fuckin' whore, you'll do as you're told. Paid you good money, didn't I? On the nose. *Before* I got the goods. Do it my way or—"

"Or what . . . ?

Smack. A brittle crack. A piercing squeal, reminding Nelson of pigs in abbatoirs. Stun guns rammed up their asses.

His breathing began to settle down. He kept quiet in the murky dark, his knees, his entire body shaking like he'd got the ague.

What the hell's going on?

"Gotcha, my pretty. Come to Poppa, there's a good li'l gal."

Nelson knew the voice; low throaty, *phlegmy*. It belonged to the hand that had dragged him down here. Its owner was breathing hard.

Wanting.

The woman shrieked again.

Nelson caught the sound of wrestling bodies, grunting, gasping. Muffled screams, then—

"No, no, PLEASE, please, somebody . . . HELLLPPP!!"

More grunting, then rapid scrabbling sounds.

Someone panting and gasping, footsteps chugging along running away into the fuckin' darkness . . . scrambling up the grass bank, sounded like.

Nelson pictured it, this desperate guy reaching up, grasping. Losing his grip. Slipping back and down into the stinking cesspit . . .

The woman's sobs grew fainter. They were fading away now into whimpering little gasps.

Nelson doubled up. He started to heave at the soft, gurgling, *bubbling* sounds that came next.

There was more grunting and—slurping. Then disgusting wet noises, growling, and a low humming, like animals feeding.

More slurps.

Vomit shot from Nelson's mouth. Gasping, struggling for breath, he clamped a hand to his mouth and ran.

He stumbled, running in awkward leaps and bounds; breathless, nauseous, his heart pounding like a mad thing.

Gotta get outa here, afore they . . .

Tears streamed down his face, into his open mouth.

His face was all shiny, runny with sweat and tears and snot.

He lurched on. Stumbling over more rough terrain, dim obstacles, jagged stumps; up another rise, then . . .

Thank you God!

He heaved himself onto the sidewalk. Panting hard, his lungs raw, hurting, pain erupting through his body—but *halleluia*, he was streetside again!

Looking over his shoulder, he spotted the pay phone he'd used earlier. He raced toward it.

His legs wobbling like jelly. His arms pumping, his breath making hissy, whistling sounds. Then:

Ahhh, NO!

He pulled up short, crying out in despair, making small, whiny noises.

"*My cleaver . . .*

"*I left it. Back there . . .*"

He gulped as a knotty hand hooked his throat.

Slipping sideways, he whirled around and wrestled free. Then, bounding forward, he turned for a moment—and caught sight of his assailant.

Jesus Christ!

A huge, bearded giant; filthy rags flying out behind.

Head down, almost *touching* him.

As the streams of inbound traffic flowed off the Bridge, haloes of light shot blinding beams into Nelson's face. Grimacing, his arm flew up to shield his eye.

His breath came in great heaving gasps.

Panic gripped. His lungs were packing up. . . .

The troll was on him . . .

Arms outstretched.

"No, you don't, buddy boy. . . . The party's *just* about to take off."

Strong, grimy hands snatched at Nelson's tunic.

Dragging it up, twisting it tight under his chin.

Nelson's head jerked back and sideways.

He felt his feet leave the ground. Found himself staring into bloodshot eyes. At long filthy dreads matted up with the troll's greasy, straggly beard.

An old-time hippie gone bad.

And MAD.

Mad for flesh.

His.

Anybody's.

The derelict leered, his wet lips pulling away from dark broken stumps. Globs of blood swung from his beard.

Unspeakable fumes fanned Nelson's face. Transfixed like a frightened deers, his good eye swiveled and opened wide. Air hissed from his sagging lungs.

Uhhh . . .

The troll gave a final violent shake, then slammed Nelson hard against the railings.

TWENTY-SIX

Deana lay under her bedsheet. Wearing black sweat-clothes. And her sneakers, with the wool socks pulled up over them.

Ready to venture forth on another midnight run.

To find Warren, get the knife back, and hopefully return it to its rightful place.

But Mom wasn't even in bed yet.

She was moving around in the kitchen, clearing dishes, running water, washing them off. Deana heard the quiet click of a cupboard door.

Mom: not wanting to wake her.

Doing her stuff and trying to keep quiet about it.

For my sake.

Hope she doesn't decide to peek in through my bedroom door to see if I'm fast asleep.

Good thing I'm not wearing my cap yet. . . .

Mom was in the bathroom now, humming quietly to herself.

Thinking about Mace?

You bet.

At last, Mom's bedroom door closed.

Then opened again.

Mom wants me to know that she's around if I should wake in the night.

Deana smiled.

Mom was so thoughtful.

Wonder what Warren's doing now?

Probably getting ready for his nightly stroll.

With Sabre, his trusty canine friend.

Maybe I should take along some pepper, to throw in the mutt's face if he attacks me.

Oh yeah.

That'd really impress Warren.

He'd hate me for it.

Oh well, scrub the pepper. Have to trust Warren to drag Sabre off me. *If* he decides to go for my throat or something . . .

Deana twisted her head sideways. She looked at the clock on the nightstand.

12:12.

Tomorrow already.

She held her breath, keeping quiet and still.

No sound from Mom's room.

Okay. Let's move it.

She swung off the bed.

Twisted up her hair and pulled a navy knit cap over it. The cap had "NY" embroidered in white on the front. She grinned a little; she always felt like a ghetto kid when she wore this one.

Looking down at her feet, her sneakers covered with the thick wool socks, she decided she looked more like a yeti.

All she needed now was a weapon.

In case Nelson was lurking out there.

Maybe the pepper'd be a good idea.

Nah.

Nelson wasn't around last night.

Probably won't be around tonight, either.

Mom thinks he's snuffed it. Maybe his body's out there at this very moment, floating in the Bay, bobbing around in the cold, dark water, being chawed by fish. Sharks even—their deadly teeth tearing off his arms and legs. Chomping on his stringy innards.

She shivered, thinking about it.

That is *really* gross.

Nelson was a weird guy, but he didn't deserve a death like that.

Deana crept out into the hallway.

She stopped awhile and waited.

Bet Mom's asleep by now.

Dreaming about Mace.

Yeah. I can see it now.

Mace and Mom. Like Bogart and Bergman in *Casablanca*. Staring into each other's eyes across some crowded bar . . .

Play it again, Sam.

Ugghhh.

Gruesome.

She felt for her door key, caught inside her sweatshirt.

It was safe and sound.

Good.

Nothing like spending the night huddled on the stoop, Mom opening the door and saying, "Why, good morning, honey. Your own bed not comfortable enough for you?"

Now for one of Deana's famous midnight runs.

"Gotta find Warren's house first," she murmured. "I reckon it's about a block away. Up the hill. Good thing I'm fit. All this running, and tennis with Mom, keeps me in good shape."

At the end of the driveway she looked up, then down, Del Mar. She felt a buzz of excitement; the thought of being alone in the darkness brought goose bumps scurrying up her body.

Yeah. It sure is scary.

Everybody's asleep. Except me. I'm awake and ready for anything.

Almost.

She couldn't see anyone around.

Staring up the street some more, her excitement took a downturn.

Del Mar. Dimly lit by too few streetlamps, making long stretches of street almost totally black. The trees were giant shadows; the houses, dark formidable places.

She suddenly felt very scared.

"Nightmare on Del Mar," she muttered. "It'd make an awesome movie. Maybe I should write me a film script someday."

Humming a little, she began to mark time on the spot. Shoulders back, knees pumping up and down.

Up down, up down, up down . . .

Usually, this exercise focused her on the run ahead.

Thank God tonight was no exception.

Feeling loose-limbed and relaxed, she began running up the incline toward Warren's house.

A shadow stepped out before her.

She gulped, stopped, and danced back into the shadows.

The shadow came toward her.

At her.

She held her breath. Moving sideways. Backward. Any way but forward.

Every move she made, the thing blocked her path.

Weaving, dodging, dancing in front of her, stopping her from moving on.

She fought back panic, her heart hammering in her throat.

Then there was this shrunken death-head swaying before her. Its eyes gleaming at her from deep, dark sockets, its wrinkled mouth drawn into a tight black O.

Backlit by a streetlamp, wisps of hair stood out around its head like a silver halo.

Maybe it just crept out from some crypt or other . . .

Nah. It's not the living dead.

It's solid flesh and blood . . .

A bent, skinny old woman!

The hag grunted, then pulled up short in front of Deana. She was clinging onto an untidy bundle in her arms. The bundle poked and jerked, then out jumped a small dog. It raced across the street and disappeared down a tree-lined drive.

"*Shit!*" the hag shrieked. "*Now* look what you've done! Harry! Harry! Come to Mommy. . . . Haaarrryyy!"

A small white head with pointed ears appeared at the driveway opening.

Harry.

Thank God.

Deana, not believing what she was doing, called out, "Come on, Harry. . . . Come here, there's a good dog!"

The tiny head darted back, then disappeared into the shadows again.

"Fuck!" The crone stepped forward, her fierce, raddled face glowering at Deana. She raised a skinny, clawed hand and whacked it across Deana's cheek.

"*Ouuchh—you bitch!*"

Deana's neck twisted up and sideways. The crack was like gunfire inside her head. Staggering back, she clamped a hand to her face.

Damn!

The punch had landed *exactly* where Nelson slugged her three days ago. Pain shot through her jaw again.

"Fuckin' *bastard* sonofabitch," she cursed through clenched teeth.

Let her find her own fuckin' dog.

Huh. Harry—what kind of a name was *that* for a dog anyhow?

* * *

Head down, still nursing her cheek, she hurried past the old woman. Breaking into a run, she slammed smack into someone else hurrying toward her.

Dazed by the impact, Deana shook her head. She heard excited barks. Then loud wuffing noises, echoing up and down the street.

Sabre.

Thank *God*.

She didn't think she'd ever be *this* grateful to hear a barking dog.

"What the . . ." Warren held on to her, tight. "It's the midnight runner, if I'm not mistaken. What brings you out here again?"

"Warren. Am *I* glad to see you—" Deana broke off with a grim laugh. "My God. What an *experience*. I can't *believe* it!"

They fell quiet for a moment, listening to the hag's shrill voice, still calling: "Harrryyyy. Come to Mommy, darling . . . !"

Deana looked at Warren. Their eyes met and they grinned at each other. It was a nice, friendly moment.

Then, with a yelp of pain, Deana clamped a hand to her jaw.

Warren frowned. "You all right?" he asked. "I could drive you to an emergency room. There's one a coupla miles from here. . . ."

Deana shook her head.

"No? Okay. Then sit here on the wall awhile. Get your breath back." He led her to a low brick wall. She lowered herself down, carefully, and leaned back into the bushes.

"It's great to see you, Warren. And the mutt. Believe me—things got a bit nightmarish back there for a while."

A large wet nose examined her knees with loud snuffling sounds. Deana smiled. Pushing the dog away, Warren said, "Sabre. Sit. Sit, boy!"

Sabre sat.

Warren dropped down by Deana's side, wrapped an

arm around her, and pulled her gently to him. Feeling safe and comfortable, she sighed and snugged into the crook of his shoulder.

Sabre squatted, bright-eyed, watching. Steamy breath plumed from his mouth like puffs of gray smoke.

"How about that cocoa?" Warren said at last.

"Sounds like a swell idea."

"Sure? What if I'm a mad rapist?"

She drew back and faced him. "I'll take my chances that you're not."

"Good. Nice to know I can be trusted."

"Didn't say that. Just meant that I'm willing to take my chances. Personally, I don't *think* you are. Anyway, even if you were, I can look after myself."

"Yep, I guess you could. You sure *look* like you'd hold your own in an emergency."

Is he joking, or what?

Maybe not.

Anyway—now's a good time to ask about Mom's knife . . .

And try out his cocoa.

"Follow me," he said.

Deana tagged behind, while Warren led the way up the driveway. She smiled. It had been *his* wall they'd been sitting on. And, like he said, there were two redwoods in front.

Sabre trotted by Warren's side.

Without quite knowing why, Deana glanced back, through a gap in the redwoods. She could just about see the street.

A car was nosing its way past the driveway.

She caught her breath.

It was long and black, with tail fins. No lights.

The glare from the streetlight hit the windows. They were black, too.

She shuddered.

It's going real slow . . . like a funeral car.

The car passed out of sight, and she hurried to catch up with Warren.

Warren was at the front stoop, reaching into his pocket. Bringing out a key, he slid it into the lock.

The door opened in on a dark hallway.

TWENTY-SEVEN

Here we go, Deana thought.

Straight into the lion's den.

The vestibule had a warm smell. A faint aroma of food hung on the air.

Pot roast—last night's dinner, she guessed.

Warren took her arm, leading her along the hall and through an entryway at the end.

He clicked on the light. It flooded a small compact area that obviously served as both kitchen and breakfast bar.

He gestured toward a pinewood chair. She sat down and scooted it along the tile floor to the table. It made a loud scraping noise. She wondered if she'd disturbed anyone.

Warren took a stool at the bar. Looking at her quizzically, he made the first move.

"Let me guess. You've come for your knife, right? I have it here. *And* your cap. Although I see you've found another one. Must need quite a wardrobe—going out, losing your things like that . . ."

"Okay, Warren. I confess. I *did* come back for my knife. It's Mom's, and she'll go ballistic if she finds out it's missing."

"Looks remarkably like a vegetable knife to me."

"So what? *Any* kinda knife is a good idea for someone out running at night."

"Sure," he said seriously. "But maybe it's *not* such a

wonderful idea. Midnight running, I mean. Especially for a young girl . . ."

"I'm eighteen. I can look after myself."

"Eighteen?" He looked impressed. "All of eighteen?"

"Look. Hand me my knife, please, and I'll be on my way."

"Knife *and* cap. You ought to thank me."

Uh-huh. Here it comes.

I have to thank him.

Serves me right for being so dumb.

For walking into his trap like a complete moron.

"Oh yeah? Thanks, but no thanks."

"I meant by accepting my offer of cocoa. Nothing more."

Warren seemed a little offended that she'd read something more into his words.

"Okay," she replied, relenting slightly. "But we'll have to make it snappy. I might be missed." As an afterthought, she added: "Mom's well in with a guy from Mill Valley PD."

"Really? In that case, a quick swig of my special brew and you must be on your way. I'll escort you, if you like. In case you meet up with Harry and Mommy Dearest again."

"Whatever." Deana was intrigued by his easy, light-hearted manner. He sure didn't *look* threatening. She glanced at Sabre, lying, head on paws, under the sink unit. His bright eyes fixed on hers.

Watching every move.

Good one to have on the home team, Deana decided.

The cocoa was great. The best she'd tasted so far.

"What's your recipe?" she asked.

"My secret," he said, and smiled.

"Well, it's tasty, I'll give you that."

He gave a smug smile, looking pompously complacent. Then he winked at her.

"Told you I got awards for it. Anyway, how about you? At high school?"

"Going to Berkeley in the fall."

"Mmmm . . . A little past that stage, myself. Though I confess, I *do* recall it with some affection."

"Oh." She looked at him. He didn't exactly *look* like he was past it.

"What do you do, then?"

"I have a bookstore. In San Anselmo. I put out searches for rare and out-of-print books. Request a book, any book, and I'll get it for you. . . . Eureka."

"Uhhh?"

"Eureka Bookstore. As in striking gold? Remember the old forty-niners?"

"Sure, sure. Got it."

"Neat, huh?" He sounded childishly pleased, explaining the name of his place to her this way.

"Cute," she replied. "Anyway, you look too young to be mixed up with old books."

"I'm twenty-two, if that helps." He smiled brightly.

"Really?"

"Yes, really. Quite ancient, aren't I? As for the bookstore, my parents left me a small sum after they died, and as I've always loved books, I decided to make them my life's work. *Voilà,* I bought myself a bookstore."

"You mentioned your sister. . . ."

"Yes. Sheena. She's out right now. Should be back around five-thirty. Home with the dawn chorus, usually."

"Stays out late, your sister?"

"Mmmm. You could say that. She works at a club. In San Jose. Hangs around in case of trouble."

"That so? She keeps fit, then?"

"Oh, sure. Used to coach for a college baseball team. Gave it up. Too much like hard work, she said."

"Must be quite a gal."

"She sure is."

"Younger than you?"

"No. A little older."

Deana began to feel uneasy. She was thinking about the car she'd seen earlier.

The black *funeral* car.

She shivered.

Okay, it was interesting enough, all this personal stuff, but she really oughta be getting on home now. If it weren't for thinking about that goddamn car, *and* worrying about Mom's knife, she told herself, she could have stayed all night, no problem.

Chatting about whatever came into their heads.

Perhaps even *more* personal stuff.

She had the feeling Warren would make a good listener. Maybe she *should* hang around a little longer. . . .

Except Sheena might object and throw me out.

If I stayed till five-thirty. Which I won't.

"I gotta go."

"Of course," Warren said. He rose and pulled open a drawer by the sink unit.

"Here's your knife." He handed it to her, handle first.

"Oh, and your cap. Sabre found it and brought it to me. You may have to launder it," he added.

Fishing around in a lower cupboard, he picked out the cap and passed it over.

Deana sniffed it, wrinkled her nose, and smiled.

"Get your drift. About laundering it, I mean."

"I'll see you home."

"It's okay. Really—"

"I'd like to see you home," he interrupted, cutting her short. "I'd worry you might meet up with a real live rapist—or worse, Mommy Dearest again."

"Okay. *If* you can keep up with me. I like to run."

"Lead on, MacDuff."

Warren held open the kitchen door for her, then looked back at the dog.

"Sabre. Stay."

"Don't think we'll need his services again tonight," he said, adding, with a wink, "Any rough stuff and we'll deal with it ourselves. Okay?"

"Sure. Let's ride."

They left Sabre glowering from his den under the sink, his eyes accusing them both. Shifting around on his butt, the mutt was obviously dying to follow.

Once outside, Warren grabbed her hand. They set off down the dark driveway, matching stride for stride till they reached the gate.

No sign of the black car.

Thank God.

Out on Del Mar, Deana filled her lungs with the warm night air.

The darkness seemed friendlier somehow, the shadows less threatening than they had been earlier.

Maybe the chat with Warren *and* his yummy cocoa did the trick.

It helped a lot that the car had gone.

Idiot. Probably nothing sinister about it.

Just some kid nosing around. Not really a threat.

She hoped they *didn't* meet up with the skinny hag and her pet pooch.

Sabre should be here, she thought. Any trouble, maybe he'd eat Harry, just for me. . . .

It was good jogging downhill with Warren, their feet slapping the sidewalk.

At least, Warren's feet slapped.

In her thick wool socks, Deana's were quiet and muffled.

And he was right when he'd said he was no stranger to running. Gets plenty of practice too, Deana thought, struggling to keep up with him.

No sign of Mommy Dearest and the faithful Harry.

Probably tucked up in bed and asleep by now.

They ran on till they reached Deana's driveway. She huffed to a halt. Warren, too.

Waiting a moment till their breath evened out, Warren said, "Well, my lady in black—here you are. Safely delivered to your door. Care to come jogging with me again sometime? Or maybe we could do something a little more formal?

"Like the movies.

"Or dinner . . ."

Quaint.

The movies or dinner . . .

Either way, though, Deana thought, feeling a strange new surge of excitement, would suit me fine.

She thought of Allan and immediately felt guilty.

"Yes?"

"Sure," she replied nonchalantly. "I'll let you know. Maybe we'll meet up when I'm out running sometime— then we could arrange a date."

She lifted a hand in salute. Warren stood awhile, watching her run up the driveway.

He turned, walked away, and was soon jogging again. Getting easily into his stride, legs pumping hard, muscles straining to keep up the punishing pace.

Between harsh, measured chugs of breath, an amused smile played on his face.

TWENTY-EIGHT

Sheena left the club early.

Pacey hadn't been any too pleased, but when she told him, "Either I go an' I come back again tomorrow night, or I go an' don't come back at all," he'd shrugged and said, "Family crisis? Sure. We all have one a' those from time ta time. *I* should know, believe me. Okay. Do it, Sheena. But don't make a habit of this. I can't afford for you not to be here."

Damn right he was, too. The other guys working the door at Pacey's Place couldn't handle it the way she could. She was proud of her physique. A powerful five ten, and stacked with it. Because of all those workouts. She gave a tight smile. Her karate was pretty impressive, too.

* * *

Tonight, Sheena had had one of her "insights."

They didn't come often, but when they did, she knew better than to ignore them. They'd been with her for as long as she could remember, but tonight's was the strongest so far.

She was uneasy about Warren.

As she swung her Chrysler coup into Del Mar, the feeling of unrest mounted. She eyed the low black job up ahead. It was easing along like it was looking for someplace. She put her foot down, the engine roared, and she released the pressure slightly. The street was like a goddamn morgue. So *quiet*. Nobody around. But hey, Warren liked it, and it was within easy reach of Eureka. . . .

Sheena cruised up the hill till she saw the two redwoods. Home.

Home? She didn't think so.

The car in front was still doing around twenty-five, thirty. Slightly annoyed, Sheena slowed down. She continued with her train of thought.

Guess I have this monkey on my back—have to keep on the move. She gave a wry smile. No place like home, isn't that what they say? *What* home, I ask myself. . . .

"Hey, buddy. Get a move on, why don't ya?"

She removed a piece of gum from its wrapper and wadded it into her mouth. The fingers of her free hand tapped the wheel impatiently.

Suddenly, the black job revved and disappeared up the street.

Nearly there now.

Sheena's breath quickened.

She felt strangely alert.

Like she was homing in on a target of some kind. She was reading all the signs. Super-aware.

This is *it*.

Her eyes pierced the darkness. Instinctively, she drove past her driveway and stopped in a dark, shadowy place a couple more yards on. While all her senses were taut, oddly *acute*, a part of her brain told her she needed a workout. One of those hard, punishing jobs when all she focused on was the pain of her hurting lungs and straining muscles.

It was a strange yet familiar feeling—more a *compulsion*, really. She always felt this way when she had one of her "insights."

Yeah. I need a workout.
But that'll come later.
After that, sleep.
Same routine every time.

She heard voices.

Peered into her rearview mirror.

It was Warren and some kid. The kid's face showed up ghost-white against her black clothes.

They were jogging out of the driveway. Laughing quietly. Looking into each other's face. Sharing a joke.

Sheena's brows raised a little.

Nice work, bro.
What happened to the "one man and his dog" routine?
The joggers rounded left and set off down Del Mar.

Sweat glistened on Sheena's forehead.

Her hands clenched the wheel.

Something was wrong.

TWENTY-NINE

Deana went to the kitchen in search of coffee. It was eight a.m., just six hours since she'd left Warren's place. All she needed was a mug of hot coffee and maybe, just maybe, she'd crawl back to bed. . . .

The flowers were standing in the sink.

"Wow, Mom. Who sent those? Don't tell me. Your new friend, ta-dah: Detective Mace Harrison!"

"Right the first time, hon," Leigh said, ignoring Deana's last remark. "They're from Mace. Aren't they just beautiful?"

Deana stared at the bunch of flowers. Exotic pink orchids mixed with sprays of white freesias. Still encased in their cellophane wrapper and tied with a pink satin bow.

Some bouquet.

Puzzled, she looked at Leigh.

"I had no idea things had gotten so far. So soon."

Leigh smiled dreamily. "You better believe it, hon. Mace and I are getting along *very* well. He's *so* kind and thoughtful. It's been ages since anyone gave me flowers like these."

Leigh disappeared into the utility room, busying around finding a vase large enough to hold the flowers. Moments later, she reappeared with a tall, elegant one, decorated with a blue and white Chinese design.

Removing the bow and cellophane, she began arranging the blooms to her liking. She hummed a tune to herself.

Deana couldn't remember seeing her this happy—so bright-eyed and her cheeks all flushed like those of a teenager in love.

Warning bells rang.

Mom's got it bad.

Worse than bad, she had this sinking feeling that Mom was more than "getting along very well" with Mace.

Leigh stepped back to admire her display and caught Deana's expression. A worried frown clouded her face.

"Deana, honey. Smile, please. Be happy for me."

"Sure thing, Mom. I'm thrilled for you. Really."

Choked, Deana turned away. She went to her bedroom and closed the door.

So Mace had been here again last night.

Jeez. What an asshole. Bringing flowers, like that. He probably stayed the night.

A thought occurred.

If he *was* here overnight, did he hear me come in this morning?

Count on it.

Mace is a cop. A real pro. And they say cops on a case never sleep. Right?

And from what Mattie said, Mace was pretty much joined at the hip to his job.

Maybe he heard me come in this morning and decided not to tell Mom. Like he's saving the news to blackmail me later. . . .

I should tell Mom about Warren.

Before Mace does . . .

She'd be real worried, knowing about my midnight trysts.

She'd worry herself sick. . . .

God. That's the *last* thing she needs, what with Nelson still on the loose and everything.

After I'd promised I wouldn't leave the house, wander off without her knowing.

I'll *have* to tell her about Warren.

Before Mace gets there first.

She'd never forgive me if that happened.

Her mind in a turmoil, Deana returned to the kitchen.

Leigh was still lingering over the flowers.

Deana cleared her throat.

"Mom. I have something to tell you. You're not going to like it. . . ."

"Oh? What is it, honey?"

Mom looks so radiant. So happy.

I *can't* spoil it for her.

"Mom," she began. Hating herself. Knowing she was about to chicken out of telling the truth. "I'm really happy for you. If this is what you want, I hope it works out for you and Mace."

Christ.

I'm such a *liar.*

A deceitful, scheming bitch lying her way out of a seriously tricky situation.

I *could* say I met Warren accidentally. That might take her mind off Mace for a while.

She pictured what would happen when she told Mom about Warren.

"And where did you meet him, honey? We both agreed you should stay in the house, not go out unless I was with you. . . . Yes, I know it's hard, Deana. . . . Oh. You met him when you were out running. . . ."

A pregnant pause.

Then: "AT NIGHT???"

Yeah.

Can you just imagine it?

Finito. No more midnight runs.

Door key confiscated.

Chained to the bed—till Mace nails Nelson . . .

Yeah. *Great.*

Like sometime, never—that's when Mace'll nail Nelson. Just so he can hang around Mom some more. *If* Nelson's still around to nail, that is.

"Mom. Was Mace here last night?"

"I told you he was, dear."

"Yeah, I know he *visited* last night, Mom. Like late. But when did he *leave?* Did he spend the night here?"

Leigh blushed.

Deana cringed. She hated embarrassing her mom like this.

"Okay, Deana. Yes. He called me after you'd gone to bed. And we talked . . .

"In the end, as we had so much to discuss, I asked him to come on over."

"Mom!"

Her hunch was right, then.

Mace *had* been in the house when she came back from seeing Warren.

Could be they were both awake when I arrived home.

In the early hours.

Two twenty-five, to be precise.

Christ!

So Mace could've heard me come in!

But Mom hadn't?

If she had, she'd have asked me about it first thing this morning.

"Where did he get the flowers from?" Deana demanded, borrowing time, not quite knowing what to say next. "That time of night?"

"Woke up old Fess Winters, the florist on Main Street. Told him he wanted the biggest bunch of the most expensive flowers he'd got. And here they are. Mace is *so* romantic, isn't he?"

Yeah. A pretty impulsive guy.

Bet Old Man Winters thought so, too.

Nice going, Mace.

No wonder Mom looks so dreamy, so starry-eyed this morning.

Orchids for the lady.

I think I'm gonna throw up.

THIRTY

When Leigh left for the restaurant, Deana leafed through the telephone directory for Warren's home number.

She came up with zilch. Ditto the Eureka Bookstore.

Should have asked him for his card.

Would've made things a whole lot easier.

Well, I didn't, did I?

Good thing, too.

I can see it now. . . .

Phone up this guy you hardly know, tell him the detective from Mill Valley PD stayed with Mom last night. Remember, the one I told you about? Yeah, that one.

And he'd say, "Okay? So what business is this of mine? Moms have a right to private lives, too, y'know."

Deana replaced the phone book in its alcove.

Wandering aimlessly into the living room, she stared through the glass wall at the panorama below.

The day spread out before her like an empty, rain-washed sky.

What shall I do?

Read a book?

What book?

How about I ring Eureka and order, say, *Get Shorty* by Elmore Leonard.

The mad adventures of small-time Miami loan shark Chili Palmer, Miss . . . er, sorry, I didn't catch your name?

Yes. That's the one. Please express it over to me.

Oh, and thanks for your trouble, Mr. Hastings.

Or maybe she should watch daytime TV?

Yawn.

A video?

There's always *Reservoir Dogs*.

She'd seen it before. Twice.

Good film, but boring old diamond heists and Harvey Keitel weren't exactly what she was looking for right now.

What about . . .

She rushed to the hallway. Grabbed the phone book and looked up "Hastings."

Dummy!

Warren was new to Del Mar a couple of days ago, so his name wouldn't be listed yet.

Three blocks away. That would probably make it in the three hundred and sixties . . .

And under the name of the last occupant.

She'd *never* work it out that way.

Shit.

Maybe she had enough to occupy her mind, thinking about Mace calling Mom, telling her I was out last night. . . .

Leigh, darling. Did you know your daughter was *out* there on Del Mar, seeing some *guy?*

He'd just love that. . . .

As she went to her bedroom, Deana pictured Warren's kitchen. Cozy. Friendly. Smelling of pot roast . . .

And Sabre, harboring dark thoughts beneath the kitchen sink.

Some dog, that.

Dangerous.

At least he rescued my cap for me.

Cap.

She'd tossed it, and her black sweats, into the hamper. They sure could do with a wash, after all that excitement.

Probably stink like hell.

"That's what I'll do while Mom's out," she decided. "Wash my black things. Get them dried and put away before she sees them."

Deana opened the hamper. Dragged out her sweats.

Her knitted cap fell to the floor.

So did Warren's card.

Showing his business address *and* a scribbled phone number on the reverse.

His home number!

"Eureka!"

Must have put it inside her cap before he handed it to her. When he scrabbled about in the cupboard under the kitchen sink.

Smart guy.

Now what?

Call the number, dummy. Even if he's not home, his sister will be. . . .

A squirm of excitement stirred between her legs.

Maybe this wasn't going to be such a boring day after all.

Do it, Deana. Go for it.

She sat on the bed, dialing out the number on her extension line.

Brrinngg . . . Brrinngg.

"Yeah. The Hastings residence . . ."

The woman's voice was deep, brisk. Businesslike.

For someone who didn't get home till five-thirty a.m., this sure was some together lady. . . .

"Er . . . May I speak with Warren, please?"

"Who's asking." A statement. Not a question.

"A friend. Just say, the midnight runner. He'll know who it is."

At the other end, Sheena gasped. A shiver played up and down her spine.

It was back.

Her premonition.

Deana heard the phone slap down onto a hard surface.

Silence. Then, in the background:

"Hey, bro. Gal here says she's the midnight runner."

Deana blushed.

My God.

Sounds like I'm some kind of weirdo.

Giving out code names over the phone.

Silence.

More conversation in the background. Garbled now. Farther away.

Then Warren's voice, slightly breathless.

"Hi. You just caught me. . . . To what do I owe the pleasure? So soon."

Deana heard the smile behind his words.

She felt foolish, not *quite* knowing why she'd called.

Of course she knew.

She'd called for the hell of it, hadn't she?

No, not that.

What she'd really called Warren for was to talk about Mace.

Come to think of it, what *could* she say about Mace without being a traitor to Mom?

"Hello? Are you there?"

"Sure . . . Hi, Warren," she said weakly. "Sorry to bother you. Tell me I'm a nuisance."

"No, I won't. What is it, my midnight lady? Hey. What's your name, anyway? Can't keep coming over all Shakespearean. It's enough to take the edge off any budding friendship."

"Deana. Deana West."

"Deana. Mmm. Nice name. So . . . Deana. How can I help?"

He sounded calm, sensible. Understanding.

She snuffled, feeling hot tears well up.

"Why don't I come over there? Cheer you up a little?"

"That'd be great, Warren, if you could. What about Eureka? Shouldn't you be there by now?"

"There's nothing spoiling back at the store. A quick call and my trusty assistant will open up. She has a key."

She?

Deana suddenly felt too tired, too exhausted to talk or even *think* anymore. The events of the last few days, never mind Mace being in the house last night, were just about all she could handle at the moment.

"I'd like that, Warren," she said quietly.

"See you in five minutes."

"Oh, Warren?"

"Yes?"

"Don't bring Sabre, will you?"

She pictured him smiling at her.

"Wouldn't dream of it."

THIRTY-ONE

"So Nelson's dead."

Leigh gripped the phone, feeling startled yet vastly relieved. She heard her voice shaking.

What Mace had to say was good, yet bad, news. He chose his words carefully.

"We have a body, Leigh. But it hasn't been officially identified yet. Nelson have any family?"

"None that I know of. Parents died in a fire when Nelson was ten or so, I believe. He never spoke of brothers or sisters. Something of a loner, I gathered."

"We need someone to identify him, Leigh. Feel up to it?"

Oh my God, she thought. *I'm not sure. . . . I need time to think about this.*

Avoiding his question, she asked, "Where'd you find him, Mace?"

"Buncha kids spotted something out on the Headlands. Washed up on the beach. Thought it was a mess of old rags at first. Turns out it was a body. Been in the water five, six days by our reckoning."

Five or six days. What's left to identify?

"Okay," Leigh gave a deep sigh. The last person she wanted to see was Nelson. Especially a *dead* Nelson. "If it has to be done, I'll do it."

" 'Preciate it if you would, Leigh. But I warn you. He's not a pretty sight."

I bet.

"Pick you up in, oh, twenty minutes?"

"Sure."

* * *

Stepping out into the hallway, Leigh went through to Deana's room. She lay in bed, awake. Leigh went over and sat on the bed. Stroking Deana's hair, she said, "Nelson's gone, honey. He won't bother us anymore."

"He's dead?"

"That's right. They found him washed up on a beach over on the Headlands. Must've jumped off the Bridge."

"My *God.*"

"I have to go identify him, honey. Mace's due to pick me up shortly. You be okay?"

"Sure. I don't envy you, Mom. Identifying a corpse. Especially one that's been in the water so long."

"Somebody's got to do it, hon. No one else around who knows him . . . Staff back at the Bayview, maybe; but when all's said and done, as his employer, it's probably down to me."

"Sure. Okay. Oh, Mom . . ."

"Yes?"

"In an *awful* kinda way, everything's turned out for the best, hasn't it?"

"Sure it has, honey. Thank God it's all over now."

THIRTY-TWO

Leigh looked at the lights sweeping down to the Bay, twinkling like stars in the darkness.

She smiled and said softly, "What a wonderful view. Know something, Mace? I'm one lucky gal."

Mace grinned. "Sure you are, Leigh. The luckiest. Fabulous house. Great restaurant. Looks. Style. Smart kid—and me."

Facing her in the tub, he traced swirls through the bubbles on her left breast. Fascinated, he watched her nipple emerge as he teased the foam with his forefinger.

His other hand caressed her thigh.

She lifted her head and took a deep breath. The warm night air was balmy on her wet skin.

She met his eyes and smiled.

Bathing together in the hot tub had been an idea she'd played around with all day.

Well, at least from lunchtime.

After identifying Nelson this morning, hot tubs, not to mention fun and games with Mace, had been a million miles from her mind.

Later, she'd reneged on that.

Why *not* chill out in the redwood tub?

With Mace . . .

Could help to clear my mind of Nelson.

The *remains* of Nelson, she corrected herself.

On the way over to the morgue, Mace told her to think objectively. "It's a corpse we got here," he'd said. "Not a human being. All you gotta do is identify some itty-bitty thing—a signet ring, clothing, anything on the body you recognize as belonging to Nelson."

One look at the gray, sodden, *eaten* face with holes for eyes, the chewed, ragged hands, and she'd gagged, found herself folding to her knees. Mace caught her and held her tight. She leaned into him gratefully.

As she fought back vomit burning her throat, her gaze returned to the sheet-covered body. The chewed stringy arms lay outside the sheet.

She saw a gold ring—Nelson always wore one on the forefinger of his right hand.

Except now it clung perilously to a flimsy gray stump that *used* to be the forefinger of the corpse's right hand. Dumbly, she nodded. As far as she could see, this was Nelson, all right.

Mace took her home and poured out a brandy. He stood by while she drank it down.

* * *

Surprisingly, Leigh wasn't feeling as wrecked as she'd expected. At least seeing Nelson's remains meant she and Deana could put him, and his sick little games, behind them now. Reluctant to leave her alone, Mace asked, "Sure you're gonna be okay?"

"Yeah. No worries," she answered with a brave smile. Seeing his concern, she added, "Really, Mace. I'll be okay."

"You make sure you rest, now. I'll drop by later. Check you out."

As good as his word, Mace arrived after dinner—complete with Dom Perignon champagne.

Deana pouted when she saw him, and stomped off to her room.

Shit.

Screw Mace.

It would have been nice to spend just *one* evening alone with Mom!

She switched on her TV, channel-hopped for a while, then decided on a rerun of *Friday the 13th.*

She'd seen it before.

But tonight, especially tonight, *Friday the 13th* suited her mood precisely.

THIRTY-THREE

Leigh planned the hot tub, intending it to be a nice, relaxing thing for them both to do. And if they moved on to *other* things—then so be it.

She figured either way would be great.

But the end result wasn't working out quite as she'd planned. For one thing, Mace still wore his white T-shirt. *And* his undershorts.

* * *

She reminded herself that it was *she* who'd pulled him into the tub. Fully clothed. And strangely, it seemed like Mace was in no rush to remove them.

Except his jeans. He'd tugged at them, under water, struggled around, then tossed them onto the decking.

She grinned.

Good thing he'd left his leather jacket and gun holster in the living room.

She turned up the bubbles.

Mace was ready to play.

But, suddenly, she wasn't.

What is it with me?

Why don't I want to join in the fun?

Admit it, Leigh. You can't get Nelson out of your mind.

Okay. He's gone. But she *still* couldn't shake off the feeling that she was partly responsible for his death.

She shuddered.

It had been so *horrible*, identifying his body this morning. . . .

Thank *God* that was all over now.

Catching Leigh's faraway look, Mace frowned. Christ, he thought impatiently, is she *still* thinking about Nelson?

Or was something else playing on her mind?

Right now, Mace had something on *his* mind.

And it sure wasn't Nelson.

"Leigh. You know how I feel about you. . . ."

"Don't spoil it, Mace. Let's just enjoy ourselves for now. Save the serious stuff for later, huh? It's been an emotional time all around, and I think we're both feeling the pressure. Let's just relax. . . ."

She slid down into the bubbles till only her head and the tops of her shoulders were visible. She felt Mace's thighs moving in the water, touching hers.

Steam rose and puffed around them. She fought to stay awake, but her eyelids were drooping. As the bubbles massaged her body, her limbs began to feel heavy.

Her eyes closed all the way.

Mace slipped down, too. Tangling his legs with hers. Under the water, his hand reached out . . .

She jerked, went taut, pressing her legs together. Waves swelled up over her chin. She swallowed a couple of mouthfuls, and for a moment her face was submerged.

She swooshed to the surface, shaking her head, running fingers through her wet hair. As she struggled around on the seat, her pale skin gleamed in the darkness.

"Mace," she snapped. "Quit foolin' around!"

"Ssshhh!" Mace put a finger to his lips. "You'll wake Deana. Do that, and she might want to join us!"

"MACE!"

Still feeling on edge, Leigh rose from the tub. The turbulent water swished and swirled around her. The cool air chilled her body. She shivered and folded her arms tight across her breasts.

Mace leaned back, admiring her slick form, glowing in the darkness above him. He whistled softly. She looked like da Vinci's Venus rising from the foam.

"Mmmm. Ms. West. D'you know you have *the* most desirable body? Stay as you are . . . I'll go get my camera."

She gave an abrupt laugh and Mace stood up, water sluicing his body. He stepped out of the tub.

"Hurry," she said tersely. She felt impatient, but managed to smile *and* shudder with cold at the same time.

"Can't wait, huh?"

He held out his arms. She climbed out of the tub, hesitated a moment, then snuggled into them. Clinging together, they shivered a little in the night air.

Murmuring into her smooth wet hair, he said, "Forget the shots, baby. They can wait. Let's go get us a drink."

Pressing into his body, she felt his erection growing,

pushing, probing her pubic hair. She leaned up toward him, her open mouth closing on his.

Slipping her hand inside his wet shorts, she found his shaft and curled her fingers around it. Sliding her hand up and down, she felt him growing stronger all the time. Her mood changed. The yearning *ache* returned.

Taking his hard-on with both hands, she pulled it to her, jabbing it against her opening.

Gasping with longing, she tightened her legs around him, her rim throbbing painfully.

"I want you in me, Mace. In me, *now*. For godsake, *Mace . . .* "

"No," he said, holding her hair, pulling her head back and up to meet his face. "No, my angel. Down here first."

Drawing back, she let go of his erection.

Her heart sank.

Smiling, he lowered his gaze, looking at his shaft, pushing her down till she was on her knees before him. "Some head first, honey," he said huskily. "Just to get things moving."

Disappointment sliced through her like a knife.

She *wanted* him.

In her.

Not this way.

She wanted him to ram *deep*—like he'd done last night.

She grabbed at him, disappointed, impatient. Holding his shaft with both hands. Feeling it jerk in her grasp.

God, she was *desperate*.

She *needed* him.

But if this is what it takes, she thought, then so be it. . . .

She took him in her mouth, sucking, swirling her tongue around his bulk, feeling the ridges, the tight silky skin.

Then gagging as he thrust himself deeper and deeper into her, holding her head hard against him.

She broke away, choking, gasping, looking up at him, her eyes bright, wide with shock.

"Mace," she whispered thickly. "That was *too* much. I nearly choked on you, there."

"You loved it, Leigh. You know you loved it."

"No, Mace. It was *too* much. Just hold me, will you . . ." She broke off, her lips trembling, hot tears falling down her cheeks. His bittersweet *taste* strong in her mouth.

She'd ached for him, *wanted* him inside her. She'd do almost anything, but, Christ, that . . . that hadn't been the most sensitive way of making love tonight.

She choked back a sob. How *could* he treat her like this? After *all* she'd been through today . . .

Shivering, she struggled to her feet, brought up her arms, wrapped them tight around her body. She swayed slightly, still hugging herself.

God. The disappointment. The tension.

It was all *too* much.

She felt cold. Utterly exhausted.

A smile played around Mace's lips. Raising his brows, he held out his arms. "Come to Mace, then. There, there. . . . don't take it so hard. But don't tell me you aren't into a little violence now and then? Thought you were a gal who'd appreciate some rough and tumble—but seems I was wrong. Sorry about that, Leigh."

His eyes glinted in the darkness and the smile, vaguely mocking a moment ago, suddenly softened to one of concern.

Her arms fell to her sides. She relaxed, moved in against him, feeling his warmth, his strong, hard body. . . .

"Come now, honey," he murmured. "How about opening that bottle of champagne I brought us? A coupla drinks and we'll start over. Huh?"

"Sure." She smiled up at him. They walked through the patio door and entered the dark living room. Maybe she *had* been a fool, she told herself. Making a stupid fuss over nothing.

Just that I'm feeling *vulnerable* tonight, is all.

"I'll go get us some towels," she said quietly.

Moving away from him, she turned on the coffee-table lamp and went to the bathroom.

Legs astride, hands on hips, Mace watched her go. Her buttocks swaying, her long shapely legs moving leisurely, one before the other, she looked like a catwalk mannequin.

Hell, he thought, she'd give most movie stars a run for their money.

She had glamor. Something he liked in a woman.

She returned to the living room, wearing a soft bulky robe, the sash tied tight around her waist. Mace thought how young and vulnerable she looked.

Too young to have an eighteen-year-old daughter . . .

She carried a couple of towels under her arm. Tossing one over, she said, "Here, don't want you catching your death. Take off those wet things, too. I'll dry them for you."

He caught the towel. He wrapped it around his waist.

Leigh began rubbing her hair with the second towel.

"*Very* sexy," he murmured, watching her through half-closed eyes as he made for the bathroom.

She quit rubbing and shook her head. Her golden hair fluffed out like a halo. Her legs were shaky. She was still feeling a little awkward about her earlier outburst.

Time to relax, she told herself.

She went to the kitchen and reappeared, moments later, with the champagne in an ice bucket. Ice chinked around as she placed it on the coffee table.

Mace emerged from the bathroom, holding his wet T-shirt and shorts. He wore a white towel robe, one that Leigh's dad used on the rare occasions he and Mom stayed over.

His tanned body showed up in sharp contrast to the white robe. Eyeing him with reluctant admiration, Leigh felt a flicker of excitement. For a long time, their eyes met.

Then, smiling, she dropped her gaze. Took his wet clothes and stepped into the kitchen.

Arranging them in the dryer, she tried to convince herself she could still enjoy the remains of the night.

THIRTY-FOUR

"Let the orgy commence!"

Leigh winced as Mace grabbed the champagne. Catching her expression, he gave a wry smile, tore off the foil top, and twisted up the wire.

The cork flew out with a loud pop.

They giggled, searching around for it on their hands and knees, their earlier tension all but gone.

"Over here," he called. "Under the TV table."

He paused, looking at the photographs placed either side of the TV. Family shots; memorable Kodak moments showing Leigh and Deana laughing into the camera, arms around each other. Two older people—Leigh's parents, he guessed.

And Deana standing alone. In a white bikini. On a seashore . . .

"I want to keep it," Leigh was saying. "Call me old-fashioned, but I think it's kinda romantic to save corks from champagne bottles. Write dates on them, names, that kinda thing. Folks do it all the time in the restaurant. . . ."

"Women!"

He laughed, tossing the cork to her.

"That's what I love about you, Leigh West. You're all woman. Beneath that cool exterior, I swear there's a soft, sensual seductress just crying to be let out."

He poured the fizz into two flutes, already set by the ice bucket. Waited till the bubbles settled before filling up the glasses.

"Here's to . . . to what?" His eyes twinkled. He paused, brows lifted inquiringly.

"To the future, Mace. A future without Nelson."

"To us, Leigh." He looked into her eyes. She flinched slightly at their intensity.

Relax, Leigh, she told herself. *It's party time. Go with the flow. Let it all happen.*

She smiled at him. "To us," she said, chinking her glass against his.

Then:

"Mace . . ."

"Uh-huh?"

"Mace, about what happened back there. I'm sorry."

"You're sorry? My fault, Leigh. Shouldn't have pressured you like that. A guy gets a little carried away sometimes. So let's say no more about it. I'm sorry. Didn't spoil our night, I hope?"

"No, of course not." Leigh gave a hesitant smile, wishing that were true.

It's been too long between men, she reasoned. *I've almost forgotten how it was with them.*

Her mind slipped back.

To Charlie. Her introduction to oral sex. Comparing Mace's macho display with Charlie's tender, boyish passion.

So long ago now.

Christ. Eighteen years, and she still remembered . . .

Her face had been sore for days afterward.

Before that, Larry Bills—her first-ever lover.

Ugghh.

She cringed inwardly, embarrassed at the memory.

After Larry, there'd been Tad Bronski, then Jake Hartmann from high school. Nice guys, both of them. Each respected her—and Jake had been deadly serious about their relationship. That is, until his folks hauled him off to Canada when his dad changed jobs.

Her mind lingered on Charlie again. He'd been a pretty hot lover—*on those two occasions.* . . .

When he'd stopped being so goddamn shy, and scared of his mother.

He'd been kinda *innocent.* A victim, somehow.

You could say that again.

A lamb to the slaughter . . .

Yet, from the first, she'd detected something *different* about Charlie.

A kind of quantity X. Something of the unknown about him.

Something ever so slightly *sinister.*

And, of course, his witch bitch of a mother.

Edith Payne.

Leigh shuddered, not wanting to start that over again.

Yeah. *All* her boyfriends had had their moments.

Except Larry Bills. He was a one-off and didn't count. Boy, was that the *mother* of all mistakes. . . .

And, of course, Ben.

Ben was a pussycat. So kind and thoughtful; he'd never do *anything* to hurt her.

Now there was Mace.

She smiled to herself. Mace was all man.

And, she had to admit, that's what did it for her.

His taut, powerful body. His *attitude.*

And his control.

Always, his tight control.

Me Tarzan. You Jane.

That's Mace, all right.

He'd been an absolute rock for her over Nelson.

Kind. At first, neither suggestive nor sexy. She'd felt safe just having him around the place—and God knows, she'd been grateful for that.

She hadn't exactly rebuffed him, either. She'd *encouraged* him, if anything.

She'd called him the other night. Practically begging him to keep her company in the long dark hours.

No prizes for guessing they'd ended up in bed.

She, tearful; he offering his special brand of comfort. . . .

So what happened tonight?

Where had it all gone wrong?

Mace took her hand in his.

"Hey." He laughed. "Don't go quiet on me, Leigh. I came armed with champagne, hoping to bring a little joy into your life."

He toyed with his glass, swilling around the remains of his drink. Knowing something still bugged her.

"Leigh. I *care* about you. You do know that, don't you?"

"It *had* crossed my mind, Mace. You spending more time here than in your own apartment, an' all!"

"Any objection to that?"

"Mace. You *know* I don't. You're beginning to mean a lot to me, too. I, we, would have been lost without your help, your advice and . . . concern. It's real good to know you're there for us."

"Is *that* all? I'd hoped there was something more . . ."

Her robe slipped off her shoulder. Her mouth opened slightly as she gave him a puzzled smile.

"Of course there's more, Mace. *Much* more. And you know it. It's just that tonight . . ."

Suddenly, he was before her, hunkering down, looking anxiously into her face. "I'd hoped there was, Leigh."

He dropped to his knees, resting his head on her lap. Feeling his warmth against her, she stroked his hair, still damp and tousled from the hot tub.

They stayed this way for a while—quiet, content, just being together.

Then he was sitting on the sofa beside her, she leaning against him, feeling relaxed and a little sleepy.

"Time to go," he whispered, his breath warm against her neck.

"Go? So soon?"

"Time to go to bed. For me to make love to you till . . . sunup, at least. I love you, Leigh West. And tonight, I'm gonna show you just how much. . . ."

Mace left before six next morning, leaving her in bed, drowsy, clinging, not wanting him to go.

"Gotta ride, Leigh. Things to do, places to go."

He kissed her warm, open mouth. It tasted sweet as honey, making him want more.

He lingered over her, kissing her neck, caressing her shoulders. His hands slid down to her breasts, feeling her nipples tense and stiffen. Tracing swirls around them with his forefingers, he tweaked them slightly. She squirmed a little, sighed, and curled into his arms.

Finally, he whispered, "Call ya later, Leigh. 'Bye."

Quietly, he let himself out of the house.

Not wanting to wake Deana.

Dipping into his jacket pocket, he hooked out a palmful of seeds. Flipping them into his mouth, he chewed around them for a while.

His lips curved in a slow smile.

Thinking about Deana sneaking in at two-thirty a.m.

As he munched, his face broke out in a grin.

Suddenly, he didn't give a monkey's shit about waking Deana. He hoped he had. He quite liked the idea of her lying there, listening . . .

Hearing him leave her mother's bed.

THIRTY-FIVE

Leigh was leaving for the restaurant when the phone rang. It was Mattie.

"Hi, Mats. What's up?"

"I'm coming over, Leigh. Be there in five, six minutes?"

"Sure. See ya."

What did Mattie want so early? I know she's supposed to be our personal bodyguard—but hasn't she *heard* that Nelson's dead?

Mattie had sounded subdued. Upset, even. Leigh frowned. What on earth was wrong?

Was it anything to do with *her?*

Perhaps Mattie needed a shoulder to cry on.

Leigh didn't have to wait long to find out.

"Coffee?"

"Sure. As it comes. The blacker the better."

Leigh set two mugs on the kitchen table. More informal here than in the living room, she decided. If Mattie had something on her mind, she'd probably prefer to discuss it in the intimacy of the kitchen.

Leigh poured coffee, passed Mattie hers, and sat facing her over the table.

Leigh added cream to her own coffee while Mattie worked around the real reason for her visit. For a while, she stirred her coffee, concentrating on the swirling black liquid.

"Not keeping you, am I?" she asked, glancing up.

"Not a bit of it. The gang's all there, back at the Bayview. Beavering away, I hope." Leigh smiled at her.

Mattie said, "Heard the news about Nelson. So you identified him?"

Leigh sighed and nodded. "Yeah. All of that. Not a pleasant experience, I might say."

"Yeah. I seen bodies that've been in the water for a while. Good thing you even *recognized* Nelson. Fish tend to mess things up."

Leigh shuddered. "Don't, Mattie. It was bad enough as it was. . . ."

"Mace told you about Nelson?"

"Yes, he did. He's been very supportive."

"I'll bet."

Leigh started at the cynicism in Mattie's tone.

"Meaning?"

"Meaning that Mace can be a *very* supportive person."

Leigh didn't care for the way she said that.

"You got something on your mind, Mattie? If you have, spit it out. I'm all ears."

Mattie hesitated for a moment, then said, "Lemme tell you a story, Leigh."

"Go on."

Mattie paused again, deciding where to begin.

"Five years ago, when I first came to Mill Valley PD, I was a raw, hurt young girl. Naive, if you like. From a li'l hick town near Lodgepole, Sequoia country . . .

"I'd met up with some guy there who *did* things to gals. To get his wicked way."

She huffed out a short, cynical laugh.

Then, with a meaningful look at Leigh, she said, "Know what I'm sayin'? On the other hand, Leigh, maybe you wouldn't *wanna* know what I'm sayin'. Even if you *did,* I'm not about to tell ya what that guy got up to.

"This I *will* say. What happened back in that small hick town made me want to get out there, smoke out all the pervs, the rapists—the *psychos* lurking in every goddamn corner of this big, beautiful country of ours . . . and give 'em hell. Or at least what the fuck they deserved—as far as the law allowed, that is.

"I joined Mill Valley Police Department. Became a crack

shot, did martial arts. One of the guys, they called me.

"Met Mace. Worked with him. He 'peared to be an okay guy, all right. Looked after me. Gave me back my confidence in human nature, I guess. Rounded me off." Her mouth curved in a mirthless grin. "I was a pretty messed-up gal in those days. . . ."

Leigh frowned. "Mattie. I'm sorry. Really sorry. You must have been badly hurt. . . . But what has this . . ."

"Got to do with Mace?"

"Right."

"Well, I'll tell ya, Leigh. I got to know Mace pretty well, bein' his partner an' all. He was my alter ego. My *shadow*. Christ. We didn't even have to *speak* to know what we were both thinking." Suddenly concerned, Mattie glanced across at Leigh, hoping she hadn't come off too strong. Dropping her voice, she looked away. "Yeah. We were that close."

Leigh sipped her coffee without even tasting it.

What *had* Mattie come to say?

Something about Mace?

If it was, she had a sinking feeling she didn't want to hear it.

"I know you're seeing a lot of Mace. And I don't blame you. Or him. You're a wonderful lady, Leigh. Money. Nice home. Great restaurant. A daughter who's a credit to you . . ."

"And?"

"You don't know Mace like I do, Leigh."

"Cut the bullshit, Mattie. Let's just get to where you're at."

"I mean, Leigh, the guy back there in Yellow Bend ain't the only one who likes to hear a gal scream."

Mattie finished her coffee. She left soon after delivering her parting shot, leaving Leigh to interpret the conversation as best she could.

Mattie'd spilled the beans, all right, Leigh thought. Leaving me with *plenty* to think about. Jesus. Most of what she'd said was beginning to make a lot of sense.

Carefully, Leigh picked through Mattie's words, going over her sketchy innuendos. And, she didn't mind admitting, it hurt like hell. For chrissake, Mattie couldn't mean Mace was a *psycho?* Could she?

Shuddering, Leigh dismissed the thought.

Sure. Mace had a macho streak.

Most men have, she told herself.

But he isn't a *sadist*, as Mattie implied. Mace was kind, civilized, and . . . normal.

Wasn't he?

Sure he was. Look how he brought me flowers, champagne. Was always around to protect us from Nelson.

But, she told herself, *I* was the one who encouraged him. He didn't jump me.

I was the seducer; he, the seduced. . . .

Leigh hesitated. She held her breath, last night's little drama fixed firmly in her mind.

Some head, first, honey. Just to get things moving . . .

A cold shudder ran through her body.

A lot of guys like their head, she reasoned.

It's all part of the foreplay.

But she'd reacted in such a goddamn *crazy* way. Like a dumb kid crying "rape."

On the other hand, if what Mattie implied was true, that whole darn episode could be a taste of things to come. . . .

THIRTY-SIX

"Hi, Mom. Thought I heard voices."

"That's right, honey. Mattie dropped by. To see how we're doin'. Just checking." She gave Deana a bright smile. "Want some coffee? It's still hot. Or will be, once I've perked it up a little."

Leigh switched on the percolator. Still thinking about Mattie. What *was* it with her? She fancy Mace herself, or something?

Way she went on, she all but hated him.

I've heard there's a fine line between love and hate.

Could be she's just plain jealous. . . .

"Hey, Mom. The coffee's perked. Pour mine while I get dressed, will you?"

"What did your last one die of, young lady?"

"The usual. Lack of breath, I guess." Deana left the room, smiling. Mom was the best. Always so cool and nice about everything.

She felt a stab of guilt.

She didn't *like* having secrets from Mom. It felt like betraying a friend.

Slipping into blue jeans and a yellow T-shirt, Deana decided the time was ripe to introduce Mom to Warren.

She'd like him. He was so sensible and grown up.

And he had his own business.

That ought to impress her.

Deana returned to the kitchen, her ponytail swinging jauntily. Mom was at the sink, rinsing out the two used coffee mugs. Deana picked up hers from the table.

Wisps of aromatic steam met her nostrils.

She felt better already.

I gotta tell Mom about Warren.

How shall I play it?

Dummy. Why not tell it like it is?

Just go for it, Deana.

"Mom."

"Yes, dear?"

"There's someone I'd like you to meet. Guy called Warren Hastings. Lives on Del Mar with his sister. And his dog, Sabre."

Leighed perked up. She turned to face Deana.

Deana had met someone so soon?

"And how did you meet this . . . Warren, honey?"

Deana grimaced slightly. The next bit wasn't gonna be *quite* so simple.

"He owns a bookstore, Mom. In San Anselmo."

Yeah. San Anselmo. Where Allan and I were supposed to have gone to the movies that night.

"I ordered a book by phone one day . . ."

She cringed.

More lies. My *God.* I can't believe I'm doing this. What *am* I—the original daughter from hell?

"But how romantic, honey. You should have told me. And is he *nice,* this Warren?"

"Yes, he's real nice, Mom. You'd like him."

"So when do I get to meet . . . Warren?"

"I'll give him a call today. We can arrange something."

"Dinner would be fine. Just let me know. I'll get something sent over from the restaurant."

Leigh's mind slid back to the night Deana brought Allan to dinner. When he'd met Mom and Dad—was it only *ten* days ago?

My God.

What can *happen* in ten days!

Your world turned upside down; a boy dead; your daughter devastated by it all.

Although she *appears* to be getting over it . . .

And Nelson . . . Thank *God* Mom and Dad hadn't been around to see it all happen.

She hated herself for even thinking this way, but it was a blessing Mom and Dad made that emergency dash to Colorado. And if it didn't seem so *awful* on Aunt Abby, she hoped Mom and Dad would stay there a while longer. . . .

Deana smiled at Leigh.

"Good thing Gran and Pops are in Boulder. They would've made things ten times worse. Pops shouting, Gran crying and everything . . . Missed out on the barbecue, though."

"What *are* you, young woman, a mind reader? I was just thinking the same thing. But never mind the barbecue, Gran and Pops *had* to go to Aunt Abby. She was seriously ill."

Their eyes met, and Leigh smiled. "Got to agree, honey. They been here, Mom and Dad could've made things a whole lot worse!"

"You gonna tell them about Allan and Nelson and everything?"

"Uh-huh. But not for a while, honey. Just let's see how things go."

THIRTY-SEVEN

It was dark on Del Mar tonight. Really dark.

A gentle wind disturbed the trees.

Scudding clouds hid the moon and stars from view.

Apart from the rustling leaves, it was quiet, too.

Deathly quiet.

Only Deana's breath sounded harsh and loud as she hurried toward Warren's house.

She hadn't called him, as she'd told Mom she would. Instead, she'd decided to slip out again. Meet up with Warren as he walked Sabre.

I'm the midnight runner again.

A thrill of excitement brought goose bumps to her skin. The hair on the back of her neck rose and prickled.

It was scary out here on the street.

In the dead of night.

It may be scary, but the thrill of running alone through the night was worth every second.

Anyway, with Nelson gone, there wasn't too much to be scared of.

Except Mommy Dearest and her dog.

Maybe a rapist or two.

And the black car.

Don't forget the black car . . .

But she was a fast runner.

She could hide in shadows, dart down alleyways, or tackle anyone who looked like they were going to attack her.

Mom still didn't know about her midnight runs.

Warren did, though.

And Mace.

Fuck Mace.

Somehow, though, she didn't think he'd inform on her. He'd keep it all to himself.

It was their little secret.

She shuddered.

She *hated* keeping things from Mom.

And she *loathed* the idea of being in league with Mace. The mere thought of it made her flesh crawl.

Anyway, she had too many midnight runs under her belt to start explaining things to Mom now.

Besides, I get a real kick out of it . . .

Could be I'm *addicted* to midnight running.

Can a person become addicted to running at night?

I guess so . . .

Nearly there now. I can see the two redwoods, their branches reaching out onto the street.

Where's Warren?

Not here yet.

Deana felt a twinge of disappointment. It had been *so* romantic, thinking they'd meet up again this way.

And he'd be really surprised, and pleased, that she'd shown up again.

Tonight, when she saw him, she intended to invite him to dinner. She felt a squirm of excitement at the prospect of him coming to her home. Again.

This time, she wanted to show off a little.

'Cause Mom really knows how to throw a dinner party.

She'd look elegant, chatting to Warren. Charming him, but not *too* much, with her intelligent conversation.

She knows about books, too. . . .

Deana ran on, her mind turning to her wardrobe. Mentally going through all of her clothes, deciding what she'd wear the night of the party.

A really big decision.

Maybe her new black dress with the low square neck? She knew it showed off her breasts and her small waist to perfection.

Well, maybe not *that* yet. Don't want to scare him off.

Black's way too formal, anyway. Because we'll go somewhere *after* the meal.

Don't bank on it, Deana.

Mom'd be suspicious. A new boyfriend *and* bunking off together already.

Like I did with Allan. The night Gran and Pops came to dinner . . .

Allan.

Deana West, you are a *shit*.

Allan dead only ten, eleven days and you're out on some midnight tryst? Meeting up with a guy you've seen only three times before . . . And don't forget. He already came to the house the other day. . . .

Mom doesn't know about that. She'd be real upset to know I've had Warren over and not told her about it. Not that anything *happened*. Didn't get to discuss Mace, like I'd planned. We just talked about books and everything. Warren told me about his store, and promised to get me a copy of *Get Shorty* by Elmore Leonard.

And now you're drooling on about going out with him *after* the wonderful dinner Mom is gonna put on—specially for the benefit of her darling daughter.

The darling daughter who *lies* through her teeth.

What a *bitch* I am. . . . Soon as I introduce Warren to Mom, there'll be no more lies. Promise.

THIRTY-EIGHT

Christ, it's even darker up here.

Deana sped up.

The wind had gotten worse. It shook the trees, whipping the leaves around in a frenzy.

Deana shivered but kept up her pace.

It was a night when almost *anything* could happen.

She ran on, her mind full of Warren. Picturing his face when she invited him to dinner. Hoping he'd say yes—after all, he *did* say he'd like a date.

Dinner or the movies, he'd said.

Remember?

How could I forget!

What a hoot, she'd thought at the time.

But, admit it, Deana. You were secretly thrilled at the idea of going out with Warren.

Sure. He *is* kinda sexy, and a date could be a lotta fun. Then Mom suggested dinner. . . .

So here she was, running up Del Mar.

Risking God knows what . . .

Her heart skipped a beat. She began thinking of the funeral car and how spooky it had looked, crawling along outside Warren's house, its windows all black and shiny. . . .

She gave a grim smile.

Probably just some jerk, cruising around . . .

She ran on.

Then, mixed in with the keening wind, she caught a faint whimper. Like a small animal was lost or something.

A hand clawed at her ankle.

Her mouth went dry.

She gasped.

Her knees sagged and she fell—onto a lumpy kind of hump.

The hand slid away.

"Who . . . What the hell . . . !"

Shit. She'd landed on a sack of household garbage.

"Goddamn stupid thing to do put your garbage out on the sidewalk," she muttered.

"Git offa me . . ."

Deana started at the weak, whiny voice.

She scrambled to her feet.

"My *God!* . . . Oh, it's you!"

Mommy Dearest.

Lying in a heap on the sidewalk.

Clutching Harry, wrapped in a blanket.

The blanket fell open and Harry rolled out, his legs in the air. His eyes jerked around. His mouth hung open, his small red tongue panting against needle-fine teeth.

Harry was in a bad way.

"Help us, please!" Mommy Dearest pleaded. "Had one a' my derned attacks agin."

The hag shook her head, her wispy hair floating in the wind. She looked a little confused.

"Should never'a come out t'night," she muttered.

"Here, let me help," Deana told her. "Lean on my arm, I'll take you home. Where d'you live?"

"Back there a ways, dear," the hag gestured behind her, somewhere up the steep hill.

"Well, hold on to me." Deana helped Mommy Dearest to her feet. "How about Harry? He looks sick, too. Want me to hold him, too?"

"Don't y'let him fall, now, will ya?"

"Course not."

The hag clung to Deana's arm. Deana held Harry tight, rolled in his blanket. Leaning into the wind, they made it up the hill a little way. The hag drew to a halt outside a fancy iron double gate.

Deana stared through the railings.

The driveway was pitch dark.

A cold shiver ran down her spine.

Could be *anything* down there . . .

Mommy Dearest lifted the latch, the gate creaked open, and Deana helped her inside. The hag kicked the gate shut with a resounding clash.

Deana did a double take.

That sure was some kick! Mommy Dearest musta perked up a little.

Still clutching Deana's arm, the hag limped her way down the drive. Deana held on to Harry. He was jerking around in his blanket, making loud, snuffling noises.

Her heart hammered. Blood pounded in her ears.

Hope to God he doesn't die on me, 'cause I really gotta go—don't wanna miss Warren. . . .

They halted outside a huge front door. Dry, straggly growth matted around the two columns either side.

"Jeez," Deana breathed. "What a *place!*"

The house was tall, dark, and deathly quiet. It looked like something out of a horror movie. She pictured Lurch, from *The Addams Family*, opening up the door . . . and Gomez hovering in the spooky hallway, grinning around his cigar, rubbing his hands together.

She squinted at a faded wood sign above the door.

She could just make out the words: "The Flora Dawes Rest Home for Distressed Gentlefolk."

Deana grimaced.

This is so spooky.

Time I was gone.

Her heart beat faster.

Gotta catch up with Warren, before it's too late.

Desperately, she wished he and Sabre were with her now.

At her side, Mommy Dearest let out a gasp. She was clutching her chest.

Deana's heart sank.

"Maybe I should just see you inside," she said quickly. "Then hurry on home. Promised Mom I'd be back by ten-thirty . . ."

With a loud groan, the door swung open. Mommy's hand gripped Deana's arm. She dragged her forward into the shadowy hallway.

Gray light sliced the gloom. Darkness fell as the door clanged shut. The noise echoed eerily through the house, and Deana's heart stood still. Panic set in. A closed, musty smell met her nostrils. She'd smelled something like it in a thrift store in Sausalito—a mix of old clothes, cooking, bodies, musty books, and other junk.

As she became accustomed to the gloom, Deana saw dozens of bright eyes staring at her. It seemed like an army of dwarfs had gathered in the lobby to greet them. The dwarfs were curious. Impatient, craning their necks to get a better view.

Jesus H. Christ!

She held on to Harry and stared closer.

These aren't dwarfs . . . they're little old women!

Like one of the living dead, a wizened hag stepped forward. She reached out a scrawny, blue-veined hand. . . .

Deana reeled back. Into the arms of Mommy Dearest.

No sign of "one of her derned attacks" now . . .

Like bands of steel, Mommy's arms grabbed her.

Harry yelped, leapt out of his blanket, and scooted into the shadows.

Struggling, panicking, Deana twisted around, trying to free herself. The hag held on tight.

"No you don't!" Her voice was high and strong.

It had an insane ring to it.

The hairs on the back of Deana's neck crawled.

Goose bumps rose on her body.

My God, the woman's a fucking lunatic. She's raving mad!

Christ! How did I get into all this? I shoulda left her to

*die out there. . . . Hell, I do one good turn and look where
it gets me!*

A horrible thought crossed her mind.

Nobody knows I'm here.

I'm trapped with all these . . . loonies!

"Say something, girl!" demanded a witch with an eye
patch and long white hair. Deana backed away.

Mommy Dearest shoved her forward.

"Best I could do," she told the hags. "Not too many
young 'uns out on Del Mar t'night!"

"What d'ya think of Mr. President?" called out a shaky
voice from the back. "Ya reckon he's onto them delin-
quents throwing bombs inta classrooms yet?"

A raucous voice shouted: "Whassyername, honey?"

"Aw, give it a rest, Clarabel," somebody said. "Can't ya
see the kid's scared? Reckon we oughta bring her inter the
back, give her a cuppa coffee 'n' a slice of pie . . ."

A low mumbling filled the hallway, punctuated by hissy,
whispering sounds. A shriek of laughter rang out.

The hags looked at Deana, waiting for her to speak.
They were like gaunt gray vultures. Restless. Needy. Hungry, like they hadn't seen young flesh in a long time.

Deana froze at the thought.

*They came for me in a pack. I guess they could tear me
to pieces.*

Oh my God!

Her eyes narrowed. She gritted her teeth.

Just let them try!

The hags shifted forward.

The white-haired one taunted her.

"Don't ya like it here, dearie? Ain't fixin' to leave us,
are ya?"

Deana saw red. She screamed, "Bank on it, you fuckin'
old witch. I'm outa here . . ."

She whirled around, but Mommy Dearest grabbed her
arm. "Mind ya manners, young'un," she snarled, "Pay
more respect to ya elders!"

Deana shook herself free. She glared at the hag.

What's the bitch got against me? I did my Girl Scout thing. Helped her when she was in trouble.

I coulda left her there to die.

Wish I had now . . .

Boy, does this place suck. . . .

If the bastard's brought me here to entertain her gang of trolls, she's gonna be mighty disappointed. Show's over, folks. I'm outa here before I get eaten alive!

A scrawny hag in a long, cotton frock limped forward. Stretching out a knobby finger, she touched Deana's arm. "Don't go, dearie," she said. "Talk to us. We won't hurt ya none. Promise. We jest wanna see some young blood, is all. Haven't set eyes on a youngster like you in a long, long time. . . . Tell me . . . seen any good movies lately?"

The old woman's eyes held a pleading look. She smiled, her face creasing into a network of wrinkles.

Deana gasped.

My God, I gotta get outa here!

She turned, made for the door, but with viselike fingers Mommy grabbed her again.

She was *incredibly* strong.

A hag at the back of the crowd elbowed her way to the front. She stroked Deana's free arm, then plucked at her sweatshirt sleeve.

"Nice top you got there, young'un. Hey, Martha. Come an' take a peek at this sweater. Sure ain't Neiman Marcus, but it's better'n the one you're wearin'!"

Martha toddled over, her head shaking with every step. "Why, yes," she said in a trembly voice. "You're right there, Betty-Lou. Think I'll have me this one. Jest my color, too."

Betty-Lou shrieked with laughter. "Black? You aimin' to wear it to ya funeral, Martha?"

Deana gasped. They'd take my *sweater?*

The *bastards*.

And there'd been a moment back there when I felt *sorry* for them!

Betty-Lou snatched at her sleeve.

She tore it down.

Exposing Deana's bare shoulder.

Mommy Dearest hung on to her other arm.

There were whistles. Hoots of laughter. Hands tugged at the flapping black cloth. Deana's left breast suddenly burst free.

She panicked, tearing herself away from Mommy's iron grip. "Lemme GO!" she yelled. "HELP!!!"

"Whassamatter, dearie? Don't ya *like* it here?"

The hags hadn't enjoyed themselves so much in ages. Betty-Lou couldn't stop cackling.

"Remember that time in Vegas, Martha? The night the lights went out at The Sands . . ."

Tearing herself free, kicking, shoving, knocking Mommy out of the way, Deana charged for the door.

With a triumphant yelp, she reached it, flung it open, and raced out into the night.

"Y'ain't bein' very friendly," Mommy Dearest croaked after her. "Gals here only want a li'l ol' chat. They get lonesome sometimes. . . ."

"Hey. You like Tyrone Power?" yelled the raucous one. Her voice got carried away on the wind. Deana caught the words "He's my favorite y'know. Did ya see *The Mark of Zorro*? Well, did ya?"

"Dear *God*," Deana muttered as she ran. "What a *madhouse*. They plan to eat me alive, or talk me to death— they'll have to catch me first!"

Way behind, she heard the inmates pile out of the house. They sounded bewildered. Confused. Gabbling to each other in high, tetchy voices. Going quiet as they hit the cool night air . . .

* * *

Deana didn't stop till she was outside the gates. Only then did she draw to a halt, panting hard, trying to steady her breath.

Wow. I'm outa there.

Goddamn bitch!

Luring me in . . .

She grimaced.

Resident fuckin' entertainer at the Zimmer City Rest Home?

Oh yeah?

Eat shit and die, you crazy old bitch!

Deana started to run uphill.

Toward Warren's house.

THIRTY-NINE

A low growl brought her skidding to a halt.

Her heart lurched.

Sabre.

And Warren, holding Sabre's lead, being yanked along as the dog rushed forward to greet her.

"Why, if it's not the midnight runner! Good to see you, Deana."

"Great to see you, too, Warren. And Sabre—how ya doin', big boy?" She smoothed Sabre's forehead. He got excited, danced back, then bounded forward, nudging his wet nose into her hand.

"Sure looks like he's glad to see you again."

"Yeah."

His eyes were curious.

He looked at her torn sweater, at the left side of her bra gleaming white in the lamplight.

She seemed awfully upset.

He took off his fraternity warm-up and draped it around her shoulders.

"What *happened* to you back there?"

Deana gave a cracked sort of laugh. *"Happened?* Tell you what happened, Warren. Nearly finished up as entertainer of the year, that's what happened."

He frowned, wanting to know more but not asking.

Laughing shakily, she held on to his arm.

"Remind me to tell you about it sometime."

He guided her to his place, his arm around her waist. She liked the way it felt. His arms around her. His jacket around her. Making her feel warm and safe.

Most of all, *safe.*

Sabre trotted by Warren's side, eyes eager and bright, his ears held high.

Guess he *is* glad to see me, she thought. Could have done with him when I visited the old folks' home. He'd have come in real handy. . . .

"Anyway, Warren," she said, quietly, pushing the vision of distressed gentlefolk out of her mind. "Are *you* glad to see me?"

He stared at her quizzically, a broad smile spreading across his features. "Yes," he said simply. "I'm very glad to see you again."

"Came to ask if you'd like to have dinner with Mom and me sometime." Adding, "Mom would really like to meet you."

"Think I'd pass the grade?"

"What's up, Warren? Running scared? You *did* say you'd like to see me again. And I said I might be out one night and that we could arrange something?"

He scratched his head. "Yep. I believe I do recall something along those lines. . . ."

"Warren—are you coming to dinner at my house, or what?"

"It'll be my pleasure, Deana. But why not use the

phone? Would've been easier than running up here in the dark . . . getting . . ."

Mauled by Mommy Dearest's buncha geriatric weirdos? You're not kidding. . . .

" 'Cause I like running. Especially at night. Developed quite a taste for it, as it happens."

"Deana. Does your mom know you're out?"

"Get to the point, why don't you, Warren? Matter of fact, she doesn't. It's just that it seems so *exciting* for us to meet in secret like this."

"Mmmm," he said, his eyes twinkling. "Guess I feel a hot chocolate coming on. How 'bout you?"

"You bet," she said, and smiled.

FORTY

Sitting in Warren's kitchen, nursing a mug of his yummy chocolate drink, Deana relaxed. It felt good to be here in Warren's home—especially in his friendly, slightly untidy kitchen.

Sabre retired to his den under the sink. He lay there, checking out Deana's movements. Then, snuffling into his paws awhile, he closed his eyes.

But his ears stayed alert.

Like sentinels on guard.

Good old Sabre. Some dog, that. She smiled.

Then frowned slightly.

If only I knew what to tell Warren.

How *much* to tell him.

Or how *little*.

And not only about tonight, either.

She thought about Mace.

Warren deserves to be put in the picture.

What picture?

Dammit. There's so *much* to say. . . .

Oh God. If only things weren't so *complicated*.

"Anybody home?" Warren watched her, his brows raised.

"Sure. Can you keep a secret?"

"Try me."

"Well, you're right, Warren. Mom doesn't know I'm out tonight. She doesn't know about the other nights, either. Jesus. She'd go hairless if she *did* know."

It was a start, anyway. . . .

"I see. Go on."

"Something happened to us. To Mom and me. About ten days ago. I can't explain it yet. But trust me it's been a horrible experience. People died. Violently. It's been bad, Warren."

He hugged his chocolate, stared into its creamy depths. Giving her time to choose her words.

"Mom's been concerned for my safety—and I for hers, come to that. We've both been in danger." Deana stopped, then carried on, more cheerfully this time. "But in the end, it turned out okay. Thing is, I don't want Mom worried about me going out at night. She's been through such a lot.

"I told her I met you when I phoned your store for a book."

Warren looked up sharply.

Deana smiled.

"*Get Shorty* by Elmore Leonard. Is modern gangster stuff something you stock?" He nodded. She went on. "So, Warren, I'd be really grateful if you'd keep our . . . nighttime assignations to yourself. Oh, also your visit to the house."

"I see. Had an idea there was more. I have a nose for mysteries." He tapped the side of his nose with a forefinger. "*Murder She Wrote* was a favorite show of mine.

"Okay," he continued, choosing his words carefully. "I'll go along with that. But let me tell you here and now, I don't like unsolved mysteries. And I don't go for subterfuge, either. Especially where Mom and daughter are concerned. So maybe, least said, soonest mended, huh? Give you time to sort things out with Mom."

Deana nodded. For a moment there, she'd been about to confide in him.

Give him the *works*.

Tell him her feelings about Mace.

But now was *not* the time to mention Mace.

Later. Maybe.

Pity.

She'd have dearly liked to discuss him with Warren.

But maybe later. *Much* later.

Get too heavy and Warren might cry off.

"So." Warren smiled at her encouragingly. "I'm invited to dinner, am I?"

"Sure are."

"Best bib and tucker?"

"Mmmm . . . Not necessarily. Smart casual, I think. Mom's kinda casual herself."

"Ah."

"So how about evening after tomorrow? You doing anything that night?"

"Er . . . Let me see." Warren took his time. Humming a little. Studying the ceiling, as if checking out the evening after tomorrow. He looked at his wristwatch. It showed 12:14.

"Let's get this straight. It's already tomorrow, so does that make our date tomorrow evening or the one after that?"

They burst out laughing. Deana felt relieved. She'd been feeling quite tense, talking about the stuff she and mom had gone through these last few days.

She was glad to relax a little.

"Tell you what, Deana. Ask your mom which night is okay, and give me a call—at the store or at home. Phone's on answer when we're out at work."

"Okay. I'll do that." She felt good and warm inside. Things were so *easy* with Warren.

"Anything else I should know? Subjects to avoid—current political situation, weather in Florida, stuff like that?" He threw her a warm smile. Then, turning serious, he added, "Given that you've both gone through a sensitive time just lately."

His gaze held hers. It was as if he were telling her not to worry. Things would turn out okay. That he'd be there for her.

"Nope. Just talk books. Sports, like swimming and tennis, Mom loves those. And movies—seventies stuff. Oh, and food. Compliment her on the food."

"Your mom likes to cook?"

"Sort of. She owns the Bayview Restaurant in Tiburon."

FORTY-ONE

Sheena studied the redwoods out back.

Not really seeing them, because her mind was elsewhere. She'd gone way back; saw her ten-year-old self in class. Big for her age, awkward, alone. Writing wasn't her strong point, but here she was, struggling with an essay on the life of a fuckin' sperm whale. She looked at her spidery joined-up writing, all blotchy with ink.

Then, behind her, the fuckin' teacher said in that cold, icy voice of hers, "Sheena Hastings. I do declare, the standard of your work gets worse. See me after class!"

All eyes turned toward her. Mary Jo Hassler sitting in the row behind, sniggered. Titters rose in waves from the rest of the class.

Her head jerked back.

Mary Jo. Tugging at her long dark braids.

* * *

She remembered how her eyes had watered up, how *ashamed* she'd felt. . . . She'd never been much good at writing.

Christ. She'd *hated* her childhood. And school most of all. Who fuckin' said schooldays were the happiest days of your life?

Whatever goddamn motherfucker it was, they wanted to come up with one more thing like that and then go blow their fuckin' brains out.

But all of that was a long time ago. Those lousy schooldays; her lousy *childhood*. Only thing kept her going was beating the hell outa them kids on the sports field. Yeah. She was the greatest at sports in those days.

THE BEST.

Was then, is now.

Pumping iron in the gym, judo, karate, kickboxing, you name it. She'd done it all—and better than most men, too. She knew all about the pain barrier. Going through it, stretching her muscles to the max. Almost passing out. She'd been there. Done that.

And when she figured her body could take no more—there were plenty of other ways to feel pain.

Oh yeah, *other ways*.

Sheena's lips curved in a triumphant smile.

In the early days, only one other person understood her. *Really* knew what made her tick.

Kat Tod, her partner.

Kat knew about pain; she'd had a cartload of it herself. Bad childhood. Bad marriage at thirteen years of age.

All of them, *painful* experiences.

Kat had gotten herself killed last October. Memory of it still hurt Sheena. It'd had been a bad business. S & M, the cops called it. Okay. That's what *they* called it. But she knew Kat was following her own path of redemption.

Redemption?

Self-destruction, more like.

Yeah.

Ended up a mess a' bloody ribbons in some shitty back alley . . .

Jesus. What a gal. She'd gotten mixed up with a real bad crowd. Rented herself out. An' paid for it in full that one last time. . . .

Sheena turned away from the window. Contemplating her "insight." Her gift for premonition, whatever. She hated it, yet loved it, all at the same time.

It was *part* of her.

What she *was*.

Love it or loathe it, that gift was an important part of Sheena Hastings. Life as a kid hadn't been a whole lotta fun, but she sure knew that her special talent—and her sporting prowess—set her way above the rest.

In the bad times, she held on to this.

Mom and Dad had tut-tutted her claims that she "knew about things before they happened." They'd chastised her. Called in the local priest. Encouraged her interest in sports.

Finally, there'd been the psychiatrist.

He'd prescribed Prozac. Why the hell *Prozac*, for godsake? She was happy the way she was. Only person who understood that was Warren. They trained together. They talked together. She was a few years older, but she hung around with him most of the time.

Warren *understood* her. Like now. He *knew* she was happy at Pacey's Place. Among her own kind. Problem people. Misfits. Weirdos. They got together, understood each other. No questions asked.

Now there was this "midnight runner." Who in hell was she? Whomever, whatever, she turned out to be, she was involved with Warren.

Without knowing why, but trusting her instincts, Sheena felt a squirm of apprehension.

FORTY-TWO

It was Thursday evening. Night of the get-together with Mom and Warren.

Mom wasn't home yet.

Warren wasn't due for a couple of hours.

In her bedroom, Deana stripped to her bra and panties.

"Hope everything works out okay," she murmured to herself. "Shouldn't be a problem. Two nice people. Civilized guys who know the score. They'll get along fine."

She peered into the dresser mirror. Inspecting herself. Practicing how she'd look. A dry run for later.

She went over to her bed. Laid out were two outfits— her final *final* selection. A maroon cotton pantsuit, and a blue jersey crossover blouse and short denim skirt.

Smart casual, she'd told Warren.

No way was the black dress an option. Far too formal for a muggy evening.

It's gotta be the crossover blouse and denim skirt, she decided. The blouse would be great, if . . .

If what?

If Warren wanted a closer inspection?

She hugged herself.

I know he likes me.

She could tell by the way his eyes swept over her in an approving, but not suggestive, way. Maybe he'd guessed she wasn't interested in sex at the moment. Understood it was too soon. . . .

Her relationship with Warren would grow, gradually and at her own pace, she decided.

She swung around. Looked into her dresser mirror again, posing, admiring her body. She eased up her breasts till the tops bulged out from her bra. She posed, hand on hip, drawing in her midriff so that her waist looked really small and neat.

Her flimsy panties stretched across her hipbones. She sure was glad she'd kept up with those abdominal workouts. They'd been a bore, but they made one helluva difference to her figure.

"Not bad!" she told the mirror. "Warren's eyes are gonna stand out on stalks when he sees me tonight. . . ."

Thick black hair tumbled around her shoulders.

Full, firm breasts brimmed out of their cups. Her nipples *almost* showing . . .

What would Warren think if he saw me now?

She imagined his eyes, watching her, longing to touch her, take her in his arms—but then, *not* wanting to, not after the bad experiences she'd hinted at.

What if Warren wanted to . . . wanted to see *more* of me? Anything's possible—especially if I kinda give him the go-ahead. Maybe I should go over myself with the LadyShave. Just in case.

She ogled her reflection in the mirror.

Then teased both breasts out of their cups, pushing them up, just a little more, till she could see the dark pink aureole of her nipples.

That's better!

She literally flowed out of her underwear now.

Almost *too* much . . .

Tossing a seductive smile at her reflection, she slowly stroked her breasts, her waist, her hips. She pushed her panties down ever so slightly, revealing her taut flat belly—and dark curly wisps of pubic hair.

She groaned, hating the wiry growth peeking out of her panties.

She paused.

What was that?

A movement. A step, disturbing the quiet beyond the open door of her room . . .

Is anyone there?

Can't be Mom . . .

She's still at the restaurant.

I'm alone in the house.

Warren?

Nah. He hasn't got a key.

And Nelson's dead.

Isn't he?

Then who else . . . ?

Catching a ragged breath, her heart leapt to her throat.

She frowned. Peered into the mirror.

A familiar figure filled the doorway.

It moved toward her.

Slowly.

Mace!

His eyes dark. Intense.

Staring at her.

His mouth hung slack, open a little. She caught a glimpse of white, even teeth.

Horrified, Deana whirled around. Her arms flew up, crushing her breasts.

Mace.

How did he get *in?*

He stood before her.

His hands reaching out.

FORTY-THREE

"Stay away from me, you creep. You BASTARD!"

Terrified, Deana backed away.

MACE!

The bastard—what's he doing here?

His arms dropped to his side. His shoulders hunched slightly. "Deana. Ssshh," he whispered. "I'm sorry. . . . Didn't mean to scare you . . ."

"Oh, no? What d'you take me for—a *moron* or something? What're ya doing in my room? In my *house,* come to that?"

"Take it easy, will ya? I said I'm sorry. What more—"

His eyes looked dark, wild.

"What *more* do I want? I'll tell ya what more. I want you *outta* my room and outa my *LIFE.* Outta *my* life and Mom's, too."

She snatched up her robe, struggled into it, wrapped it around her body, holding it tightly closed.

"You're a fuckin' creep. You know that?"

Mace backed away, hands lifted, palms up.

He looked dazed. But his eyes still looked wild.

And his mouth still gaped open like he was in a trance. His brow and upper lip were shiny with sweat.

God, he looks so *weird.* What's up with him?

Seems like he's having a tough time with his words, too. He was stumbling around, trying to find the right ones.

Not much like the Mace she'd known up to now.

Where had his control gone? One thing about Mace. He was always so *in control.* Of himself and situations.

It was weird, the way he was now.

"Er . . . Look, Deana," he said thickly. "I'm going. Right? I wasn't here, right? No . . . no need to tell Leigh . . . I'll tell her myself. Later . . ."

"You *bastard.* You come in here spying on me, and now you tell me to keep my mouth *shut?*"

"About the size of it, Deana. Stay mum—and so will I."

Suddenly, he was getting more lucid by the minute.

The old Mace.

The one she *hated* so much.

Deana held her breath. Tried to calm down. Wouldn't do to get him riled up. Way he'd looked a few moments ago, he might just *turn* on her. . . .

But she had to know exactly what he meant.

"Whatdya mean—and so will you?"

"We both have our little secrets, honey. Don't we? Like you sneaking back into the house around two-thirty a.m. You tell your mom about that, did ya? Or your visits to that house with the two redwoods in front?"

She picked up her hairbrush from the dresser, and he backed off.

"Okay. Okay. I'm going. Sorry for coming on to you like that. It's just . . ."

He faltered. Looking bewildered again.

"It's just *what?*" prompted Deana.

Don't think I'm gonna be able to handle him like this. God, Mom, where are you, for chrissake?

This was a different Mace, all right.

An *iffy* Mace.

"Nothin'. Nothin' at all," he muttered.

His voice was low. She could scarcely hear it. Like he was talking to himself.

He turned and made for the door.

Then stopped dead.

They'd both heard the same thing. The muffled sound of an engine; a car pulling up outside.

The sound of a door slamming shut.

Mom.

Thank *God.*

Mace turned. Put a finger to his lips.

As he looked across at her, he was back to normal. All business. Fierce. Intense. In control.

The old Mace.

"Ssshh. I'm warning you, Deana."

The finger sliced across his throat.

Deana held still.

She watched him go.

What if Mom found her like this, half-dressed—with Mace hurrying down the hallway? She's gonna think something fishy's going on.

Shit. This had to happen tonight, of all nights!

The night Warren was coming to dinner.

The night when she'd *prayed* everything'd go according to plan.

What the fuck was up with Mace, anyway?

He hadn't *looked* as if he were about to rape her.

He'd just *stared* in that awful *creepy* sort of way.

Okay. He knew about my sneaking in at two-thirty. But how did he know I'd visited a house with two redwoods in front?

Did he know about Warren?

The thought that he did made shivers run up and down her spine.

How much does the bastard *really* know?

She heard voices.

Mom saying, "Why hello, Mace. Didn't expect to see you today. . . ."

"Courtesy call, Leigh. See how you both are, an' all."

"My, this is a real treat. So soon after . . ." Mom's voice softened into a murmur.

Silence. More murmurs . . .

Kissing.

How *could* she?

But of course, she doesn't know yet.

About Mace's surprise visit to her darling daughter.

And I can't *tell* you about it, Mom.

Can't *warn* you about Mace.

Christ, Mom. He's *real* bad news, and I can't tell you. *Because he's blackmailing me!*

Deana felt like throwing up. Mace could sneak in, spy on her, scare the shit outa her, and then cozy up to Mom like he meant it.

Christ, what a *crud!*

Deana was angry. And scared. She'd seen a whole different Mace back there. And it was not a pretty sight.

It sure was *spooky,* the way he'd *gaped* at her.

Not exactly like he wanted to rape her, either.

More like he'd never seen a woman half-naked before.

Which is a load of bullshit.

She knew that.

Mace must've had *scores* of women.

Guys like him take women, use 'em, and throw 'em away. . . .

God. *Mom!*

Coming this way.

Deana straightened her robe, flung her hair over her shoulder, and busied herself putting the pantsuit back in the wardrobe.

"Hi there, honey!"

Mom put her head around the door.

"Hi yourself, Mom. Just deciding what to wear tonight."

"Yeah. I bet. Take you all afternoon?"

"Something like that . . ."

"Good of Mace to call on us like that. Although he *did* know I was working all day. I've really spent too much time out of the restaurant lately. Had a lot of catching up to do: ordering, consulting with Carlo . . . all of that. Carlo's doing a good job, too. Not like Nelson, of course, but . . ."

"You okay, honey?"

"Why, sure, Mom. Just want to make a good impression tonight, is all. What d'ya think about my *final* choice?"

She held up the soft jersey top and denim skirt.

"You look great in all your things, dear. I'm sure Warren will think so, too."

She looked at her wristwatch.

"Must fly, darling. I'll leave you to it. . . . Must go have a shower; smarten *my*self up a little, too."

Leigh stepped into the hallway.

As ever, Deana thought, watching her go, Mom looks wonderful.

She paused. Waiting for Mom to say something about Mace.

Like, how'd he get in?

Or, did *you* let him in, honey?

Dressed, or should we say *un*dressed, like that?

Or maybe Mace has his own key?

Mom wouldn't have given him a house key so soon in their relationship.

Would she?

Mom and Mace had been an item for less than two weeks. . . . That's all. She *wouldn't* give him his own key.

But she *is* pretty well struck on him.

Mom poked her head around the door.

"Mace been here long, honey?"

Here it comes.

Darling daughter does the dirty on Mom.

Again.

"Five, ten minutes, is all."

"Good thing you were around to let him in."

"Yeah."

Bull's-eye. The twenty-four-thousand-dollar question answered in one go.

Mace hasn't got a key.

Not yet.

"If I'm in the shower when Tony calls with the food and wine, see to him, will you, darling?"

"Sure, Mom. Leave it with me. Mace gone?"

"Yep. Duty calls, he said. Asked him to join us, but he said he'd gotta ride."

Gotta ride!

Huh. I'll bet.

She frowned.

Just what was Mace up to? He'd sure started to act strange. Not his usual self.

Showing a side she and Mom hadn't seen yet.

Don't *want* to see it anymore, either.

Obviously, Mom thinks he's okay.

And she wouldn't tolerate a *weirdo*.

Would she?

She'd gone along with Nelson. And *he* was a weirdo.

But his meals were something else. That's what he was

there for—to cook good meals. Mom couldn't *really* complain about him.

Look what happened when she did. . . .

What would have happened if she hadn't?

Christ! This is leading nowhere fast.

Gotta get ready.

Warren'll be here before I'm dressed, at this rate.

She listened to Mom splashing in the shower.

Humming to herself.

Happy.

Not knowing how spooky Mace could be.

What'd happen if I told her about him sneaking up on me? How do you *tell* your mom her boyfriend's a Peeping Tom? That he gets off staring at your half-naked daughter?

Come to think about it how the hell *did* he sneak up on me?

Mom hadn't given him a key.

So how'd he do it?

Get in through the window?

What window? All their windows were intruder-proof. They opened only so far. And no farther.

He could have stolen a key.

The spare one Mom left under the magnolia bush by the front stoop?

Maybe he was simply being what he was. *A good cop.*

He'd made an impression of the key under the bush, and had another one made, Deana thought.

Intruders do that all the time.

She'd read about how they did it.

Lesson One: Don't leave your house key under the magnolia bush.

Wonderful.

Mace going around with a key to *our* house!

Deana's mouth went dry. Her heart leapt to her throat.

Mace can enter our home whenever he feels like it!

Whenever he wants to scare the pants offa me.

Our home isn't safe anymore.

Deana dressed carefully. She brushed her hair and put on her makeup. But her heart wasn't in it.

All she could think about was Mace.

Creeping into her room again.

When Mom was out and she was all alone.

FORTY-FOUR

Deana was setting place mats on the dinner table when the doorbell rang. It echoed through the hallway.

She froze.

It has to be Warren—but how can I be sure?

Could be Mace!

Nah. Mace wouldn't return so soon after spying on me. Would he?

That's just the kinda awful thing he *would* do.

She heard Mom go to the door.

Open it.

She was talking, her tone bright and friendly.

A low voice, interspersed with Mom's highs, indicated an animated conversation was taking place.

Whoever it was, was standing in the hallway.

She heard Warren's voice and huffed a sigh of relief. She raced through the living room into the hallway.

"Hi, Warren. You two met, I see!"

Mom was shaking Warren's hand. She looked flushed and bright-eyed—as she always did with guests. That was the nice thing about Mom. She knew how to make people feel at home.

"Hi there, Deana. Your sister was just making me welcome."

He winked at Deana.

Mom laughed, flushed some more, and went off into the kitchen.

They were alone.

Warren eyed Deana approvingly. "My," he said. "You look stunning tonight." His voice dropped to a conspiratorial whisper. "You should wear blue more often. Much more becoming than black."

Deana grinned. She put a finger to her lips. "Don't you dare . . ."

Warren smiled and crossed his heart.

"Mum's the word," he mouthed.

Deana led him to the living room. She motioned for him to sit on the sofa.

"Dinner isn't quite ready yet," she said. "Care for a drink?"

"Mmmm. Whatever you're having would be great!"

Warren looked around, taking stock of the room.

As if he hadn't seen it before.

"Fabulous view you have over there." He nodded in the direction of the glass wall.

"Yeah. That's what everyone says. White wine?"

"Sounds good to me," Warren said, smiling at her.

She went to the kitchen and returned with two glasses of Chablis on a serving tray.

He's a handsome guy, she thought, watching him take his glass. In a clean-cut kind of way. Dark slicked hair, gray suit, white shirt. A club tie of some sort.

Underneath all that, she sensed his taut, well-honed body. A squirm of excitement stirred between her legs.

Wondering how he'd look bare-ass naked.

"So you own a bookstore, Warren?" Mom said over dinner.

"That I do. For my sins." Mom looked at him inquiringly. He laughed. "Sorry—a figure of speech! I love my work, Ms. West . . ."

"Leigh, please," Mom said with a smile. "Makes life a lot simpler."

"Leigh. Nice name, if I may say so."

Deana glared at him.

Warren smiled back, sending her a sly wink at the same time.

I *know* he's just being friendly, she thought. And Mom does have this effect on people. I should be used to it by now.

But she *did* feel a little on edge.

It's that asshole Mace, she decided.

Suddenly appearing like that.

Scaring the pants offa me.

Well, not quite.

But he sure had me spooked there for a while.

What had *really* spooked her, though, was the way Mace had looked.

Zoned out.

Unsure.

As if he'd been *really* sorry about going into her room like that.

She stole a glance at Mom. She looked happy enough. Perhaps she hadn't ever seen Mace as I saw him this afternoon.

Maybe I should let it stay that way. . . .

Deana wanted to forget, but found she couldn't. Mace coming at her like that was something that worried her a lot.

Warren and Mom were talking books. How Mom liked historical novels and biographies; she'd been searching for something on Bob Dylan. Warren said he'd look out for this really good one he'd heard about.

"Wonderful meal, Leigh," Warren said, wiping his lips on his napkin.

"Thanks, Warren. Glad you enjoyed it. Duck à l'orange prepared this way is a Bayview special. Goes down well with the clientele."

"Mom," Deana put in. "Would you mind awfully if Warren and I went for a drive somewhere?"

Leigh's face paled slightly.

Watching her, Deana almost changed her mind about going for a drive with Warren.

She's remembering the night of the family party. When Allan and I left her to it with Gran and Pops.

"Mom. We'll be back in an hour or so—won't we, Warren?"

"Er, yes, of course. Would you mind, Leigh? I always hate to eat and run. But perhaps you'd both do me the honor of dining at my place sometime soon?"

Leigh smiled at Deana. "Sure," she said. "That would be wonderful, wouldn't it, darling?"

"Yes, Mom. It would."

After they left, Leigh cleared away the dishes, piling them up, intending to wash them later. She took out a bottle of Chablis from the fridge and poured herself a glassful.

Strolling back to the living room, her mind was full of Deana and Warren. Mmmm. She liked Warren. He seemed mature and sensible; probably a safe date is what Deana needs right now. *After all our problems, she could do with some relaxation.* . . .

She switched on the TV.

Maybe I should call Mace. . . .

Or maybe I should take some time out by myself. Relax. Chill out.

Like an irritating insect, the tub scenario still lurked in a corner of her mind.

Afterward, though, Mace had made up for it.

They really *were* good for each other.

She was sure of that.

Her eyes followed the flickering screen, not really seeing what was there. She came to, focusing on David Letterman interviewing some celeb from *Friends.* . . .

Leigh made a face. Reflecting that she must be the only person on the planet who wasn't into *Friends.*

There *must* be something else worth looking at. . . .

She played around on the remote, finally settling on an old Steve McQueen movie. Smiling to herself, she remembered she'd had this humongous crush on Steve McQueen after watching *The Great Escape*.

Steve on his motorbike . . .

Ultra-*sexy*.

Taking another sip of Chablis, she watched the screen some more. Not really understanding, now, why she'd been so over the moon about dear old Steve.

Her eyes strayed to the framed photographs on the TV table.

Something odd there . . .

One was missing.

The picture of Deana wearing her first bikini.

Showing off. Posing on a rock, her dark hair blowing in the breeze, the sea rolling in behind her.

Leigh remembered that day down at Point Reyes Beach. The first time she'd realized Deana had suddenly become a woman . . .

The same day Deana had reminded her of Charlie.

There'd been something about her smile. That small cleft in her chin. The way she stood there. At one with the elements.

Nature girl, Leigh had called her.

Now the photograph was gone.

Perhaps Deana gave it to Warren as a keepsake.

I'll ask her later.

Leigh felt a twinge of regret.

That photo had been a good one of Deana.

One of her favorites . . .

FORTY-FIVE

Friday, July 16

Lisa Bonetti was eighteen years of age. She had long dark hair, and a tall, athletic build. She played tennis, enjoyed swimming, and was a hotshot at archery.

Due to go to UCSC in the fall, Lisa was the apple, as they say, of her father's eye.

At 3:01 she was on her way to Kathy's Diner on Main Street, to meet her friend Margy for coffee and donuts. She'd missed out on lunch, so she was looking forward to a couple of Kathy's fresh apple donuts. She had no idea she was being followed.

The black car cruised by a couple of times then drew up alongside as she hurried along the sidewalk.

"Miss!"

The black window slid down; an elbow, then a man's face appeared. The man looked both serious and concerned. He glanced up, nodding briefly.

"Lisa Bonetti? I'm Detective Joe Napier, San Jose PD." The man flashed police ID at her and returned it to the inside pocket of his leather jacket.

He leaned across the passenger seat and swung open the far-side door.

"Ms. Bonetti, your father's in Cedar Heights. Had a near-fatal heart attack around two this afternoon. News came through as I was going off my shift. Chief asked me to drive you over to see him."

The girl paled. She frowned slightly.

"But there must be some mistake. . . . I mean, my father was okay this morning when I left him. He took his pills as usual and walked down the driveway to wave me off. . . . I've spent some time in the library—didn't think to call and check. . . . Er, who phoned your office to say he was ill . . . ?"

Her face was ashen now. Clearly, news of her father's attack had come as a bad shock. The man in the car smiled, then said gently, "Lady name of Lydia Ashmont, your next-door neighbor I believe, phoned us to say pass on the message to daughter Lisa that Tony's in the hospital. Right? You *are* Lisa Bonetti? And your father *is* Tony Bonetti?"

"Sure. Take me to him. And *please* hurry."

Lisa stepped into the car, leaned forward, and placed her purse by her feet. She fastened her seat belt, settled back, and turned to look at the driver.

"How long will it take?"

Smiling, he said, "Not long, Ms. Bonetti. Not long." He touched the remote button and the driver's window slid up with a neat, whirring sound.

He reached into the glove compartment, his side of the car, and produced a hypodermic syringe.

Turning to face the girl, he smiled into her eyes and emptied the syringe into her arm.

She gave a small gasp and slumped back in her seat.

Anyone seeing her would have said she was asleep.

Roughly, the driver lifted her head, making sure she was out for the count. He felt around in his jacket pocket, brought out a few sunflower seeds, and palmed them into his mouth.

Taking a brief look in the rearview mirror, he released the hand brake and eased away from the curb.

Chewing on the seeds, the man glanced at the clock on the dash.

3:05.

His lips curved in a smile.

Whole thing'd taken around three minutes.

Lisa Bonetti's naked body was found four months later, in a remote, seldom-used spot on the Marin Headlands.

Birds and other marauding wildlife had not made indenti-fication easy. However, of one fact there was no doubt—the body was carved open from the throat to the pubic bone.

Soft tissue was mostly gone. But the vaginal cavity contained a wad of decaying organic material. The victim's severed tongue, heart, and other internal organs were shoved inside it.

Tony Bonetti was heartbroken at the discovery of his daughter's remains. Bright and early one morning, unable to come to terms with her terrible fate, Tony took his old service revolver, gripped the muzzle between his teeth, and blew his head clean off.

FORTY-SIX

"Where to? Anywhere special in mind?"

"You choose. I'm in your hands."

"Okay. Hold tight. Just close your eyes and relax!"

Deana pushed back into the seat, snugging against the soft upholstery. Nice car, she thought dreamily. A two-seater Porsche coup.

A tangy whiff of leather hit her nostrils.

She felt a little shaky. Slightly out of her depth.

It was the first time she and Warren had been together like this. Up close and *really* together. Sure, she'd been to his house. Drunk his scrumptious cocoa. Become best buddies with his dog. A gal can't get much closer, she told herself with a slow smile.

She stole a glance at Warren's profile. Straight nose, firm chin. Lit up now by a passing car. He looks kinda sexy in that white shirt, she thought, the way it shows up against his tan.

The night was warm and sticky, and Warren had discarded his suit jacket, loosened his tie, and rolled up his sleeves. His forearms were strong, matted with dark hair, and well-muscled. She watched his hands holding the wheel loosely. Imagining how they'd feel wandering over her naked body . . .

Stop that!

Still, she couldn't help thinking about it. A picture leapt into her mind. Warren, running his hands over her shoulders, holding her breasts, squeezing her nipples. His mouth opening onto hers . . .

A thought struck her. She frowned. Who knows, Warren might decide he was too old for her, smile kindly, and say, "Good-bye eighteen-year-old ex-high-school kid Deana. Go find somebody your own age. . . ."

Warren felt her gaze and smiled. His eyes flashed as he turned to look at her.

"Will I do?"

"Do?"

"Yeah. You've been staring at me for the last coupla miles. . . ."

"Sorry. Just thinking that you look kinda sexy. In the dark. With that intense expression on your face, you seem so intelligent and . . . mature, somehow."

"I hope by that you don't mean I'm too decrepit for a young gal like you?"

"On the contrary, I feel *safe* around you. Felt it that very first time you invited me to your house. You have this, I don't know—*gravitas,* I guess you'd call it."

"Wow! Sounds heavy."

They'd dropped down to a crawl, climbing along a rutted road. For the first time she looked out the window.

Her breath quickened. She shivered. Almost panicked. Goose bumps scurried up her body.

"Warren . . ."

"Uh-huh?"

"Where are we going?"

"I thought we'd maybe go over to Stinson Beach. Take a stroll in the moonlight . . ."

Deana's face turned ghostly pale.

"Why, Deana, what is it?"

They'd arrived at a clearing now.

The clearing. The parking area for the outdoor theater . . .

The Porsche purred to a halt.

"Warren!" she wailed. "How could you *do* this to me?"

"Do what, Deana? For godsakes, what d'you mean?"

Dismayed, he looked at her. She'd drawn up into a small tight ball, her hands held clenched to her face.

"You brought me *here,* Warren. How did you *know?* Why did you bring me *here?*"

Tears coursed down her cheeks.

Then he got it.

Whatever had happened to Deana a short while ago, had happened here, in this clearing.

He pulled her gently to him, making soothing noises as if she were a child waking scared from a nightmare. She shook, sobbed, and cried all at the same time, her face wet and shiny with tears.

He waited till she'd calmed down a little.

"Take me back, Warren," she said quietly. "*Please.* Take me away from this place!"

"Sure, honey. Just don't *cry* anymore. You're safe with me."

Deana snuffled, and he produced a tissue from the glove compartment. She took it, gratefully, and dabbed at her face. "I must look a real freak," she said with another sob.

"You look wonderful, Deana. You always do."

"Thanks, Warren," she said, still sniffing loudly. A pause, then: "I think I owe you an explanation."

"Not necessarily. But I can guess. Something to do with what happened to you—and your mom?"

She nodded, her lips still trembling.

"No need to explain. Don't want you upsetting yourself any more. I'm just sorry I chose this place, is all."

"Not your fault. *I* said you choose. Didn't say anything about *not* going anywhere near Mt. Tam. So don't blame yourself. You weren't to know. But can we go home now, please?"

"Sure," he said, turning the key in the ignition, still looking at her anxiously. "Sure you're okay now?" Deana nodded, snugged back into her seat again, and stared out into the night. Remembering Allan.

How he'd opened the car door for her, and how there hadn't been a cat in hell's chance of him escaping.

Then the old Pontiac, whooshing by, lifting him off his feet.

Allan. Allan . . .

Another sob shook her body. Vivid pictures flashed through her mind. She saw herself running away from Allan.

Saving my own skin . . .

He could've been *alive*.

Maybe I could've *saved* him.

Don't think about it anymore. . . .

She gasped.

Something . . .

Someone was back there, in the bushes. The car moved on past. Warren maneuvered it slowly, carefully over the ruts.

Still Deana could see it . . . the white face, with dark holes for eyes. No, not dark holes. It, whatever it was, had an eye. It had looked at her. Its mouth gaping wide . . . Its scrawny hands parting the bushes . . .

Then it faded into the dark beyond.

She turned around. Stared hard.

Saw nothing.

She frowned.

The face had been a lot like Nelson's. Thin, white. Eerie. Positively *ghoulish* in the dark shadows.

It *can't* be Nelson, she told herself.

Nelson's dead.

Mom identified the body.

Her breath evened out. Her mind had been playing tricks again. Coming here hadn't been one of Warren's greatest ideas.

Glancing across at him, she met his eyes. He smiled gently. "Okay now?"

"Okay," she said quietly.

She was still shaking, though.

Thinking about Nelson.

But a *dead* Nelson, she reminded herself. Hope I can sleep tonight. Hope I don't see him again. Walking past my window, waving his hatchet.

Bullshit, Deana.

Pull yourself together.

Nelson's dead.

This is two weeks on. We're safe now. Mom's okay. She's got Mace, 'n' I've got Warren to keep me company. I hope. Unless I've scared him off by tonight's little performance.

"And as we lie here," Allan's voice whispered in her head. *"Our naked bodies all sweaty and tangled . . ."*

Oh my God.

Stop it.

Allan's dead. *Gone.* Please God don't let me go over *that* again. . . .

She looked at Warren, felt the bumps and jolts as the car sped downhill, bouncing over the ruts. He met her gaze, smiled, and said, "You've got me now, Deana. I'll take care of you."

FORTY-SEVEN

"Leigh, tell me about your pregnancy. The early days, when you were making out, all alone . . ."

There was enough of a pause for Leigh to look up, puzzled.

"Go on," she said quietly.

"Sorry, Leigh. Does my asking questions upset you? I'm just interested in *you*, is all. I want to know *everything* that ever happened to you. That make sense?" He tilted his head, smiling quizzically.

Leigh returned the smile. "Sure it does, Mace. But I already told you all there is to know about my misbegotten youth. I was a bit wild. Got pregnant. Those days folks took it a little more seriously than they do now. I was sent away and—well, you know the rest."

Leigh shrugged, then smiled. It was an end to the matter, as far as she was concerned. "Why don't I get us another bottle of wine from the fridge." She left the sofa and made for the kitchen.

Reaching for clean glasses and setting them on the serving tray, she began to feel good and warm inside. She was glad she'd changed her mind and called Mace when Deana and Warren had left after dinner.

She'd wanted to relax. What better way to do it than with Mace by her side?

Ten o'clock.

Another hour or so and Deana'll be back. Must remember to ask her about the missing photograph. Not tonight, though. Leave that until tomorrow.

Bring her home safely, Warren, she thought with a shiver. *Please God, don't let it be like last time. . . .*

She looked up, saw Mace standing in the doorway.

"Hey," he said, coming forward. "Let me open that for you."

"Thanks. Nice to have a man around. To open things, and . . ."

"Oh, yeah? And what else, may I ask?"

"Oh, to open things and just *be* around the house, I guess."

They took their wine through to the living room.

Lingering by the glass wall, Leigh told him, "As for my story—if you must know, there's not much more to say. I got knocked up. I wasn't the first. Won't be the last. Girls do it all the time. I wasn't in love with the guy, so there was no question of him being involved. . . . He died anyway."

Mace stayed silent. They crossed over to the sofa. He took her glass and set it down on the low table.

Then he moved in against her. Their lips met. . . . Pressing close, she could feel his hard-on, bulking up, growing big inside his jeans.

"Perhaps we should take the wine into the bedroom," he whispered. "Relax a little, take in some TV, and . . ." He bent down, his mouth finding hers, his tongue edging in, hard, searching.

He felt her flinch away slightly.

"Sorry, Leigh. Only if you want to, of course."

"Mace, you *know* I want to. Just a little worried about Deana, is all. She went out after dinner. With Warren, her new boyfriend. They should be back soon. She said maybe an hour or so."

He eased away from her, searching her face. "Hey. She shouldn't worry you like this. Y'know? Maybe I should have a word—"

"No, please don't," Leigh cut in with a short laugh. "Warren's okay. Really. He's mature and very sensible. Deana's perfectly safe with him."

"She still shouldn't do this. Not so soon after Nelson an' all."

"Really, Mace. Everything'll be fine. Honestly. I feel it right here." Leigh touched her heart. The silk robe she'd changed into earlier gaped open, showing the soft curve of her left breast.

Mace grinned. "Do that again and I warn you, I won't be responsible for my actions!"

"That's my Mace. Mmmm. You're *so* masterful at times."

She stood up, took his hand, and pulled him toward the bedroom.

"Er, the wine?"

"What wine?" she said with a sly smile. "We'll enjoy that later!"

She went ahead of him into the dark bedroom, her robe sliding to the floor.

He picked it up, tossed it over the bedrail. "Come here, you crazy woman. Come to Poppa." He grabbed her by the waist and flung her on the bed. She reached out to switch on the bedside lamp, but his hand closed over hers.

"No," he murmured. "We don't need light. We got hands. We got touch. Ve-erry sexy, so they tell me . . . and a guaranteed turn-on!"

"Okay. Okay. Just *give* it to me, Mace. Hard and long."

He looked down. Her face was a pale blur, pleading.

"Am I hearing this right? You saying 'give it to me.' Any way. Any how?"

"Sure. Why not? Just *do* it, Mace." With trembling fingers, she began struggling with his jeans. Unzipping them, pulling them down. She reached out, felt his coarse curly hair, shuddered, and curled her hands around his shaft. Sighing and moaning a little, she breathed, "My God, Mace. *Give* it to me."

She was panting now.

Pulling him to her.

Wanting him.

Whichever way he cared . . . She shrugged down under him, feeling his weight straddling her, leaning over, his hair

falling forward. In the dark, their eyes met and held. . . .
She grabbed his penis with both hands. Close up, it was
huge. Engorged. She rammed it into her mouth. Hard.

He pulled away. . . . "No," he said softly. "Not that way.
The way *you* want it."

She gave in, straightened out, and he lay on top, covering her face with kisses, tracing his tongue gently over her
mouth, her neck, then slipping down to her breasts.

He cradled them in his hands, caressing them. He went
down again. Taking small quick licks, his tongue playing
around her nipples, feeling them go rigid. She wriggled
beneath him, pressing onto his shaft, feeling the moist
warmth rising. . . . He went in deeper and deeper. . . . She
rose to meet him.

Moaning, panting, she rammed herself onto him. He responded, pressing deep, shafting her with long, hurting
strokes. He came quickly, flooding her with hot, releasing
bursts. Finally, he pulled away. Moving off her. Falling back
on the bed, breathing hard, his body slick with sweat.

She lay there, staring into the darkness, still panting
softly. At last, her breath evened out. She felt full, satisfied. Complete.

A clicking sound came from the hallway.

They tensed, holding their breath.

A light clatter of heels on the clay tiles.

Deana.

Home.

Leigh breathed a sigh of relief.

Mace turned his head, smiling into the darkness.

Leigh's face was a soft white smudge in the gloom.

A gray light crept in from the window, playing across
the bed. Trembling shadows from the trees outside shifted
around, touching the walls, the ceiling.

"Deana's home," she whispered, finding his hand. He
took hers in his and squeezed it. "Okay. I give in," he whispered back. She turned on her side, facing him, curving in
to his body. Feeling the sweat, slick and warm on their skin.

Mmmm, she thought, smiling softly, everything is just so *perfect!* Her eyelids began to droop. She felt spent, happy, relaxed.

Mace dropped a kiss on her shoulder, then lay back on the pillow, watching the shadows shift on the ceiling.

Soon, their breath became a steady rhythmic sound. Still holding hands, though more loosely now, they slept.

Leigh jerked awake for a moment, remembering the thrill of how they'd made love. And that Deana was home. Asleep by now, she guessed, lifting her head from the pillow.

2:55.

God, it's so *hot.* A shower would be nice. Drenched with sweat, the bedsheet clung to her like a live thing. Plucking it away from her skin, she felt the night air chill her body. Pushing down the sheet, carefully so as not to wake Mace, she let it lie a moment, crumpled, damp and cool across her thighs.

She glanced down at her body, gleaming pale in the darkness.

Do it, Leigh. Go get yourself a shower. . . .

Holding her breath, she worked her feet, slowly, pushing down the bedsheet some more. Turned to look at Mace. Still sleeping. She pictured him on her, his come pumping deep inside her.

A tremor of excitement flicked in her groin.

She felt so tender there. And sore.

His warm semen still seeped between her legs. He's some *hunk,* she thought dreamily; that blond hair, those dark eyes. And his body . . . Tight abs. Well-muscled arms. His just *being* there made her want him all over again.

Her glance swept down his body, his chest rising and falling as he slept. It was the first time she'd taken a real good look at him naked.

But something was wrong.

Even in the gloom she could make out the thick black hair covering his arms, chest, belly, and down between his legs. She looked at his penis, lying pale and shrunk now, in a *mass* of pubic hair. Her glance switched to his face. Clean-shaven, as ever.

A chill began in her stomach.

This was a *different* Mace.

A stranger.

He stirred, feeling the air chill his skin. His muscles tightened; he hugged his arms around him. Then his eyes opened. He lifted his head. Looked down at himself.

Uncovered.

Naked.

With a growl, he leapt up.

"What in *hell* are you doing?" he demanded. She drew back, startled at his tone. Terrified by the sudden anger. His mouth came open and his eyes flashed dangerously.

Suddenly he was on top of her.

His fist coming down . . .

Smashing her face . . .

Knocking her into the pillow. Then more blows, to her throat, breasts, stomach . . .

She heard herself gasping, weak little sounds. . . . He still straddled her, laying into her body again and again, pummeling hard.

Leigh threw her hands around her head. Trying to stifle her screams . . . Then, rolling into a ball, she turned away from under him and slid off the bed.

Standing, trembling, shivering, terrified, her arms hugging her body.

Mace sat up. Staring at her. Breathing hard. Suddenly, the fight left him and he drooped forward, shaking his head.

"Leigh, I'm so sorry," he murmured. "*Please* believe me. You woke me—I was having a helluva nightmare. Leigh, you *have* to forgive me."

"A *nightmare?*" Leigh backed away. She grabbed her robe from the bedrail. The silk clung to her damp skin. Struggling into it, she dragged it around her body.

Remembering Mattie's words:

"The creep from Yellow Bend ain't the only guy who likes to hear a gal scream . . ."

"You'd better leave, Mace," she said, her voice quiet and shaky. "I think we both need some space. Time to think things through."

He grabbed the bedsheet and held it up to his chin. But she turned away, not wanting to look at him anymore. Not wanting to see him, or remember him this way. Angry. Violent. Punching her. Beating the daylights out of her.

She heard him searching around for his things. She switched on the light and walked into the bathroom. Hoping Deana hadn't heard her cries. Heard him laying into her.

Please God she hadn't heard that.

FORTY-EIGHT

"Mattie. We need to talk."

"We do?"

"Yeah. Time to spill the beans, Mattie."

"About friend Mace?"

"Right. Maybe there's something else I should know?"

A pause.

Then Mattie said, "I'll be right over."

Mattie was off-duty, and the way she looked when she arrived at the house took Leigh off guard. Red blouse tied at the waist and denim cutoffs. She strode into the hallway, her long tanned legs taking her straight to the kitchen. She looked like a high-school kid on her way to the beach.

"What's the matter, Leigh? Got a problem?"

Leigh followed, then busied herself making coffee. It was eight in the morning and she hadn't fixed breakfast yet. Deana was still in bed.

"Yeah. You could say that. Take a pew." Leigh motioned

to the bench by the kitchen table. "Last week, you implied that Mace had 'another side' to him. Maybe a black side. An *iffy* side. Care to tell me more about that?"

Mattie took the mug of hot black coffee Leigh placed before her.

"Where shall I begin?" She spoke slowly, giving a tight smile. "Guess the beginning's about the best place?"

Mattie looked up, peering into Leigh's face.

"Well, shitski, honey! Where'd you get *that?*" She gestured toward the bruise already showing purple on Leigh's cheek.

With a self-conscious gesture, Leigh's hand went to her face. "Does it look *so* bad?" she asked anxiously.

"Bad enough," Mattie replied, shaking her head.

Leigh gave an embarrassed grin. "Maybe I should put on some more makeup. I'll do that before Deana shows. Don't particularly want her to see me in this state. As it is, she can't stand the sight of Mace."

"Look," Mattie said briskly. "Mace is good at his work. You might say too good. He wants somebody, he goes out there and nails 'em good. Yeah, he's well-respected back at the department. But beneath all of that there's a certain something that says potential rogue cop—know what I'm sayin'?"

Leigh gave a short, harsh laugh. "I get the picture," she said. "Have you *seen* Mace flare up? Go stark, staring crazy?"

Mattie took a swig of coffee, then looked Leigh in the eye. "A coupla times. One day he put a guy in the jug; the guy calls out for a lawyer. Unfortunately, he caught Mace going off shift. Mace goes straight in there and slugs the guy out cold. Guy lying there, still out cold, and Mace starts kicking him. Couldn't stop. I had to drag him off. It wasn't easy. Then Mace turns on me. I get a bruised jaw for my trouble. He apologizes, says he doesn't know what came over him."

Mattie shrugged her shoulders.

"Next time, he slugs a girl in a club. Broke her jaw, turns out. Anyway, he shows his ID, tells *il patron* the girl's makin' a nuisance of herself. Girl's fired on the spot. Mace walks free. No hassle. No problem."

Leigh listened in silence, then said, "Uh-huh, seems like our Mace is bad news. Like he's two separate people. Never took me to his apartment, y'know . . . I did wonder why. Maybe he's got somethin' to hide? Know what? I'd sure be interested to know what makes him tick."

Mattie swung her leather shoulder bag around to her front. She lifted the flap, dove into it, and came up with a key. Waving it before Leigh's eyes, she said, "How about we have ourselves a little adventure?"

"You mean *that's* Mace's house key?"

"Sure is. I happen to know he's out on a case right now. Should take him all day . . ." Mattie's eyes challenged her.

"Why not?" Leigh said.

Mace's apartment was in darkness.

Leigh suppressed a shiver. What *had* Mace got against good honest daylight? What *was* he, Count Dracula or something?

The apartment was very neat. *Too* neat for a bachelor pad, she thought. No magazines. Straight lines of paperbacks in a cheap wooden bookcase. No mess, no beer cans, no evidence of takeout food.

Nothing.

She frowned. It was unnatural.

Place is like a damn funeral parlor. Especially with the blinds all drawn like this.

She shuddered. There was something about the neatness of it all that spooked her.

Mattie glanced around. Leigh smiled. Good ol' Mats. Casing the joint. Once a cop always a cop . . . Bet nothing escapes her notice.

She was right.

"Place hasn't been slept in these last coupla nights."

"How can you tell?" Leigh felt guilty. Of course Mace hadn't spent the night at home for a while. He'd been with her, hadn't he? Well, last night, anyhow.

"Desk calendar says July fifteenth," Mattie said. "It's now July eighteenth." She went through to the small kitchen area. She opened the fridge door. "The milk's past its sell-by date."

Leigh's eyebrows went up. "Looks like Mace isn't the only good cop around here," she remarked dryly.

"Hey. How about this?" Mattie, at an open drawer of Mace's computer desk, was waving some photos.

Leigh perked up. Photographs, especially missing ones, held a particular significance for her right now.

She looked at the photos fanned in Mattie's hand. Mainly art shots, nicely lit ones of people, places, water, rivers, the sea, rocks, and some amazing skies. Most in mono; some in full color.

"Our Mace hopes to make the big time one day," Mattie explained. "He's got an award somewhere. Told me about it once. The Smith-Griffon Award for Best Seascape or something, I remember."

Mattie returned the photographs to the drawer and opened another one. She came up with bundles of letters and bills.

Leigh began to feel uneasy.

Suppose Mace walked in?

At this very moment.

She imagined footsteps hurrying down the corridor outside. A key scraping in the lock.

The door opening . . .

"Mattie. We really oughta go now. I don't feel good about this whole thing."

"*You* don't feel good, huh? Come on over and look at these. Then tell me you don't feel so good."

Mattie's tone was serious. Leigh's heart skipped a beat.

Mattie sank into a soft leather sofa, holding a large scrapbook on her knee. Leigh went over. Turning pale as she stared at the pages Mattie was flicking through.

Bodies.

Dead bodies.

Carved.

Placed in awkward, symmetrical, *artistic* positions.

Bodies of girls. Twisted. Writhing in their final death throes. Bloody. Naked . . .

Page after page of photographs.

Mono press shots. The blood all black and glistening.

A few in startling full color.

Head shots, showing the final agonies.

Faces pleading. Mouths wide. Screaming for the man with the knife to stop. *PLEASE . . . STOP . . .*

Leigh gagged, vomit lurched in her throat. She felt herself fold at the knees. She collapsed on the sofa.

"Wowww . . . ," breathed Mattie. "We gotta get outa here. . . . But wait a minute, there's something else. A letter . . ."

Leigh looked over Mattie's shoulder at the bunch of creased, handwritten pages she was holding.

And read the words:

"I, Edith Payne, hereby . . ."

My *God*—not *Charlie's* mother . . .

Quietly, the door opened.

FORTY-NINE

"Why, ladies. This *is* a pleasant surprise," Mace said. "You wanna read my private stuff?" He snatched the crumpled pages from Mattie. "Here," he said, thrusting them at Leigh. "Take a look, sweetheart. Ring any bells?"

"Mace, I'm sorry. . . ."

"Oh, don't be sorry, honey. I don't mind you sneaking in here. Poking through my private things—"

"Wasn't Leigh's fault, Mace," Mattie broke in calmly. "*I* had your key. *I* decided to pay you a visit. Don't blame Leigh. She came along for the ride."

"Came along for the ride, huh?" A corner of his mouth lifted. But he wasn't amused. His eyes were cold, dark as bottomless pits. Whatever it was he felt, he was holding it in. Keeping everything under control.

As always.

"So, Leigh. Thought you'd nose around, did you? Time you knew anyway. Time you paid the price. Finally. After . . . what is it now? Eighteen, nineteen years?"

"What d'ya mean, Mace? Eighteen, nineteen years?" Her heart lurched. Damn right she knew what he meant. What was he, Charlie's avenging angel, or what?

Mace relaxed a little, easing into the game, getting conversational. "Read it," he said. "And watch it all make sense, baby. Just a little reminder of that wonderful summer, all of those years ago."

Slowly, Leigh took the letter from him. Meanwhile, Mattie's eyes considered Mace. She was tense, ready to pounce if need be. One false move and she'd drop him. She knew she could, but she also knew that Mace was on the alert. She held still. Waiting.

"Go on, sweetheart. Read it. Put some coffee on, Mattie. We could be here for some time."

He set himself down, legs astride a hardback chair. Grinning. Watching Leigh. Enjoying her discomfort.

"Hey, baby. Don't mind me. Settle back in that easy chair, why don't ya? Just want to see your pretty li'l face when you read what Deana's granmama has to say!"

Mattie glanced at Leigh. Her eyes said, "You okay?"

Leigh nodded, briefly.

She sat on the edge of Mace's armchair. With trembling lips, she looked at the yellowed pages. Ma Payne had a good hand. Legible. Of the old-fashioned copperplate school. Charlie said she'd been a teacher. . . .

Leigh drew a deep breath. Quickly, her eyes scanned the pages, scarcely believing what she read:

"I, Edith Payne, hereby state the True Facts regarding my Three Children and the Terrible Events that took place after their Birth.

On December 15, in the year of Our Lord 1963, I gave birth to three babies. Jess, Charlie and Tania. Their father was my husband Charlie Payne. My, but they were three fine healthy babies! Beautiful as ever three babies could be. My Gifts from Heaven, I called them.

Firstly, I should state that I came to Lake Wahconda as a teacher. I taught the children of the lake people hereabouts. It was here I met and married Charlie Payne, a man of native Indian descent, and of little means and education. I tried to teach him to write, but he didn't take kindly to this and soon gave up trying. He was a man content in his traditional ways.

Charlie said little when the three babies came along, but from the start, he seemed fearful of our little girl. All the babies had a good head of dark hair, but Tania had more than the boys. Charlie insisted she was a child of ill-omen, mumbling some tale that a female child covered in black hair was a bringer of ill fortune. When he was liquored up, he spoke of this old legend, telling that a woman mating with a wolf at Full Moon would give birth to such a child.

Charlie Payne was a simple man. He stood by his beliefs, and nothing I said could change his mind. Tania must die, he vowed, to save us all from misfortune. He was set on this path. I begged him not to kill our daughter, but he was deaf to my pleas.

I knew he would soon kill Tania, so I stole Mary-Ann Baker's baby while she was at the lake washing clothes. The child was barely a week old. I dressed her in Tania's shawl and placed her in Tania's cradle. I hid my own daughter in the woods. Charlie Payne took Mary-Ann's baby, hacked off her head and sank her weighted body into the lake.

This was a terrible thing to witness, and in my distress, I told him he'd killed the wrong baby—that this one was not ours. He demanded to know where I'd hidden Tania. Distraught, I told him in the woods. He went to find her. I hurried to the woodshed, took the ax and followed him. In his drunken state he tripped and fell in the undergrowth. I hacked him as he lay, screaming for mercy. I just hacked and hacked till he was dead.

After the disappearance of her newborn, Mary-Ann Baker drowned herself in the lake. Folks still say they hear her ghost moaning in the night as she searches for her little one.

Teaching class and making baskets brought little enough money to support my children. People hereabouts were next to dirt poor themselves. So I gave away two of my little ones. I gave Jess to my friend Ellie Burke and her husband Tom, in Duluth. I believed Ellie would give him a good home and look after him well, as she herself had not been blessed with children. I gave my daughter to a family of travelers. They seemed good, honest folk who vowed they would care for her.

I kept my baby Charlie. I loved him with all my heart, and as best I could, kept him away from all that is bad and wicked in this world.

When my boy Charlie was almost grown, he took up with a no-good whoring slut. A vacationer she was, out for any innocent young boy she could lay her hands on. She seduced, then murdered him and walked free of this terrible crime. Accidental Death, they called it. But I know different.

I pray that someday, God will repay this Jezebel in full for her wickedness. May her slate NEVER be cleansed of the terrible wrong she did my Charlie and me.

Let it be known, this statement is for the eyes of my son Jess Payne only. Tania is long gone. Wherever she is, I hope she is happy.

May God forgive me. All I want now is to Rest in Peace.

Signed: Edith Mary Payne.

FIFTY

Stunned, Leigh let the pages flutter to the floor. She heard Charlie's voice telling her "it" was in the lake. But hadn't he mentioned a *brother*? Maybe that'd been his own conclusion.

If he'd been told he had a twin, he might've naturally thought "it" had been a brother. And it looked like Ma Payne hadn't been in any goddamn rush to explain otherwise.

And who was Jess? Where does *he* fit in?

Mattie shot a quick glance in her direction. It said, *Leigh. We gotta get outta here. Fast.*

Agreed.

But first, we waltz our way past *Mace?*

Are you kidding?

"Where's that coffee, Mattie? We sure could do with a shot here." Mace watched Leigh's face. Saw her bewildered, agonized frown. Saw how the past had leapt alive for her, prodding and poking her in all the most vulnerable places. He was enjoying the prospect.

"Time she learned the truth about her in-laws," he

thought, smiling softly. "The *real* truth about the genes her precious daughter inherited."

All that *Payne* blood running through Deana's veins.

His lips curved. His eyes glittered, black, sloelike.

Leigh got it, all right. No problem. The truth came at her thick and fast. She raised her head. Saw the smear of sweat gathering on Mace's upper lip.

"He's getting off on this," she told herself. "He's enjoying every minute of it."

She knew it now. Jess was *Mace*.

Charlie's brother. Deana's uncle.

Oh my God, I don't believe this. Please let it be some terrible mistake. . . .

She thought about the insanity in the Payne family. Edith Payne, screaming at her, eyes dark and wild. Seems like Charlie's pa was mad, too. Liquored up, and on another planet. A killer. Of a tiny baby. A baby hacked in such a horrible way. *And Mace.* Hard. Cruel. Raging when she'd uncovered him last night. Seen his black body hair.

Must've bleached the hair on his head to appear blond to the outside world. Trying to hide, *eradicate,* all trace of the familial black growth.

And Deana.

Oh my God, my darling daughter. Her thick black hair. The *body* hair she was always complaining about. From her father's side. From the Payne side.

She pictured Deana, her own dark-haired daughter—the vision merging with Edith Payne's Tania. But, she told herself gratefully, Deana had no manic streaks, no strange ways; nothing to say she'd inherited the "bad" Payne blood.

Thank God, Deana had West genes, too.

I was a bit of a rebel though, she reminded herself, recalling the hippie days, the demos, her anti-everything buttons pinned all over her clothes. . . . A teenage rebel she'd definitely been.

But Deana hadn't caused her *that* much trouble. Had she?

* * *

"Coffee. Black. And plenty of it!" Mattie brought in three steaming mugs on a tray.

"Gee, thanks, Mats." Mace grinned. "Just what we need. A shot of good ol' caffeine to get us all spiced up and rarin' to go. What say you, Leigh darlin'?"

"Coffee. Sure," Leigh said uncertainly. What a *nightmare*. Looks like he's not going to let us go. So how do we get out of here in one piece . . . ?

"Y'always did make great coffee," Mace went on. "Am I right, Mattie?"

"Okay, Mace. Quit the bullshit. Whatever it is you and Leigh have got going here, I'm outta this place. You comin', Leigh?"

"That's where you're wrong, Mattie. You an' Leigh ain't goin' anywhere." Mace reached behind. Fingering his holster.

"Mace. You're making one big mistake."

"Come now, Mattie. You know better than to go against ol' Mace. You *know* who's boss around here."

"Quit playin' around, Mace, I put one call through and the cops'll be buzzin' around here like flies, an' you know it."

"Think so, Mats?"

"Know so, Mace. Just stay cool and let us pass."

"You were breakin' and enterin', Mattie. And you, Leigh. Wouldn't have thought it of you. So ladylike an' all."

"Mattie. Meet Mace, Deana's uncle. Surprised, huh?" Leigh gave a mirthless laugh. She was playing for time. Trying to catch him off guard. What then? She'd no idea. *Go with the flow. Take our chances, I guess . . .*

"Thought there was something more to our friend than he made out," Mattie put in, looking at Leigh. She turned to Mace. "Let us pass, Mace. You want to continue your illustrious career at the department? Let us by and we won't say a word."

"Mmmm. Not bad, Mattie. Not bad at all. Taught you

well, didn't I? Tricky situation, and you turn the tables with a slick remark. Won't work this time, Mattie baby. You're talking to the master. I got me two perps here. On a breakin'-and-enterin' charge. I got me a result."

Leigh's mind worked overtime. She was sure Mace planned to finish what Charlie Senior had been unable to do.

She remembered Mace's theory about Nelson. "He might come back. Finish where he left off," he'd said.

Charlie Payne Sr. didn't get to kill his black-haired baby girl. So now Mace wants to do it for him. No Tania around? So what about Deana, Charlie's black-haired daughter?

Oh my God. *Deana*.

I gotta get on home. Protect her. Send her away. Like Ma Payne sent Tania away.

Well, not *quite* the same.

Talk to Mace, she decided. Persuade him to let us go. But don't let him know I'm onto his little game.

She turned to Mattie.

"Mattie, why don't you clear away the coffee things? Mace and I need to talk."

A brief glance at Leigh and Mattie took the hint.

Right. I go out into the kitchen. Deposit the mugs. Leigh keeps Mace talking. His back's turned to the door and I come out, guns blazing . . .

"Well, now, Leigh. Thought we'd finished talking for good last night. Nothing much left to say." He tilted his head, watching her, his eyes half closed, skimming her body, undressing her as she stood before him. Like he'd done so many times before. How she'd *enjoyed* him doing that.

She blushed slightly, annoyed with herself for the predictable reaction. "Mace," she whispered. "I'm so sorry for the way I behaved last night. . . ." She took a step forward. Playing for time. Looking guileless, innocent.

She smiled at him. That special, intimate smile she often gave him.

Except it wasn't working today.

He was tense, alert. Listening. But not to Leigh.

He whirled around. Grabbed Mattie's hand, the one holding the gun. He twisted it up. The gun pointed skyward.

"Yo! Gotcha, Mattie baby. Can't cheat ol' Mace. Should know that by now!"

"Oh no?" Mattie's left leg shot out in a karate kick to the groin. He dropped her arm, danced back, and came up with a sideways chop to her neck. Mattie gasped, whirled away, but dropped her gun. Leigh sprang forward, snatched it up, and jabbed it against Mace's head.

Mattie dove into her back pocket, opened a pair of cuffs, and snapped them around his wrists. Grabbing the gun from Leigh, she swiped the handle end across Mace's head.

A short "Uhhhh" burst from his lips as he folded to the floor. He collapsed in a heap.

Mattie grabbed Leigh's arm and they both made for the door. They heard Mace groan, turned, and saw him shake his head. They didn't wait; they bolted, disappeared down the hallway, and raced out into the street.

Driving back to Del Mar, Mattie said, "So what is it with you and Mace? Care to tell me?"

Leigh hesitated, then said, "It's a long story, Mattie."

God, my life's one procession of "long stories."

She took a deep breath. "Here goes. When I was eighteen, I went to visit an aunt and uncle in Milwaukee. Out in Lake Country . . ." She told her tale, briefly and to the point, ending with Charlie's death and how she'd found herself pregnant.

There was a long silence.

Then:

"Wow," Mattie said with a low whistle. "That's one helluva story. . . ." She paused. "So now Mace has this thing about dark-haired girls. . . ."

Looking at each other, the same thought occurred to them both.

"But all the time," Mattie went on, "Mace is really

searching for Tania. Meanwhile, he can't find her, so *any* dark-haired girl will do."

In her mind, Leigh saw the gruesome pictures in Mace's scrapbook. "Don't, Mattie, please," she whispered. "I don't want to think about it. . . ."

"Leigh. We gotta get to Deana. Fast."

"Oh my God," Leigh breathed, her eyes filling up. Her mind raced, considering the awful possibilities if Mace got there first. She felt trapped. Helpless. This was one helluva nightmare, all right.

If Deana was a target.

Maybe she wasn't.

Maybe Tania'd show up.

Like that's gonna happen. . . .

Mattie changed gear, making a right into Del Mar. Driving up toward Leigh's house, she wondered how she was going to deal with this one. They had no positive proof Mace was involved in murder. Without it, she knew the department would never believe her. So he saves gruesome pictures. Could be the scrapbook's something he picked up someplace.

No accounting for taste.

She'd have it out with Mace. . . . Oh yeah? She grimaced. She could see it now. Mace saying, "Gee, thanks, Mattie, that was some slug you threw back there. . . . Guess I owe you one for that."

For a moment, she saw herself lying at his feet, her lifeblood spilling out, soaking the carpet. . . . Maybe dead.

Hell no. It wouldn't be like that.

Mace was no killer. He had a temper and a weird taste in pictures, but they were buddies, weren't they? They could always talk things through. She'd suggest he take time off, she'd cover for him. . . . She'd wheedle the truth out of him. What he intended to do . . .

"Mattie."

"Uh-huh?"

"Why d'you call people Charlie?"

Mattie gave a hoot of laughter. "Why do I call people Charlie, huh? I guess that holds a little resonance for you right now. Yes?"

"You could say that."

"Well, it's like this, Leigh. Remember little ol' Yellow Bend? Like I told you, where I came from?"

Leigh nodded.

"S'far as I remember, seemed like everybody was called Charlie in that goddamn town. So, talk to a person whose name you didn't know—I reckoned if you called 'em Charlie, you'd be right on the nose!"

"Makes sense. I *think.*"

"So you thought I knew about *your* Charlie, did ya?"

"It's possible Mace could've told you!"

"Huh!" Mattie snorted. Then: "Okay, Charlie. You're home." Showing her even white teeth in a broad smile, she turned into the driveway. The battered Ford rumbled to a halt at the front stoop. Leigh got out of the car, closed the door, turned, and leaned in through the open window. Mattie liked the window open. Cleared out the fumes, she'd told her.

"Thanks a lot, Mattie. Looks like, between us, we brought matters to a head. Mace-wise that is. You gonna be okay?"

"Sure." Mattie grinned. "Leave Mace to me, I can handle him. Just watch out for that daughter of yours."

Leigh wondered if Mattie *could* handle Mace. After all, things *had* taken a turn for the worse—he could get nasty. She hesitated, then asked a question she'd thought about for a long time. "Mattie. Have you and Mace ever . . ."

"Nope." Mattie smiled back. "Wasn't that kinda relationship. Tried it on a coupla times, but he wasn't having any. At the time, I guessed he must've been 'funny' that way. Y'know? As in gay? Turned out I was wrong. He fell for you all right, Leigh!"

"You think so?"

"I know so. 'Bye. Take extra care, you and Deana. I'll keep you posted."

It was late afternoon. Time for a shower, Leigh decided. Then I'll prepare supper. Wonder what Deana had for lunch?

She eased the key into the lock. The door swung open.

"Deana," she called.

No reply.

Her heart racing a little, Leigh bit her lip.

No worries, she thought.

Maybe Deana went over to Warren's place.

FIFTY-ONE

The sun was going from the front of the house.

Fingers of shadow spread across the hallway.

Leigh held her breath; a twinge of dread plucked at her stomach.

She listened.

Heard a slight flutter . . .

Probably a bird outside . . .

Then:

Light footfalls scurried behind her.

A hand clawed out roughly, catching her hair, cupping her mouth.

Cutting off her cry of "HELPPP—"

Struggling wildly, she broke free. Twisting away, she swung around.

And gasped, her heart lurching, the color draining from her face. Her legs trembled.

She felt herself swaying.
It can't be.
It was . . .
Nelson.

FIFTY-TWO

"I'd best be getting on home. Mom'll be worried. I called to say I'd be back by ten."

Warren glanced at his watch. Ten-fifteen.

"I'll drive you," he said, adding, "I'd be happier that way."

"Okay. Thanks."

They stepped into the darkness. It was cooler now. And quiet—except for the breeze stirring the leaves around them. Deana thought about the funeral car and shivered.

Inside the Porsche, she said, "Mom worries about me these days. Since . . . *it* all happened. I guess I should really be home, keeping her company."

"Y'know, that's what I love about you, Deana. You're so nice to your mom."

"Oh yeah? How about all that poetic stuff? Skin like milk, eyes like deep pools, etcetera, etcetera."

"Oh, so you want Dark Lady of the Sonnets?"

"Mmmm, Shakespeare. Now you're talking—although I'll have you know, Warren Hastings, *my* reputation is whiter than white. Compared to the Dark Lady's, that is!"

An excited tingle began in her stomach. Warren hadn't mentioned the word "love" before. Allan had, when they talked about the *Friday the 13th* movie, the night he got killed. "I love the way you squeal and cover your eyes . . . and peek through your fingers," he'd said.

But when Warren said "love" in that quiet, sincere way, the word took on a whole new meaning. He said it as if he really meant it.

As she stole a glance at him, her excitement mounted. She hardly dared breathe. He slid the key in the ignition and started the car. Reaching the end of the driveway, he made a right and slowed down. He brought it to a halt.

Turning to her, he said softly, "Y'know, I *do* care about you, Deana. I care a lot."

He's gonna kiss me, I know it. . . .

She swallowed hard, and whispered, "And I like you, Warren. You've been great this last coupla weeks or so." Then, as an afterthought: "And Mom likes you, too."

She cringed inside, and made a face.

And Mom likes you, too!

What a *dork!* As sweet nothings go, Deana West, that sure takes the biscuit!

She gave a wry grin.

"Great," he said, winking at her. "A guy always likes to know he has parental approval!"

She grew embarrassed. "Why d'you always make a joke of everything?"

"Nerves. When things get serious, I resort to humor. Which, I might add, doesn't mean I'm any the less serious about you—*if* you get my meaning?"

"Sure I do, Warren. That's why I like you. You're so . . ."

"Mature?"

"Well, yeah, that's the word—now you're joking again!"

Their eyes met. She caught a ragged breath. Her heart pounded. Deliciously aware of his proximity, she reached over and gave his knee a tentative squeeze. Looking deep into her eyes, he began tracing a fingertip down her cheek.

She shivered, pressing her thighs together, feeling the sharp tingly buzz between them.

He stopped stroking, pulled her forward, and kissed her softly on the lips.

Her breath quickened and she leaned into him, her breasts crushing against his chest. Her nipples stiffened.

Her heart raced. It was like they'd been searching for each other all of their lives.

She squirmed and wriggled closer. His hand caressed her knee, then slid along her thigh, kneading the firm, naked flesh.

Deana sighed and reached down to touch him, smiling softly as his hard-on jerked under her hand. Hesitating a moment, she found his zipper, peeled it down, and reached inside. Her hand closed around his erection. It felt strong and hard. Her fingers traveled its length, caressing the tip. It was smooth, warm, moist. Their lips met again, his tongue found hers, and he sucked with long hard strokes. Still holding him, she moaned into his mouth, her hand jerking in a steady rhythm.

This is so fantastic, she thought. *I don't want it to stop. Ever.*

Good thing I'm wearing my wrapover . . . and left off my bra.

His hand slipped inside her blouse; it felt warm against her breasts. Massaging them gently, feeling their weight, running his fingertips over her nipples.

Her lips found his again; she was gasping, *wanting* him so much. He came away, found her breasts, and freed them from her soft jersey top. She pushed a nipple into his mouth. He nuzzled hungrily. Her eyes closed . . .

Then snapped open.

A rap on the windshield, Deana's side of the car, caught them off guard.

They heard a high, simpering giggle.

Deana bolted upright, taut, alert. Dragging her top across her breasts, she pulled away from Warren.

Who the hell?

Mommy Dearest . . .

In a trilby hat, set at a rakish angle. Wearing a dark, tailored jacket, a floppy handkerchief flowing from its breast pocket. Her hands, in shabby white gloves, poked through the open side window.

With a gasp, Deana drew back.

"Christ!" Warren muttered, staring at the apparition. "What's *she* doing here?"

The hag's eyes narrowed.

They looked *different* tonight. Ringed with smudgy mascara, they reminded Deana of black hairy spiders. "My God," she breathed. "Nightmare City made flesh . . ."

Better say *something*.

Anything.

Like what?

Howdy. How're the old folks back home?

She managed, "Where's Harry?"

The whiskery chin jiggled at them.

"Harry died. Little runt went tits up on me. Weren't nothin' I could do."

"Oh. Sorry to hear that. You must miss him."

Jesus *Christ!* What am I, stupid? Sitting here talking to this *maniac*? I should be grabbing my cell phone, calling the cops . . .

Mommy Dearest batted her lashes in a grotesque wink.

"Caught ya at a bad time, did I, dearie?"

"You *asshole!*" Deana exploded. "Y'know I could report you for abduction? Serve ya right, too. And y'know the cops could get ya for keeping those old broads locked away like that? They almost *ate* me alive back there. . . . How come the authorities let you run a home, anyhow? You're a mad, sick old fuck and should be locked away yourself!"

Mommy's head came forward, her eyes glaring. They leveled with Deana's. The hat slipped, tilting to one side. She looked weird, scary—like she was about to tear open the car door and drag Deana away.

Back to her abominable brood . . .

Deana shrank into her seat.

Warren touched the remote. The window whirred up.

Grinning like an animated zombie, the fag-hag from hell pressed her skinny nose to the glass. Quickly, Warren turned the key, revved the engine. The car leapt forward.

A little way down the street, he peered into the rearview mirror.

The fag-hag was gone.

"So Harry popped his clogs."

" 'Bout the size of it. Smart move. Wherever he is, he's gotta be in a better place than in that weirdo's freaky rest home!"

Warren shot Deana a quizzical glance. He guessed all this had something to do with her experience the night she invited him to dinner. He decided not to ask.

She gave him a weak smile. "Wearing that stupid hat, she looked like that gay English guy, Quentin Crisp. . . . God, what a *hoot!*"

"You're not kidding!"

"Well, that's Mommy Dearest," she said faintly. "Or should I say, *Daddy* Dearest? What a *freak!* No idea she was a transvestite." Remembering the hag's strong, scrawny arms tight around her, Deana murmured, "What d'ya reckon? Is it a 'she'—or a 'he'?"

Warren gave a thin smile. "Who cares? Just make sure we avoid her in future, that's all."

"Agreed. Apart from that, she *did* interrupt something rather special. Don't you think?"

"Mmmm. You're right there. We started . . ."

"Started what, Warren?"

"We started something I'd rather like to finish later. How 'bout you?"

"Yeah," she said softly. "Me, too."

Deana went quiet for a moment. Then tears welled up. Slowly, they fell down her cheeks.

Warren stopped the car.

"What is it, Deana? Not something *I* did, I hope?"

"No. Nothing like that. What we did was all so . . . wonderful. It's just that everything seems to be *happening,* is all. One thing after another. Especially tonight, coming face-to-face with that freaky old witch again. And then there's Mace. . . . I don't know, I'm so *scared* of him. And of what he's doing to Mom."

She almost said, "And how he came to my room . . ." but stopped herself, reluctant to spoil things by discussing Mace tonight.

Warren drew her to him and kissed the tip of her nose.

Looking into his eyes, she said quietly, "You're all right, Warren. Y'know that?"

"You, too," he replied. "And don't forget, whatever happens, I'll always be here for you."

Leigh met Deana at the door.

"What's up, Mom? You look as if you've seen a ghost."

"I just did, honey. Nelson."

Deana's jaw dropped. She stopped in her tracks.

Oh my God. Not Nelson!

What the hell *is* happening to us?

FIFTY-THREE

"He's sick, Deana. He wanted money . . ."

"Where is he?"

"He left. I called Mattie—I feel awful about that. He was just a pathetic human being. Real sick."

"You called Mattie? Not *Mace?*"

"No, honey. Not Mace."

Something in Leigh's tone made Deana hesitate. There was a tension in it she didn't like. If there's a problem with Mace, she thought, I need to know about it. "Mom. About Mace—" she got out.

"How's Warren?" Leigh interrupted, a little too quickly. Deana closed her lips. Maybe now wasn't the time to say anything about Mace.

"He's okay." She pictured the fag-hag and her band of

trolls, tucked away in the twilight zone. Best keep *them* under wraps, too. Mom doesn't look like she can take any more shocks.

She led Leigh to the living room. "Guess you could use a drink," she said, going over to the wet bar and decanting a cognac into a balloon glass. "Anyway," she said, rapidly changing the subject. "How're things at the office?"

"Er . . . I didn't go today, hon."

"No?"

"No. Something came up."

"Oh? Like what?"

"Deana, better grab yourself a drink, too. There's something I should tell you."

Brriinngg . . . Brriinngg . . .

Leigh's heart lurched.

"The phone, Mom," Deana reminded her gently. "Shall I get it?"

"No, dear. It's probably for me."

It was.

Mattie.

"We got Nelson, Leigh. He's in a bad way. Something terminal, I guess. But he'll be looked after, where he's going. Don't you worry about him. Thing is, looks like he's still harboring some kinda grudge. Swears he's gonna get you—when he comes out. Which he won't, of course. Come out, I mean."

"Thanks for that, Mattie," Leigh said. She gave an uneasy laugh. "Makes me feel a whole lot better. I don't think."

"Nelson's going noplace, Leigh. Trust me—and you can take that to the bank. He's real sick, and he's behind locked doors. So, no chance he'll bother you or Deana, ever again." Mattie hesitated, then asked, "You okay? Musta been quite a shock. . . ."

"Yeah. *Right.*" A pause. "And Mace?"

"He's gone, Leigh. Vacated his apartment. Skedaddled. Vamoosed."

"Oh my God . . ."

"Keep your doors locked, Leigh." Mattie spoke quietly. Leigh, catching the urgency in her voice, felt a little faint. Mattie was asking, "Has he got a key to your place?"

Leigh's heart missed a beat.

"Yes . . . No. I don't know. I never gave him one. But he knows where I keep a spare."

Mattie's silence spoke volumes.

"Maybe you should have a minder," she said. "I'll get somebody over there. Whoever it is, I'll bring them over myself, so when I call, you'll know it's okay."

"Right." Leigh shivered, bringing a hand to her throat. "This is getting worse, Mattie."

"It will do. Until we nail Mace. And doing that won't be easy. He's one slippery chick."

"You're not kidding," Leigh murmured, then said, "Okay, Mattie. See you soon."

"That Mattie?"

Leigh nodded. Hugging herself, leaning against the door frame, going over the conversation. Deana studied her, frowned, and said, "Mom, you look awful."

Leigh managed a bright smile. "Gee, thanks, honey. That's all I need to know."

"Here, take a sip of this." Deana handed the glass of cognac to her mother. "You look as if you need it."

"Thanks." Leigh took a swig and winced. "How people can *drink* this stuff, I'll never know."

"Mom. You had something to tell me. . . . What is it?"

Leigh sighed. She wasn't feeling up to repeating the whole thing over again.

"It's a long story, honey."

Here we go again: *"Here lies Leigh West. Hers was a mighty long story . . ."*

She sighed, and felt sick, going over what happened today. But Deana *has* to know. Best get it over with now. . . .

Easing into the sofa, she took a sip of cognac and shuddered. At the other end, Deana faced her, her legs drawn up, chin resting on her knees. Her glass lay untouched on the table.

An uneasy silence hung on the air.

"Honey," Leigh began in a quiet voice. "You've always wanted to know more about Charlie, your father. Well, today I learned the truth of the matter—straight from the horse's mouth. Or, put another way, straight from the pen of Edith Payne, Charlie's mother."

Wide-eyed, Deana stared at Leigh. "And?"

"When I was your age, I was a bit of a rebel. Mom and Dad packed me off to Aunt Jenny and Uncle Mike's in Milwaukee. It was there I met your father. . . ."

Leigh's hand reached out to touch Deana's. She gave a hesitant smile.

At last, the tale came tumbling out. All of it. No holds barred. Leigh hoped to God Deana could deal with it. She watched her daughter's face, afraid she'd see disgust, bewilderment, even contempt. Afraid things between them might never be the same again.

But what Leigh saw was Deana growing up before her eyes. She'd been listening intently, a small frown creasing her brow as she absorbed the details.

"And you never *once* suspected that Mace was Charlie's *brother?*"

"Never. Not in a million years would I think such a thing could be true. Until . . ."

"Until what?"

"Until I saw Mace's body last night." She felt a little awkward talking to Deana like this, but as she'd gotten this far, she felt she had to carry on. "You know, like he's a blond? Well, he had *black* hair. Pubic hair and stuff? He was a different person. He has a tan, but with the black hair, his bronze body looked so *natural*. . . . Like he was born with it—nothing to do with the sun."

She paused, realizing Deana would spot the link.

She did.

Black hair. Black *body* hair. Like her own. Deana grimaced. The awful truth was beginning to hit her.

"And I'm *related* to that *creep?*"

Gently, Leigh said, "That's right. He's your uncle, Deana."

"Oh my God!!!"

The doorbell rang. Shattering the silence.

Their hearts raced.

Leigh rushed to the hallway.

Mattie was on the stoop.

"I'm alone, Leigh. Decided to go it alone. I know Mace's mind better than anyone." Quickly, she stepped inside the hallway. "We put out an all points," she explained. A moment's pause, then quietly she asked, "Does Deana know?"

Leigh nodded.

"How's she taking it?"

"Well, I think. Probably hasn't hit her yet. When it does, there'll be repercussions—bound to be. But at the moment, she's okay. It's quite a story for her to deal with, Mattie."

"Yeah, a pretty tough one to swallow, I agree. But she'll pull through. She's a sensible gal for her age. Best she knows what we're up against; that way she'll be aware of what *might* happen."

"The devil you know, et cetera."

Mattie frowned. "Something like that," she said quietly.

They went into the living room.

"Hi, Mattie."

"Hi yourself, Deana."

"Deana, huh? Sure that's not *Charlie?*"

"No, honey. No more Charlies. Enough of them around as it is, huh?"

Leigh broke in. "Hey. It's been a busy day—and night. How about a nightcap before we turn in?"

"Sounds good to me. Thing is, I don't reckon I'll be doing much sleeping. . . ."

"Me neither," Deana put in.

Leigh went over to the sound system. She put on some Sinatra. Sexy ol' Frank. "My Way" was her favorite. A good one to relax to at the end of a hard day.

They chatted and laughed. Trying to chill out. Trying to ignore what had happened earlier. But, beneath it all, their minds were on Mace. Wondering where he was.

What he was doing.

Finally blocking him out of her mind, Deana switched over to Warren. Thinking about how they almost made love.

Yeah. Almost.

Then she pictured Mommy Dearest and her band of old broads.

Forget her, she told herself. *She's history. . . .*

Deana's thoughts slipped back to Warren.

Wishing he were here. Promising herself she'd tell him the whole story just as Mom told it to her.

A terrifying thought crossed her mind.

Warren could be in danger himself. . . . Mace *knows* about him. Knows where he lives, too.

He might threaten Warren.

Harm him, even.

Oh God—that couldn't really happen. Could it?

"Mom," Deana said hurriedly. "What about Warren? Mace knows about him being my boyfriend and everything." She turned to Mattie. "D'ya think he's in any danger?"

"Warren?"

"Yeah. I met him recently. He's a nice guy. Has a dog called Sabre. And a sister called Sheena. She's a bouncer at a nightclub in San Jose."

Mattie's ears pricked up. This was a new angle. One that could complicate matters.

"Perhaps we should warn this . . . Warren? Got his number?"

"Yeah."

"Best give him a call, Deana."

"Okay."

Deana went to the hallway. She dialed Warren's number. Two short rings. Then:

"The Hastings residence. How may I—"

"Warren?"

"Hi, Deana. How ya doin?"

Her heart warmed. He sounded so calm and *sensible*.

"Warren. Sorry to call so late. But we, er . . . might have ourselves a situation here. Mom's boyfriend—pardon me, *former* boyfriend Mace, from Mill Valley PD?" Deana rolled up her eyes and made a face. Come on, Warren. You *must* remember. . . .

"Yes?"

"Well, I can't explain now, but he's on the run. Gone apeshit. And he *knows* about you. We thought he might try to contact you."

"Really?"

Deana got worried. If only she didn't have to involve him like this. Worst-case scenario, it could mean good-bye to Warren. And they hadn't even made love yet. Not *properly,* anyhow.

"Deana. Are you and Leigh okay?"

She breathed a sigh of relief. He didn't *sound* as if he was about to disappear out of her life forever.

"Sure. We have a police officer here." Turning, she looked through the doorway and smiled in Mattie's direction. "She's keeping guard over us."

"Deana. I'm coming over."

"You sure? What about Sheena?"

"She's not due in until five-thirty."

"Yeah. You said . . ."

Putting a hand over the mouthpiece, she told Mattie, "Warren's coming over. Okay?"

"The more the merrier!"

Deana spoke into the phone.

"Sure, Warren," she said. "But be careful. Bring your car down the driveway. We'll be waiting for you."

"Right. Be there in about fifteen minutes?"

"Sure. Oh, Warren?"

"Deana?"

"What about Sabre?"

"I'll leave him here. Intruders come a-callin', they might change their minds and go home."

Deana giggled. "Sure. Let Sabre guard Sheena. Or should that be the other way around?"

At the other end, Warren smiled grimly.

"Intruder breaks in here, Deana, it'd be a question of who gets him first—Sheena or Sabre!"

FIFTY-FOUR

The phone rang out.

It seemed louder than usual.

Mattie motioned to the women to stay seated. "I'll get it," she said quietly.

Alert now, Leigh and Deana heard Mattie pick up the phone. "Yes?" she said. Next time she spoke, she sounded mad.

Mattie listened intently, feeling her blood rise. "But I'm on police surveillance here. Tell the chief go fu—"

"This *IS* the chief, Blaylock." The voice thundered in her ear. She jerked the receiver away from her head. "An' I'm ordering you to git the hell outa there. Just git that tight little ass a' yours over here, pronto. DO YOU COPY?"

"But these people are in dang—"

"Those *people* can have alternative surveillance. I'll assign another officer to the job. I'll have one over there in a bit, Mattie. Something just showed up here. We need you and your goddamn womanly instincts t'help us out. Got me?"

"Okay. Okay," Mattie said wearily. There was no stopping the chief when he was in a lousy mood. "I'll be right over."

"Sorry, guys. Gotta go. Chief's in an uproar back there. Sounds like something big with a capital B's just broke out. Another murder, I guess. He's sending over an officer, pronto. So I'm gonna have to say goodnight.

"Doors and windows have been double-checked, but no harm done if you check again. Do *not* open doors—or windows—to *anyone*. Right? I'll give the guy a code word. What d'ya suggest?"

Deana perked up. "How 'bout 'Eureka'?"

Mattie shrugged. "Eureka it is. I'll call ya soon as I'm through with World War Three goin' on back at the ranch."

Mattie left. After she'd gone, Leigh and Deana hadn't much to say. In the semidarkness, the living room suddenly seemed scary. Shadows, trembling in the flickering light from the TV, became potential intruders. And even with the sound turned low, they felt that tonight, *Psycho* was a bad choice of movie to watch. But they let it roll on, neither of them feeling inclined to switch channels.

11:28.

No Warren.

And no replacement bodyguard, either.

The phone rang. Shattering the stillness. Smashing into their thoughts.

Leigh looked across at Deana.

"Mattie said she'd call. That must be her now." She got up, straightened her back, and went into the hallway.

Deana heard her say, "Can't *you* deal with it, Tony?"

Leigh's grip tightened on the phone. She was stunned.

Tonight of all nights. There *had* to be a major problem at the Bayview.

"I'm a waiter, Ms. West. Not a bouncer," Tony reminded her.

"Call the cops, then."

"They're coming out just as soon as they can. Thought you needed to know that. Before you get here."

"But, Tony. Can't *you* deal with it?" Leigh persisted wearily. Her hand brushed her forehead. She felt sick.

"They want *you*, Ms. West. They specifically said for you to be here. Christ! All hell's breakin' loose. . . . My God—you better get over here fast!"

Leigh sighed. She'd no wish to leave Deana alone. But it looked like she had no choice. . . .

"Honey, there's a fight at the restaurant. Apparently, the place is being trashed as we speak. Police are on their way over. I gotta go, honey. I hate to leave you here alone, but . . ."

"I'll be okay, Mom. I'll stay *glued* to my seat. Anyway, Warren's on his way over. So is the replacement officer." Deana gave a weak smile. "I'm gonna be *okay*. Really. Jeez. Sorry about the restaurant. Tonight of all nights. Hope it isn't *too* bad."

"Thanks, honey. Knew you'd be sensible about this. Call me the minute Warren shows up—don't open the door to anyone else. Except the officer, of course. And don't forget the password."

"I won't, Mom. Take care. See ya later."

Leigh started the car, unable to shake off her misgivings. She hated leaving Deana like this. But the Bayview—how come it was being *trashed*?

Who would *do* this?

Not something her usual clientele would get up to . . .

At the top of the driveway, she made a left and turned down into the street. Be glad when this whole thing's over, she thought. Can anything *else* go wrong tonight?

Good thing I didn't mention Mace's scrapbook to Deana. God. She would have been so *scared*. . . .

* * *

Deana snuggled into her armchair.

Thinking, Where's Warren? Said he'd be here in fifteen minutes. It's way past that now. . . .

She switched channels. *Psycho* had been a real bad choice. She channel-hopped, and found a low-budget sci-fi movie. She stared at the screen. So far, all the action seemed to be happening in a spaceship, with some crazy alien crew leaping around in tight suits.

Boring . . .

She switched off the TV.

Everywhere was spooky quiet.

The shadows, shifting around in the semidarkness, grew scarier by the minute.

Seemed like the house had taken on a life of its own. The trees outside rustled and sighed. The moving shadows they made, crouched like animals ready to pounce.

A low rumble jolted her upright. Huhhh. Goddamn water cistern again!

She slumped down, huffing a sigh of relief.

But—what was *that?*

A faint click . . .

Her mouth went dry.

Her heart raced. Her breath came out in short, harsh bursts.

Then silence again.

It was *so* eerie.

Even the trees weren't rustling.

She relaxed, switched on the TV.

Psycho was still on.

It'd reached the part where Norman Bates was talking to his dead mother in the attic.

The movie was almost finished. . . .

What then?

Warren should be here by now. . . .

The doorbell's gonna ring any minute.

Maybe I should call. Something could've have gone wrong. . . .

She heard movement, a faint rustle behind her.

She stiffened. Froze. Her mouth dried up again.

"Hey. Sugar. How 'bout a cuppa coffee for your uncle Mace?"

His voice was soft, warm, familiar.

She jerked around.

"You," she gasped.

"Who else, darlin'?"

Mace grinned, friendly like. He opened his arms, palms held out. As if to say, *Hey. Here I am!* Like the night in her room. The night Warren came to dinner.

Mace. The bastard!

She'd handled him then. But she wasn't too sure she could do it now.

Knowing what she did.

Remembering what Mom had told her.

Her legs felt shaky. Her breath jerked out in quick, shallow gulps. Trembling, trying to play it cool, she steadied herself.

"Coffee? Sure. Take a seat, Mace. I'll go see to it right away."

She got up, made a move to the kitchen, thinking, If I'm quick I could use the extension in there. Call Mom, the police, Mattie. Warren. *Anybody.*

Mace watched her go, chewing on seeds, a loose smile playing on his lips.

Deana clattered around in the kitchen. Fixing coffee. Setting mugs on a tray. An eye on the phone all the time.

Do it now do it now.

What if he's watching?

Fuck that.

Just do it. She did it.

Lifted the phone.

Dead as dirt.

"Well now, sweetheart." He was behind her, making a snipping motion with his fingers. "Them li'l ol' wires are all cut. Uncle Mace couldn't take no chances. Not with a smart young gal like you around."

He moved forward, catlike. Grabbing her hand. Twisting it behind her back. Holding it there. Tight.

She was hurting, but no way would she let him see it.

He pulled her close, their bodies touching.

She winced, catching a whiff of mulchy breath.

Goddamn seeds . . .

He grinned.

Slammed his free hand across her mouth.

Kept it there.

She struggled, trying to come up for air. Beneath his hand, she tore open her mouth, trying to say, "Warren'll be here any minute."

Only it came out like some weird mumbo-jumbo.

"Really. You do surprise me," he said with a curt, amused laugh.

He frog-marched her into the living room. Flung her facedown onto the sofa. Rammed a knee hard into her spine. Grabbing a handful of hair, he jerked her up and back, and wound a black silk scarf tight around her head. It cut into her eyes, across the bridge of her nose.

Leaving only a slight airway.

She panicked. Struggled. Barely able to breathe.

Pausing, he stepped back, watching her mumbling, kicking, gasping for air. Then, dragging a coil of twine from his jacket pocket, he began to wind it around her arms.

She still wore her blue top.

The one Warren had put his hand inside earlier.

The tie had worked loose; the soft cloth slipped from her shoulders.

He gaped at her for a moment, seeing the rise of her soft round breasts, a glimpse of dark nipples, feeling himself rise, jerk, and grow hard.

She looked so . . . good and sweet. Scared. Vulnerable.

He smiled tersely.

Later, he promised himself.

Plenty of time . . .

He spoke softly. "Take it easy, sweetheart. You should know better than to fight with Uncle Mace."

Deana lay quiet. Wondering what in hell he planned to do next. Straining hard to hear his movements. Trying to guess what was happening.

A blanket dropped over her head. She struggled, feeling the twine bite into her arms, sweat break out and stream down her body. She gagged against the coarse, prickly cloth as he bound it around her.

More twine. Then he was hoisting her onto his shoulder.

Bumping along, she felt his biceps, flexed and hard, beneath her, the jolts and sickening thuds to her stomach and breasts. . . . Heard the click of his cowboy boots on the tiled hallway . . . Felt a draft of air on her legs and feet. Her mules had gotten lost in the struggle.

They were outside now, the cool night air flowing fresh around them.

She found herself swooping as he swung her down, setting her upright on the gravel.

OUCH!! Shit!!!

Jagged stones jabbed and bit the soles of her feet. . . .

She heard the click of the trunk opening. Felt herself lifted, tossed into it. *Rammed* inside it. He was tucking in the blanket. The sharp edges of a toolbox or something jabbed her chest.

She gave a sharp gasp of pain.

The lid slammed down, cutting off whatever air there'd been. She found herself inhaling coarse, prickly fibers. They caught in her throat. She began coughing.

Christ, I'm gonna choke to death. . . .

Suddenly, she was panicking, spluttering.

She swallowed hard.

Again. And again.

Soon, her throat muscles were under control. . . .

Thank God!

But it's so hot . . .

"I'm gonna suffocate in here. I'm gonna DIE. Nobody'll find me till it's too late. . . ."

She felt vibrating throbs as the engine turned over. Heard it slip into gear, move up the driveway. Mace made a left and she slid a little, her foot tensing against metal. . . . Jesus, she thought, *I'm suffocating. . . .*

Panic welled up again.

Don't scream. . . .

I do, and I could start choking all over again.

Her hands strained against the twine.

No way would it give. . . . Desperate, gulping sobs rose in her throat.

She began to gag, choke . . .

Streams of sweat drenched her body.

Lie still. Save what air there is. . . . He can't drive all night. He has to stop. Please God make it soon!

They were traveling over rough ground.

Bumping over ruts and rocks, her body shaking, jolting up and down.

Nauseous waves swept up from her stomach . . .

The scarf bit into her face.

Sweat, slick and hot, oozed from every pore.

My God. WHERE ARE WE?

Don't tell me. Mt. Tam. I know it—sense it. Goddamn fuckin' place. I HATE it. I get outa here, I'll NEVER, EVER come back to this freakin' place again. . . .

More bumping. More ruts.

The car pulled to a halt.

Her heart lurched.

What now? Is this where I get it? Right where Allan got his?

The trunk lid swung up.

Thank God.

Cool air streamed in.

He was pushing her, then rolling her forward. Feeling around for something. A weapon?

Christ! He's gonna kill me!

He picked her up.

Hoisted her onto his shoulder.

She was bouncing and flopping around again, like a sack of laundry.

He stopped.

He was fiddling with a door lock, stepping over a stoop, his boots stamping across a wooden floor. Then she went flying through the air, landing on a springy mattress. She heard, *felt,* the harsh metallic squeak of bedsprings. . . .

He was loosening her ties now. Peeling off the blanket.

Thank God thank God.

Now I can *breathe.*

Get this thing off so I can see, maybe I can talk him out of killing me.

The scarf stayed put.

So did the twine around her wrists.

Oh, the goddamn *heat!*

Her skin felt slick. Slimy.

Uggh . . .

If only I could *see!*

In her mind, though, she could see the headlines:

GIRL, CAPTURED BY MANIAC UNCLE!

Lost for weeks out in the wilderness, the eighteen-year-old's emaciated body was found by hikers today. Looked like she'd starved to death. Slowly.

Or maybe hacked to death, quickly.

What's it to be, folks?

"Gonna leave ya now, sugar. Uncle Mace has gotta ride. Places to go. Things to do."

She felt his lips on her forehead.

And his kiss.

Light, soft.

She caught his sour breath.

"Back soon, honey," he whispered.

She heard the *click, click* of boots as he walked away, a door snap to, a key turn in the lock.

The car engine revved, then raced. It moved away. She listened till the sound faded.

She was alone.

Hey, come back! Don't leave me like this!

Save your breath, Deana.

Maybe he won't be too long. . . .

She waited.

And waited.

S'pose he never comes back. S'pose he just leaves me here to rot. . . .

It was almost light when Mace returned.

FIFTY-FIVE

"Deana! Deana! Leigh! Open up!"

Warren thumped the door so hard, he thought he'd bust his knuckles.

"Christ, where *are* you, Deana?"

It's like Sheena said. . . . They've gone. . . .

What had Deana meant by "Mom's boyfriend's on the run . . . and he's gone apeshit?" And why did she emphasize "he *knows* about you?"

Sounded like anything could've happened. . . .

Probably had.

They could both be dead.

"Oh my God. Not that . . ."

Sheena had arrived home early. A couple of minutes later and he'd have hit the road, driving over to Deana's.

"Warren, maybe I won't be goin' back to Pacey's no more," Sheena said quietly. "He kinda objects when I leave him in the lurch."

She seemed preoccupied. He knew that look.

Only too well.

His mouth went dry.

"Sheena! For chrissake, tell me what's up? What was so important you left the club early?"

She said she was scared. Had had one of her *feelings* . . .

He saw beads of sweat on her upper lip. He'd never seen her this tense before.

"You're not gonna like it, Warren, but this gal o' yours, she's in deep trouble. I feel she's in a place that's small— and dark. Yeah. It's real dark in there, and she . . ."

She hesitated, knowing what this was doing to Warren.

His face went white. "For God's *sake*, Sheena, she *what?*"

"Call the cops, Warren. Let them deal with it. It's none a' your business. Don't want you getting yourself killed on account of some gal you only just met!"

But Warren was out the door. She heard the Porsche burst into life.

"Deana, if you're in there, open up. PLEASE!"

Twin headbeams swooped down the driveway. Warren squinted, bringing up a hand to shield his eyes.

Leigh's car screeched to a halt. The near-side door swung open and she jumped out.

"Warren!"

"Leigh! You're safe. . . ."

"Yeah. But what about Deana?"

"What d'ya mean, Leigh?" His heart lurched, and sank like a stone.

He *was* too late. He'd known it all along.

He stood aside while Leigh prodded the key into the lock. The door fell open. They rushed inside.

The hallway was dark.

They ran to the living room. Trembling light from the TV threw uneasy shadows into the darkness. A talk-show host laughed, holding a mike close to a grinning member of the audience. . . .

"Deana! Deana, darling! You there?"

Leigh darted into each room, calling, her heart sinking, her legs all shaky.

When she returned to the living room, her shoulders were hunched. She looked drawn, defeated. Exhausted.

Oh my God, thought Warren. *Sheena's right. I shoulda called the cops.*

Leigh caught his concern. "Did you only just *get* here?" she demanded, her face hostile.

"Yeah, Leigh, I'm sorry. I got held up. . . ."

"My God, Warren. You got held *up?* Don't you *see?* Mace arranged all this so he could take her. . . ."

"What happened? And where were *you,* Leigh?"

Leigh broke down, sobbing. There'd been no fight at the Bayview. All had been quiet when she got there. Just another civilized night. Customers enjoying their meals, paying their checks, saying their goodnights. No "all hell breakin' loose" as Tony said. . . . Tony? It hadn't been Tony who'd phoned her. It had been a hoax caller. And she'd bet her bottom dollar it'd been Mace who'd done the calling. . . .

The phone rang.

Leigh sprang forward, grabbed it. "Yes?" Her voice was terse.

Mattie.

"Thank *God* you're okay, Leigh. Have to report there was no emergency back here. Musta been a hoax call. Chief signed off early. Went home to his wife. She'd gotten sick. Nobody here's aware of any emergency. Don't ask me why . . . Leigh? You and Deana okay?"

Leigh met Warren's eyes. Hot, frightened tears began to well up.

"Deana's gone, Mattie. She's not here."

A moment's silence, then:

"It's Mace. Y'know that, Leigh, don't ya?" Mattie's voice rose. "Goddamn fuckin' asshole Mace. Jesus! Our friendly master mimic Mace. The shit fooled us all."

FIFTY-SIX

Almost sunup.

Mace eyed his wristwatch. "Maybe a half hour till it gets light," he muttered.

Gotta move it. Though I shouldn't worry, he told himself, I got nothin' but time. He set his holdall down on the stoop and pushed the key in the doorlock.

He grinned. This was a real good place for his "other activities." Nobody, but nobody'd come this way in weeks.

The air was cool and clear, the dew still heavy on the rough grass humps along the track. He scanned the terrain. Mountains on one side, well-wooded with dark, impenetrable pines. The cabin, hidden in rocky territory, was almost impossible to access. He'd used the dirt path, betting not many others would attempt it—wouldn't want to. You could wreck a vehicle driving over the rough tracks hereabouts.

He glanced over to his right. Into the wide misty space beyond. Before that, though, came a sheer drop to the valley below. In the growing light, he heard the distant sound of roaring water. The river. He'd done some whitewater rafting down there a coupla years back. When he first discovered the cabin . . .

Yessir. One lonesome place. But, like the trooper he was, he always covered his tracks, so nobody'd ever discover his "other activities." He'd been fortunate to find such an isolated spot.

He went inside the cabin.

"Hi, honey. I'm home!" he sang out.

Silence . . .

Then a muffled sob from the bed.

"Well now, Deana darlin', how ya doin'?"

He set down his holdall and went over to Deana. Humming a little to himself, he untied and peeled off the silk scarf. He released her wrists from the twine.

Deana gasped, scrunching her eyes, peering into the half-light.

Saw him standing over her.

Giving her one of his twisted smiles.

"PLEASE, MACE. TAKE ME HOME!" she blurted.

"Why, sure enough, y'are home, sugar." Mace looked a little surprised, hurt she was thinking otherwise.

"Where *am* I?"

She rubbed at her wrist, wincing as she went over the burn marks. Her hands still felt dead.

"You're tucked away nice 'n' safe where nobody can find ya, honey."

Deana looked around at the cabin. A tin bucket stood in the corner. *Coulda done with that hours ago,* she thought, aware of the dark patch, now cold and uncomfortable, between her legs. She saw packs of bottled water, an open cardboard box, a rickety hardback chair—and Mace's holdall, directly in front of her.

Shuffling till her back was against the wall, she took in the gray tick mattress. Old brown stains made big patchy patterns across it.

Blood?

There were more stains than mattress.

She stifled a gulp of fear.

"Mace, what are you going to do to me?" she asked, despising the tremor in her voice.

"Haven't decided yet, sugar. But take my advice, don't you worry your pretty li'l head about it." He walked over to the cardboard box, took out a wrapped bread roll, and handed it to her. "Here. You must be hungry. Some time since you last ate, huh?"

She took the roll, peeled off the wrapper, opened up the top layer, and peered inside.

"Won't hurt you none." He watched her closely, an amused grin on his face. "Can't guarantee it'll be Bayview quality, but it's as good as you're gonna get."

He picked up a bottle of water, twisted off the top, and passed the bottle to her. "There," he said. "Salami on rye and a swig a' water and you'll be fightin' fit in no time at all. Mmmm . . . Looks good," he said, and nodded at the sandwich. "Don't mind if I have one a' those myself."

Helping himself to a roll and fresh water, he sat facing her, astride the hardback chair. He broke off a wad of bread and shoved it in his mouth. "Guess you must be wonderin' why you're here," he said, chewing around on the food. "Why I'm taking such a special interest in my pretty li'l niece?"

"You could say that," Deana said slowly, not taking her eyes off his face. How could she *ever* have fancied him? He looked like an over-the-hill biker with his leather jacket, bleached hair, and crumbs falling down his front.

Scratch over-the-hill biker.

Mace is one hundred percent cop, Deana, an' don't you forget it. A cop gone bad—and mad . . .

Her heart began to hammer.

Mace chewed on his food, smiling at her like he knew something she didn't.

Deana didn't like the way he did that. She shivered.

"Tell ya a little story?"

"If you must."

"Gotta keep y' entertained, honey. Can't have ya gettin' bored, now, can we?"

She made a face. He had to smile. The kid had guts, he'd give her that.

"I tell you a tale, then I take your photograph. Deal?"

He offered a hand and she took it, warily.

She didn't much like the sound of "photographs," but at least it didn't seem like he was going to kill her yet.

He got up and stood looking through the cabin's murky window. "Guess your mom told you about Edith Payne's letter?"

"Er, sure, she told me about it. . . ."

"I'll go one better, sweetheart. I'll tell ya *my* version!"

Turning on his heel, he faced her. Looking into her eyes, saying nothing. Just staring like she was a stranger he'd never seen before.

Then giving her that twisted smile again.

She glanced away, feeling nervous, uncomfortable. Why the hell didn't he sit down and get on with his story?

As if he'd read her thoughts, he set himself astride the chair. He began talking.

"How d'ya think it feels to know that your own mother kills your pa, then gives you to somebody who couldn't care less whether you lived or died?"

His eyes glowed at her, burning with a hate she didn't understand.

Shrinking from his gaze, she said slowly, "Don't know how that'd feel exactly, but . . . I guess it'd be awful. . . ."

"You don't know how that'd feel exactly." His voice rose a couple of octaves, mimicking her words.

Curling his mouth in disgust, he resumed his tale.

"Well, I'll tell ya, Deana. It feels bad. Real bad. It makes you hate a person so much you wanta make 'em suffer— the way you suffered. All those years."

Deana stayed quiet.

"My pa didn't have a chance. He was sick. And drunk. No wonder, with Edith Payne for a wife. My pa believed he was right. And I guess he was. . . . No girl should be like sister Tania. Dark and . . . covered in hair . . ." He slumped forward over the chair. His face creased up. He looked beat.

Deana's mouth stayed shut.

Maybe he's gonna cry.

Then I can hit him with something and escape. . . .

Casually, she looked around. Saw nothing she could use as a weapon. Except the chair . . . and he was sitting on that.

"I searched for my sister, y'know. Didn't track her down, though. But not once have I given up hope. She's out there. Somewhere." His voice rose. "Causin' grief and makin' things bad for somebody else, I guess. Yeah. I KNOW she's still out there—somewhere . . ."

"So, what d'ya intend doing when you find her, Mace? Or should that be Jess?"

Right on, smart-ass! That should get you killed okay. You wanna die? Carry on this way and you'll get your wish . . .

He lifted his head, and his eyes leveled with hers. They seemed oddly vacant, yet they glittered with a wild, dangerous look.

Deana shuddered.

Christ, I got him riled again. What am I, a fuckin' moron?

His mouth quirked in a humorless twist.

"Well, now. Ain't *you* the funny girl? Just call me Uncle Mace, honey. That'll be fine by me."

"Sorry, Mace. Didn't mean to upset you," she said in a small voice.

"You didn't upset me none. Me, I'm just your nice, friendly ol' uncle Mace."

"You joined the police so's you could find Tania? What did you do before that?"

He grinned. "Smart kid, ain't ya? Oh, I bummed around 'Frisco, working bars—pumpin' iron. Knew all the gyms in the Bay Area. Boxed a little; this 'n' that. Then Mom got sick. She was an old lady by then. I went back to Wahconda, but she was dead already. Only inheritance she left was the cabin I was born in—and that letter. . . ."

Deana almost felt sorry for him. He sure was a mixed-up guy. Yeah. Sick. Dangerous. But sad, too.

Suddenly, he was on his feet, staring out the window again. His hands went up to his hips, his jacket lifted, and she caught the bulge of his hip holster.

"Mace?" she ventured quietly. "Why don't you let me go home? Keeping me here isn't gonna do you any good. People'll be looking for me. They find me and—"

"Find you? What makes you think anybody's gonna *find* ya, sweetheart?"

"Well, they'll search for me. Probably trace me to here."

"No way. *Nobody* saw you go. *Nobody'll* find you here. Reason I use this place is because nobody ever comes up here. 'Cept me."

Then he was standing over her. His legs apart. Grinning. Stroking her hair. Smoothing the dark strands resting on her shoulders. Over and over again.

She winced.

Too scared to move.

Her eyes leveled with his crotch.

Saw him jerk inside his pants.

God, no. He's gonna rape me. Please God. NO!

He grabbed her head, pressed it to him. His hard-on rose some more. She felt it throb against her face.

Breaking away, she squirmed back across the mattress, edging off it, landing on her knees.

She scrambled to her feet.

"Just let me go, Mace. Before we both do something we'll regret." Her eyes wandered to the chair. One quick smash and it'd be in pieces.

I could use one of the legs to hit him with.

Kill him, if I have to.

Oh yeah? You an' whose army?

His eyes mocked her. "Don't do anything stupid, Deana. Remember, I could break ya pretty li'l neck, just like that."

He swiped the air with a swift karate chop.

She blinked. Picturing his hand coming down, whistling toward her.

Watch it, Deana.

Maybe I'll get him while he's asleep . . .

If he falls asleep . . .

She shivered, suddenly getting the feeling he was reading her mind.

Instead, he looked confused, bewildered. Shaking his head. Heaving a sorrowful sigh.

"I'm gonna have to put y'away, Deana. Y'know that?"

"Put me *away?* Whaddya mean, put me away?"

"Put you someplace where you'll come to no harm. Where you'll be safe. Come to Uncle Mace, li'l girl."

He beckoned, smiling. Like he was offering candy to a baby.

She glared back. Not moving.

"C'mon, sugar. Uncle Mace might turn nasty if Deana doesn't come when she's called." His voice had a singsong lilt to it.

"So, whaddya gonna do, Mace?"

"Something I shoulda done right from the start." He picked up the twine from where it had fallen earlier. She watched him advance, slowly, winding it around his hands.

She backed away, stumbling against the cabin wall, her arms shooting out, spread-eagled against the wood slats.

"C'mon now, Deana. There's a good girl."

Fascinated, she watched him twist the twine around his fingers. Her hand rose to her neck.

"No, Mace. Please don't," she panted. "DON'T DO IT, MACE!"

She lost it . . . somehow got caught up in a swirling black cloud.

Screams rang out, shattering the deathly quiet. . . .

Vaguely, she wondered who it was, crying out like that. The screams died.

Then she heard sobs . . . tiny, whimpering sounds.

FIFTY-SEVEN

"Just calm down now, honey. Uncle Mace ain't gonna hurt ya. Yet." He stood over her, busying himself with the twine. Wrapping it neatly, tightly, around her legs. The way he went about it, she could tell he'd done it before.

Probably many times.

She struggled, trying to kick out at him, but all she did was make futile little scuffles with her feet.

Goddamn shit's hobbled me—like a horse!

Tears of frustration streamed down her cheeks.

Mace's mouth curved in a bright smile.

"Now, now, darlin'. No struggling. A gal could get hurt that way."

He slapped her face. Her head jerked up, sideways, then flopped. Her hair swung around her shoulders. Giving a little cry, she gasped, ready to give him a mouthful.

Thinking better of it, she clamped her lips tight.

No use goading him. I could wind up dead.

Gonna wind up dead *anyhow.*

"Hey, sugar," he whispered. "Didn't y'care·for that?"

No reply.

Catching the defiance in her eyes, he whacked her again. With the back of his hand.

Seems like Uncle Mace is having himself a rare old time.
Stay with it, Deana

He wants you to crack. Break up. Plead for mercy. Okay. Like he'll wait forever. No way is the shit gonna see I'm scared. . . .

He studied her face; saw the tears, her clenched jaw. The defiance still there.

His smirk broke out again.

"That's a good li'l gal. Uncle Mace don't like gals who get flighty. . . ."

She wriggled her feet.

The twine sliced into her calves and ankles.

She pulled a face. Struggling only worsened the pain.

Mace is one sick fuck, she fumed inwardly, *but he sure knows how to tie a person up.*

In desperation, she stared at her legs: pale, puffy, crisscrossed with twine. "Dear God, Mace," she gasped. "This *hurts*—I'm gonna get gangrene if you don't untie me."

Suddenly, the full realization of what Mace *could* do hammered home. The damage . . . the *pain* he could inflict.

She began to shake.

"Scared, honey?"

Her lips stayed shut. She shot him a sour look.

"No reply, huh? Maybe you'd care for another crack?"

The next one rocked her jaw.

Harder this time.

Starting up the pain where Nelson had slugged her two weeks ago.

"Uuugghh . . . ," she gasped, shaking her head. She felt a gush of blood spurt and rise inside her mouth, but her top teeth seemed to be embedded in her lower lip. She eased them free. Blood flowed out and down her chin.

Do this one more time, the fucker's gonna break my neck.

Cringing with pain, her hand flew to her jaw. Her lips felt slick and rubbery. She scowled, clenched her teeth, and muttered, "Up yours, shit-face."

His brows lifted slightly.

"Let's pretend I didn't hear that, sugar. . . ."

She glared at him. But he seemed distant, as if his mind was on other things. It was.

Tilting his head, he looked at her, admiring his handiwork. The swollen eyes, bruised mouth, cut lips, the trickle of blood sliding down her chin . . .

Then, reaching forward, he slipped her blouse off one shoulder.

Not satisfied with that, he pulled it down some more, until her breast peeked out.

Deana cringed. Went taut. Goose bumps squirmed all over her body.

Gently, Mace fingered her breast, tracing swirls around it, touching up the hard dark nipple.

Her stomach shriveled. She pulled away from him, scarcely breathing.

His eyes held hers for a moment.

Daring her to move . . .

She lurched forward, thinking about screaming, throwing herself at him, clawing at his face, blinding him with her nails. . . .

Then he was stepping away, like an artist assessing his masterpiece.

Deana gave up. She went still.

Now for the final touch . . .

That long black hair.

His hands came at her, reaching out, holding the dark shiny strands between his fingers . . . savoring the silky feel. Then he fussed around, arranging it over her shoulders.

"Mmmm—huh!" He seemed pleased with the effect. Humming under his breath, he took a little time poking around in the holdall. He brought out the Nikon and several unopened reels of film.

No need for Polaroids today. The light's okay.

Everything should go according to plan.

He was about to create another Mace Harrison masterpiece. A surge of satisfaction, *anticipation,* welled up inside him. It felt good and warm.

Lifting his eyes skyward, he gave a cynical smile.

"This one's for you, Daddy," he whispered.

FIFTY-EIGHT

Mace bunched his lips in a fake kiss.

"Smile for the birdie, sweetheart," he murmured, putting the camera to his eye. Moving back slightly, he extended the lens and adjusted it, twisting it around between finger and thumb.

He wanted *all* of Deana in the frame. First off, standing against the cabin wall. It'd be the perfect foil for her pale, bruised body. Plus the fact there'd be no giveaway clues . . .

Just Deana and the shitty ol' pinewood wall.

Deana: tears coursing down her cheeks, jaw hanging loose, bloodied lips all swollen . . . eyes dark, frightened, pleading . . .

He aimed to cover every angle.

Left side . . .

"Stay still, sugar."

Front.

Then the right side . . .

"I'm comin' in now . . ."

He zoomed in. Getting one or two head shots in close-up.

Engrossed in his work, Mace clicked away for fifteen minutes or so, changing the film when necessary.

That done, he replaced the camera in the holdall.

Deana blurted a gasp of relief. She slid down the wall, feeling the floor cold and damp beneath her buttocks. She felt wrecked. Salt tears welled, spilling down her cheeks, nipping at her cut lips.

Eyes on Mace the whole time.

Watching him warily, like a mouse in the thrall of a cat.

Mace beamed, showing his rows of straight white teeth.

"How 'bout breakfast?" he said, zipping up the holdall. "I'm starvin'!"

Over at the food box, he brought out a sandwich. "Here," he said, peeling down the wrapper. "Take a bite."

Deana couldn't stop the rush of blood rising to her head.

"Get some therapy, Mace," she spat through thick, puffy lips. "Think I'm gonna do *exactly* what you want? Go fuck yourself. You're a goddamn sicko and you know it! When they find me, you're gonna fuckin' pay for what you've done!"

Mace shrugged his shoulders, set himself astride the hardback chair, bit off a chunk of bread. He began to eat, grinning around his food, crumbs flying from his mouth.

He pointed the sandwich at her.

"You don't wanna eat, then don't eat. And I ain't gonna kill you. Yet. Things to do first. But you'll regret not eatin', sugar. Could be *days* 'fore I decide to . . ."

She trembled, holding on to her voice, keeping it low and level trying to form the words without showing how much he'd hurt her. It wasn't easy.

"Before you decide to do what?"

"You'll see, sugar. You'll see!"

Done with his sandwich, he bent down and picked up the blanket. Opening it out, he threw it over her head, held it tight over her shoulders.

Deana spluttered, screamed.

Kept on screaming and struggling.

Pulling her close, calming her down, Mace was amused. He huffed out a short laugh. "May as well stop that, honey. There's no one around to ride to your rescue—least of all that prick of a boyfriend a' yours. Whassisname? Warren? Huh! Warren *cocksucker* Beatty?"

Mace was in jovial mood; he chuckled to himself, like he had just made the joke of the year. Still holding Deana tight.

Then, snatching away the blanket, he grabbed at her

top, gripped it tight, twisting it around till she almost choked.

He wasn't laughing now. Instead, he had that wild-animal look again. Baring his teeth, he lifted her off the floor, slammed her against the wall, and held her there.

A mirthless grin twisted his mouth.

He let go. She slumped forward. Then, quickly, he began winding the blanket around her.

Holding her up with one hand.

Unbuckling his belt with the other.

Snapping it like a bullwhip, looping the belt around her, trapping her arms.

Drawing it tight.

Buckling it up.

Still holding her upright.

Deana wasn't screaming now—she'd almost stopped breathing.

Can't breathe . . . and scream at the same time.

Gotta breathe.

Short, shallow huffs.

Panic welled. Her head hurt.

Sweat oozed, slick and hot, from every pore.

My God. He really, really means to kill me!

I'm gonna die, and no one'll ever know. . . .

Hoisting her onto his shoulder again, he shifted around, his bulk kneading her guts as he balanced her weight. Her head swung low, and the blood throbbed and pounded, hard.

He stepped forward, catching her head as he went out the door. Smashing it sideways with a sickening thud.

She felt blinding, flashing pain. Her head spun. . . .

A rush of vomit surged in her throat. . . .

Mace was outside now. His breath coming quick and heavy as he traveled over rough terrain—undergrowth, bushes—snagging his boots. With each step, each lurching jolt, his shoulder humped into her belly, pummeling her aching gut. She gasped, heaved, not knowing how much more she could take. . . .

Through the blanket, the sun scorched her back. Nausea rose again. She retched, forcing it back down.

Then she hit dirt, feeling hard knobbly humps beneath her buttocks. She rolled over, steadied herself . . . and came to rest on her back.

Listening to Mace stomp away.

Seconds later, a door opened.

Mace returned. Hoisted her onto his shoulder again.

A sudden draft caught at her legs. Earlier, jolting along on his back, it'd been hot.

Now . . . it's icy cold. . . .

Where am I? Where's he taking me?

Deana started to cry.

Wishing that Warren were here.

If—when Warren finds me, he'll get even with Mace. Pound his brains out. Tear him apart. Kill him with his bare hands. Then he'll take me home.

She smiled faintly, feeling Warren's hand caressing her thigh, his mouth hard on hers, moaning as her fingers curled around his shaft . . .

Dank, earthy odors stole through the blanket, curling into her nostrils. It was cold here . . . wherever it was. . . . Damp and so *cold*.

A sunless place.

Oh my God!

She plummeted down. Hit something that gave under her weight; it felt soft, but not springy.

Like a mattress on a hard dirt floor.

She heard Mace's breath, huffing out in short, sharp grunts. Felt him pulling at her middle, picking at the belt, loosening it. Unwinding the twine from her legs . . . Pulling the blanket from her face.

Christ, the *stench* . . . Bad, rancid dirt beneath her, water slick on the walls . . . She focused her eyes, but it was so *dark*, she couldn't quite see where she was.

Uhhh . . . It's so COLD!

Like the grave . . .

Shuddering, whimpering, she dragged the blanket to her. Fierce, fiery, *tingly* pain seared her legs as the blood came pumping back.

Tears spilled down her cheeks.

"Let me go, Mace. PLEASE," she blurted. "I've done nothing to hurt you. I kept quiet about you coming into my room like that. Mom doesn't know a thing. . . . When I get outta here, I promise I'll never tell."

"No sweat, sugar. Uncle Mace *knows* you won't tell." His voice dropped a notch. It went quiet, calm, confiding. "Best listen up, kiddo. You won't tell, 'cause—you're—going—NOPLACE. Geddit?"

His eyes glittered, shining in the dark.

She stayed quiet.

A chill crawled up her spine. The numbness, the tingling, the pain in her legs were nothing to the fear she felt now.

Her heart hammered.

Goddamn maniac! He's gonna kill me! I'm gonna die here and nobody's gonna find me. . . .

In her mind she pictured Mace carving, gouging all her intimate, secret places—then tearing her apart . . . slurping on her flesh with fiendish glee, sucking his lips, his bloodied fingers. . . .

Her hands flew to her face.

Feeling grateful relief that he'd done with her.

For the moment.

She heard him stomp away.

Then she was crying, with hard, hurting sobs.

Peeking through her fingers.

Catching a slice of daylight as he went out the door.

The door slammed.
A scattering of debris hit the floor.
A key rattled home.
With a harsh scraping sound, it turned in the lock.

FIFTY-NINE

The thing came closer . . .

Moving quietly with animal stealth.

She heard its raspy breathing.

Felt its foul breath as it hung over her bed . . .

From out of nowhere a cloth fluttered down.

Covering her face.

Clinging so tight, it was like a second skin.

A surge of panic set her screaming, tearing at it.

All the while, the thing watched.

She saw the huge veined wings spread out behind it. . . . Ropes of matted hair. Small darting eyes. Spiky teeth. Curved, clawed hands reaching down.

Her screams turned to whimpers and died. She lay rigid with fear. Sweat, like globs of blood, oozed down her body. She opened her mouth to cry for help, but no sound came. She tried again, straining, willing her voice to work. Her jaws ached; her throat was like sandpaper, dry and parched.

As she twisted and turned, the hands gripped her neck, tighter and tighter . . . until . . . she was falling . . . into deep dark space. . . .

Leigh struggled awake, tearing the bedsheets from her slick, damp body, clutching at her neck, looking around for that eerie nightmare creature. . . .

The curtains billowed softly. Cool air played on her sweat-soaked skin. . . .

Still not convinced she was alone, she stared anxiously into the shadows, seeing familiar things—her wardrobe, dresser, wicker chair, hamper . . . pictures on the wall . . .

She sighed. Her breath evened out. Everything's okay, she told herself.

Then:

No it's not. . . .

Panting again, she peered into all the gray creepy spaces, into the shadows where *anything* could hide. . . .

She trod the bedsheet down with her feet.

Feeling her nightgown up around her neck, cutting across her throat, almost strangling her. This hadn't happened since that last nightmare, when Edith Payne had grabbed her, shrieked at her by Charlie's graveside . . .

Charlie's funeral.

Now it could be Deana's. . . .

NO NO NO!!!

STOP THAT. RIGHT NOW!!!!

Deana's safe.

I know it I know it. I'd know in my heart if she was d . . . Can't say it. *WON'T SAY IT . . . !!*

The realization that Deana was gone engulfed her once more. This was the second terrible night of drugged, blacked-out sleep. Sleep broken by hideous phantoms. Ghosts invading the night like demented harpies.

Leigh's heart sank. Mattie said she'd call the minute she had news . . . when any clue, no matter how small, showed up. There'd been nothing.

Zero.

Zip.

She knew the cops were on the case, and with Mattie on their tails they'd stick at it. . . . But there'd been no sign of Mace. No sign of Deana.

Leigh swung her legs off the bed. The night air began to chill her skin. She shivered, feeling worn, unutterably weary; waiting for news. Mattie had insisted, you're more use at home than out there, looking for Deana. She may call. . . . You gotta be ready. . . .

She'd waited. But there'd been no calls from Deana. Just anxious ones from Warren. Reassuring ones from Mattie.

There were two cops in the house. Guarding her. Watching out for intruders. Checking the office now and then for updates on the case.

None so far.

In her heart, she knew Mace had what he wanted.

Deana.

A surrogate Tania.

Oh God, Deana, don't rile him.

Use your intelligence. Spy your chance. . . .

Spy your chance?

With a rogue cop, a trained killer, a *maniac* like Mace for company?

Dear God please help my baby girl.

Leigh got to her feet. She swayed, put a hand to her forehead, fell back, and flopped on the bed.

Reaching for the glass of water on the nightstand, she saw the small brown container of sleeping pills. . . . Her hand strayed forward, but she snatched it back.

I gotta stay awake.

Deana may call.

Don't want to sleep anyhow . . . not with these nightmares. . . .

Pulling on a robe, she went to the hallway, feeling ice-cool tiles beneath her bare feet. She padded into the living room. Dawn had broken; its pale gray light made eerie moving patterns on the carpet.

She looked around . . .

Caught her breath . . .

Something was wrong.

The place was quiet.

Too damn quiet . . .

Okay, Officers Halliwell and Bodine were probably catching a few z's. One in the den, the other in the kitchen, where she'd left them . . .

But somehow, it wasn't the peaceful quiet of people asleep. This was more an overall, deathly hush. Like the world was holding its breath. Waiting for . . . what? Armageddon?

Impatiently, she shook her head and huffed out a long, low breath. Don't be a fool, she told herself. You're hyped up. Worried out of your skull about Deana.

And fearful that . . .

Something isn't quite right. . . .

She screamed.

Loud and long.

Even as she screamed, she remembered Edith Payne, shrieking like a wounded animal when she discovered Charlie's broken body all those years ago. . . .

"Oh no, oh NO!!!" Leigh sobbed out frightened little cries, her hands crushed to her chest. Her knees folded and hit the carpet with a sickening jolt.

She scrabbled over to the TV.

Grabbed at the photographs fanned out on the floor.

Horrified at what she saw . . .

Terrified.

DEANA!!! Oh NO!! . . .

A dozen or so black-and-white shots.

Deana, her face all bruised, lips cut and swollen. Eyes puffy, almost closed. Hair arranged neatly across her naked shoulders . . . curling around her breasts.

Oh my God . . . Deana!

Leigh snatched up a print, pressed it to her mouth, sobbing, her tears making smudges, carving lines down the bromide. She stopped. Looked at the others.

Picking them up, slowly, one by one. Her stomach twisting, her tormented eyes seeing the damage Mace had done . . .

Oh my God . . .

Must tell Mattie. There may be some sort of *clue* hidden in the photographs. Somehow. Some*where*.

Mattie would find *something*.

She knew Mace like no one else did.

Leigh stumbled to her feet, clasping the photos to her breast. Something else caught her eye.

Another photograph. One she knew well. Deana at Point Reyes Beach. In her new white bikini. Laughing at the camera.

Fuckin' bastard Mace.

He'd had it all along.

Deana *hadn't* given it to Warren. . . .

Oh, shit! The goddamn fuckin' evil beast! What a fool I've been—harboring a psycho like that!

Guilt welled up.

If she hadn't fought with Nelson.

If she hadn't taken up with Mace.

If she hadn't gone to Aunt Jenny's in the first place.

Grow up, Leigh. This isn't your fault.

But maybe you should have listened to Deana. She'd never liked Mace anyway.

Now Deana was held captive by Mace.

And her dork of a mother never even *guessed* that he . . .

Leigh hurried into the hallway. To rouse her bodyguards. Tell them that Mace had sneaked in . . .

Could still be here . . .

Her blood ran cold.

The house was eerily quiet.

Huh!

Some bodyguards . . . Allowing an intruder to sneak past them . . . Come to that, they should be around; they must've heard me walking about?

Leigh quickly discovered why the two cops were silent. They lay sprawled in pools of blood, congealing loops of it sliding from gaping slits in their throats.

* * *

"Mattie. Mattie!!!" Leigh cried into the phone, willing her to pick up. She didn't. Hurriedly, Leigh yelled at the answering machine. "Mattie. Please come over as soon as you can. Something's happened here. Something serious. I want you here. NOW!"

Christ! No, Mattie. Just a conversation with her answering machine . . . A great start to the day—all alone in the house with those awful images of Deana playing on her mind—not to mention two stiffs for company.

Warren! He'll know what to do. . . .

Letting the prints drift to the floor, Leigh went through her little black book with trembling fingers.

She found Warren's number. Dialed it.

Knees shaky, heart in her mouth, she prayed for Warren to speak to her.

"The Hastings residence." A woman's voice.

Sheena.

"This is Leigh West. I must speak with Warren."

"You got it, sister." Sheena's response was instant. Like she was waiting for Leigh's call.

A moment's silence then.

"Leigh. Warren here. What is it?" His voice rose. "Deana?"

"Warren, please come over. Someone's been here. An intruder. It *has* to be Mace. And . . . the two officers . . ."

"Yes?"

"They're dead, Warren. They've been murdered."

"Christ." Warren's voice was terse. "I'm coming over, Leigh. You called the cops?"

"I phoned Mattie. She's not in. Left a message for her."

"Mill Valley PD?"

"No. I'll do it now. . . ."

"Stay right there, Leigh. I'll phone the cops from here, and I'll be over in a coupla minutes. Don't touch a thing."

"He left photographs, Warren," Leigh went on, sobbing.

"The *bastard!* . . . I'll be right over, Leigh. . . ."

* * *

Sheena turned to Warren. "I'm coming too. I need to know what's going on."

"Best stay put, Sheena. Might just complicate matters, you being over at Leigh's house."

Leigh gave a heavy sigh and shivered. She felt chilled to the bone.

Pulling her robe around her, she found the belt and tied it tight. Thank God for Warren, she thought. Deana was right. He's such a sensible, capable guy. . . .

She glanced toward the front door, wanting, *willing* him to be there. To tell her everything was going to be okay. He'd find Deana. . . . Bring her home. . . .

She looked at the prints scattered at her feet. She bent to pick them up.

A hand slipped around her waist.

She gasped, jumped.

Froze.

SIXTY

The hand tightened.

Another clasped her arm.

They brought her up.

Pulled her around.

Lips closed on hers. Gently . . .

Mace.

"Why, hello, sweet thing," he said softly. "How ya been?"

"YOU! You BASTARD! What're you doing here . . . ? And where's Deana? Tell me where you've hidden her. TELL ME!" Shaking off his hands, she grabbed his biker jacket, jerking him close. "Just tell me what you've done with my daughter. You'll *never* get away with it. TELL ME—WHERE IS SHE?"

"Hey, steady on, there. And let go a' me. Can't tell you where li'l Deana *is*, but I *do* know she's alive and well. . . ." He thought about it, blew out breath slowly, and shook his head. "Y'could say she's several country miles from bein' all *right*. But she's okay. At the moment," he added with a grin.

"Where? Just tell me *where* she is, Mace!"

He backed off, into the shadows, his eyes glittering in the half-light. Suddenly, out of nowhere, he had a knife in his hand.

His eyes narrowed.

Pointing the blade at her, he whispered, "That's for me to know—and our little friend Warren to find out."

"Warren? Why Warren? All of Mill Valley PD is looking for Deana . . . never mind Mattie . . ." She looked at him uncertainly. . . . Where *is* Mattie? she wondered.

Her heart froze.

She *must've* picked up my message by now. . . .

"Really?" Raising his eyebrows, he sent her a chilling smile. "Wouldn't count on that if I were you!"

He turned. Disappeared into the kitchen.

She heard the back door open, then snap shut.

Stunned, she wondered what Mace had meant.

I wouldn't count on that if I were you. . . .

Surely he hadn't. . . .

SIXTY-ONE

The doorbell rang. She leapt. Her stomach clenched. . . .

Who . . . ?

She looked around, half expecting Mace to appear. . . .

"Leigh, Leigh! It's Warren. Open up!"

Sobbing with relief, she ran to the door, slipped the chain from the catch, and opened it.

She stood there, swaying, tears making silver trails down her cheeks. For the second time in the last half hour, she felt her knees fold under her.

Warren lunged forward. Grabbed her waist. Kicking the door shut behind him, he guided her to the living room and helped her onto the sofa.

It was almost daylight, but not yet light enough to see clearly. Flashing a brief smile at Leigh, murmuring, "A little illumination wouldn't go amiss," he turned on the TV lamp. Its warm yellow glow lit their part of the room.

He asked gently, "Feeling better now?"

"Warren," Leigh said in a small voice. "I can't tell you how relieved I am to see you. Did you call the cops?"

"Yeah. They should be here any minute now."

"I didn't want to get you involved like this."

"I *am* involved, Leigh. With Deana." *More than you know,* he thought grimly. "Try not to worry—we're gonna get her back in no time."

"I'm not so sure, Warren. You may change your mind about that. Take a look at these. . . ." Leigh jerked her head at the photographs spread on the table. Tears welled up again.

Warren's face darkened as he scanned the pictures. He went cold with shock and anger. "My GOD!" he breathed, his voice rising. "He left THESE? The guy's a psycho, a sadistic fuckin' maniac! How could he *do* this—to her . . . then take pictures . . . and bring them here . . ." His voice broke off.

"You're telling me. I couldn't sleep . . . came into this room—and found these here on the floor. As well as one he'd stolen earlier. I called Mattie. She wasn't around . . . so I left a message on her answering machine. Then I found the two officers. . . . God, it was just too awful."

"You need a drink." He went over to the wet bar.

They heard thumping on the door.

"Police, Ms. West. Open up!"

Warren left the bar. "I'll get it. You stay here."

Leigh nodded dumbly.

She heard Warren open the door, introduce himself. Then men's voices. One said, "Where are they?"

Leigh got up. She met the cops coming down the hall.

"They . . . they're . . ." She cleared her throat. "One's in the kitchen—the other's in the den. . . . Through here, Officer. And you are?"

"I'm Officer Craig and this is Officer Bronson, ma'am."

They showed their IDs and disappeared into the kitchen.

Warren looked at Leigh's pale face, her dark-ringed eyes, and wondered if he should call her doctor.

"You okay?" he asked quietly, following her to the living room.

"I'm so worried . . . and there's something I didn't mention, Warren. Mace was here. He was in the house when I called you. He implied something might have happened to Mattie. Hope to Christ it hasn't."

She looked at him anxiously.

"Maybe he got to her. Like he got to those cops in there. . . ."

Warren's jaw tightened.

The phone rang.

Leigh hurried into the hallway. She picked it up.

It was Mattie.

Leigh gasped a sigh of relief.

"Got your message, Leigh. What happened? It sounded serious."

"It was. *Is*. Halliwell and Bodine were murdered. Mace got to them, Mattie. The cops are here now. So is Warren. Any news of Deana?"

Leigh closed her eyes tight. Please God let there be news. *Good* news.

" 'Fraid not, Leigh. I'm comin' over ASAP. Tell you what I know. We can compare notes. . . ."

Leigh put the phone down, hoping Mattie had something constructive to say. Like she'd got a plan, had an idea—anything that'd save Deana from Mace.

By the time Mattie showed, the bodies had been taken away. More officers were poking around. Checking doors, windows. Taking prints.

Mattie's eye caught the photos scattered on the coffee table.

"Just run it by me, Leigh," she said quietly. "What happened?"

Leigh repeated everything she'd told the officers.

Including the fact that Mace had already been in the house when she'd called Mattie.

Leaving them to it, letting Leigh get on with her story, Warren went to the kitchen and made coffee. A few minutes later, he brought in three steaming mugs, and cream and sugar on a tray. He set the tray before them.

"It's been a terrible experience for you, Leigh," Mattie was saying.

Leigh remained silent, then said, "Mace implied something may have happened to you, Mattie."

"He did? Well, it hasn't. Don't intend that it should, either. As for the photographs, Leigh," she let out a deep sigh, "what can I say—that it's Mace up to his old tricks again? Yeah," she said, shaking her head, her lips tight, remembering the scrapbook they'd found at his apartment. "We sure gotta find badass fuckin' Mace in one helluva hurry."

Diving into her shoulder bag, she picked out a folded plastic sack and protective gloves. She drew the gloves on, easing them over her fingers.

Glancing at the photographs, she separated them with her fingertips. Staying silent for a while. An icy chill creeping through her body. This looked like the business. She hoped they weren't too late.

Slowly, she gathered the prints together.

Shook open the sack, slid them inside.

"I'll get these over to the lab. Have forensic check them out. Could be, apart from Mace's dabs, some little thing—fibers, DNA, soil deposits—that might give us a lead. We gotta catch him, Leigh. . . ."

"Don't I know it!" Leigh choked back a sob. "That's my daughter out there, Mattie. Sure . . . we're gonna catch him, all right. But I can't just wait here! God, Mattie," her voice rose, "I can't just do *nothing!*"

"What *can* you do, Leigh? We got trained people out there. We know what he's up to—given his family history an' all. He's tracking down his sister. . . . Meanwhile, he's . . . Christ, we're talking serial ki—" She broke off, embarrassed. "Sorry, Leigh—shouldn't have said that. Anyhow, we brought Ava Sorensson in on the job. Maybe she'll come up with something."

"Ava Sorensson?"

"Yeah. She's a criminal psychologist. Best in the business. If she can't crack Mace, nobody can."

"Well, if she can help . . . ," Leigh murmured doubtfully. Then: "Mattie, it's time Warren knew the story behind all this." She gave him a hesitant smile.

"It might help," he put in wryly.

"Sure," Mattie said. "That figures. Let it roll, Leigh."
Warren settled back and listened.

SIXTY-TWO

Deep in thought, Warren left for home, leaving Leigh with Mattie. And a team of cops. Wishing they'd move their asses, get out there, comb the countryside or whatever it was they were supposed to do. But just find Deana.

He prayed she was still alive. . . .

Christ, she'd better be. If I knew where the hell to look,

I'd find the bastard myself. . . . Warren sat at the dining table, head down, scanning a map of the West Coast, hoping some divine hand would guide him to where Deana was hidden. . . .

He wasn't having much luck.

Frowning, he traced a finger around the Bay Area, up to Mill Valley, then San Rafael, then down again to the Santa Cruz Mountains. . . . Sighing impatiently. Knowing he hadn't a hope in hell of finding Deana this way . . .

"I know where your girl is, Warren. . . . At least, I think I do."

His head came up. He threw Sheena a sharp glance.

Standing there, her back to the picture window, she looked pale and somehow disoriented.

"Well?" he asked tersely. "Tell me. Right now, Deana's probably being beaten up, abused—Christ only knows what else the bastard's doing to her. She's in real danger, Sheena, so whatever you think you know, let's have it, before it's too late."

"Y'ain't gonna like it, bro." Sheena's pallor made him wonder what the hell she'd "seen." Usually, he didn't set much store by her "feelings," but right now, any lead was better than none—and by the way she looked, she may, just may, have hit on a clue.

"She's in a dark place . . . could be underground. Whatever, wherever, she's in a dark, enclosed space. And," she added quietly, studying his face, not liking the haunted look in his eyes. "She hasn't long to go, Warren. She knows it, too."

Warren leapt up and raced to the window. He grabbed her shoulder.

"Can you tell me where this . . . dark place is? Can you see any landmarks—*anything*?"

She shook him off. Going quiet again, before resuming her story. "I keep getting these deep, desperate *fear* feelings. It's dark, and I can't see . . . I just know she's in danger. Someone's aiming to kill her. But not before he's . . . *done* things to her. . . ."

"Christ—anything else?"

"She's in the wilderness, Warren. Metaphorically and physically . . . D'ya know what I mean?"

"Jesus, sis. We've gotta tell Mattie about this!"

"She's a cop?"

"Sure. She knows the sicko who's doing all this stuff to Deana. In fact, Leigh, Deana's mom just told me the whole story. Sounded far-fetched, but it's all kinda linked in with Deana's disappearance."

"A story, huh?" Sheena frowned. "A 'far-fetched' story. . . . You better tell me about it. . . ."

"So Ma Payne got rid of her kids? 'Cept Charlie. Jess turned into Mace and now Mace wants to kill Deana, because he can't find sister Tania—meanwhile, any black-haired gal, but especially Deana, will do.

"Jess, aka Mace, can't forgive Mom for killing Pa—and for giving him away like that. . . . Am I right?"

"That's about it, sis. This guy Mace is one fucked-up psycho. He *does* things to women. Then carves them up, apparently. Leigh said she and Mattie found a scrapbook at his apartment with pictures and press cuttings of his gruesome deeds. . . . God only knows what he's doing to Deana right now. At this very moment . . ." He faltered. "Maybe you can figure it out, Sheena. I certainly can't!"

Warren paced up and down. Working things out. He'd go find Deana himself. But first, he had to decide which route to take.

Sabre sat, ears pricked, watching from the doorway.

Sheena's eyes leveled with Warren's. Sending him a cool glance, she said, "I know how this Mace character feels, Warren."

"You WHAT? What the hell are you saying, Sheena? You can *understand* why this sick fuck is doing the things he does?"

"No, not that, bro. All I'm sayin' is, I *understand* this Mace character hatin' his mom for givin' him away. Remember, Warren, I've been in the same position myself. I was adopted, too, don't forget!" She turned, stared out the window, her anger showing. He could tell that by the way she squared her shoulders, held her back ramrod straight.

Sure, he remembered she'd been adopted. They both had. Just that he'd never felt the need to discuss it with her before. Far as he was concerned, Sheena was his big sister. Had been for as long as he could remember. And they'd both been treated equally by Mom and Dad—that had been their way.

Sheena turned from the window, her face harsh with concern. "Understandin' the *feelings* of this guy is the only thing that strikes me right now, bro. I'm sorry, believe me. And sure, if you think it'll help, I'll talk to your Mattie woman."

SIXTY-THREE

The door opened.

Deana flinched, twisting away from the blast of light.

She stumbled, tripped. Fell backward onto the mattress.

"That pleased to see me, huh?"

"Mace. I need water. *Please* lemme me have some water. . . ."

"Hey. That's nice. I like to hear my li'l girl saying pretty 'please.' "

"Screw you, Mace."

"Now, now. Don't you go blottin' your copybook. Say sorry, Deana—or do I have to smack your butt?" He put down his holdall and swaggered slowly toward her. A vague gray light snaked in through the dirt-streaked window, lifting the gloom, filtering across the grimy mattress. Deana crouched back in the shadows, hands clasping her drawn-up knees. Hugging them tight to her chest.

Mace bent down. He peered at her, smiling, his teeth a white slash against the dark of his face.

"Saw your mom today."

Her eyes widened. Her breath quickened.

"Wanna know how your mother *is*, sweetheart?"

She gulped back a sob.

"How is my mother, Mace?"

"Frightened, sugar. Your mom's one very frightened lady."

Tears welled up. Hearing him say "mom" like that made her want to cry.

Mom, oh Mom . . . You gotta come an' get me. Please!

Despair, and a seering desolation swept over her. She broke down, blurting shuddering sobs into her hands.

"Come, come. Here, I got you somethin'."

She glared at him with red, swollen eyes.

He held up a film-wrapped sandwich. Shook it in her face. "C'mon. Eat. Don't want y'dyin' on me now. Eat like a good girl."

"I want water. Gimme some water, Mace!"

"You'll get your water when you've had this."

She reached out, grabbed the sandwich, peeled the film from the bread, and stuffed one end into her mouth. She started chewing, then choking, her throat was so dry.

"Hold it!" He held up his hand. "Now, wouldn't that make a pretty picture for your everlovin' mom to see? Her little girl eating up her food?

"Stay like that, sweetheart. Don't ya move, now." He rummaged inside the holdall, bringing up the Nikon.

Lifting it to his eye.

Playing around with the lens.

Adjusting the flash.

Squinting into the viewfinder, firing off a few shots.

* * *

Done with that, Mace straightened his back. A wide beam lit his face. "Y'take a good photo, sugar, I'll say that for ya. Your mom's gonna be real pleased to see these."

"Where d'you get off, Mace? If y'think Mom's gonna break down before your eyes, you better think again, shit-face. She's one tough lady, and don't you forget it."

"Mmm-huh. Know what? Y'could be right, honey. But let me tell you one thing. . . . You're bad blood. Y'know that? Only one thing to do with bad blood, an' that's git rid of it." He dropped the Nikon into the holdall and zippered it shut.

Deana shuddered. The bread stuck in her gullet. She began to choke again.

Careful, now. Don't rile him any more. . . .

"Yeah, you're bad blood, sweetheart," he went on in a calm, conversational tone. "Pa wanted you dead, Mom saved you and then hacked him, *killed* him, for doin' what he *knew* was right. After that, y'could say most of us Paynes came to a bad end. Pa murdered. Me farmed out to those good, God-fearin' folk in Duluth. . . . Charlie dead after fornicatin' with that whorin' slut. An' you . . ." His eyes accused her. His face was a dark, wild mask. Spittle hung from the side of his mouth.

Terrified, still coughing, Deana edged back into her corner.

Change the subject. Attract his attention. Anything— just make him stop this crazy goddamn crap. . . . It's driving me nuts. . . .

"Mace. I want some water, please. I *need* water." She coughed some more.

"Water? WATER? I ain't got no water." Mace shook his head, trying to clear it, shut out the memory of his mother's face, the superstitious fears. . . . The dark, desperate feelings of anger.

He'd avenge Pa's murder, all right.

Rid his soul of Tania.

He glared at Deana. His eyes taking in her long dark hair. Her white shoulders. Remembering how she'd looked half-naked, that day in her room. How her breasts heaved and wrestled, tumbling out of that too-tight bra of hers.

Tania . . .

Taunting him.

Laughing at him.

Bawling at him to go away.

You BASTARD, she'd screamed.

Yeah. Tania has ta go. . . . She brought a curse on us Paynes. . . . Pa shoulda killed her right at the start. . . .

"Mace . . . What're you gonna do?"

Stupid damnfool question, but she had to keep him talking. Keep his mind on the straight and narrow. Keep it from wandering. She'd seen this film—what was it called? She couldn't remember now, but the girl in it kept talking to this crazy guy, to stop him from throwing her over the cliff. She'd talked and talked till the cops came an' took the crazy guy away.

In her mind, she pictured this happening to her.

Mace'd have his hands around her throat, squeezing the life outta her. . . . Then she'd start talking. Maybe arguing. For hours on end. Mace'd give up, go away, an' then Warren an' Mattie and a gang of cops'd show up and take her home. . . .

As if . . .

Her blood ran cold.

"Do?" Mace asked, surprised. "Why, go a-callin' on that whorin' slut, sugar. After I've rid me of sister Tania . . ."

Reaching down into the holdall, he drew out a hunting knife.

Drawing it from its sheath, he held it up to the window. Then, smiling softly, he wiped it on the seat of his pants.

SIXTY-FOUR

Saturday, August 14

The girl up ahead caught his eye.

She was stacked—tall, athletic-looking, with long dark hair caught up in bunches. The bunches bounced jauntily against her candy-pink sweatshirt. A tennis racquet swung in her hands. He eyed her long, shapely legs swinging down the sidewalk.

Her feet, in white socks and sneakers, almost danced in her hurry.

A glimpse of tight white shorts peeking out from beneath the sweatshirt got him going. He felt himself rise, go hard.

"All *right*," he murmured to himself, a loose smile playing around his lips. "The kid's a honey; a real live dancin' queen. Most likely gaggin' for it, too."

Already wreckin' lives, spreading her filthy evil all over town . . .

His gaze fixed on the swinging bunches. Long and black, they curled a little at the ends.

Thinking ahead to her tennis date, smiling to herself a little, the girl didn't see the black Tornado cruise by, nor the driver slouched in the dark interior, wearing reflective shades, his left arm hanging out the window.

The car slid to a halt some twenty yards ahead of the girl. Through his rearview mirror, the man watched her swing toward him.

Drawing level with the parked car, she looked in the open passenger-side window. Saw the man at the wheel. Wearing a black leather biker jacket and one of those funky sports wristwatches that did everything 'cept play "The Stars and Stripes."

He was chewing, his jaw working around with a steady, rhythmic movement.

Later, in one of his three rented Bay Area apartments, Mace surveyed his work. Dipping his head from side to side, appraising his latest killing, assessing the need for a little more embellishment.

He grinned, his white teeth glistening in the soft light from the bedside lamp.

One less evil bitch, he told himself.

In the small cramped space the realty office had euphemistically described as a living room, the blinds were drawn. And not only against the glare of the midday sun.

Mace eased the knife from the slit in her throat. It came away with a sharp, sucking sound. Fresh blood welled, pumping over her shoulders. Matting the long strands of hair. Making a pool on the pillow behind her.

She groaned, moved slightly. Her legs made small jerky tremors. Bubbles gurgled gently from the mouth-shaped slit. Her fingers twitched, then lay still.

Her lids fluttered gently, then opened.

The eyes staring up at him were blank, glazed.

Dead already.

Mace hefted the knife like a dagger. He raised his arm, visualizing the long clean slit he'd carve from throat to pubic bone.

His hand came down, slicing the firm white flesh, the blade juddering slightly as it hit the breastbone. Like a jacket unzipped, the torso sagged open.

More blood seeped from the "mouth," easing onto the pillow . . . till the dark hair floated in a small black lake.

Mace paused, then hacked some more. Edging up the skin with the tip of his blade, flapping it open, peering at the hot steamy coils within.

He could *smell* her evil.

Warm, mulchy, sour.

Sniffing, breathing it in, he grinned, then flicked the skin back again. Kneading it into place with quick, practiced fingers. Patting the breasts, hanging loose, lolling sideways, away from the incision.

He fondled them, squeezing the soft dark nipples.

Frowning.

They'd been so *taut,* so *ready,* a half hour ago. When she'd squirmed beneath him, strong and agile. Yeah. She'd given him a hard time, all right, but he'd made it, ramming her, jerking his come into her moist warmth.

How she'd bucked, squirmed, screamed out.

Shoulda given her a double shot. . . .

Not "liquid ecstasy," though.

This time he'd used his trusty hunting knife. "Yessir," he muttered, panting a little, remembering. "It'd been a real pleasure, slicing that smooth white throat."

He'd shut her mouth, once and for all.

And he'd made another. One guaranteed to stay open, no matter what. . . .

He liked that.

A harsh laugh blurted from his lips.

Never did catch her name. . . .

Probably something like Debbie, Jennifer, or Susan.

Typical middle-class product.

He took a wild guess. . . .

Wealthy daddy. House in Pacific Heights. Tennis and the beach all summer. UCSC in the fall. All set for a big exciting career in Daddy's L.A. office.

Maybe . . .

Not anymore, though.

With that black hair . . . she'd've always been evil. . . . Doin' bad things the resta her life . . .

He'd done the world a favor.

He'd gotten rid of one more Tania.

* * *

Hate twisted his face. His teeth clenched.

He turned away. Busying himself with his holdall, throwing in the almost empty vial of GHB, the syringe . . .

He brought out the Nikon and began taking shots. Full-on. Sideways. Then zooming in for a close-up of that gaping "mouth." It'd be a real change from the others in his scrapbook, he told himself.

A medical shot. *Like a do-it-yourself tracheotomy guide on the Internet.*

He gave a short laugh.

His bloodied fingers stained the camera.

Streaks of blood smeared his face.

Tugging the knife from the body, he threw it into the holdall. The Nikon followed, clattering against his spare service revolver, more vials of GHB, the pack of unused syringes.

Then, picking up opposite corners of the bedsheet, he pulled them across the body, knotted the ends, top left to bottom right. Top right to bottom left. A slim hand, slack and bloodied, slid out through a gap. He shoved it back inside the bedsheet.

Hoisting the bundle off the bed, he paused for a moment. Figuring out the means of disposal. He could stash it in the wardrobe. Leave it in an underpass. Or wait till dark, put it in the car trunk, and toss it over a cliff someplace.

Slumped in an armchair, a can of beer in one hand, the TV turned low, he waited till dark.

SIXTY-FIVE

Sheena stared at her reflection in the dresser mirror.

She looked pale, shaken; felt chilled to the bone.

She'd been stroking her hair with an ebony-backed brush. Now it lay where it had fallen, in her lap.

Slowly, she set the brush on the crystal tray in front of her. The tray held combs, bobby pins, and a couple of hair bands.

Her eyes went to a small wooden doll, hand-carved, dark with years of handling. The doll stood propped against the mirror.

She was seeing a brightly painted wagon. A woman, passing the doll to a small girl perched up front. The child was maybe two, three years of age. A man and woman sat either side of her. The shackled horse stamped and snorted, anxious to be gone.

Sheena sniffed. She smelled the horse's breath, grassy, steamy, hot. Felt the child's wonder, excitement at sitting up so high, at the horse shifting around. All the time wary of those strange people wrapped in furs by her side . . .

The thin-faced woman in the long gray dress wore an apron tied at the waist. She was saying, "Here, child. Don't you forget this, now. It'll keep ya company in the long nights ahead. . . ."

Sheena began to shake. Her breath hissed out low and shallow. . . . Sweat beaded her forehead, her upper lip. She felt its flush warm her armpits, then spread hot and slick down her body.

She went over the scene again. Recalling each detail. Figuring out its purpose, its meaning.

Knowing full well . . .
She was that child.
The doll was hers.
The thin-faced woman, her ma.
Edith Payne.

Her mind was picking up on something else.
A different scene this time.
The cold, dark place where Deana was.
Familiar territory . . .
Wild. Isolated. High in the mountains.
Along a rough dirt path.
One of many such paths.
Water thrashed and rumbled below.
She reached out, touching the girl on a mattress . . .
In that cold, dark place . . .
She *was* the girl on the mattress.
Feeling confused, in pain, desperate, knowing she couldn't hold out much longer . . .
I'm gonna die and nobody'll ever know . . .

Sheena leapt up.
Raced into the living room.
"Hey, bro!" she called out. "Make it snappy. We'd best take the Chevy."
Warren looked up, his face pale.
"You've 'seen' Deana? Where is she, sis?"
"I know the area, Warren. She's a few miles from here. Somewhere in the mountains. In Santa Cruz country . . ."

SIXTY-SIX

"You comin' with me?"

"I'm not sure, Mattie. There could be news of Deana. . . . Do I *have* to be there?"

"Shitski, Leigh. You *gotta* be there!"

Mattie drove Leigh to the Bayview.

They were quiet, their faces tense, serious.

Thinking about Deana.

And the upcoming meeting with Ava Sorensson.

Hoping she'd come up with some clues for them to work on. *Any clue,* however small, would be welcome. So they'd know where to start.

The cops had gone through Mace's Tiburon apartment with a fine-tooth comb. Apart from his dabs, some photographic equipment, and the goddamn scrapbook, the place was clean.

He's still out there, though.

Leigh shuddered.

And Deana . . . tortured, abused . . . Christ knows what by now . . .

She stifled a sob.

Please God she's still alive.

Life just couldn't get worse.

Like a survivor clinging to a shipwreck, she clung to the knowledge that Deana was strong, athletic. She was also feisty, resourceful, intelligent. Leigh gave a wry smile. She'd just described herself at that age.

Yeah, she acknowledged. *Deana's tough. But would she be a match for Mace . . . ?*

Leigh gave up trying to banish the scary scenarios playing in her mind. She felt shot to pieces. Her head throbbed.

She hadn't slept again last night. Nor for nights, it seemed, before that. Not since the day Deana disappeared.

Mattie swung into the Bayview parking lot. The old Ford shuddered to a halt. They climbed out and made their way to the front door on Main Street.

Ava Sorensson was already there. Seated at a window table overlooking the harbor. Outlined against the daylight, her profile was lean, clear-cut. She wore her fair hair smoothed back from her brow.

Now forty years of age, Ava had gone to law school, gained a master's degree in criminal psychology, and then had set up a lucrative practice in Boston. The black pin-striped pantsuit and black-framed eyeglasses added to the crisp DA-in-waiting look.

Turning, she met Leigh's gaze.

Nodding to Mattie, she rose from the table and held out a hand to Leigh. "Ms. West. I'm Ava Sorensson. I guess Mattie's filled you in as to why I'm here?" Her mouth curved in a friendly smile. Leigh's eyes focused on the bright red lips and straight white teeth. As well as being the best in her field, Ava Sorensson was also a looker.

"Please sit down, Ms. Sorensson." Leigh returned the smile and sank into a wicker chair at the table. "It's Leigh, by the way. May I call you Ava?"

"Why, of course." The psychologist settled back into her chair.

Mattie made a grab for the menu. "Let's eat," she said. "Then we get down to business."

Mattie and Ava chose baked swordfish with a salsa garnish. Feeling shaky and vaguely nauseous, Leigh declined food but ordered a bottle of chilled chardonnay. Playing around with the bread sticks in a basket Tony placed before them, she hoped her tension wasn't showing too much.

Halfway through coffee, Ava dipped down and rummaged in her briefcase. She hauled out a sheaf of papers.

"So," she said, looking over her eyeglasses, first at Leigh

and then Mattie. "We have a rogue cop on the loose. A rogue cop with an unusual history. An ethnic, superstitious father, who was also a drunk and a potential child killer.

"Way I see it, our subject, given away as a child, swears vengeance on the mother who slew his father. The mother who later farmed him out to strangers.

"He's also seeking the sister his father set out to kill."

Ava took a sip of coffee, glanced at Mattie, and said, "Long and short is, we have a serial killer here—any update on where he might be?"

"You mean, you have no *idea?*" Leigh burst in. She'd been waiting for this "brilliant" criminologist to come up with some wonderful clue. And now she's asking *us* where Mace could be?

Diners began to sit up and take notice.

Leigh lowered her voice.

"You're the expert," she said tersely, across the table. "We thought you'd point us in the right direction. You've done profiling Mace, now *you* tell *us* where he's likely to be. My daughter's out there . . . and Christ knows what he's done—*is* doing with her."

"That's understood, Leigh." Sorensson was sympathetic. She'd experienced the wrath of anguished family members in the past, so she was more than ready for Leigh's outburst.

"I'll do my best," she said gently. "I haven't encountered many such cases, but having studied this guy's history, I found it . . . quite interesting." She paused, then said, "His crimes are symbology-based."

Mattie raised her brows.

Ava continued. "Let me explain. Psychopaths often identify with an aggressive role model—in this case, Payne Senior. It's my guess that had he lived to tell the tale, he would undoubtedly have abused both Mace and his siblings."

"So where's this going, Ava?" Leigh asked, her voice beginning to rise again.

Mattie laid a restraining hand on her arm.

"As we know," Ava continued, "Payne Senior was murdered by his wife Edith, and Jess aka Mace now appears to identify with the *myth* that is his father. He puts himself in his father's place. *Assumes* the persona. *Is* Payne Senior.

"At the same time, hating his mother for killing his father, never mind for her rejection of himself—by passing him on to the family in Duluth. Because of these issues, plus the superstition surrounding his dark-haired sister, Mace sees women as evil, untrustworthy people."

Ava paused, glancing at Leigh, assessing how all this was affecting her. Leigh was pale but seemed in control. She decided to continue. "All Mace's pathological maternal hatred, plus the desire to avenge his father's murder, is now directed toward his 'evil' sister Tania.

"In the absence of the real Tania, Mace is systematically working his way through a series of dark-haired women. With each killing, he's avenging Payne Senior's death and, in effect, carrying out his father's plan to murder his sister. . . ."

Ava's eyes leveled with Leigh's. "I'm sure you understand, Leigh. We're dealing with a dangerous psychopath. A man with a mission. We desperately need to bring him in. . . ." She bit her lip. "Like many psychopaths, Mace Harrison is an intelligent man. John Gacy, Ted Bundy, and others disguised themselves as law-enforcement officers in order to gain access to their victims. And very convincing they were, too. Mace Harrison doesn't need to *act* that part. He already is, pardon me, *was* a well-respected cop, who did his job in exemplary fashion."

Mattie's face was taut. "Damn right," she muttered. "That sick fuck was the cleverest sonofabitch I ever did meet!"

Leigh felt faint. Her head began to swim.

"Please, Ava," she whispered. "Tell me where you think Mace is—and where he's hidden Deana!"

Sorensson placed a warm hand over Leigh's icy one. She smiled gently and said, "I'm afraid I can't tell you where your daughter is, Leigh. But I think I know where

Mace is headed. It's my guess he'll return to his roots, his old stomping ground. . . . Go back to where it all began."

"You mean . . . the lake? Lake Wahconda?"

Ava nodded.

Shaking, and on the verge of tears, Leigh looked at Mattie.

Then she was staring past Mattie's shoulder, at two people entering the restaurant.

A red-haired girl.

And a big guy with a beard.

She blinked and swallowed, hard.

After all these years . . .

Cherry Dornay and her brother Ben.

SIXTY-SEVEN

Deana lifted her head.

Her face was a vague blur in the darkness.

Her stomach clenched; she stared at the door.

The crashing, splintering sounds got louder.

Oh my God! Who is it? What's happening?

Nursing her head, she bit her lip, making her mouth bleed all over again. The blood tasted warm, salty. . . . She felt it slide down her chin.

Then the door burst open, shattering the dark with a blast of light.

Outlined against the sun, a figure stood in the opening.

"Deana? Deana!"

A man's voice.

She was *almost* sure it was Warren—coming to take her home.

What if it's not?

She crouched back in the shadows, her eyes fixed on the man. He moved forward, peering into the darkness.

It could be Mace. . . .

Said he'd come back. Use his knife on her. Cleanse her sins away. Rid her of her bad blood . . .

The man got closer.

She cringed, still not making out who it was. . . .

Maybe a figment of my imagination—been having some really weird dreams lately.

A pause.

Yeah . . . That's it. I've gone stark staring crazy!

Her hands shot up, covering her face, her fingers making a narrow V.

She squinted through it, breathing hard.

I might be in an insane asylum right now. . . .

Cringing back, she saw someone else behind the man . . . a tall woman with long black hair. Dressed in black. Denim cutoffs. Iron Maiden T-shirt . . . Deana's eyes leveled with the woman's long, well-muscled legs.

"Deana! It's me, Warren," the man said gently. He was standing over her now. Then lowering himself, kneeling . . . reaching out.

Deana screamed.

"Don't touch me. *Please* don't touch me. . . ."

Her screams trailed off into tiny whimpers. She pressed blood-streaked hands to her mouth, her eyes desperate, pleading.

"Warren? Is it *really* you?"

She peered at him through narrowed eyes.

"I guess they do things like this to mad people," she said slowly. "Fuck about with their brains . . . Like get their hopes up, then . . ."

A cold, wet nose snuffled at her knees.

"Down, Sabre. Sit!"

Warren—and Sabre.

Oh thank you God thank you God!

Warren's voice came low, urgent. "Gotta get you outta here, Deana. Fast. Can you walk?"

Dumbly, she shook her head.

"No? Then I'll carry you. . . ."

He bent down, lifted her in his arms.

She flinched as he held her, her body hurting all over. . . . Still not believing Warren was here. That he'd found her. Just when she'd given up hope he ever would . . .

The woman's voice hissed out.

"Gotta hurry, Warren. I can hear an engine. . . ."

"Open the car door, Sheena. I'll be right over."

Sabre loped ahead with the woman.

Picking up speed, Warren ran the last couple of yards over dry, sparse grass roots and scrub snagging his boots, fresh mountain air keening at his lungs.

Frowning anxiously, willing him on, Sheena stood by the open door of the Chevy. The vehicle the other side of the ridge was getting closer. They heard its engine chugging, whining, the tires skidding over rough dirt road.

Hunching herself into the driver's seat, Sheena revved up the Chevy, eager to be gone. Looking back anxiously as Warren laid Deana across the backseat, pulling a blanket over her.

He climbed up front beside Sheena.

Sabre, panting out hot steamy breaths, leapt in and curled around his feet.

Warren slammed the door shut.

Sheena, her white-knuckled hands clenching the wheel, stepped on the gas, swung the Chevy around, the tires squealing and racing as they hit ruts and rocks.

Then she let it ride, manhandling the wheel with strong, capable hands.

The black customized Commando mounted the hill. It headed toward them.

Through the dust-covered windshield, they saw Mace, his teeth bared, snarling. He was picking up speed.

Sheena drove at him hard and fast. Aiming to go straight through the Jeep or knock it off the mountain path. Mace hesitated slightly, then rammed the gas pedal to the floor.

Sheena yelled, "Hold tight!"

She went for Mace.

The Jeep swerved to the left, then skidded to a halt, showers of dust belching up behind. The left-hand door swung open. Mace slid out, jerking his revolver out of its holster.

Scurrying, crablike, darting behind rocks and bushes, he dropped on one knee, both hands on the gun. He got Sheena in his sight.

Aiming to take her out, he pulled back the trigger. . . .

Warren ducked. Sheena drove. Smashing into the blacked-out Jeep. They watched it teeter, then topple over the ridge with a rattle of dirt and stones. Shots rang out. Whining by. Missing them by only a fraction.

Quickly, Sheena zigzagged the Chevy out of range. Hanging on to the wheel, speeding, slipping, sliding down the trail in a shower of dust and stones.

Warren straightened up.

He peered through the rearview mirror.

Mace was gone.

SIXTY-EIGHT

"Leigh, we got Deana."

"Christ, Warren! You've GOT her?"

"That's right, Leigh. Is Mattie there?"

"She sure is," Mattie snatched the phone from Leigh's hand and yelled into it. "I should tan your butt, Warren Hastings. Why the hell didn't you *tell* me about this before you went chasing off? You coulda wrecked this case, y'know that? Coulda got Deana killed . . ."

"Sorry, Mattie. There just wasn't time. We had to go. Anyway, we're coming in now. And Deana's alive, okay?

She's had a rough time, but s'far as I can see, her injuries look kinda . . . superficial. Can't say for sure, though. . . . She's a little bewildered. Got an injured jaw. Black eyes. Otherwise okay."

Wrapped in blankets, Deana lay on the sofa, Leigh by her side, holding and stroking her hand.

"How did you find me?" Deana asked Warren. Her words came out thick and slurred. She was weak as a kitten, couldn't stop shaking, not yet believing the nightmare was over.

Warren's brows went up. He looked across at Sheena, standing silent by the glass wall, staring out at the view. "Over to you, sis," he called out with a grin.

She turned nonchalantly, lifted a shoulder, and tilted her head. "Yeah. Right . . . ," she said, looking at Deana. "I'll tell y'about it sometime. Just say I wander around those parts myself now and again. When I need to think, get my head straight, know what I mean? I just take out the old Chevy and have me a little campin' trip up there in the mountains."

"Yeah, but . . . that . . . that place I was in, it was so well hidden. . . . It couldn't have been easy."

"Persistent li'l gal, ain't ya? Let's just say my woman's intuition played a part—it led me to where you were."

Leigh broke in. "And I'm sure glad it did. I can't *begin* to thank you both. . . ." She paused, still stroking Deana's forehead, throwing Sheena a grateful smile.

Looking over at Mattie, she said, "So, what do we do now, Mats? Take Ava's advice, fly out to Wisconsin? How about backup?"

"Don't you worry about that, Leigh. FBI, local troopers, you name it, every fucker with a badge is about to descend on Lake Country as we speak. I'm shippin' out later today."

"And I'm coming with you," Leigh said.

Mattie looked doubtful.

Warren met her eyes.

Quietly, he said, "I think Sheena should also go along."

There was a pause while Mattie did a double take.

"You do? Why?"

"Apart from being pretty useful when it comes to one-to-one combat," he winked across at Sheena, "she has a . . . vested interest."

Mattie's eyes narrowed.

"Whadyamean? A *vested interest?*"

"I'm Tania," Sheena said. "Mace's sister."

SIXTY-NINE

The lake looked pretty much the way she remembered it.

The same clear, bright air. Inlets, sandy coves, sunbathers stretched out like fish to dry. Dark stands of pine to the south. Water lapping gently around the pilings. The sputter of motorboats. Canoes, one or two rowboats . . .

Charlie's was green, she remembered.

Could I forget . . . ?

And loaded with baskets.

The sound of vacationers laughing, shouting to each other from the smartly painted piers, floated across the water. Bringing up an arm, shielding her eyes from the sun, Leigh saw them, the size of ants, from her side of the lake.

A motorboat with a water skier tagging behind, zipped by on a crest of white foam. . . .

Leigh smiled softly, remembering how it had been, eighteen years ago. After the accident, Uncle Mike and Aunt Jenny moved camp. Away from Wahconda. They'd sold the cabin and summered in Colorado from then on.

Back in the eighties, they'd retired to Florida.

Carson's Camp was under new management. All modernized and spruced up with a change of name—Lakeside

Holiday Homes. In place of the old log cabins were smart new ones, in varnished pinewood, with porches, loungers, and barbecues out front.

Over to her right, Leigh could see the new cabins, shiny yellow in the sunlight. She saw a twist of smoke, caught a drift of grilled burgers hanging on the air. Nothing really changes, she thought with a smile.

Squinting into the sun, her eyes scanned the lake.

They picked out a green rowboat.

Her heart lurched. For a moment, she felt the same tense excitement of eighteen years ago. When she'd spotted Charlie out there. Charlie, bare-chested. Wearing his funny hat, with its high rounded crown, wide brim, red feathers tucked in the headband . . .

Charlie.

Waiting offshore.

Silent.

Unmoving.

Paddles resting in the oarlocks as he watched her showing off, posing in her white bikini . . .

She fingered her sea-thing, nestling in the cleft between her breasts. It felt so *right* to wear it again, here, at Wahconda. The place where once she'd truly believed it was her good-luck charm. Despite the way things had turned out. This trip, she'd slipped it around her neck, figuring it deserved another chance. . . .

"Penny for them?"

Mattie was smiling at her.

"Mulling over a coupla things," Leigh said, a rueful smile playing on her lips. "As you do. But that was then. Right now we got business to attend to."

Mattie didn't miss a beat.

"Nothin' like old times for bringin' on a case of the jitters, eh?"

"Tell me about it," Leigh said with a wry smile.

Mattie studied the far end of the lake. "So those people

back there at the Bayview—the gal, that your friend Cherry Dornay?"

Leigh nodded.

"Mmmm . . . Nice hair. And the guy?"

"Ben. Cherry's brother. A good friend from way back when I was in San Diego having Deana. Yeah, he was a very good friend. . . ."

She sighed.

Thinking about Ben.

Her knight in shining armor, she'd called him.

A bunch of kids strolled by. Wearing swimsuits, towels hanging around their necks. Laughing and joking on their way to the lake.

Leigh watched them pass.

Her lips curved in a smile. "Ben was a great guy. The best. But I walked, Mattie. Eighteen years ago—and again yesterday, back at the Bayview . . ."

"You have a lot on your mind right now, Leigh. And I get the feeling your Ben'd understand just why you walked out the door—when you've a chance to tell him, that is. D'ya think you might get it together again someday?"

"Maybe. In my own time. When I'm good and ready."

They'd made reservations at the Lakeside. At the height of the summer season they were lucky to get two cabins—a double and a single. Sheena and Mattie chose the double. Leigh took the single.

They ate burgers and fries in the bright, airy restaurant. Red-check cloths on the tables. Red-check curtains at the windows. Mostly, this time of day, the place would be humming with activity; right now it was deserted, except for a young couple sitting quietly in the corner drinking coffee, a map spread out before them.

Sheena was uneasy, on edge. She played around with her food. Finally, pushing her plate aside, she said she needed a run. Promised she'd be back in half an hour.

Mattie watched Leigh's face. She was looking strained, pale. The tension of the last few hours was beginning to take its toll. She hoped Leigh would be up to it when they came eye-to-eye with Mace.

If they came eye-to-eye with Mace.

Hope to God we do. Maybe we're on a wild-goose chase.

Sorensson could've goofed.

Mace could be back there on Del Mar.

Stalking Warren.

Watching Deana.

Deana had pleaded to join Leigh and the others, but the doc advised a twenty-four-hour hospital checkup. That done, Warren was to look after her at his place. Mattie had arranged for a round-the-clock watch on them both.

Leigh assured Deana she'd be back in a couple of days. She hated going, but felt she needed to be on the spot to help Mattie catch Mace.

For the umpteenth time, she satisfied herself that Deana was in safe hands.

Until a small voice in her head whispered:

Oh yeah? Just how safe is safe?

Leigh felt cold and sick inside.

Nothing fazed Mace, she knew that.

If Deana or Warren was to be found, Mace'd do it. . . .

Shit, Leigh. Pull yourself together—they'll be okay. Go out there; do your thing. As in help Mattie nail Mace.

Between the three of them, she had every confidence they would.

Sheena alone was a one-woman army. . . .

Mattie was also a pretty tough cookie.

And Ava assured us Mace'd be here.

Ava could be wrong, the voice piped up again.

No way, Leigh told herself. He *is* out here. Regressing. Reliving his childhood days. Thinking about God knows what.

She recalled Sorensson's face, pale, intense. "Be convinced, Leigh," she'd said. "Harrison's moved on. The West Coast's behind him now. He's out there in Lake Country. . . ."

"We get some sleep, then plan a course of action," Mattie told them before Sheena left to go running. "We're on a covert operation—and it's a team effort. Leigh, if you think of anything, let us know. Such as likely places where Mace could be—and Sheena, you're welcome to come up with your ideas. Any 'feelings' you may have . . ."

They parted.

With severe misgivings, Leigh went to her cabin. She turned on the shower and undressed. Easing out a little as she stepped under the shower, soaping herself, feeling the warm water sluice her body. It felt good and, for a short while, relaxing.

Toweling herself dry, she put on her only change of clothing—a loose navy sweatshirt and pants.

But as she lay on the bed, her former unease returned.

She tossed around, staring at the ceiling; all the while bad memories, fears about meeting up with Mace, and escalating concerns about Deana whirled through her mind.

She sighed.

One thing was for sure.

With all this going on in her head, she didn't feel much like sleeping. . . .

SEVENTY

A hand curved slowly around her neck.

"It can be like this again, Leigh," he told her.

So tenderly, she almost believed him. . . .

Wanted to believe him.

His eyes glittered down at her.

His mouth hung open.

Her heart hammered. She drew back, her hands flying to her face.

"I loved you," he whispered. "Things just got a little mixed up, is all. . . ."

Her eyes snapped open.

SEVENTY-ONE

"MACE!"

"I'm here, sugar. And y'came all this way to say hello? I'm touched, darlin'. I truly am."

The late-noon sun dipped behind the trees, but it was still hot. The cabin was deep in shadow. Shafts of light from the open window pierced the semigloom.

A light breeze from the lake bellied the curtains.

Leigh gasped. How the hell had he gotten to her? The door was locked . . . and the windows . . . ?

Shit!

Like a fool, she hadn't checked the windows.

Her eyes darted back to Mace.

A different Mace now.

Plaid shirt. Combat pants—your average guy taking a well-earned summer break. A little fishing. A few beers . . . It figured, all right. Dressed like that, he'd pass unnoticed in a crowd.

His hair was darker, longer; the blond surfer streaks were gone.

He was a stranger.

A dangerous, unpredictable intruder.

Her blood chilled at the thought.

He swayed a little. A hunting knife hung loosely in his right hand.

"You shouldn't've come, Leigh. Nosin' around. Disturbin' a man payin' his respects to the place of his birth . . ."

His voice was flat, toneless.

Slowly, Leigh edged up the bed, flinching as her back caught the slatted rail behind. She pulled away from him.

Scarcely daring to breathe.

Sweat, slick and hot, flowed down her sides.

Mace leaned in, his knife making circles near her face. His eyes were deep pits. Grape-black. Glinting into hers.

Hypnotizing her.

Tearing her eyes from his, she thought, *I've gotta break the silence—keep him talking. . . .*

"You did some awful bad things to Deana, Mace. Why did you do it?"

"She was a whorin' little slut, that's why. She deserved to die." He spoke slowly, his voice slurring slightly. "She's out of the way now. Yessir, where she is, little bitch won't be causin' no more grief."

"Deana's still alive, Mace."

"Wrong, Leigh. I killed her. She had to die. . . ."

He's killed her! THE BASTARD'S KILLED HER. . . . OH NO!

She shot upright, her heart racing.

Reaching out her left hand, edging it sideways toward the water glass on the nightstand, she extended a finger. Nudging the glass a little; cringing as it crashed to the floor.

In the silence, it sounded like a bomb going off.

Mace came in with his fist.

Mashing her jaw.

Whipping, *cracking* her head sideways.

Making a low "Uuggghhh," she slumped back on the pillow.

Out cold.

Wrestling her onto his shoulder, he went through the kitchen bar to the front door. Unlocking it with one hand, closing it behind him, he hurried out back.

SEVENTY-TWO

The cabins were behind him now.

Still running, he turned, snatching a look over his shoulder. Through the trees, he saw the cabins recede into the distance.

All clear.

He stumbled on, through another deserted copse, stepping over branches, chugging through rough grass.

Soon, the grass gave way to pebbles.

Okay so far . . .

Out of the trees now, the late-noon sun caught him off guard. Squinting into the light, he shook his head, trying to clear the noise, the clutter, the nonsense inside it.

He made his way to a secluded inlet.

Reached the rowboat.

Lowering Leigh into it, he pushed the boat forward.

It shushed quietly along the sand and slipped neatly into the sparkling water.

Leigh groaned.

Leaning over, he slapped her face. Her eyes opened, stared at him groggily for a moment, then closed again.

She was out. Okay.

He stepped into the boat, settled down, eased the paddles from the oarlocks, and stroked out across the lake.

SEVENTY-THREE

"He's got her, Sheena. I heard a crash, went to investigate, and she'd gone. It could only be Mace. Do you see anything out there?"

Sheena, mobile pressed to her ear, listened intently.

"I'm approaching the lake now, Mattie. . . . Can't see anything this end. . . ." Her voice was hurried, breathy, as she jogged over uneven scrub and pebbles.

Drawing to a halt, she scanned the water. "There's a guy in a rowboat. Dark hair, plaid shirt . . . Stroking like hell . . . He's looking over his shoulder. . . ."

She paused, then said quickly, "Mattie. It's Mace. Travelin' south. Heading for the pines out there."

"You sure about that?"

"Sure as I'll ever be. The guy's in an awful hurry. Hey, didn't Charlie have a hideout around here—like the place he died in? And yeah. There's something in the boat, Mattie. Like a pile of clothing or . . ."

"Sheena, keep an eye on that boat. I'll pull rank, requisition a launch. Rowboat. Inflatable. Whatever."

Sheena kicked off her sneakers and waded into the lake till she was breast deep. Then, lifting her arms, she struck out after the rowboat.

SEVENTY-FOUR

Slowly, Leigh opened her eyes, trying to focus on the room. Everything blurred before her.

Her lids closed again.

Gingerly, she felt her jaw. It moved around freely—a little too freely for her liking. Pain shot through her face, stars exploded like fireworks in her head.

Her eyes opened. They darted to Mace.

"Recognize where y'are, darlin'? Recall this li'l ol' place, do ya?"

Leigh went cold. She began to shake.

She was lying on a palliasse of some sort. It was lumpy, hard, with no give to it—like it was filled with straw or something.

She closed her eyes again. Shutting him out. *Smelling* the place . . . The damp, earthy, *moldy* odor . . .

Her eyes snapped open.

THIS WAS IT!

THE HOUSE.

WHERE CHARLIE DIED . . .

The nightmare began again.

Screams echoed around and around in her head, like those other screams, all those years ago.

Edith Payne's screams. When she'd discovered her son Charlie, lying broken and bleeding. His head caved in . . .

"Never did take the old place down," Mace was saying. "Left it here to rot. Gotta tread careful now. . . . Could fall down one a' these biiiig holes. . . ." He grinned at her, standing on the edge of one, jumping up and down, testing the old boards, judging how much they could take.

She shuddered, feeling them shake, vibrate; hearing debris crumble and fall into the void below . . .

Mace gave a hollow laugh.

"All comes floodin' back now, darlin'? Day you killed my brother Charlie?"

His fist came at her again. Smashing her head back to the mattress. He stood there, grinning and chewing, hearing her groans, her small, soft cries.

Then he was down, grabbing the neck of her sweatshirt, twisting it around his hand, bringing her up close till her face touched his.

Her stomach lurched with fear and loathing.

His grip tightened.

SEVENTY-FIVE

"STOP! Police! I got ya covered, Mace!"

Mattie.

Right behind him.

Both hands gripping her gun.

Shoving it into his back.

His hands went up.

Carefully, still keeping him covered, she reached for her belt. Unhitched the cuffs. Snapping one open, she moved forward to slip it onto Mace's wrist. . . .

Then Sheena appeared. Wet from her swim.

"Save it, honey," she told Mattie, not taking her eyes off Mace. "He's mine."

Droplets pooled around her naked feet. She glowered at the back of his head.

Mace stiffened, his hands dropping a little, poised for action.

Sheena was ready.

"Jack off, Mace," she snarled. "Or should that be Jess?"

Mace froze.

Then his shoulders and hands relaxed.

"Sister Tania," he said quietly. "We meet at last."

He swiveled around and stared, a bemused smile tilting his lips. Taking in the long black hair, sleek and wet, dripping over her shoulders. The tawny skin gleaming in the shadows . . .

She was like a warrior queen, risen from the sea. Dressed in black: Apache-style band around her head, Guns N' Roses T-shirt clinging to her body. Her breasts and nipples standing proud beneath.

His eyes played around her breasts, then dropped to the tight leather shorts showing a couple of inches below her top.

"Seen enough, punk?"

He didn't reply. His eyes still traveled over her. They were hungry. Taking in the shiny, well-muscled arms. The long shapely legs, planted firmly apart.

A slow smile curved his lips. He shook his head as if to say "Well, whaddya know . . ."

"So it's Tania," he drawled. "After all these years."

Her eyes leveled with his. Daring him to move.

"Time to turn in ya stripes, Mace," she said softly.

Slowly, her hand reached back, easing up her T-shirt, feeling for the knife in its holster. It rested warm and hard against her damp leather shorts.

"C'mon now, sis. This is your brother here. Don't wanta harm your own kin now, do ya?"

Suddenly, his arm went up and Sheena was staring at a 9mm Sig. Sidestepping neatly, she brought up her knife. Whirled it through the air. It landed, quivering, in his biceps.

Blood spurted a little, then slowly, steadily, pumped down his arm.

His face darkened. He made a grab at the wound. The knife shook a little but still held. The Sig hit the floor with a clunk, and Sheena lunged forward, forcing his arm back and down.

Mace snarled. She snatched back her knife.

"My move, punk," she said with a brief smile, wiping the blade across his shirtfront. She leapt back, crouching, weaving from side to side, tracing circles in the air with her blade.

Spying his chance, avoiding the knife, Mace bounded forward, throwing a sideways kick at her face. He missed.

Then aimed a karate chop to her throat.

Sheena danced away, still crouching, knife in hand, arms outstretched, still weaving from side to side.

Mace saw red.

"I'll get ya, bitch!" he spat out, his eyes bulging.

He aimed and missed again, his arm slicing through thin air.

Mattie closed in, clips at the ready, edging her way around the hole, while Sheena went for Mace with her knife. Looking wildly from one to the other, he tripped and lost his footing.

Leigh gasped, "Oh my God!"

The hole. The one Charlie went through.

They watched Mace go, in a cloud of dust and splinters, his legs swinging around in the deep black void, his hands scrabbling, grasping at the soft rotted wood.

They heard him whimper, then gasp out, "Help me help me . . . help . . ."

Fascinated, they watched the wood crumble and break away in chunks as he grabbed it. Then he dropped, screaming into the dark below.

A final bloodcurdling shriek and a dull squishy thud told them when Mace hit the deck.

Dust motes danced from the gaping hole, caught in a shaft of the dying sun.

They stared at each other in silence.

Then Mattie's gaze dropped to the floor.

She saw the Sig and picked it up.

"Mmmm. Nice piece," she murmured, tucking it into her belt.

SEVENTY-SIX

"Mom!"

"Yes, honey. We're back."

Leigh didn't want to believe her ears.

"Er . . . How was Boulder?" she asked faintly. "And Aunt Abby, of course."

Drinking black coffee in the living room, Deana and Mattie perked up.

"Fine, dear. Boulder's hot and Abby's taking her beta blockers. But I have to tell you, honey, it's *wonderful* to be home again!"

"Sure, Mom. Dad okay?"

Jack West broke in. "I'm fine—and how's that granddaughter of ours? She been behaving herself?"

"Sure, Dad. Deana's okay, and she's right here. Want a word?"

Leigh caught Deana's eye, jiggled the phone at her, and mouthed, "It's Pops. You wanta say hello?" Deana nodded, made a face at Mattie, and walked over to Leigh. She took the phone.

"Hi, Pops. How ya doin? Aunt Abby better?"

"She sure is, darlin'. But, like your gran says, we're real glad to be home. So, what's my favorite granddaughter been doing all summer?"

"Well, er . . . Oh, just messin' around."

"Just messin' around, huh? When your gran and I are unpacked and showered, we'll be right over, then we can have a nice long chat. So don't go rushing off, young lady. Like you did at my birthday dinner!"

"Okay, Pops. I'll be here. . . ."

The doorbell jangled.

Mattie raised her brows. Deana and Leigh exchanged glances. Leigh's heart sank. How could she *ever* explain to Mom and Dad all that had happened since they went away to Boulder?

With a resigned sigh, Leigh went down the hallway and opened the door.

"Oh . . . Hi, guys!" Her voice picked up a notch when she saw Warren, Sheena, and Sabre on the stoop. Warren was holding a couple of books.

"It's so *good* to see you both again!" Leigh was saying in a relieved voice. Warren stepped inside, and Sheena followed. Sabre trotted behind.

When they were all in the living room, Warren told Deana, "I brought the books you asked for. Elmore Leonard for you, and Dylan Thomas for Leigh. Maybe you'll get a chance to read them now."

Deana threw him a wink. "Nice timing, Warren," she said. "Gran and Pops are back from Boulder and they're due here any minute."

They arrived a half hour later.

Deana made for the kitchen to heat up the coffee.

Warren followed.

After the introductions, Mom lowered herself down on the sofa. Shooting a fearful look at Mattie and Sheena— Mattie in her MVPD sweatshirt, denim cutoffs, and gun holster, and Sheena, Amazon-like . . . long flowing hair, tight black tee, leather shorts, and studded belt.

Leigh glanced at Mom's face—red and mottled as she stared, first at the women, then at Sabre, tucked in tight, by Sheena's bare legs.

Leigh rushed over to the wet bar and poured out liberal measures of J.D.'s into two balloon glasses. She handed them to her parents.

There was an awkward silence.

Leigh's bruised face glowed as she met Mom's glance.

"Now, young lady." Dad, glass in one hand, massaging the back of Mom's neck with the other, threw a meaningful look at his daughter. "I think you have some explaining to do. . . ."

Christ *Jesus,* Leigh groaned inwardly. It's Wahconda and Charlie all over again.

Not quite.

It's Wahconda and Charlie, *eighteen years on.*

What goes around comes around. . . .

Clear as crystal, the words of the song popped into her head, making her smile. She felt a million years old. Very wise, and somehow philosophical about all that had happened this summer.

Sitting cross-legged at the far end of the sofa, she smiled at Mom, took a deep breath, and said:

"Remember Nelson? He of beef Willington fame?"

Taking a sip of brandy, Mom nodded slowly. . . .

In the kitchen, Deana gave Warren a cheeky grin. "Looks like we got ourselves a situation out there!" She paused, head tilted to one side, then said, "So, lover boy, you came over to deliver our books?"

"Right."

"That sure is one *lousy* excuse! Admit it, Warren Hastings, you just couldn't keep away!"

They smiled broadly, and their eyes met.

Suddenly, they weren't laughing anymore. They were deadly serious.

"God, Deana. It's been a helluva long time." Warren's voice was low, breathy. "Too long." He held out his arms. "Wanta finish off our . . . unfinished business?"

"Mmmm. Don't I just. . . ."

Deana snugged into him, pressing close, her arms tight around him. Their lips met. His searching, impatient; hers puffy, bruised, and hurting like hell. She pressed into him some more, feeling him stir and rise against her belly. Moaning, she felt the teasing ache between her thighs.

Damn right, she thought. It's been a long, long time. . . .

Too long . . .

She trembled as his hand stole inside her blouse, shivering as he reached for her naked breast. He held it, squeezed it a little, his thumb stroking her taut nipple beneath the filmy cloth.

She moaned, squirming, wanting more—did a little exploring of her own. Easing in against him, she peeled down the zipper of his pants. Her hand closed around him, feeling his hard-on, strong and warm. . . . They moved against each other in a steady rhythm.

Then, abruptly drawing away, she whispered, "Later, Warren. Later. Soon as Gran and Pops are gone, we can . . ."

"Promise?"

"Mmmmm," she sighed, a surge of joy welling inside her.

"I'll hold you to that," he said, kissing the tip of her nose.

She smiled softly, and her arms tightened around him. . . .

AFTERWORD
OR
HOW THINGS
TURNED OUT

by Deana Hastings

Everybody has a dream. Well, pretty much everybody I knew at Berkeley had one. Something to pin your hopes on, y' know? Mine was to write the great American novel. Oh yeah? I know, I know . . . but seriously, that's why I read American lit. And considering the stuff we'd been through that summer of '99, I figured I'd enough material to write several novels. So that's what I do.

Write novels, I mean.

Couldn't have done it without Warren, though. Had his support all the way—once we decided to "finish what we started" the night we saw the last of Mommy Dearest.

We married soon after I graduated, and our first joint project was to coauthor a nonfiction work, *Lore and Legend of Native America* which later, would you believe, became a smash-hit TV series!

Since then, as well as running Eureka, Warren's written a couple more books. Pretty serious stuff: *Shakespeare and the Dark Lady*, based on his theory that she was actually an illegitimate daughter of King Henry VIII of England.

Next up was *The Secret Side of Edgar Allan Poe.*

That went down really well in the U.K. We were *so* thrilled when it hit 3rd place in the *Times* nonfiction bestseller list. We're keeping our fingers crossed for upcoming film rights, too—maybe starring Johnny Depp? He's still my favorite actor, by the way.

Our second joint project, and most successful to date, were our triplets—yeah, *triplets*, how about that?

Spooky, eh?

We named them Jack, Warren Junior, and Helen. And get a loada this. At birth, Helen had a head of *thick, black hair*. The nurses swore they'd never seen anything like it before!

Jeez. I'm trying not to dwell too much on that. For now, she's simply our darling little daughter. . . .

Anyhow, six months after the Mace ordeal, Mom met up with her old pal, Ben Dornay. They married a couple of weeks later. Ben Junior came along ten months after that.

Then Mom opened three more restaurants along the Coast; phew, that woman is truly amazing—she has *so* much energy! Ben Senior realized *his* dream, also (everybody has one, right?), and founded the successful computer animation studio Megatron. The man is pure genius!

Right now, they're enjoying the good life in Beverly Hills and, in the best movie tradition, are living happily ever after. Mom and Ben make a perfect couple. I've never seen Mom look so content—and that's fine by me. She sure deserves it!

* * *

As for Mattie and Sheena—well, they got together shortly after the Mace affair and now live in San Diego. Mattie's gotten her own personal security company, hiring herself out, and her team of bodyguards, to some pretty important people: Hollywood stars, government officials, heads of state . . .

Sheena opened up Movers & Shakers, a club in West L.A., a twenty-four-hour hangout for gays and other kindred spirits. The club attracts major celebs—incognito, of course—and I'm told it's a huge success. As a legacy from her Pacey days, Sheena often stands on the door. Keeping her hand in, she calls it.

And yeah, Sheena and I get along fine—after all, we *do* have something in common, apart from Payne blood. Like die-hard sports! When she drops by our place in Mill Valley, she gives me kickboxing lessons—and I take her out on my "midnight runs." With Warren, of course. He worries about the weird characters sneaking around at night. *Men!*

Oh, and Sabre comes, too—except when his hips act up. Then he stays home and takes it easy. He's just reached his tenth birthday—and I'm told that's pretty good for a German shepherd dog!

RICHARD
LAYMON
COME OUT
TONIGHT

Sherry's getting nervous. When Duane left for the 24-hour Speed-D-Mart, he said he'd be back in ten minutes. But that was twenty minutes ago, and that store isn't someplace you'd generally want to go at this time of night. Then Sherry hears a noise from up the street. It could have been a car door slamming. Or a backfire. But it sounded like a gunshot.

Sherry tells herself she has nothing to worry about. Still, she puts on her clothes and heads out into the night. She's afraid of what she'll find, but she has no idea of what's really in store for her. If she did, she never would have left the safety of her home. And she never would have met a madman named Toby Bones....

RICHARD LAYMON

RESURRECTION DREAMS

Back in Ellsworth High there was definitely no one weirder than Melvin. All the kids made fun of the way he dressed, the way he acted, everything about him. Vicki was the only one who stood up for him, but even she was horrified when he dug up a dead body and tried to bring it back to life with power from a car battery.

That was years ago, but Vicki still has nightmares about Melvin. Now she's back in Ellsworth and she knows she'll have to see Melvin again. He's just been released from the institution and he's acting even weirder than ever. His experiments with the dead have progressed, and as soon as he can get Vicki where he wants her, he can make his most twisted dream a reality....

TO WAKE THE DEAD

RICHARD LAYMON

Amara was once the beautiful Princess of Egypt. Now, 4000 years later, she and her coffin are merely prized exhibits of the Charles Ward Museum. If you were to look at her today, you would see only a brittle bundle of bones and dried skin. But looks can be very deceiving, as Barney, the museum's night watchman, finds out. . . .

Barney is the first to make the shocking discovery that the mummy's coffin has been broken open. But he doesn't have a chance to do anything about it. Amara is once again freed from the cramped confines of her coffin, free to walk the earth. Free to kill. Nothing can satisfy her bloodlust. And no one can stop her. You cannot kill what is already dead.

✂ ☐ **YES!**

Sign me up for the Leisure Horror Book Club and send my FREE BOOKS! If I choose to stay in the club, I will pay only $8.50* each month, a savings of $7.48!

NAME: _____

ADDRESS: _____

TELEPHONE: _____

EMAIL: _____

☐ I want to pay by credit card.

☐ **VISA**   ☐ **MasterCard.**   ☐ **DISCOVER**

ACCOUNT #: _____

EXPIRATION DATE: _____

SIGNATURE: _____

Mail this page along with $2.00 shipping and handling to:
Leisure Horror Book Club
PO Box 6640
Wayne, PA 19087
Or fax (must include credit card information) to:
610-995-9274

You can also sign up online at **www.dorchesterpub.com**.
*Plus $2.00 for shipping. Offer open to residents of the U.S. and Canada only. Canadian residents please call 1-800-481-9191 for pricing information.

If under 18, a parent or guardian must sign. Terms, prices and conditions subject to change. Subscription subject to acceptance. Dorchester Publishing reserves the right to reject any order or cancel any subscription.

GET FREE BOOKS!

You can have the best fiction delivered to your door for less than what you'd pay in a bookstore or online. Sign up for one of our book clubs today, and we'll send you *FREE* BOOKS* just for trying it out...**with no obligation to buy, ever!**

As a member of the Leisure Horror Book Club, you'll receive books by authors such as **RICHARD LAYMON, JACK KETCHUM, JOHN SKIPP, BRIAN KEENE** and many more.

As a book club member you also receive the following special benefits:
- **30% off all orders!**
- **Exclusive access to special discounts!**
- **Convenient home delivery and 10 days to return any books you don't want to keep.**

Visit **www.dorchesterpub.com**
or call **1-800-481-9191**

There is no minimum number of books to buy, and you may cancel membership at any time.
*Please include $2.00 for shipping and handling.